Also by Mike Holst

A Long Way Back

Nothing to Lose

No Clues in the Ashes

Best Wishes
Mike Holt

Justice for Adam

by Mike holst

iUniverse, Inc.

New York   Bloomington

JUSTICE FOR ADAM

Copyright © 2009 Mike Holst

This is a work of fiction. All of the characters, names, incidents, organizations, and dialogue in this novel are either the products of the author's imagination or are used fictitiously.

iUniverse books may be ordered through booksellers or by contacting:

iUniverse
1663 Liberty Drive
Bloomington, IN 47403
www.iuniverse.com
1-800-Authors (1-800-288-4677)

ISBN: 978-1-4401-6061-5 (pbk)
ISBN: 978-1-4401-6062-2 (ebk)

Printed in the United States of America

iUniverse rev. date: 8/24/2009

Acknowledgement

I wish to thank Nancy Felknor, and Gloria Smith for their editing skills and advice. As always, in all of my books, and all of my writings, a special thanks to my wife Kitty for her encouragement and help.

Authors note

My motivation for writing this story was because of an act of selfish brutality and murder that took place in Minnesota, involving a sexual predator and a young woman from our community. Sexual predators are men who strike fear into every woman's heart, and the hearts of families and friends everywhere. They are to our society what the grizzly bear is to the animal kingdom: unpredictable, frightful, and rarely tamed.

Our legal system and the litigious world we live in becomes the second part of this problem, and we constantly disagree about how to treat these people and what to do, or not do, with them. All too often they are ignored, have their hands slapped, and are released back into society to prey again.

Although this book is a work of fiction and was constructed totally from my imagination, it shows how one man handled it when the courts failed him, and how a small town came to support him. It shows too, the depths of pain and hurt that come from these selfish acts, not only to the victims, but also to those who love them. It shows how all too often our legal system runs amok with loopholes and technicalities that do little to help the innocent, and all too often help only the guilty. There are so many things we may never get right in today's legal world, but that is what is nice about fiction. We can rewrite the rules, and make it right, can't we?

Mike Holst

CHAPTER ONE

The solitary leaf still hung there, stubbornly, on the highest limb of that gnarled old cottonwood tree. It had been many days since all of the other leaves had given up their fight and fluttered down to the forest floor. The green chloroform that had once been the leaf's lifeblood had long ago bled out, and now it flickered in the waning October sunlight, a dull anemic yellow with a border of brown decay around its shriveled edges. A small jagged tear on one side was a subtle reminder of a passing summer storm, a month or two ago.

Entombed in a small black cocoon and fastened to the back of the leaf was a pupa, the offspring of some dead insect. Waiting there, in limbo, the cocoon would remain like that until the heat of next summer's sun would return once again to this mountain valley, waking it to finish its metamorphosis.

Still, that frail thin stem that had fed the leaf, and held it there from the time it had budded through the summer and fall, refused to part. So there it remained, the only leaf attached to the skeletal tree.

Adam Holton sat, nestled into the carpet of its fallen leaves, with his back to the tree, and smoked his last Marlboro. He was physically exhausted, temporarily mentally unstable, and he needed to sit down and rest. He had been on the run for three days, and was still not sure he wasn't being followed. His shirt was wet with sweat, despite this forty-degree October day. Part of it was from the physical beating he had taken while on the run, and part of it was from the knot of fear that was eating at his gut. Every time the wind blew, or a pebble moved, he reacted. His breath was still coming in gulps, despite the fact he'd been sitting for five minutes against the sturdy cottonwood, after half sliding - half running down the hillside from the railroad yard where he'd abandoned the freight train he had stowed away on. The water gurgling in the creek below him looked inviting, but it was too open here and he would have to go downstream where there was more cover if he wanted to refresh himself.

Adam's tattered backpack lay at his feet, with everything he had left in the world stuffed into it, including enough food for a few days, if he ate sparingly. There were a few pairs of socks and some underwear hastily stuffed inside another dirty flannel shirt. There was a wrinkled envelope with a few hundred dollars he had managed to extract with his ATM card before they froze his account, and there was a loaded 9-millimeter Smith and Wesson automatic pistol. It was hardly the weapon of choice in this Montana wilderness. The rest of the contents consisted of pictures, letters, and two blankets rolled and tied to the bottom of the bag, all wrapped up inside a dirty cameo poncho.

Adam closed his burning eyes for just a few minutes. It had been two days since he had last slept, and almost as long since he had eaten. He unsnapped the side pocket on his pack without opening his eyes, and feeling around, came out with a Snickers Bar that was half smashed. Shedding the wrapper, he bit the bar in half, and chewed the half in his mouth slowly and deliberately, as if he were in a trance. Chocolate colored saliva drooled out of the corner of his mouth into his whisker stubble, and down his chin. Then, at last done savoring the flavor, he swallowed. Stuffing the other half in his mouth, he resumed chewing.

He wiped his chin with the back of his hand, and then licked it off, before falling asleep shortly after he had finished.

He slept for two hours, until the chill from the disappearing sun woke him. He was shivering uncomfortably. Pulling his collar up on his denim jacket to ward off the cool mountain breeze, he stuffed his hands in his pockets, deep in thought, while his mind wandered back over the last few days.

Adam had been driven to do what he did, no doubt about it. Every man has a breaking point where he can no longer tolerate the injustices that have been heaped upon him, one after another. Rational thinking becomes the exception, not the norm, until one day you just snap. His day had come on July 13, 1996.

He slipped deeper in thought, even beyond that fateful day, and visions of Amanda came out of the dark recesses of his mind, causing a slight smile to spread across his tired face.

Mandy. Beautiful Mandy. Oh my God how he had loved her. Adam had worshiped the ground she walked on, the very air she breathed. She was as perfect as God had ever made, and she had loved him back so perfectly. He couldn't get enough of her, and he started and ended each and every day with thoughts of Mandy. The love for him that she showed in every move she made just drove him deeper in love with her, day-by-day and minute-by-minute.

July 21st would have been the day that they said their vows and publicly acknowledged the overwhelming affection they had for each other.

They had picked out her wedding dress together, and bad luck or not, she had modeled it for him. To see her like that had taken his breath away, and he lived for the day she would wear it for the entire world to see. He lived also for the night he would carefully take it off her, and they would be as one.

The invitations to friends and relatives had been out for two months, with the church reserved, and the reception arranged. Amanda's parents were also overjoyed with their only daughter's choice of a mate, as Adam's family had been with her.

Then, Mark Stevenson, a third degree sexual predator who had been released from prison only weeks before, spotted Mandy leaving her job at the bank. And the nightmare began. Two days after she disappeared, her battered body was found stuffed in a culvert outside of town. Found by Adam, who had searched nonstop from the moment she hadn't come home.

The police had not yet declared her a missing person, despite Amanda's parents' and Adam's pleas that something bad had happened.

People come up missing all of the time, they said. *Maybe she had gotten cold feet about the up-coming wedding. It happens,* they reasoned.

Adam was in a trance, his spirit broken. The girl he loved with all his heart was gone. She had been his reason for living, and his hope for the future. This beautiful person had been savagely raped and strangled, then stuffed into a mud-filled culvert full of garbage.

A week later, they buried Mandy in the church cemetery, and on the very day she was to have been married in that small church, they arrested Stevenson.

At first he was belligerent, claiming he knew nothing, but two days later he smugly confessed, giving clues that only the police knew, to confirm it. A week later he was set free on a technicality.

His confession was thrown out, and ruled inadmissible in court. He recounted how he'd been coerced by the police to confess to the crime. His lawyer smiled and assured the public that his client was innocent of all charges. They held a press conference full of theatrics, and the media came and ate it up.

A week later, Stevenson was back in court on another charge unrelated to the murder, and when he walked out of the courtroom doors into the brisk Minnesota air, he was met with 180 grains of lead from a 30-06 hunting rifle right between the eyes. Stevenson's head exploded on the courthouse steps, splattering his attorney with brains and gore.

There had been no question as to who had done it. Deputies, standing on the street after the shot was fired, had seen Adam standing above them. He left the rifle, with his prints all over it, on the roof of the Federated Building across the street. A building he had worked in, as a physical therapist, and knew well.

The sheriff started the chase, but lost him. Then the highway patrol had taken it up and chased him across three states, before he disappeared in Missoula, Montana, leaping from a freight train he had boarded in Jamestown, North Dakota where his truck had blown the engine. Little did he know they were chasing him for speeding.

It was three hours now since he had left the train. Adam stood up, hanging wearily onto the tree, his forehead pressing against the rough bark. Then his arms went around the tree, and he shook the tree, screaming: "Mandy!"

Far above him, the solitary leaf on the tree broke loose and floated downward, settling briefly on Adam's head before sliding to the ground. It was letting go, and telling him to let go also, but Adam would never do that. He was far from finished.

CHAPTER TWO

Adam followed the creek deeper into the mountains. He was enough of a woodsman to know what getting lost was all about, so he was careful to stay close to the stream. For now it was his way to seclusion, but he knew eventually he would need to come out. Somehow he needed time to think this out.

He was actually in a long narrow valley that doglegged to the left and then ran up into the Rockies. Looking to the northwest he could make out the high snow-covered peaks hidden in wispy clouds. It looked cold and forbidding up there, and with each day that went by, that cold was creeping closer to this valley as winter was ready to grip Montana any day. Right now, however, he was going to have to ignore the weather. He needed a few days to think about where he was going with his life.

Adam's fear of those who had pursued him had throttled down a few notches. At this moment he didn't believe they were following him, but on the other hand, he knew that people lived around here, and strangers like him needed to be given a wary eye. For the time being he would avoid contact with everyone, if possible.

He saw smoke in the distance and decided to investigate. Walking through a mature white pine forest it was hard to keep an eye on the smoke, and he had to climb a tree from time to time to make sure he was still walking in the right direction. It appeared to be some kind of a controlled burn, as it seemed to not grow in size or intensity.

Adam had been raised in northern Minnesota where forest fires were not unusual, but one thing it did mean, is that people were usually sent to control them. If this fire was unattended, he could use the heat for a while. Building a campfire had been a risk that he had been leery of doing.

The woods thinned out and now it was more scrub trees and brush. The smell of smoke was heavy in the air, but with the wind at his back it was tolerable. At last Adam was in the area that had burned over. The ground was black, and a heavy puff of ash seemed to explode from the ground with every step he took. Stumps and wood debris still smoldered and burned everywhere.

There was a lot of rock in the area, so he tried to stay close to cover as much as he could. He had seen no one around, but he wasn't taking any chances. At last he came to a small patch of un-burned brush and grass that, for some reason, the fire had skipped right over. It was a good place to spend the night, and the smoke from his campfire would blend right in with all of the other smoke.

It was nearly dark as he made camp and cooked a can of Dinty Moore's beef stew he had stashed in his pack. As hungry as he was, tonight it tasted better than he ever remembered it tasting before.

After eating, he walked back down to the stream to wash up, spooking a pair of mule deer that scampered out of the stream and startled him. They ran about fifty feet up the hillside, their hoofs clicking on the rocks, then stopped and stood watching him over their shoulders. Their coats were now turning grayish brown for winter, instead of the reddish hue that they had in the past summer.

Somewhere, high overhead, a flock of geese flew honking intermittently, as they looked for a place to rest for the night on their trip south for the winter. Right now he could hear them, but not see them.

The stars were shining brightly and the night air was fresh and crisp. Too crisp for the light clothing he had on, and Adam went back to his campfire to warm up. Stirring the coals with a stick, he mulled over his future. He could keep walking, but to where? Somewhere, someplace, somehow, - he was either going to have to work, or steal, to survive. Should he move on, - or should he try to put down some roots for a while?

Adam spent most of the next day just gathering his wits about him. He had been on edge for too many days, and it felt good to relax. Wandering down to the stream, he stripped down to his underwear and washed up. The cold water almost took his breath away so he made it quick. That afternoon he had climbed up the slope behind him to get a better view of the valley. Far to the east he could see cattle grazing on a large grassy plain. He watched the cattle for some time, but never saw any hint of human activity. Tomorrow he would take a closer look.

Adam made up his mind that he was going to have to find work to survive. There would be no surviving in this part of the country without food and decent shelter. He could keep going and move farther south, but the chances of finding something as remote as this, were best right here. The more people around, the better the chance that someone would be looking for him.

He was no cowboy, but he had lived on a farm back in Minnesota when he was younger, so he was no stranger to that kind of life. If things went to hell in a hand basket, well, - he had the gun, and he would just have to deal with it, he reasoned, but also knowing he didn't have it in him, to risk hurting innocent people.

Linda Pendleton struggled, after her husband died, to keep the ranch going. She and her husband, Dan, had come to this valley twenty years ago and went from a few head of beef, to a herd of over five thousand. They had gone from a two-room log cabin they built themselves, with a few primitive tools, to a sprawling ranch house and several outbuildings. In the past, as many as twenty people had worked for the Pendleton's on the Lazy L Ranch.

Then, two years ago, Dan was diagnosed with cancer and had wasted away, despite all of the love and care Linda could provide. His once rugged frame and handsome looks had been devoured from the inside out. He had been cremated, and his ashes spread on the western pastures of the Lazy L, where he had spent so much of his life.

Linda's brother Arnie had moved in with her to help out after Dan's passing, but he was not in the best of health, and was getting up in years. Linda was faced with mounting bills and no money to hire good help and last week Arnie had moved into town.

Linda didn't look forty-two years old. Long days in the wind and sun over the years, had given her a ruddy complexion, but her face was firm and free of wrinkles. Her long blond hair was turning darker with age, but it was still thick and wavy. Her body was firm and well proportioned. Her breasts and hips had not changed much over the years, and she still had a striking figure.

She and Dan had one child, a boy named, Lee. Lee and Dan had been her world, and then, when Lee was ten, he had fallen from a horse and was killed. Linda, broken hearted, would not try for more children. When Dan died, it ended that chapter of her family, and now all she did was try to survive from day to day.

Today, she rode along the western side of the range with Ramon, on all-terrain vehicles, looking for stray cattle before the roundup. The days of horseback riding was a thing of the past, although they still had a few horses and mules they used in the winter. In a couple of weeks they were going to ship this entire year's crop of steers, keeping only the young stock and cows. The money would help them make it through the winter, although the price of beef was drastically low this year.

Ramon Garcia had only been with her for four years and had become one of her most trusted employees. He was young, but he had been raised on ranches and knew what he was doing. He was also a hothead, but Linda knew how to control him, and she did.

Ramon had been riding ahead of Linda, when he stopped and pulled the field glasses up from around his neck, holding his hand up for her to stop. "There's someone down there along the creek. I think he heard the ATV's and slipped back in the brush."

"Probably just a drifter, or a fisherman, Ramon," Linda answered. They were not that far off the interstate, and from time to time, hunters and fishermen did come on the ranch property. It was almost impossible to post it for trespassing because of the size of it. For the most part, sportsmen did not bother Linda, anyway.

"Why don't I go down and see if I can shag him out," said Ramon. "You might as well wait here and then we'll double back. I have a feeling that any steers that are unaccounted for aren't in this part of the range. That fire would have spooked them away from here."

Because the terrain was rough and rocky, Ramon decided to abandon the four-wheeler and walk in. He brought along his Winchester Model 94 carbine, out of habit. Two years ago, a grizzly had attacked him and he was lucky to still be alive.

Adam watched Ramon walking toward him. His first impulse was to run, but there was little cover after the fire, and on those four wheelers they would surely catch him. A second thought told him that these were not lawmen, so he probably had nothing to fear, and maybe this would work out for him.

Adam walked out of the brush and headed towards Ramon. When they were about fifty yards apart, he could see the rifle. But if this was going to work, he was going to have to keep cool.

Ramon was the first to speak. "Are you lost?" he asked.

"No, no. I'm just passing through. I was walking the interstate, but I decided to come down here and camp out. Is that ok?"

"Suit yourself," said Ramon. "I would think you could find a better place to be than this burned off area full of smoke and ash."

"Yeah, I can see why you would think that, but I came here because I had no matches and I needed a fire," Adam answered. "Gets damn cold around here at night."

"Well, you probably should move on before more than the cold gets you. Lots of grizzlies around here." Ramon was noticing Adam's light clothing and lack of supplies.

"Is this a ranch?" Adam asked, ignoring the comment. He had moved closer to Ramon and was shading his eyes from the bright morning sun.

"Why do you ask?" Ramon had placed the barrel of the rifle on the toe of his boot and had his hand over the end of the stock.

"I could use a job. At least for awhile."

Ramon stared at Adam for a few seconds, and then said, "You're in luck. The boss is with me." Right now he was not sure he liked Adam, but Linda did need the help, and it would make less for him to do.

Adam stuck out his hand. "Name's, Aaron," he said. "Aaron Holton."

"Ramon Garcia," Ramon said, shaking his hand. "Come with me."

Ramon walked ahead and Adam followed, back up the trail until they came to two four wheel ATV's parked on a wider trail. Just as they came even with the vehicles, Linda stepped out from behind some rocks.

The sight of a woman out here, made Adam look around quickly. *Was this some kind of a trap?*

"This is Aaron," said Ramon. "Says he is looking for work."

"Hi," said Adam. "Nice to meet you, Ma'am."

"What brings you to these parts, Aaron?" Linda had stepped closer and Ramon was now sitting on the four-wheeler sideways. He had put the rifle away.

"You might say I am running away from some things," Adam said. "It's a long, complicated story." Then seeing that Linda wanted more of an explanation he added, "My wife died, and I just had to get away."

"'I'm sorry about that. Have you worked on a ranch before?" Linda's dark blue eyes were riveting.

"Not really," said Adam, "but I was raised on a farm so I know how to act around livestock. My last job was as a physical therapist, but I'm not sure there's much call for that, out here."

"Hop on that four-wheeler behind Ramon and let's go back and talk. If you want."

The Lazy L office was in one corner of the house, with an outside entrance at the side. A long, dark brown leather couch was by one wall with a matching chair sitting a few feet away. Large windows looked out over the range in front of them, which right now was filled with livestock grazing, unaware that their days on the range were nearly over.

Ramon left Adam alone with Linda, and now the two of them sat on the couch, one on each end, turned just enough to be facing each other. It felt good to Adam to be inside and out of the cold.

"You have an accent, Aaron," she said as she handed him a cup of coffee.

Adam smiled. "Must be Minnesotan, if that's a proper word. That's where home was."

"You mentioned you had lost your wife. Was it sudden?"

"Yes," Adam said. "Very sudden. I—" He started to say more, but realizing he was building a tangled web here, that could come back to haunt him, he stopped.

"Do you think running from it is the right thing to do?" Linda now stood and walked behind the big oak desk in the center of the room, but didn't sit down behind it. She picked up a paperweight of an old Conestoga wagon from the desktop and blew the dust off it. "Sorry," she said, and smiled.

Adam caught the warmth in her smile and smiled back, a little more at ease.

"I'm hoping for a new beginning," he said. "It has to come with a change of scenery."

There was an awkward silence for a moment as Linda stood looking out the window, seemingly in deep thought. Then she turned back to him and said. "I normally don't hire drifters, but it's hard to find people right now, and we do have a fall roundup coming on. If you like, you can go down to the cattle barns and see Ramon. Tell him I said to put you to work. Your pay will be thirty dollars a day and room and board."

Something told her if she asked him to identify himself further, he would walk away, and for some crazy reason she didn't want that to happen.

CHAPTER THREE

Sheriff Joe Adcock looked at the 'wanted' poster of Adam Holton on his desk. He didn't know if he should hang it up, file it, or throw it away. The trail was getting colder, but he wasn't too upset about it. The world was better off without Mark Stevenson, even if blowing somebody's head off with a big game rifle had to be discouraged.

Stevenson's attorney had not been seen since that fateful day, when he scampered back inside the courthouse covered with brain tissue, and threw up all over the lobby. He felt sure he was the next target.

But Sheriff Joe knew Adam Holton was long gone. The last sighting of him had been on a security camera in a bus depot, in Billings, Montana. No record of him getting on a bus was found, or for that matter, even buying a ticket.

Adam Holton was a well-liked young man, and one of Aspen County's "up and coming" citizens. He had sung in the church choir, was a member of the local Jaycees and the Young Republicans. He had ridden in last year's Fourth of July parade on a hay wagon, dressed as Paul Bunyan, and tossed candy to the kids, along with Mandy, who was dressed as Lucette, Paul's imaginary girlfriend. They had seemed so happy together.

For many years, Adam's family and Joe Adcock's family had been good friends, and Adam's dad had worked on Joe's reelection campaign, until he passed away last year. His mother died a few months later of a broken heart.

"You know Percy, sometimes I think the law does more to get in the way than to dispense justice." Joe was talking to his deputy, who had just come into the office. "I'm not talking about you and me as the law, Percy, - I'm talking about the Courts."

He thumped his finger on the 'wanted' poster lying in the middle of his desk. "This young man had a bright future, and now he's a fugitive. All because the courts couldn't get their shit together and keep that pervert, son-of-a-bitch in jail. Mandy didn't deserve to die, no how. No one deserves to go through what she did."

"Here," he tossed the 'wanted' poster of Adam across his desk. "Take this down to the post office and get it faxed around the country. Especially the Dakotas and Montana. I'm going over to Gert's for coffee," Joe said, grabbing his hat off the hook by the door, and heading out.

Adam tossed his bag on the bed in the bunkhouse. Ramon told him to walk around and get familiar with the place, and then tomorrow bright and early, they would head out on the range. He also told him to go to town and get some warmer clothing, or he was going to freeze to death.

"There is an old Ford pickup parked by the office you can take. The keys are in it." Then, as an afterthought, he said, "Stop and see Linda, and see if there's anything she needs while you're there. You got money?"

"Some," Adam said.

"Well if you need an advance, tell Linda. I'm sure she'll give it to you."

Adam showered and changed his clothes. There was a washing

machine in the bunkhouse, and he threw in his dirty clothes before he left.

There were about twenty beds in the room but it looked like only a few were being used. The rest had bedding stacked on the ends, but they were not made up. A gas furnace in one corner was blowing faintly, mounted high over a table that held a couple decks of cards, and a pinochle board. On a shelf in the corner, a dusty television set brought a fuzzy picture of Matt Lauer doing an interview on 'The Today Show.' There was no audio and the caption on the screen said, "mute."

The bunkhouse was set on the back of the property, about a hundred yards behind the main house and office. Behind the bunkhouse were the cattle barns, silos, and grain bins. In the winter it took a lot of feed to keep the operation running. A good part of the ranch was devoted to growing the corn and alfalfa hay that kept the place going during the winter months. The barns and bins were bursting with this year's crop, as the harvest had just been completed a few weeks ago.

Adam walked from silo to grain bin, past stacks of square hay bales covered with plastic sheeting. There was a long metal building, open on one side, where the combines and machinery sat parked for the winter. This was so much bigger than anything he had seen, growing up in Minnesota.

Linda cupped her hands around her coffee cup for warmth, as she watched him walk across the center courtyard towards the house. She remembered her husband Dan twenty years ago, and this young man was a dead ringer for him. He even had that same swagger in his walk.

There was an air of confidence that showed through in this young man, although right now it was seemingly clouded with uncertainty. Adam stamped off his boots next to the back step, and raised his hand to knock, when Linda opened the door.

"Ramon suggested I go to town and get some warmer clothing," he said.

Linda gave a little laugh, and said, "Ramon knows what it's like in

Montana in the winter, Aaron, and I agree with him. I need to get some groceries, so I'll ride along if you don't mind. Let me get my coat." In the back of her mind, she thought, *I don't need to lose my truck.*

When Linda came back she had her coat on, and was carrying a man's leather coat with a wide sheepskin collar. "This used to be my husband's, why don't you see if it fits you? You look about the same size."

He slipped the coat on, and it fit perfectly. "Are you sure he won't need it?" Adam asked.

Linda smiled, and said, "My husband died two years ago, Aaron. He would want you to have it."

"I'm sorry," Adam said. He was extremely nervous. He didn't want to be around other people right now, but there seemed no way out of it. He was also having a nicotine fit and couldn't wait to buy a pack of smokes.

"That's all right, you didn't know. What do you say we hit the road?"

The pickup truck was covered with a coating of dust that seemed to leak in through every crack and hole, as they drove the dusty road to town. It was not that far, but it was accessible only by this long, dusty frontage road that ran alongside the interstate. Linda asked Adam to drive while she made out her grocery list.

About a mile down the road, Linda, who had been quiet and absorbed in her list since they had left the house, said, "Tell me about your wife."

It caught Adam off guard, and for a couple of moments he didn't know how to respond. Finally he said, "She was my life. My reason for living."

"How long were you married?" Linda had turned to face him, sitting sideways on the seat. Her right hand was pulling slack on the seat belt harness, while her left hand was on the seat back next to Adam's shoulder.

"Not very long," he said. "Not very long at all, but we knew each other for a long time."

"Did she die suddenly? I don't mean to pry, you just seem upset, and I want to be a friend."

Some sand caught the tires in a rut, and Adam wrestled with the steering wheel for a moment.

He turned to look at Linda with a somewhat pleading look that said he didn't want to talk about it. "It was very sudden. I never got a chance to say goodbye."

Linda patted his shoulder in a small sign of comforting, but said nothing. She turned in the seat and looked out the side window. "I bet it snows before the week is out," she said. "The radio this morning said it snowed last night in the higher elevations."

The store they shopped at was called Cowboys' Fleet. It was a big department store with everything from groceries, to clothes and hardware: a one-stop shopping trip. While Linda picked out groceries, Adam found some flannel shirts, some long underwear, a pair of new jeans and some insulated boots. That was all he figured he had money for right now.

When he caught up with Linda, she had her cart full of groceries so she started filling Adam's cart too, until they were both overflowing. It took a lot of groceries to feed six hungry men, and one woman.

"That should do it for awhile," Linda said, and they got in the checkout line. When the cart was unloaded enough to get to Adam's purchases, Linda put them on the belt with the rest of the stuff. As Adam reached for them, she put her hand on his, and said, "my treat." He protested mildly, but she would hear none of it, and wrote a check for everything.

As they went out to the truck, a few flurries were coming down and there was a definite chill in the Montana air.

Adam spent the rest of the day walking around the ranch with Linda, while she showed him where everything was kept. There was a large livestock barn with birthing stalls, and even a small infirmary for injured animals. There was even a special room where artificial insemination was done. Each head of beef represented a good deal of money, and everything possible was done to keep them healthy.

There was another barn for horses and mules. It was mostly empty now, but in the past it held almost thirty animals. About one fourth of this building was filled with tacking.

"Do you like to ride horses?" Linda asked, as she ran her hands around the muzzle of a large black Arabian stallion that had stuck his head over the side of the pen, and nickered at her. "This is Blaze," she said, before Adam could answer her question. "He was Dan's favorite, and he kind of lives a sheltered life right now."

Adam could see the hurt in her face, when she mentioned Dan's name. She quickly changed the subject.

There were five horses and three mules in the barn, and Linda explained, "normally, they wouldn't be in here, but the man came today to trim their hoofs and we haven't turned them back out to pasture yet. They just aren't needed as much anymore; with the coming of the four wheel ATV's.

"I love horses," Adam said. "We always had a couple around the farm."

There were several buildings full of feed, water tanks, and implements. There was another building loaded with building material, fence posts and tarps, and in one end, several all terrain vehicles and trailers.

"The men are working up in the high lands today, and tomorrow you'll be working up there with them. There are a lot of bales to still bring down before the snow gets too deep. Almost all of our feed is grown up on the plateau. Because of the bears and wolves, we can't leave livestock up there. Several years ago, Dan had a road built going up there, but its steep, and in the winter hard to manage, so we truck all of the hay down here."

"Ramon mentioned, rounding up steers."

"Yes, probably next week we'll ship about a thousand head. It's a big job, but you'll enjoy it." She poked Adam playfully on the shoulder. "We'll make a cowboy out of you yet."

"I better get supper started," Linda said. "We had a cook up until a couple of years ago, but we had to let him go, and now I'm the chief cook and bottle washer."

"Guess I'll go clean the barn," Adam said. "I need to do something to earn my money. Thanks for the clothes." He wanted to say more, but the words just seemed to escape him. This lady was being very kind to him, and he didn't know why. Tomorrow when he was with the rest of the boys, he had a feeling things would be different.

Linda just smiled, walked outside, and headed for the house. She had had a lot of men work here over the years, but for some strange reason she felt different about this one. She turned and looked back when she was about half way across the yard. Adam was still standing there watching her walk away.

Joe Carter had been County Sheriff in Missoula for about twenty-two years now, but this was to be his last term, and it ended in three weeks. He and his wife Joann had spent their last winter in this cold, mountain community. They had bought a small condo in Tucson, and he couldn't wait to get there. Little did he know he would be living less than a mile from Joe Adcock, a sheriff from Minnesota, who was also retiring and moving south to a warmer climate.

He sat at his desk, opening the mail with a letter opener that resembled a little samurai sword. How many of these 'wanted' posters had he seen over the years? Not only sent on paper, but also over the Internet. Most of them were given a cursory glance, and filed in the round container next to his desk, but every once in a while he would see one that he felt was worthwhile to hang up, for one reason or the other.

The poster read, **Wanted for illegal flight to avoid prosecution for murder.** He read the description underneath. **Adam Holton, age 26, 6 foot 1, 180 lbs. Brown hair and green eyes. Last seen at the bus depot in Billings, Montana on October of this year. No prior record but should be considered dangerous.**

Adam's picture showed a handsome young man with a wide smile. The picture had been taken standing next to a young lady, whose face had been blocked out. Joe studied the picture. What would make an innocent-looking man like this do what he had done? How many times over the years had he asked that same question?

The radio was blaring with another county's emergency and he got up to go turn it down, leaving the poster on the corner of his desk. Just then, his barber, Cal Winters, walked in and yelled, "Coffee time!"

Joe slammed the door shut behind him, as he and Cal headed over to the Rusty Nail for coffee. The burst of wind from the door closing, swept across his desk, and the 'wanted' poster flicked off onto his chair, and then onto the floor under the desk, just out of sight.

"Just two more weeks until the election, Cal. How are things looking with the election right now?"

" I wish I had a handle on it, Joe, but right now it's just too close to call."

Cal's son, Tony, was running for sheriff against one of Joe's deputies, Ryan Markinson. For Joe, it was a no-win situation. Ryan would make a good sheriff and had always done a good job for Joe, but on the other hand, Cal's son was like part of the family. Joe had known him since he was a toddler. Tony was a successful lawyer, and no one could understand why he wanted be a sheriff, and leave all of that.

"Well," Joe said, "win or lose, the county is going to get a good sheriff."

"Not as good as we had," said Cal, and slapped him on the back. "I am going to miss you, you old fart!"

They sat at the bar on the same stools they always sat on: two old friends in the twilight of their lives, soaking up the friendship.

"How's Linda Pendleton doing?" Cal asked.

Joe blew on his coffee, his big hands cradling the heavy mug. "You know, Cal, I guess I really can't say. She used to stop in from time to time after Dan died, but I ain't seen hide nor hair of her for nigh onto six months now. Guess she's just too busy trying to keep that place running out there."

"Got to give her credit, Joe. Not many women could do what she's doing. I thought somebody would get interested in her by now. She must be pushing forty-five, but she doesn't even look forty yet."

Joe looked around at the near-empty bar and cafe. He was going to miss this. He was going to miss it a lot.

When Ramon and the boys drove in that night, it was nearly six, and it was dark before they came into the bunkhouse to clean up for supper. Except for Ramon, the other men ignored Adam, or "Aaron," as they knew him. Ramon came over and sat down at the table with him, where he was greasing his new boots.

"Tomorrow, I want you to drive the fork lift, loading bales. Do you think you can handle that?"

"Not a problem," Adam said. "What time do we start?"

"Six a.m. I know it's Sunday, but it snowed up on the plateau last night, not a lot, but enough to make it greasy. We have two or three more days before we have all of the bales down, and there's a big storm in western Washington that's headed this way."

Adam did not answer, but nodded his head.

Linda had supper ready when they all filed into the house. There was a huge platter of ribs, fresh corn on the cob, and two big baskets full of baking powder biscuits, plus a bowl of fresh honey to dip the biscuits in. It was the best meal Adam had eaten in a long time, and he made a pig of himself, slowing down only when he caught Linda smiling at him over her coffee cup.

He smiled back at her. "That was so good, Mrs. Pendleton. You don't know how good it feels to eat a home cooked meal."

"We don't eat this good every night, Aaron, - and please, call me Linda."

All of the men seemed to leave at once, as soon as they were done eating. Only a couple of them commented at all about the food. Adam had heard some of them speaking in Spanish, and thought maybe they didn't speak English.

Adam brought an armful of dishes out of the porch and into the kitchen, where Linda was running water into the sink.

"Just stack them there," she said, pointing to an area next to the sink.

"Can I help?"

Linda turned and faced him, her hands covered with soapsuds. "You're getting to be too good to be true, Aaron."

She washed, and Adam, taking the dishes from her and rinsing them in the hot water dried them. Several times their arms touched and Adam was aware of her skin on his. Not in a sensuous way, but aware of the closeness, all the same. Something he missed: someone to be close to.

Adam could hear the wind long before he crawled out of bed. Ramon was up, moving around the bunkhouse, and a couple of the other men were sitting on the edge of their beds, rubbing their eyes.

One of them, called Sampson, obviously in reference to his huge size, stood looking out of the window. His hand was in the back of his long johns, scratching his butt, while his face had a look of contentment. Apparently he had found the right spot.

Adam stuck his head out the door to survey the weather. A sliver of a moon showed through some high wispy clouds that seemed to be rushing by in the darkness. In the distance, the same moonlight reflected off the snow-covered mountaintops. They looked cold and forbidding.

There was a brisk north breeze, and an old tin windmill, across the yard, rattled with its effects. Daylight wouldn't be for an hour yet, but a sodium lamp mounted high on a pole in the middle of the yard, lit the area with an eerie yellow glow. Adam could hear it humming as he stood in the doorway.

He looked toward the house, and saw that the "eating" porch, off the kitchen, was lit up. He could see Linda's shadow going back and forth behind the shades. When the shades went up, it was the sign that breakfast was ready.

"Close the door, asshole. You born in a barn?" Sampson was not in a good mood this morning.

Breakfast was sausages, and pancakes with fresh strawberries on top. Beside each plate was a bag lunch for that man. They ate fast, as Ramon was in a hurry to get up to the plateau and get going. If they had a good day today and tomorrow, they just might get done.

Linda had put the food on the table and left, but Adam could hear her moving around in the house.

"You come with me, Aaron," Ramon said, as he slid his chair back from the table. Adam stuffed the last of his pancakes into his mouth, and then suddenly realized Ramon was talking to him. He was going to have to get used to his new name.

There were several vehicles warming up when Adam and Ramon got out to the yard: three trucks with lowboy trailers behind them, one large diesel tractor with forks on the front of it, and two hay wagons attached to tractors.

"That tractor with the forks is yours," Ramon said. "When you get up there, pull the pin and drop the trailer by the first line of bales. It takes about forty-five minutes for each trip back we make, so you'll have some waiting around to do. Try to push as many bales together as you can while you're waiting, so you can load faster when we get there."

Adam had driven lots of tractors before, so in no time he was familiar with the controls, and heading up the mountain road behind the convoy.

The road was one-lane wide and covered with snow and ice. Several times the truck in front of him lost traction, and he had to wait for it to get going again. The road ducked in and out of the mountainside, and around curves, so sometimes there were taillights ahead of him, and sometimes he felt like he was the only one out there. His tractor was the slowest of the vehicles; so keeping up was out of the question.

At last, he broke out onto a flat stretch that had about a fifteen percent grade uphill. And then, there it was in front of him: the land they called The High Plateau. He could see the trucks about a mile ahead of him, and they appeared to be parked, waiting to be loaded.

The bales were huge, and weighed almost a thousand pounds each, but the big tractor handled them with ease. Ramon stood by and gave hand signals to show him how to place each bale.

At last they were all loaded and they headed back. Adam could see a long line of bales in the emerging daylight as he started gathering them up and putting them in one location. Alone with his thoughts he worked methodically, smoking Marlboro's and placing bales. He would no sooner get a pile of bales arranged, and the trucks and trailers would return.

The work became automatic and his mind wandered to other things: the life he once had, and the violence he was running from. But often it came back to the present, and Linda. Right now, she had given him hope and purpose. He was not sure how long it would last, but he hoped it would be for a long time. For now, he would take it one day at a time.

At noon they went into a machinery shed that had been built into the hillside and ate their bag lunches, with cups of steaming coffee. Adam sat by himself on the head of a large combine. The wheat that had been grown up here had long ago been harvested and stored in the grain bins back at the ranch. The equipment, for the most part, was stored up here, rather than risk the treacherous drive back down the mountain trail that Dan had built long ago.

The others sat around a homemade table, made with a half a piece of plywood and a large wooden spool. Their chairs were empty five-gallon pails. They chattered incessantly in Spanish, breaking into rounds of laughter from time to time, paying little or no attention to Adam.

Ramon stood by the door, looking at the sky and his watch. He must have eaten his lunch earlier, because he had none. It bothered Adam that he talked to him only when it was necessary to do so. He didn't seem rude, but he would never win any awards for congeniality, that was for sure.

Adam finished his sandwich and an apple that was in the lunch bag, along with a fresh, sticky cinnamon roll wrapped in wax paper. The same lunch they all had. Pulling out a paper towel that had been stuffed in the bottom for a napkin, he found a pack of Marlboro's wrapped inside it. Slid into a slit in the cellophane, was a note that simply said: *Thanks for the help with the dishes. Linda.*

CHAPTER FOUR

The sun was setting behind the mountains when Sheriff Carter walked out behind the building to get into his cruiser and head home, a ritual he would do only a few more times. He stared at the brown stucco building that he'd spent so many hours working out of, and a flood of memories washed over him, some good, some bad. The decision to retire had not come easy, but there comes a time in every man's working life when you pretty much have seen and done all you want to see and do. It was time to move on.

He had arthritis in his knees that seemed to get worse in the cold damp winters, and the thought of moving south, to warm sunshine, was an inviting idea. The downside: his love for this Big Sky country, and all of the friends he had made over the years. If only he could bundle them up and bring them with. Some of them, like Dan Pendleton, had already gone to their just reward. The thought of Dan made him remember he needed to go see Linda before he left. Maybe tomorrow. Tonight, he just wanted to get home to a hot meal and his wife's friendly chatter.

There was about an inch of snow on top of the cruiser, and Joe reached across with his forearm and cleaned off the windshield. The sky looked gray to the west, and he remembered the forecast this afternoon that had predicted a winter storm brewing west of the Rockies. Right now, it looked like it was going to hold together and hit them sometime tomorrow. He would have to make sure his snow blower was gassed up when he got home.

Inside the office, Ryan Markinson was sitting at the sheriff's desk, just trying to get the feel of it. Tony Winters was a worthy opponent for the up-coming election, but Ryan was confident he would win. He had been Joe's right arm for over ten years now, and most of the people in the county knew and trusted him. Besides, Tony was a lawyer, not a lawman. Most cops didn't have much time for lawyers, but Tony and he had always gotten along.

He leaned back in the chair, bringing his long legs out from under the desk to put them on the corner of the desk. Ryan saw the paper lying on the floor where his feet had been, and putting his feet back down, reached under the desk and picked it up. It was a 'wanted' poster and just one of hundreds that came through the office each year. He studied the face on the poster for a moment, and then laid it on top of the desk while picking up the ringing phone.

It was Joe. "Hey, Ryan, I just got home and the weather seems to be kicking up a little out there. Maybe you should make sure a couple of the cars have chains on them, in case anything happens in the mountains tonight. You know, it always takes a couple of storms before the damn fools around here know it's winter."

"Gotcha Joe. I'll call over to the County shops right away, and I'll get some sandbags in the trunks too. Have a good night, Joe."

"Thanks Ryan, I will." Joe pulled into the drive and killed the engine. Ryan had been a good and faithful deputy and he was going to miss him.

Ryan stood up and adjusted his gun belt. Once again he looked at the 'wanted' poster he had retrieved. He reached down, picked it up, crumpled it into a ball and threw it into the wastebasket. It was time to hit the road and get something done.

Linda was busy getting supper ready and getting it all into the pickup to bring up to the crew. They had had a good day, and Ramon had called and told her if they worked late they could probably finish, so she decided to bring supper up to them. The way the snow was coming down, they might not be able to get back up on the plateau tomorrow. Several times the trucks had gotten stuck and Aaron had pulled them out with the tractor. Only the constant trips back and forth, had kept the road open.

Adam stood on the step of the tractor waiting for the trucks to come back one more time. He watched down the road for lights, but so far hadn't seen anything but darkness and shadows. Then, through the swirling snowflakes and darkness, came just two headlights. At first he thought it was Ramon, but then he saw it was Linda's pickup, and he remembered that Ramon had said she was bringing supper up to them.

The road went straight over to the machinery shed and that's where she was heading, so Adam put the tractor in gear and headed that way. They arrived at almost the same time.

"Oh, I am not ready for this," Linda said, as she got out of the truck. "I cannot believe how treacherous that road is, coming up here. I hope no one slides off before you guys get done."

Adam smiled and started the small generator that provided electricity for the shed. "It is getting bad," he said.

They stood in the doorway watching for the trucks to return. Adam noticed how rosy her cheeks were, and how the snowflakes stuck to her long eyelashes. She turned and smiled at him. "It is kind of pretty. I guess winter is what you make of it. The same can probably be said for life, huh, Aaron?"

Adam did not make the name connection right away, again, but quickly recovered. "Yes, you're right. Life is what you make of it," he repeated her words. "As for winter - being from Minnesota, I'm no stranger to winter."

Linda reached up and brushed the snow off his face. "I see headlights.

Let's get the chow in here. You guys can bring the pots back when you come."

The stew was hot and tasted so good. Ramon sat with Adam for once, and they talked a little bit about their backgrounds. "I started working for the Pendleton's about four years ago. When Dan died, I thought I would have to move on, because Mrs. Pendleton and I just were not a good mix. But I guess we have developed a better understanding of each other. At least I hope so."

Adam smiled. "She seems nice to me."

"You know, she does seem to have taken a shine to you, Aaron." He stopped talking for a moment and stared at Adam as if he was looking for the right thing to say. "Good for you, Aaron," was all that came out. "Let's get done before we *are* snowed in."

By the time they finished eating, the snow was a blinding blizzard. Adam looked out across the vast grassland, now knee deep in snow, and saw Linda's taillights on the pickup slowly fading away as she made her way down the road to the ranch below. They scurried to load the last load of bales. Without any weight on the trucks, they could move very little in the slippery snow, and Adam was forced to drive around from vehicle to vehicle until they were all loaded, and could move under their own power.

"We need to winterize that tractor before we go down, and then you can ride with me." Ramon was standing in the doorway of the tractor cab, practically shouting to be heard over the engine and the wind. Adam nodded his head, "yes," and drove the big machine back to the shed where it was stored.

The two men hurried to add some additives to the fuel tank and then, with things buttoned up, headed down the trail one last time.

"Even if the others were right in front of us, I doubt if we would be able to see them in this mess," Ramon said. "Man, this crap is coming down. We're going to have cattle to tend to, tomorrow."

"This weather real hard on them?" Adam asked.

"They're all right for a few days, especially if the temperatures stay up, but they need food and this snow pretty well hides it. We might have to round some of them up and get them into a better area where we can feed them."

Ramon was fighting the steering wheel in the ruts that other trucks had made. "Damn!" he said. "Coming up here, Chico told me he almost lost his trailer over the side when it slid off the road. Now I know what he was talking about."

Not far below them now, they could make out the lights of the ranch, and Adam was resting easier. It was nearly midnight and everybody was tired. The other trucks and trailers were parked outside of the bunkhouse, still loaded.

Ramon shut off the key and said, "Let's get some sleep. We can unload in the morning."

It was warm in the bunkhouse, and it felt good. They had all gotten more than a little wet, and it felt good to get out of their outerwear. Adam sat on the edge of his bunk and ran his hands through his hair. Everyone else was already sleeping and he walked across the room to shut off the light. He stopped and looked out the window toward the ranch house, and noticed that the lights were still on in most of the house.

Man, doesn't she ever stop? he thought. For a second, it didn't register, but then he realized Linda's pickup was not there, either. In fact, it was nowhere in the yard that he could see.

He walked over to Ramon's bunk and shook him. "Hey, Ramon, where's Linda's truck? It's not parked by the house."

Ramon sat up and angrily said, "How the hell do I know where her truck is, man? Maybe she went to town or something. Go to bed and quit your damn worrying about her. She's a big girl, she don't need you to look after her."

Adam walked back to the window and looked out once more. Something was not right. He slipped his clothes back on, and stepped outside. The snow was up to his knees as he walked across the yard. When he got to the house, the door was unlocked so he went into the porch. He stood inside the doorway for a moment and listened. It was quiet, - the only noise was an appliance running in the kitchen. The long eating table was empty. Normally, she set out the breakfast dishes the night before.

Outside of helping Linda in the kitchen the other night, he had never been in the rest of the house, except the office. What he saw in the kitchen, however, only confirmed his fears. Dirty pans and kettles were on the stove, and the sink was full of dishes and silver. She would never leave it like that.

Adam walked through the large living room. There was a lamp on an end table next to a short white couch, and on the table there was a half-open book with a pair of reading glasses in it for a marker. At the end of a short hallway on the opposite end of the long room, there were two large bedrooms - one on each side, - and Adam headed that way. He glanced out the big picture window that looked out over the front of the ranch. The snow was coming down so hard he could only see a few feet. He had fears of a gun safety clicking off and someone challenging him as to what he was doing there, but he could see from the hallway that both bedrooms were empty.

The house was empty. She had either gone somewhere else, or never made it back. He ran out the back door into the yard. The main road coming in was drifted high with snow. Linda would never have gone anywhere else in this storm, and would not have been able, even if she'd wanted to.

He ran back to the bunkhouse, but Ramon, angrier than before, told him, "Go to bed, or get the hell out of the bunkhouse!" Adam looked at the other men in their bunks, and realized, without himself speaking Spanish, they were useless to him.

Linda had been cautious as she came down the steep, mountain road, and had the truck in low gear and four-wheel drive. Then, the truck's front wheels had slid into the icy ruts left from Chico's trailer, and she was powerless to stop it. She was in four-wheel drive, but without any weight in the truck, it would not jump back over the rut, and before she could stop or even think what to do, she was hurtling over the edge.

The truck fell about 20 feet before it crashed into some rocks; nose first, with a sound of crunching metal and breaking glass. The force of the impact slammed Linda between the steering wheel and the door, up against the dash, knocking the wind out of her. She seemed powerless to help herself, and grabbed for anything she could find. But there was nothing.

Her forehead hit the windshield, bending her neck back so far, that for a brief second, it felt like an electrical current had run through her body. Then the truck rolled onto its side and slid another ten feet, up against a large white pine, caving in the roof and squeezing her even tighter into the small area she was in. The truck was lying on the driver's door, and she was pinned in the very bottom of the cab. For a second, it was incredibly noisy, as the jack and some tools crashed down from where they had been stored under the seat, and landed, for the most part, behind her.

Her left arm was pinned under her and broke between her wrist and her elbow, with a snap like a willow branch. Her left shoulder dislocated, and her collarbone broke in a compound fracture that left a piece of it protruding out of her turtleneck sweater. The turn signal lever had jammed into her right side, between two ribs, breaking both ribs and puncturing her right lung. The rest of her somehow survived unscathed, but the damage was severe enough. Mercifully, she was unconscious.

When Linda awoke for a split second, she felt the pain in her punctured side almost immediately. That, along with the jolt from her spinal cord being pinched, caused a small, involuntary groan. Then everything was spinning red and green circles. White flashes of light went off behind her eyes as if a camera had gone off in her face, followed by blessed unconsciousness again.

For about ten minutes she remained unconscious, but then slowly she came out of it. It was difficult to breathe with only one lung and she felt like she was drowning. She tried to scream, but then realized how useless that was, and stopped. From where she was lying she could look straight up the mountainside, through the busted windshield, at the side of the road where the truck had rolled over. The relentless snow was now being blown right into the hole where the windshield had been.

The rest of the men were coming by soon and they would have to see her lights. There were dash lights on; there must be other lights outside, burning. Had they already passed by while she was unconscious?

With her right arm she tried to feel around in the dark, but she was hopelessly trapped, and the more she struggled the more she fought for air. Her arm was over the steering column, so there was not much she could do to help herself.

Snow and cold were filtering through the busted windows and she was so incredibly cold. Her clothing had been pushed up around her neck and her back and stomach were bare. Only her bra remained in place. Below her waist she had no idea what was going on, and she couldn't reach down there. Everything appeared to be ok; there was no pain, only a feeling of everything being squished together.

There was a sweet smell, and something hot was burning her right foot, and she realized it was antifreeze from the ruptured radiator, or a heater hose. Then there was a buzzing, sparking sound, and a smell of wiring burning. The thought of fire panicked her even more than she already was, and she briefly struggled again. Then the dash lights went out, and the sound went away. Except for the wind, it was deathly quiet.

Linda started to cry. She was going to die here. No one could find her in this storm, even if they knew she was missing, which they didn't. She hadn't brought a phone, even though she had thought about it.

She thought about Dan. At last, her family would be together now. Her struggles to make a living had come to an end. She remembered people saying that when you freeze to death, you just get tired and fall asleep. *It was painless, they said.* She had often wondered who had been resurrected to bring back the good news. *"Please God,"* she prayed, *"don't let me suffer."*

Adam was trying to think. There was no sense trying to drive anything back up there. There was no sense calling for help, because it would bring the very people who were hunting for him. He was on his own. He wasn't going to provoke Ramon again. He neither trusted nor liked him, and the last conversation told him to not push his luck. Not even a four wheel ATV could get through this. Maybe a snowmobile could, but if they had one he didn't know where it was. Adam pushed his way through the snow to the barn. Maybe, just maybe, a horse or mule could get back up that road. He had never had much to do with mules, although he had heard they were very sure-footed, something that would come in handy on a night like this. But stubbornness was also a trait of theirs, and he just didn't have time to deal with that. He walked over to Blaze's pen. Blaze eyed him over the top of the stall. He had that wide-eyed look horses get when they are on edge, and this horse had been that way all day. Animals can sense when the weather is bad, and Blaze had no desire right now to be anywhere, but in his warm stall.

"Easy, Boy." Adam held out his hand to the big stallion while stepping inside the pen. "You and I have a job to do, Big Guy." Adam stroked the big horse's neck and chin, while he slipped on the halter. He could feel the tension in the stallion's neck.

Blaze tapped his feet on the concrete floor in nervous anticipation of what was coming next, but when Adam led him out of the gate, he followed with no problem. Adam walked him down the wide aisle to the tacking area where he had laid out a saddle and blanket. Blaze was not sure what was going on, but he was extremely nervous, and turned to go back to his pen. Adam had to pull with all of his strength to get him turned back again.

At last they were ready. Adam turned up his collar, and buttoned up against what he knew was waiting outside that door. There was a sheltered area just outside the door; a roof-covered pavilion, and Adam took him there first, to let him settle down a little. Several beef cattle were lying down in the area trying to get out of the weather, and the horse stepped gingerly, trying to avoid stepping on them. The cattle were nervous too, and a chorus of bawling greeted them.

The roof was high enough that Adam could mount the horse, so he did and sat patting the big stallion's neck, trying to reassure him. It had been a while since he had ridden but, like riding a bike, you never forgot how. Only a few feet in front of them the snow was swirling off the roof, adding to a big drift that hid the corral fence. It had to be four feet deep.

The temperature was not that bad, but the cold was a wet cold, driven by the wind, and it seemed to penetrate right through his clothes. The snow was letting up a bit, but the wind was still rushing down from the mountains and sweeping the valley.

CHAPTER FIVE

Ryan Markinson had pulled all of the patrol cars off the roads for the night. As the night supervisor, it was his responsibility to keep his officers safe, as well as the people they served. A large snowplow had been brought in, but for the most part, crime takes a vacation when the weather is like this. Medical emergencies and stranded motorists would be their biggest worry. The highway patrol had closed I-80 several hours ago and the townspeople just plain knew better than to be out in weather like this.

Across the street from the sheriff's station was a large truck stop, called *The Junction*, and every available parking place was filled with 18-wheelers of every shape and size. Their diesel engines, idling through the night, were causing smog that stung the eyes despite the wind that was moving it away. The rows of yellow and red clearance lights on the trucks gave the whole scene an almost holiday atmosphere.

"Five bucks says some of them truckers will get drunk and start fighting before morning," Ryan said to Cheryl Pribnow, another deputy. They were standing holding their coffee cups looking out the window, almost mesmerized by the winter scene playing out in front of them.

Cheryl smiled and said mockingly, "Your are such a positive person, Ryan."

He laughed and gave her a good-natured tap on the shoulder. They had worked together for over ten years, and knew each other like a book.

Linda wasn't getting tired, and she wasn't giving up. Not yet anyway. She was shivering violently, however, and had never been this cold in her whole life. She found that if she stuck her head out the broken windshield, she could move forward a little, which relieved the cramping in her legs that were folded under her. But the turn signal lever, which had penetrated her side, was still in the way, and still partially inside of her. The pain, when she moved this area of her body, was excruciating. She could tip her head just far enough to see down there, but it was too dark to see the source of her pain.

Then she saw the tiny penlight, clipped to her key chain still in the ignition. *If I could just bend my right arm a little farther I might be able to reach it.* She was talking to herself now, which was good. She had talked herself out of problems before.

Linda moaned out loud as she moved the wrong way, but she had to try, or she was going to freeze to death very soon. *I need to think about this. What if I tried to just get the light off the chain? But I can only get this one finger in there. That'll never work, and I take a risk of dropping the light.* At last, she got her index finger through the ring up to the first knuckle. Linda hooked her finger on the key chain and tugged on it. The key would not come out because it was still in the on position. She wrapped the chain holding the flashlight around her finger, and bent her wrist backward so far, she screamed from the pain, until at last the key clicked back to off.

It took her only a couple more minutes, and she had the keys in her hand. *One step at a time,* she thought.

The penlight had a button on the end, and when she pushed it, the tiny beam of light was shining right in her face. Linda laughed with her small victory. She moved the beam of light down to her aching side, and tipping her head once more, she tried to make out the mess she was in. There was a mixture of blood and some yellowish fluid running down her side and collecting at her belt in some kind of gross, congealed mess.

It made her cough to look down at it, and that hurt so bad. She held her breath to stop coughing.

Oh God, please make the pain go away. Please help me get out of this mess. She closed her eyes and bit her lip to help mask the pain; a reflex action that she realized no one else was there to see.

She tried again, but her coat and clothing, bunched up around her neck, was in the way and she was getting exhausted from her struggles. It was so hard to breathe. It felt like somebody was squeezing her chest on her right side. *Oh Dan, I'm sorry; I don't want to die yet, honey. Help me, Dan, if you can.* She was sobbing now. *I know you hate it when I cry, sweetheart, but it hurts so damn much. I have to stop and think. I have to quit my damn bawling and think.*

There was nothing to do with the clothing except pull it over her head and out of the way, behind her head, with her right hand. She would put it back as soon as she got this damn thing out of her side.

At last she was looking at the trouble. The long, thin turn signal lever had gone into her side, right under her breast. It went deep at first, puncturing her lung with a broken rib bone. Right now though, it was still in her side, but just under the skin. Linda could make out its shadow just under the skin on her chest. She flattened her breast with her hand to get a better look at it. *I'm glad that was not hanging any lower than it was.* The thought made her smile through her pain.

Oh my God, I am cold. So cold. I have to get my clothes back in place, and soon. But here I am, harpooned on this damn thing and I can't move enough to get off from it.

Then she remembered the times she had sat in the truck while driving down the road, and absent-mindedly unscrewed the lever from the column. *It comes out. That's right! The damn thing comes out!*

She was going to have to do it with her left arm. Broke or not, it was pinned to her body, right under the wound. She hardly had to move it.

Her right arm, draped over the column, would never bend back that far.

Linda reached up and turned the lever ever so slightly. It was loose. The pain in her broken arm was not as bad as she feared. Not as bad as this damn thing turning inside her body. *So painful. Oh my God, I'm going to pass out before it's loose. Oh my God, Dan, I am going to pee my pants.*

Slowly it moved, and she screamed and moaned, but at last it was loose from the truck: still inside of her body, - but loose from the truck. She could not bear to remove it. Earlier blood and fluid had run from her side and drenched her jeans, but right now it was only oozing a little. The warm feeling in her pants told her that she had indeed wet herself. *Well, that's just great, Dan. Forty-five years old and I pissed my pants. Now to try and get out of here.*

Linda pulled herself up, far enough now that her head and shoulders were out of the truck, and she could get her right arm back on the left side of the steering column. She held the *penlight* in her mouth while she pulled her clothing back down. *Oh, that feels better. Not so cold, but I am getting tired now. I need to put my face in the snow to warm it up. Just need to rest for a while, Dan, and then I'll walk home and take a hot bath. I'll curl up in that comforter your mother made for us, and just rest for a while. Aren't you proud of me, sweetheart?*

She pulled herself almost halfway out of the truck and was lying with her back to the hood. Her head drooped almost to the ground, the flashlight still gripped in her mouth. Linda no longer realized it was even in her mouth. *Dan, come sit here beside me, honey. I know it's a bitch out here tonight, but I just need to rest for a while and then we can go home and you can make me a hot brandy and I'll relax in the tub. Where's Lee, sweetheart? If he's around, bring him along.*

Blaze was struggling, and Adam had all he could do to keep the horse heading into the wind. At first the big horse had almost frolicked in the snow, but now he was scared, and just wanted to get back to the warm barn. From time to time Adam had to reach around and clear the stallion's eyes of snow and ice. His warm hands helped to calm Blaze down a little.

It was about a two-mile straight ride before they started up the winding road to the grassland. The horse became more confident, moving easily through the area, almost as if he forgot his fear and was happy to be running. But as the grade got steeper, Adam could feel the tension coming back in his mount.

At the bottom of the hill there was a small pine forest that provided some shelter from the wind and snow, but it quickly gave way to rock and scrub trees. Beyond that it was a three-mile trip to the plateau.

There were times when Adam could see for forty or fifty feet. Then the wind would start swirling the snow again, and they would have to just stop and wait it out. The big horse would turn around, with his rear to the wind, while they waited. He had been in storms before.

Adam dismounted once to clean off Blaze's face, and reassure the animal that they were going to be all right. He had no idea how far they'd come, or how far they had to go. Adam had only made the trip up and back twice before, so he wasn't familiar with any of the landmarks.

As they neared the top, the grade flattened out before it flowed into the meadow and he could feel it doing that now. That in itself, was discouraging because he had seen nothing, - and if Linda had run off the road, it must be behind them. The road was wide enough up here. It seemed doubtful she had had trouble above where he was.

Adam stopped and turned Blaze around once more as a large gust threatened to dismount him. He could feel the big stallion stiffen up under him as he fought the wind, and Blaze shook his head nervously, and whinnied. He just wanted to be out of here.

Adam needed to think for a moment. If Linda was up here, she wouldn't survive for long. The window of time that he had to find her was closing rapidly. Was he going to waste more time going up, or should he head down and check the area again? He looked at his watch; it had been over an hour since he had left the barn.

He rubbed his eyes to clear the ice that kept forming on them.

When he looked again, the wind relaxed for a minute. For just a brief second, he thought he saw a faint flicker of light. It was below him and to his left, on a steep grade, and in a bend on the road. Adam nudged Blaze forward and closer to the edge. Maybe it was just a shiny rock or a piece of metal, but there was no moonlight that could have reflected.

Blaze was nervous so close to the edge, and Adam backed him up before he spooked, but not before, out of the corner of his eye, he saw the light again. This time longer than before, and this time, there was no mistaking it.

In order to get there, they had to ride down to the end of the switchback and come back again. It was not directly below them, - but below the road under them. The grade was too slippery for him to just go over the side on foot. He might end up several hundred feet down if he started sliding.

Adam was worried about losing this spot, so he counted the horse's footsteps until they rounded the curve and then counted them coming back. When they were about at the same distance, he stopped and dismounted. There was no light to be seen, but there was a roll of barbed wire fencing lying on the ground, that had been in the back of the truck next to the tailgate. He had seen it there when he took the coolers out, up at the shed. Adam didn't have a light, but he had brought a rope, - and tying himself off to Blaze, he started down the slope. He just had to hope and pray that Blaze stayed put.

He found the rock that the truck had hit first, - and the rest of the things that had been in the box. The coolers, some shovels, two bales of straw and some sandbags, for weight. Where had the truck gone?

He inched his way around the rock, but there was a drop of perhaps a hundred feet on this side of the granite slab. He pulled his way back up, and going around the rock the other way, the wind stopped blowing long enough for him to see the truck against the tree: the only thing between it, and a long way down.

Adam inched his way down the slope slowly and, just then, the horse moved up above him, pulling him back a few feet. He yanked on the rope to get Blaze's attention, and started back down. When he reached the back of the truck, he tied the rope off and slid, one hand-hold at a time, along the side of the truck on the downhill side, until he came to the roof and the tree. He had to hope the truck didn't move, or Blaze was in serious trouble, as would he be.

Peeking around the roof, and the tree it was leaning against, he saw Linda, half in and half out of the windshield, lying in the snow. The tiny flashlight was still shining beside her head.

Ryan and another deputy were making an emergency run on a woman in labor, just north of town. The huge snowplow cut easily through the drifts as they threaded their way around abandoned vehicles. An ambulance was following them with two paramedics on board.

Although it didn't happen a lot, he had already assisted on three baby deliveries in his fourteen years as a deputy. Not something he cared to do, but still something that he felt comfortable doing.

He would have felt better if Cheryl had been in the office, instead of a male deputy, but she had just left minutes before the call came in to assist the Fire Department on a car fire. Cheryl was starting to grow on him, and he caught himself thinking about her more and more.

Ryan was a single dad. Not an easy job in today's world. There had been a time when he thought he had the perfect marriage, but it had all come tumbling down when Wendy, his wife of twelve years, had taken an overdose of sleeping pills. Wendy had been troubled all of her life, because she had been molested when she was a young girl. Ryan thought that with a new start, and lots of love and encouragement, she would be able to put that part of her life behind her. But it was not to be.

She left him with an eight-year-old son, Dougie, who right now was the center of his life.

Cheryl, on the other hand, was a strong woman who had never married, but also had a son from a jilted lover. Ryan and Cheryl spent hours comparing kids' stories, as they liked to call it. They had just not taken that step yet, to expand their friendship. They were both being very cautious.

The excited father was standing outside on the driveway, hollering:

"Hurry, she's on the couch." A paramedic and the two deputies rushed inside, but one look told them everything was going to be fine. The baby, a little girl, was already delivered and the mother was holding her, despite the cord that was still connected to the placenta inside her. The decision was made to transport both mother and child to the hospital, so they were loaded into the ambulance.

Ryan took the father with him in the squad car, and the other deputy rode in the ambulance. It would give Ryan some time to get the information he needed, and give the father a moment to settle down.

At first, Adam thought she was dead. He took off his glove and reached out his hand, his fingers trembling, to touch her cheek. His other arm held tight to the truck, as it was a big drop right behind him. Then Linda moaned, and said, "Dan."

Adam scampered around the tree the rest of the way on his hands and knees and put his face close to hers. "Linda, It's going to be all right. I'm going to get you out of here."

She didn't answer, but seemed to be asleep or in a coma. He picked up the tiny light and shined it inside the truck to look at the rest of her body. It looked like she would slide right out with no problems. The only problem was the drop immediately behind them. One wrong move, and they would both be gone.

Just then the truck shuddered and moved, and Adam heard the horse above them calling out.

"Easy, Blaze!" he hollered, and scampered backwards to untie the rope. The last thing he needed right now was the truck being yanked around by a nervous horse. They would all be over the edge if that happened, including Blaze.

He had the rope in his hands as he made his way back to Linda. He was going to need Blaze to help them get back up the slope. Right now, his biggest fear was that the horse would spook and run off. He just hoped and prayed he wouldn't and he hoped the way he had him tethered would convince the horse that he was tied.

Adam shined the light in Linda's face. She was hardly breathing and he needed to hurry. He reached in and pulled her out farther, so her upper body was up against his chest, her back towards him.

Adam wanted to get Linda around the truck and on the other side, and then he could check further on her condition. He realized he might be hurting her, but right now he had little choice. The flashlight was safely in his coat pocket under his gloves. Using his feet to push them both, he inched his way backwards, until they were even with the front of the truck. Blaze pulled again, and Adam yanked back before he could go far. The horse stopped.

Adam sat on the rope to keep it taut. That horse was all that remained between death and tomorrow, for both of them.

Her head hung back, with her eyes tightly closed, and on her lips was the slightest smile, almost as if she was enjoying every minute of this. Retrieving the flashlight, he panned her body for obvious wounds. The left arm was deformed, so it must be broken, and there was blood on her jeans that looked like it had run down from under her sweater. Her breathing was labored. Not just shallow, but labored and raspy.

Adam raised her sweater and saw the wound still seeping. A broken rib protruded from the wound, and there was something else he could barely see. It looked like a piece of metal from the truck. Every time Linda breathed a bloody bubble formed at the hole in her side, and Adam knew that wasn't good.

There was nothing he could do to help her here, so getting on his knees, he picked her up in his arms, - still with the rope in one hand, - and started up the hill. The grade was steeper the farther he went, and he slipped and fell to his knees several times. Only the rope wrapped around his right hand kept him from sliding back where he had come from, or worse yet, over the edge. With every step Adam took, he had to keep wrapping the slack around his arm. Blaze needed to know that Adam was on the other end of that rope.

Suddenly the rope went slack again and Adam stopped in his tracks. What was Blaze doing now? He talked to the horse, moving about above him. Clicking his tongue loudly he hoped he could be heard over the wind, but there was no response. Linda moaned and stirred in his arms,

44

and he went back on his knees and held her tighter, trying to blow his warm breath on her face. Adam put his mouth over hers, lightly, to feel if she was exhaling and he could feel a slight rush of air against his cheek from her nose. Her mouth was soft, and although it was no time to feel sensuous, the thought was there.

Blaze whinnied, and when Adam looked up, the horse was looking over the edge, about twenty feet above him. There was a cloud of snow swirling around the big stallion's head and he reared back slightly, as if to say, *come on Adam get it together. It's damn cold up here.*

"Hang on, big guy, I'm coming!" Adam shouted to be heard over the wind. He started up once more, holding Linda as tight as he could against him, and with every step he took, Blaze retreated, keeping the rope tight.

A few feet from the top the slope was grassy underneath, and his feet slipped from under him, but Blaze quickened his pace pulling both of them over the edge and onto the road.

Adam was lying on his back, holding Linda on top of him. The big horse reached down and nuzzled her hair. "You did it, big guy. You got us up here. Now, let's get us home." Adam stroked the horse, and then grabbing his mane, he pulled both of them up.

Across the road the land sloped up again, strewn with rocks. Adam moved towards a rock about three feet high, and struggled to climb on top of it, but not without first laying Linda down on it, and then picking her up again, when he was on top.

Blaze understood, and came over to the rock, and Adam lifted Linda onto the saddle, and then untied the rope. He leaned her forward against the horse's neck, and steadied her with one hand, while he got on behind her. Then, holding onto her with both arms wrapped around her chest, Adam started Blaze down the trail, gripping the saddle tightly with his legs. The reins were dragging, but he didn't even try to get to them, - the horse knew where to go.

CHAPTER SIX

At the hospital, the new mother and child were brought into the emergency room to finish things up. The father had been asked to wait outside in the waiting room for a few minutes, and Ryan was talking softly to the obviously shaken man, while he tried to complete his report. The young man had stuffed his mouth full of chewing tobacco, and was holding a paper spit cup between his shaking hands as he answered Ryan's questions, - Address, phone number, etc.

A lone janitor dressed in gray Dickeys, and with a large ring of keys attached to his belt, pushed a mop back and forth in the corner of the room. The sweet smell of Pine-Sol disinfectant was reminiscent of a high school locker room. Over the public address system, a soft voice was paging Dr. Larson to the Emergency Room.

An old Indian was sleeping on a couch across the room; otherwise the waiting room was empty. The Indian's face was a virtual road map of wrinkles and scars. His face held a look somewhere between pain and fatigue. His eyes were closed, but his mouth was open enough to display a line of yellow, jagged teeth, most of them just fragments. The old man's fingers were stained almost orange from tobacco use, and his unkempt hair had been pulled into a greasy ponytail and tied with what was left of an old red bandana

Ryan walked over to the admittance desk. The woman behind the desk looked up from the McCall's magazine she was reading, and said, "Yes, Deputy?" clearly irritated by the interruption.

Ryan nodded his head in the general direction of the old man, and asked, "What's his story?"

She hesitated for a second, but then said, "He got caught in the storm and needed a place to sleep it off. He's all right."

"Just checking." Ryan turned and walked back outside into the parking lot. A front-end loader was busy pushing snow into a pile in one corner of the lot.

The county snowplow that had led them to the hospital was still parked there, and Ryan walked over and knocked on the door, waking up the dozing driver.

"Thanks for helping us out," he said. "Would you mind giving the guy a ride back home?"

"Sure, no problem," he said. "Tough night out here, tonight."

"Yeah, it is," Ryan, said. "Not fit for man or beast, and I hope no one else has any damn problems tonight," He walked over and settled into his cruiser. "This is 4-14, and I'm clear of the hospital and returning to the office," he told dispatch.

"Ten four," came the reply. "You're clear at three twelve."

But there was a man, - and a beast, - and a dying woman, - who were struggling against the cold and snow on a lonely mountain road, picking their way back to safety, one step at a time.

Adam could no longer feel his fingers inside his gloves, but he didn't dare let go of Linda long enough to flex them. The snow had let up, somewhat, but the wind was not any better and the temperature was falling rapidly.

His hands were locked together around her chest, and her chin was resting on the top of his hands as she slumped forward, her head bouncing with every step the horse took.

Blaze seemed to sense the seriousness of the situation, and moved somewhere between a walk and a trot, his head bobbing as he pressed forward. The big stallion was covered with snow and ice, and he too, was feeling the effects of the storm and the load he was carrying. He shook his head from side to side, to try and clear his face.

Adam had no idea where they were, and could only hope that the horse would find the way home. He had started to shiver himself, and tremors shook his body as he concentrated on staying on top of the bouncing animal. He had his face buried in the back of Linda's neck, trying to exhale what heat there was in his breath, down the back of her neck. There was little else he could do.

For a moment, it looked like trees alongside of them, and Adam remembered the forest at the lower levels. That was a hopeful sign. But it must have been just a small patch of woods, because now they were looking at granite walls again, and he knew they were not that far down the slope.

It seemed like an hour later, but actually was probably not more than fifteen minutes when Adam made out the real woods ahead. The trees here sheltered the trail, the going would be easier, and there was a lot less snow for Blaze to struggle through. Adam wanted to stop and check on Linda, but the horse would not respond to his commands to stop. He just kept plodding on, as if he was in some kind of a trance.

What good would it do to stop; my hands are frozen and useless. If I do let go of her I may never be able to grip her again. Every moment we spend out here is just one second closer to death, and the prudent thing is just to get the hell out of this weather, and inside some place where it's warm.

He imagined that he could feel her heart beating through the arteries in her neck, where his chin rested, but then, it could just be his own heartbeat too.

He cursed Ramon for not helping him, and decided if Linda died, there would be a day of reckoning. He had evened the score once before, and he could do it again.

The horse was getting weaker, and Adam could feel his steps

48

faltering, He tried to talk to the animal and encourage him on. The horse gave no sign that he heard him.

Adam had no idea where they were when Blaze finally settled to the ground. He didn't fall over; he just knelt down as a camel would, to let you off. His head was still up but it was obvious the animal could go no farther.

For a few moments Adam tried to think what to do next. He slid off the animal's back, pulling Linda with him, and they lay in the shelter of the big stallion. Maybe Blaze could give her some shelter and he could walk for help. But then, maybe the horse would revive and walk away, and Linda would be lying here alone. Even if he found help, would he be able to find Linda and Blaze again when he came back?

Adam stood and walked a few more steps in what he felt was the right direction. He stuffed his hands down the front of his pants to warm them, but he might just as well have shoved a board down his pants, for all the feeling he had left in them.

He went back to Linda, and now the horse was lying down flat on the ground. Adam knew he had to get her out of there. She wasn't as heavy as he thought she would be. Maybe he was having an adrenalin rush, - and how long would that last? For a minute the wind slowed down, as if resting itself for the next big blow. It became strangely quiet, compared to the roaring they had been listening to, and then he heard a different sound. It was the squeaking of the blades on the windmill. He started walking in the direction of the sound and then he could faintly make out the yard light. Blaze had brought them to within a hundred yards of the house.

Adam started moving faster with her. It wasn't running, but a fast trot. He tripped over something and fell, but quickly he was back on his knees, and then standing and moving again. Then the roof of the barn came into view, and he knew the house was just to his left.

He tripped over the bottom step and fell forward, with both of them crashing into the door. Linda moaned, and Adam screamed: "Yes! Yes! You are alive!"

Back at the office, Ryan, Cheryl and one other deputy sat around the table in the small lunchroom. A sleepy-looking news anchor on the television was encouraging everyone to stay inside until the winds let up.

They were playing gin rummy and not really paying any attention to the television. The room still smelled of microwave popcorn, and Cheryl shoved a handful into her mouth as she giggled and laid her cards down

"That's Gin, boys. Pay up!"

Both men had their hands in their pockets, digging for change when the portable radio sitting in the middle of the table crackled and came to life.

"Squad 4-14 are you still on the air?"

Ryan reached over and squeezed the button on the hand-held as he brought it to his mouth.

"4-14. Go ahead, dispatch." *Damn, not another fool out in the storm,* he thought.

"4-14, we just got a 911 call from the Pendleton ranch. Are you familiar with that? The caller seemed to be disoriented and couldn't give me any help with an address, but just said it was the Pendleton ranch, and a lady was dying and they needed help fast."

"I know where it is," said Ryan, "but it will be awhile before we can get there, if we can get there at all. Call them back and see what the problem is, and maybe the hospital could give them some advice about what to do for her until we can get there."

Cheryl was already on the radio to the county plow operator that had assisted them earlier, and he said he would head that way, along with another plow that had just came on duty.

A call to the hospital was set up, for advice, and the helicopter was put on standby, although the word right now was that they couldn't fly in this weather.

Ryan and Cheryl left the other deputy to mind the fort, and took off in Ryan's cruiser to rendezvous with the plow.

When Adam had finally stumbled through the porch and into the house, he was exhausted. He dumped Linda on the couch in the living room, oblivious to her injuries, because he could go no farther. For a second he knelt beside the couch, gasping for breath, his head resting on her thighs.

Then, reaching for the phone on the end table, he punched in 911. His frozen fingers misdialed twice, but at last the voice said: "911 emergency, how can I help you?"

"We need help!" Adam gasped.

"What kind of help, sir, and where are you at?"

"The Pendleton ranch. Mrs. Pendleton has been in an accident, and she has this wound in her chest. She was also caught outside and I think she may have hypothermia. Her hands and face look like they're frozen."

Without waiting for an answer, Adam hung up the receiver. Linda hadn't moved since he put her down. Her head hung back and her mouth was open. When she breathed, it was labored and raspy. Her cheeks and forehead were a waxy yellow, and her hair, which had been wet, was frozen.

Adam turned on the lamp that was on the end table with some difficulty, because his fingers still felt like they weren't even his. The light showed a large, bloody stain on her sweater from the wound in her side, and he lifted it to look at the wound once more, as the phone on the end table rang.

He stared at it for a moment, and then picked up the receiver. Hello was the only word he could think to say.

"Sir, this is the emergency operator and I want you to know that help is on the way. But right now, if someone is seriously hurt, you need to do what you can to help him or her. Do you understand me?"

Adam stared at the phone for a moment and then answered, "Yes."

"Sir, I have the hospital on the line with me and they're going to talk to you, so please don't hang up."

Adam hadn't said anything yet because he still wasn't thinking straight, when a male voice said, "Hello, are you there?"

"Yes," Adam managed to say.

"This is Dr. Kevin Larson at County Hospital. Can you tell me what kind of an accident this lady has been in, and what are her obvious injuries?"

"She slid off a mountain road in her truck," he began. "She has a wound in her chest with broken ribs showing. She's having a lot of trouble breathing, and there's some kind of metal rod still stuck in her chest. She's also very cold."

Dr. Larson stopped to think for a second, and then asked, "Can you hear air escaping from the hole in her chest when she breathes?"

"Not right now," Adam replied, "but when she was on the mountain, I could see bubbles of blood coming out."

"Is she conscious?"

"No."

"How long had she been outside, and was she dressed warm?"

"I don't know how long it was, but she only had a light jacket on, and we had to get back off the mountain on a horse, and that took a-----"

"Look, sir. What's your name?"

"Adam." *Shit, he had used the wrong name. Too late now*

"Adam, get her into a warm bath. Can you do that? Not hot, just warm, - you need to warm her body up. But before you get too much water in the tub, you need to cover that wound in her chest with some kind of plastic, - like a sandwich bag. Tape it in place. Can you do that?"

"Yes," he answered.

"Then get her undressed and do it, and then come back and talk. Don't hang up the phone. I'll stay on the line. Now go."

Adam ran into the bathroom and started the tub running. His hands had no feeling, so he had to put his whole arm under the faucet to gauge the temperature. He pushed the stopper in place and ran back to the couch.

It would be easier to remove her clothing on the couch, so he pulled at her frozen bootlaces, but his fingers still wouldn't work. There was a sewing kit next to the end table, and opening it up, he found a scissors right on top and cut the laces, then pulled her boots off. Next, he pulled her sweater over her head, taking the jacket off at the same time.

There was also a plastic bag full of buttons right where he had found the scissors, and he dumped them out, and laid the plastic over the ragged wound.

Tape. He needed tape.

Back in the bathroom, he checked the filling tub, then opened the medicine cabinet and found a roll of white adhesive tape.

The wound seemed to extend beneath her bra, so Adam cut the bra off with the scissors. Cutting strips of tape; he taped the plastic in place. He then pulled her jeans off, but left her white cotton panties on. He had invaded her privacy too much already.

Adam carried her into the bathroom, and slipped her into the tub. Rolling up a bath towel, he put it behind her head and then, slowing the water flow, he went back to the phone.

"Doc, you there?"

"Yes. Yes, Adam, go ahead."

"I have her in the tub and she seems to be about the same."

"Good. Well, Adam there's not much more I can do to help you with her. Just stay with her in case she wakes up. She might be scared. The ambulance will be there soon, I hope. Good luck, my friend and I'll see you back here."

Adam sat on the floor next to the tub with his hands in the water. His hands burned as the feeling started to return, and he could also feel his face burning as it thawed out.

For the first time, his gaze fell to her breasts, but he wouldn't let it linger there. They were small but firm. He remembered the first time he had seen Mandy's breasts and how it had excited him. Mandy had been embarrassed, and it embarrassed him to invade her privacy. Oh, how he had loved her. *Why couldn't I have helped her like this?*

Adam could see the deformity in her lower left arm, which was almost certainly broken. Her legs and feet looked fine. The left side of her white panties was stained with blood that must have run down from the wound in her side.

Linda's breathing seemed to become more rapid, but there was still no sign of her feeling any pain, - or waking up. He reached down and let out some of the water, and then re-filled the tub. He thought about the horse, and wondered if he was still alive? But he couldn't leave Linda to go find him, and he wasn't even sure where he was.

The plow could go no more than a few miles an hour in some places because it wasn't even clear where the road was, but in the areas where the wind had blown the surface clear, Kelsey gave the big truck the gas. They were a small parade as they headed into the countryside: two plows, followed by an ambulance and a patrol car.

It was over twenty miles to the ranch, and then a few more up the winding road to the house.

Ramon was awake early, before the alarm went off. This early snowstorm had caught them by surprise and there would be lots of problems today. The first, and most important, would be to check on the cattle on the range to see how they had weathered the storm. There was also lots of snow to move, clearing the yard and the driveways.

He stood in the bathroom, relieving himself, and brooding. Aaron had pissed him off last night. Ever since Aaron had come here, Ramon had the feeling that Linda was sweet on this guy. Maybe it was the fact he was white. Maybe she was having a middle-aged crisis. Whatever the case, Ramon was going to clear the air with both of them, - and soon.

He left the bathroom and turned on the light in the bunkhouse. Choruses of Spanish swear words came from the men in the beds, but Ramon ignored them. They would work for a couple of hours clearing snow and then have breakfast. He walked over to the window and looked out. Drifts were everywhere, and the rooster tails of blowing snow coming off the tops of them, were evidence that the wind was still blowing hard.

Then he noticed Aaron's empty bunk. Quickly, he turned to look at the house and saw the lights on. Had he spent the night with her?

Dressing rapidly, he pulled on his boots and headed for the house. The other men sat looking at each other, not knowing what to think.

Adam heard the back door open, and thinking help had arrived, scrambled to his feet and walked through the living room to find it was only Ramon.

"Where is she at?" Ramon spit the words at Adam, pointing his finger in his face as he crossed the room towards him.

"She's here in the bathroom. No thanks to you, we both nearly froze to death, and there's a horse out there, either dying or dead, who has more common sense than you ever had!"

Ramon brushed by Adam and stood in the bathroom doorway looking at Linda in the tub. He saw the bandage on her chest and her broken arm. He stared at the bloody underwear, and looked at her head titled back on the rolled up towel, her mouth open wide as she struggled for every breath.

"What? How?" His face was a question mark, and the angry look had gone.

"She ran off the road on the way back from bringing supper up to us. I saddled the stallion and rode him up to look for her, because there was no other way."

"Where is the horse?"

"I don't know," said Adam. "Close by, but out there somewhere. He carried us as far as he could, and then he collapsed. I called for help and they're on the way. The doctor told me to get her into warm water, so it's not what you might think."

"Stay with her, and I'll get the men out and clear the road and yard." Ramon hesitated, the apology was right there on the end of his tongue, but he couldn't say it.

Adam walked back into the bathroom, and Linda's eyes were open, and she was looking around as if she didn't know where she was. He sat down on the floor next to the tub and put his hand on the side of her face. "It's going to be all right. Just lie still. Help is on the way."

She looked down at her near nakedness, but made no attempt to hide it. The look of fear on her face faded away, and through her pain, she smiled faintly, but said nothing.

CHAPTER SEVEN

It was 4:45 a.m. when the big plow broke through the last drift and turned in to the drive that led to the ranch house. Just ahead, Kelsey could see the yellow flashing lights of the front-end loader that was coming toward him, with Ramon at the controls.

The men had cleaned out a good portion of the yard and the walks to the house. The ambulance pulled around the now-waiting plows, and parked next to the back door.

One moment Adam was alone with Linda by the tub, and the next minute, the living room and bathroom were filled with a gurney, oxygen bottles, and first aid kits. The two medics and the two deputies were methodically making preparations to get Linda loaded into the ambulance.

They removed Linda from the tub, wrapped her in warm blankets, and put her on the stretcher. Her eyes were open but she still remained mute. Shock, the medics had diagnosed. Her eyes kept searching for Adam, but they wouldn't let him near her. In the next room, one of the paramedics was looking at Adam's frostbitten face and hands, and was urging him to come into the hospital too.

"You could lose some fingers if you don't take care of this. Your ears are almost as bad." He had Adam sit on the couch and he held the lamp up to his face to get a better look.

Ryan walked over to where Adam was sitting. "You work for Mrs. Pendleton?" he asked.

Adam nodded his head, yes, but said nothing.

"What's your name and what do you do here?"

"I do whatever I am asked," Adam answered, deliberately not giving out his name.

Ryan did not ask again, but rather told him, "You better go in and get yourself looked at. We can talk more later about the accident."

"Aaron, please come with me." Her voice startled Adam. Linda was right in front of him now, as they were wheeling her out. She held her hand out and he took it. The medics stopped for a second so they could talk. It was good to hear her talk, but now her face was screwed up in a painful expression, and tears were running down her cheeks. A slight sob came out as she said, "Please, Aaron, I need you."

Adam rode in the front seat of the ambulance with the driver, but he sat sideways so he and Linda could talk. There were sliding glass windows between the front and the back, and he had opened them. She couldn't see him, but she knew he was right in front of her. She kept her hand up next to her face, and Adam reached through the opening and grasped it. The sun was just starting to come up over the horizon in the east, as they pulled into town following the snowplow.

Once in the emergency room, they were separated. Linda was taken upstairs to an operating room designed just for hypothermia victims, and to have surgery on her broken bones and punctured lung. For the present, she was listed in critical condition. Adam sat in a chair in the ER while a doctor worked on his hands and face. They would be keeping Linda in the hospital for some time, if she survived, but Adam was being patched up and sent home.

"I want you to apply this salve to your hands and face for the next few days." The doctor handed Adam some tubes of the same salve.

"You'll have a lot of irritation and peeling skin, but otherwise I think you should recover without any problems. Do you have any questions?"

"Not about me," Adam said. "How can I find out how Linda, -- ah, Mrs. Pendleton is doing?"

"Why don't you just stay here for a little bit and I'll try to see what I can find out. Is she family, or a friend of yours?"

"No.—I mean, yes. Not family, but she is my friend."

The doctor patted Adam on the back. "Hang in there, I'll be right back."

Adam looked around the small cubical in the emergency ward. There were several other gurneys but they were all empty. In fact, he was the only person in the room. A phone was ringing at the desk, but no one was answering it. There were the usual oxygen hoses and heart monitoring equipment, and a locked cabinet was on the wall behind him, with several bottles of salves and pills in it.

He looked down at his red and blistering hands. How was he going to be able to work like this? Maybe it was time to move on. He was glad the police hadn't stayed around. He felt like a hunted animal would feel, seeing hunters in the woods. His only defense was to flee, but first, he wanted to make sure Linda was all right.

Adam heard footsteps in the hallway, and the doctor was back.

"They're just finishing up with her right now. They had to close the hole in her chest, and repair her lung, but it went well. Her temperature has been restored to a normal range. She took several units of blood, and the risk for infection is always there with an injury like that, but all in all, she's doing well. They *are* going to keep her in ICU for a couple of days to monitor her, and then she'll need some additional time here, at the hospital. I would suggest you go home, if you can get home. Call tomorrow and see how things are going."

Adam slid down off the gurney he had been sitting on. "Is there a phone I can use?" he asked.

He called three taxi companies before he found one with a four-wheel drive that said they would try to get him home. The weather was clearing, and the wind had died down.

Ryan went off duty at 7 a.m. Both he and Cheryl had kids to get home to, and it had been a long night. They walked out into the early morning Montana air together, and he walked her as far as her car.

"Cheryl, do you think you can get through to your house?"

"I live closer than you do Ryan, but why don't you follow me? It looks like the plows are moving." The street in front of the office was clean, and some traffic was moving with people trying to get to work.

Cheryl lived about three miles away on a major road, and when they got to her house, Ryan got out and helped her clean off her driveway. He ran the blower while she shoveled behind him.

As soon as they were done and the equipment was put away, Cheryl said, "Come on in and I'll make some coffee. Give the plows a little more time to get your road clear."

"Sounds good," he said, following her into the neat, one story rambler.

The house smelled clean, almost a soapy smell. He was standing on a clean blue rag rug right inside the door.

Ryan took off his boots and sat at the kitchen table. Cheryl disappeared around the corner and came back wearing a pair of blue jeans and a baggy sweatshirt that said, 'Go Broncos,' on it, a reference to her old alma matter. "That feels better," she said. They sat on the same side of the table, drinking their coffee, and eating day old cinnamon rolls.

"Did you think there was anything strange about that guy who rescued Mrs. Pendleton?" he asked.

"Strange, how?" Cheryl asked. "He was awfully quiet, if that's what you mean."

"No, no, I don't mean that. He just seemed to want to avoid me, that's all. I think he deliberately avoided giving me his name."

She swallowed her coffee, and wiped her mouth with the back of her hand. "You and I both know, Ryan, that half of these guys that work on these ranches are drifters, and running from something. Sometimes it's the law and sometimes it's a wife."

Ryan didn't answer her right away. He was looking at the neat kitchen walls with a coffee cup collection hanging on wooden pegs. A towel was folded over the oven door; the place was spotless. How he wished his place looked like this.

"Right, Ryan?" Cheryl was still looking for an answer to her comment.

"Yes, you're right. I guess I just thought I'd seen him somewhere before, but probably not."

"I better hit the trail and get home." Ryan was standing and pulling his coat back on, though he hadn't been there much more than five minutes.

"Already? Do I smell bad, or something?"

Ryan smiled, shaking his head, no. "It's nothing, - I just need to get home. "Thanks for the coffee."

Thanks for the help, and thanks for caring about me." Cheryl held her hand out limply.

Ryan smiled and said, "I can use your vote."

She laughed, and then, as if on impulse, she reached up and kissed him on the corner of his mouth. "Take care, partner, and you have my vote."

The kiss did two things. It made him feel a little closer to Cheryl, and it made him forget about Adam.

Cheryl stood in the window watching him drive away. She felt good, when she was around him.

When Linda awoke, she was still groggy from the anesthesia. There was a tube down her throat and her chest felt like it was on fire. A machine behind her was giving off a beeping sound, and there was an IV tube dripping slowly into her right arm. Her left forearm was in some kind of a cast, almost too heavy to lift off the bed. The lights were dim in the room, but she could make out other beds, beside her and across from her. They all appeared to be empty. A nurse was sitting with her back to her, at a desk in a glass cubicle working on charts.

Something was also uncomfortable in her crotch, and reaching down with her right hand, she felt the catheter tube that was there, and it was taped to her leg. Bringing her hand up her body, she could feel a band of heavy bandages across her chest. Another plastic tube came out of the bandages and went under the bed.

She stared at the ceiling, trying to make sense of where she was and how she had gotten here. She remembered the crash and being trapped in the truck. The terrible experience of that piece of metal stuck in her chest, and being so cold, but it was all foggy after that. Except, she remembered being in the bathtub in her house and Aaron sitting beside her, but she didn't remember why. She recalled the ride to the hospital and Aaron talking to her in the ambulance, but shortly after getting to the hospital it was all a blank.

She coughed, and it hurt so bad she moaned out loud, and the next second there was a nurse at her side, checking her bandages and talking to her about how lucky she was to be alive. Linda couldn't answer her with the tube down her throat, but she reached up and grabbed the nurse's arm, pleading with her eyes to get the tube out.

"Tomorrow," was all she would say. "Tomorrow, if everything goes right. You need to rest, dear." Then she injected something into the IV and Linda felt herself slipping away again.

Because the roads had been plowed on the way in, the ride back to the ranch was uneventful. The sun glared off the white landscape, and the Indian driver with his wrap-around sunglasses had little to say. That is until they arrived, when he said, "Twenty three dollars, please."

Adam fished a five, and a twenty out of his front pants pocket and handed it to him. The money was still wet, as was his clothing, and he couldn't wait to get out of them.

The driver laid them on the other seat with a slight look of disgust, saying nothing.

"Keep the change."

Adam walked over to the house first, while squinting in the bright sunlight. He needed to get something to eat before he did anything. It was early afternoon.

The yard and the road were cleaned of snow. All of it was piled in a huge mound beside the horse barn. There was no sign of the other men anywhere.

When he reached the porch, he turned and looked toward the mountain they had come down from, early this morning. It looked quiet and peaceful. The pine trees were covered with so much snow that it threatened to break their boughs.

Then he thought of Blaze. Had he survived? Adam didn't think so, because the big horse had laid down just before they left, and looked like he was close to death.

He walked back down the steps and started in the direction they had come from last night. He would have to find him and give him a decent burial. They wouldn't have made it without him.

Adam walked almost to where the road started to rise up to the foothills, but there was no sign of the horse. The slight breeze and the sun made his blistered face ache, and he walked backwards to protect himself. He could be under a drift anywhere. They might not find him until spring.

He stopped to light a cigarette, and his pants leg caught in a loose strand of barbed wire next to a gate he remembered riding through last night. He walked back the way he had come and then he saw some hoof prints. They had to have been made after the wind died down, or they would have blown away. They were heading toward the open corral and the back of the horse barn.

Adam was running now and whistling for the horse. When he got to the area that was not fenced in there were several head of beef cattle that had taken shelter behind the barn, but no Blaze.

He walked amongst the cattle, which for the most part, ignored him. Some of them were lying down and others were milling about bawling for feed, and then, - there! - lost in the sea of Black Angus cattle, was Blaze. He was lying down next to the barn, with his back against the wall in the sunlight. The saddle and blanket were still on him.

The big horse's eyes were full of matter, and his ears were bleeding from being frozen. At first Adam didn't think he could get him up, but finally with a lot of pushing and prodding, the big stallion got shakily to his feet. Adam led him inside the barn to his stall.

He gave him some warm water to drink, stripped him from his tacking, and brushed out the rest of the snow and ice. He groomed Blaze's face and ears and fed him sugar lumps and sorghum that he found on a shelf. He also found some bag balm that he massaged into his ears, much to the big horse's dissatisfaction. There seemed to be no other obvious injuries, and it would remain to be seen, if he got sick. *Maybe Ramon would know what Veterinarian to call. - If he would talk to him.*

Suddenly the hunger was back, and he realized he hadn't eaten yet, so he headed over to the house. The sun was high enough in the October sky so that the roof line on the house was dripping water from thawed snow, despite the fact it was only 20 degrees out. All of the breakfast dishes still sat on the table, so he collected them and went into the kitchen. The stove was covered with greasy pans, so he ran water in the sink and started cleaning up.

He had no idea where the others were, or when they would be back, so at least he could cook and clean in the meantime.

Adam found himself thinking of Linda as he stood at the sink, washing kettles. It had been nice the other night when they had stood here together doing dishes. She made him feel good about being here. She just made him feel good, period. He stood looking out the window with a towel in one hand and three dinner plates in the other. *Please let her be ok, God.* It was the first time he had prayed in a long time.

When the men got back from the range, Ramon came into the house, where Adam was just finishing up making supper for them.

"Where were you all day?" He spoke sharply as he came in the door, stomping the snow off his feet.

"They wouldn't let me go from the hospital until almost three, and

I didn't know how to get a hold of you guys, so I just kind of cleaned up here and made some chow for tonight." He stood staring at Ramon and wiping his hands on the white apron he had put on.

Ramon just stared at Adam for a moment, and then said softly. "You look like shit, man." He was staring at the blisters that were forming on Adam's face. "How is Mrs. Pendleton?"

"Last I heard, she was holding her own. They told me they would call if there was any change and I haven't heard anything."

Ramon sat down at the end of the table and ran his hands through his black wavy hair. "Look, Aaron, I'm sorry I didn't take you seriously last night. You did a great thing, man, and I wasn't much help. Why don't you just take a few days off and get healed up."

"If you can stomach my cooking, I can handle that part of the chores," said Adam. "Meanwhile, we have a sick horse I need you to look at."

The two men knelt in the straw and looked at Blaze. He looked worse than he had this morning. It took both of them, to get him to his feet.

"I'll call the vet," Ramon said, "and in the meantime, I am going to give him some antibiotics. We might have to put him down."

Linda was awake, but still under the influence of painkillers. She was so full of tubes and wires it made it hard to move. She remembered the tube in her throat from before, but now it was gone. Her eyes moved around the room taking in everything she could see while lying flat in bed. She moved her toes under the covers to try and see what worked and what didn't. She pulled her knees up a foot or so, bending her legs, and that seemed to go all right. Raising her arms despite the IV tubes, she looked at her hands, and the cast on her left forearm. She did remember seeing her arm broken and deformed in the truck.

She moved her head from side to side and although she was sore, it seemed to be ok. Her face felt hot and flushed, and she felt her cheeks with her fingertips. There were some kind of sores on her nose and cheeks. Almost like she had been burned. She wanted a mirror, but the top of her nightstand had only a small oval bowl with a toothbrush in it and a bottle of some kind of prescription drug.

Her chest was sore and it hurt to try and raise herself up on her elbows, but she tried anyway. Now she could see over the foot of the bed into the nurse's station, where two nurses, male and female, were reading a chart and laughing. But she could only see them, not hear them. There had to be some way to get their attention.

Tired of holding herself up, she sunk back into the pillow, and then her ear touched something plastic clipped to the pillow. Linda held it up to study it. It was some kind of remote. She pushed a button at the top and a television, mounted on the wall across the room, turned on. Pushing another button at the bottom, made the female nurse turn and look her way, and she came out of the cubicle and to her bedside

"You're awake," she said softly. "How do you feel?"

"I think I'll live," Linda answered. "Can I have something to drink?"

The nurse smiled, and asked, "Water or juice?"

"Juice would be great."

She had a glass of apple juice and then about half an hour later, they brought her some Jello. "You'll be moving down the hall to another room," the nurse said. "You're doing great."

Adam and Ramon walked back to the bunkhouse together. He thought about asking if he could take the truck into town to visit Linda in the hospital, but suddenly he was exhausted. It had been forty-eight hours since he'd slept. He had been through a lot, emotionally and physically. The other men were sitting around a table playing poker and paid no attention to Adam and Ramon as they walked in.

He sat on the edge of his bed, and then thought he would lie back for just a moment, to rest his eyes. The veterinarian had arrived and Ramon took the vet out to the horse barn to look at Blaze. That was the last he remembered.

When he woke up it was still dark, and someone was snoring in the next bed. He got up and went into the bathroom to relieve himself. Looking at his watch, he noticed it was 4:15. Adam looked in the mirror and could hardly believe what he looked like. Red crusty sores were cracking open on his cheeks, and the bottom third of his nose was almost black. His ears were also turning dark, and oozing a mixture of blood and some other kind of yellow fluid. He remembered the salve they had given him at the hospital and went back to his bed to retrieve it from his jacket pocket.

After rubbing the salve carefully into his painful sores, and washing his hands, he put on his jacket and stepped outside to light a cigarette. He should start breakfast soon, but first he wanted to go check on Blaze. Adam crossed the barnyard in the dark, his feet crunching on the snow. There was a faint light on in the horse barn, and somewhere behind the barn a calf was bawling.

A solitary light bulb burned over Blaze's pen just inside the door. It gave off just enough light for him to make out the form of the big stallion lying flat out against the back wall of the pen. Adam stood for a moment and watched the horse, but he saw no movement. He unhooked the gate and went in, crossing the straw in the pen, and knelt beside the still form of Blaze. His eyes were open in a death stare, his tongue protruded from the corner of his mouth.

Adam stroked the black stallion's neck, and then sat down in the straw with his back to the horse, leaning against him one last time. This horse had saved their lives. He had carried them until he could go no farther. He, and he alone, had found the way back. He ran his hands through the mane, and slowly rubbed the massive shoulders.

His eyes welled with tears that burned when they ran through the sores on his cheeks. He had never felt more alone than he did right now. It seemed that everyone and everything he became attached to, was cursed. He tried not to cry, but it came anyway, and he turned and put his arms around Blaze's neck and hugged the horse lying in the straw beside him one last time, before standing and walking out, leaving the pen gate open.

CHAPTER EIGHT

Ryan backed his cruiser out into the street and headed for the office. Today would be a busy day with accidents. It was always that way after the first real snowfall. It always took people awhile to get used to driving on ice again for a few months.

He stayed on the side streets taking his time, his car jerking around in some frozen ruts. Even though there had been a lot of snow it was too early in the year for it to last. He was almost an hour early, but getting in early would be good. He had things to get caught up on.

High on the hill to his left, Memorial Hospital was all lit up and he thought about Linda Pendleton being brought in yesterday, and wondered how she was doing. Ryan made a mental note to stop by there later today and see if she could remember what had happened. His report was still incomplete on the incident and he needed to file it.

He also thought about the man who had been brought in with her, and how he was doing. Ryan needed to find out his name. He had seemed to be somewhat elusive, and keeping to himself. There seemed to be a similarity between him and someone else he had seen, but right now it didn't ring a bell. That was the trouble with this job, you meet so many people, that sooner or later their faces all seemed to melt together.

The back lot was clear of snow and Ryan's parking place with the sign **RESERVED FOR FIRST DEPUTY,** was waiting for him. He eyed the place next to his that read, **RESERVED FOR SHERIFF.** Two more weeks and that might be his.

There was a stack of mail waiting for him on his desk, and after grabbing his coffee and getting comfortable, he dove into it. Cheryl would not be in today. It was her day off, so he could keep his mind on his job.

He sorted the mail into two piles: one for the trash, and one for the 'in' basket to go through later in the day. The pile for the 'in' basket was small, just three letters and some invoices. The rest was junk, and he fired it at the wastebasket, knocking it over instead of getting it inside.

Ryan crouched to pick up his mess, stuffing it all in the basket except for one balled up piece of paper that had been in the basket already, and had rolled a few feet away. As he picked it up the phone rang, and it was David Pierce, a local attorney who wanted Ryan to meet him for lunch.

As they chatted, Ryan tossed the ball of paper in the air in front of him, finally swatting at it, catching it in his right hand. His forefinger and thumb un-creased the paper, and he recognized the face.

"Dave, I'll call you back," he said. He laid the poster on his desk and ironed it flat with the heel of his hand. *It sure looked like the same man. Could it be?*

Ryan was at his desk and dialing up his Internet search engine. Maybe there was more information available on Adam Holton.

Linda was becoming more alert by the moment. If all went well she would be getting some real food for lunch. Right now she had the phone lying on her chest as she dialed the ranch.

The phone rang as Adam was just about to start supper. He wiped his hands on his pants and reached for it, but hesitated for a second. *Should he answer it or ignore it? He really didn't want to talk to anyone, but then it might be Ramon calling and telling him when they would be in. He said he would call.*

Adam picked it up answering, "Lazy L Ranch."

"Aaron, is that you?"

He was startled. Linda was calling? She was well enough to call?

"Yes, Linda is that you?" Adam looked around to make sure he was alone although he knew he was.

"Aaron, God, it's good to hear your voice. Are you all right?"

"Yeah, yeah I'm fine. It's you we're all worried about." He walked from the kitchen to the lunchroom carrying the phone and sat down on a chair.

She laughed. "Thank you for that, but I'm going to be just fine! Thanks to you, Aaron."

Adam didn't answer at first because he was at a loss for words, and then before he could say anything, Linda spoke.

"Aaron, will you bring me some things tonight? I might have to be here a few more days and from what I heard, all I had on when I got here was a pair of wet panties, and they even took them away."

Adam smiled, and scratching the back of his head, said, "They told me to put you in warm water and I tried to---"

"I know the whole story, Aaron, and God bless you for what you did. But I want you to go into my bedroom, and in the top drawer of the dresser at the end of the bed you'll find some decent pajamas. On the back of the door is my robe, and bring my purse off the desk in the office."

"What do I drive?" he asked softly.

"My car is in the garage. The keys are in it, and you tell Ramon that I asked for this, and also ask him what is going on with the ranch right now, so you can fill me in."

Adam wasn't going to wait for Ramon, and didn't want to talk to him. If he left now he would be back in time to get supper ready. He went into the bedroom to gather up what he was supposed to bring to the hospital. It seemed wrong for him to be in her bedroom. The bedroom was wallpapered in soft floral tones. The bedspread and the drapes matched the wallpaper. The room looked like she had just straightened it up, with everything in its place. The dresser tops were bare except for a small jewelry box and two pictures; one of a small boy, and the other of Linda with a man he presumed was Dan in a younger day. He went to the dresser she had described and opened the top drawer on the left. It was filled with underwear and he quickly closed it as if he shouldn't be looking at that. The next drawer held her pajamas. He took two pair and closed the drawer. He nearly forgot her robe and had to go back and get it, rolling it and the pajamas under his arm. Then he went to the office where her purse sat on the corner of her desk. Grabbing the purse and his jacket, he went out the side door and into the garage. The car was a vintage Cadillac, probably from the early 70's. Adam had never seen it before and it didn't look like it had been driven much. It was white, with red leather upholstery, and a big set of horns, from some steer, was mounted in the middle of the hood.

He could smell her scent in the car, and something in the back of his mind was hinting that he wanted to see her for more reasons than just bringing her pajamas, but he quickly dismissed the thought.

Adam had been able to let his guard down a bit in the last few weeks, and it seemed as if he might have a future again, or at least a purpose in life.

Not knowing the Missoula area, Adam wasn't sure how to get to the hospital, but he spotted the blue hospital signs off the interstate and followed them right to the emergency room door. He drove around the block once to make sure it was the right hospital, and then saw some familiar landmarks, so he pulled into the visitors' lot.

Ryan decided to stop at the hospital on his way home from work. He knew Linda pretty well, but it had been awhile since he had talked to her. Dan and Ryan had been acquaintances and worked on some political action committees together, before Dan's death.

He also had some oxygen tanks to drop off at the hospital, so he parked in the back by the emergency entrance. The early afternoon sun was warm, and steam from the melting snow was coming off the blacktop, as he parked his cruiser and headed inside.

Linda was sitting on the edge of her bed when Ryan knocked on the door, and she quickly made sure her gown was covering her before she said, "Come on in."

"Well you sure look a damn sight better then the last time I saw you," Ryan quipped, as he came into the room.

"I feel a lot better than the last time you saw me." She reached out and took his hand. "Good to see you, Ryan. How goes the election, or should I say how goes the campaigning?"

"I haven't done much campaigning. Lets hope it doesn't hurt me. Just been too busy with the storm and all." Ryan sat down on the only chair, and pulled it up in front of her. The bed was higher than the chair, so Linda was sitting looking down at him.

"Linda, I did stop to see how you were, but I also wanted to ask you a couple of questions. I have to file a report on this accident."

She looked down at him and smiled, but didn't reply.

"Tell me how you drove off the road, and then tell me how you were rescued by, ----What is his name?"

"Aaron Holton. He just started working for me about three weeks ago. Seems to be a find for me. Good help is hard to come by nowadays. But the accident, yes. I had just brought supper up to the men. It was snowing hard, but I have driven up there a hundred times."

Ryan shifted nervously in his chair. For a second he contemplated standing up, because he wasn't comfortable sitting down low while she talked over him, but he stayed put.

"I don't know what made me run off the road, but all I know is, I could no longer steer. Snow ruts, or something, grabbed the tires. I knew it was a long way down, where I was going over, and I remember trying to lie on the seat, and then I saw this rock through the windshield and that's all I remember for awhile. I just know if that rock hadn't been there, lord knows what would have happened. It was a long way to the bottom."

The sound of the door opening caught Ryan's attention, and he turned to see a doctor in a white lab coat coming in.

"Oops, sorry," the doctor said. "Didn't know you had company."

"No, it's fine. Deputy Markinson was just asking me some questions about the accident."

"She's lucky that someone found her when they did. She was close to death when I saw her. Adam, getting her into that warm water, also had a lot to do with getting her body temperature back up."

"Adam?" Linda asked. She looked at Ryan, and he too had a puzzled look on his face, but he was quiet.

"Yes," the doctor replied, "the young man who found you. I talked with him on the phone from your house, and he said his name was Adam."

Linda was quiet. She was confused now, and had to think for a moment.

"Well, I think I'm going to let you out of here in a couple of days. We need to get that tube out of your chest and have you fitted with a brace for those broken ribs. By the way, here's your turn signal indicator that we took out of your chest. We cleaned it up a little."

"That was stuck in her chest?" asked Ryan.

"Sure was," said the doctor. "But it was good it stayed there, because she was sucking a lot of air into her pleural cavity and that's not good. Let's turn around," the doctor said, indicating to Linda he wanted her to face the other way.

"Should I leave?" Ryan asked.

"No, no, just need a quick look at her chest here. He had simply pulled the top of her gown down to look. "Looks fine," he said. "We'll take that tube out in the morning." With that, he put her chart back on the end of the bed, and left the room.

Linda slipped under the covers, and Ryan now stood beside the bed.

"I better leave," he said. "I have some other errands to run and it's getting late."

"Thank you for stopping, Ryan, and when I get well, and this election makes you the next sheriff, we'll have to have lunch."

Ryan squeezed her shoulder and put his hat back on. He had been holding it in front of him the whole time. He winked and left the room. Had he stayed one minute longer, he would have run into Adam.

Ryan was anxious to get home to his son, but he needed to go back to the office once more and pick something up. Aaron Holton or Adam Holton - he had to know for sure. What he was going to do, if it was Adam Holton, he wasn't sure yet. He took the steps two at a time, hitting the door with his shoulder so hard that it smacked against the side of the building. It was just a few steps to the cruiser.

Linda was staring out the window when Adam came into the room, and looked startled when she saw him. His frostbitten face and ears were a mass of scabs and weeping blisters, but the smile behind them tugged at her heart.

She had thought she would just ask him straight out the minute he came in the door, who he really was, but now the right words eluded her. Up until now she hadn't realized how bad he was hurt himself. She remembered seeing him for a few minutes in the intensive care unit, but the drugs had made everything so vague and foggy she wasn't sure what was real, and what was a dream.

Adam laid the clothing and purse on the end of the bed and Linda reached tentatively for his hands. They were a mess, with peeling skin and swollen to almost twice their original size.

Aaron, or Adam, she thought to herself, - it made no difference to her now. There would be time to talk more about it later. Right now, the feelings she had for him, that had stayed right below the surface, had come to the top, and she was so touched.

Linda's chin quivered ever so slightly and her eyes started to fill with tears, until they could hold them no more, and they spilled over and ran down her cheeks. Adam used the back of his hand to wipe them away, and then held her head to his chest and stroked her hair. They stayed in that pose for several seconds, and then he reached down and tilted her chin upward so she could see his face.

"Aaron, I love you for what you did for me." Her voice was quivering with emotion. "Please, say it is all right for me to feel this way."

Adam turned and sat down beside her on the bed. So far he had not uttered a word.

"Linda, I want to love you back, and maybe I do and don't realize it. I do have special feelings for you. I know that. I know there's something there, but, and I don't know how to say this, something happened in my life a few months back, and I guess I don't know how to get over it. I want to get over it, but I just don't know how. I've done some things to make the situation worse, so there may be no way to resolve it anymore. When you get better we can talk more about it, but for now, what is left unsaid would be best said. For now, I need to think, and we both need to heal."

Once again, he tipped her chin up and wiped her eyes. Then he bent forward slowly and kissed her softly on the side of her mouth.

"I better go," he whispered. "I hope I brought the right things for you, but call if you need anything else. I haven't seen Ramon today but when I do, I'll tell him to call you." He kissed her once more, but this time on the cheek.

At the door he turned, and Linda said, "Thank you, Aaron."

She sat on the edge of the bed holding a pillow to her sore chest. It had been a long time since she'd thought about anyone else but Dan with the kind of feelings she felt now. Maybe it was just infatuation with a man because he saved her life. The more she thought about it, the more she realized it was more than that. But was it right?

CHAPTER NINE

Ryan stood inside his office and stared at the poster in his hands. His first urge had been to rush back to the hospital and ask Linda if this was her hired man. But then he thought it through, and reconsidered. Right now, if Aaron was Adam Holton, he had a duty as a sworn officer of the law to bring him in, but for some reason he wanted to know more about him, and why he was wanted.

On the back of the poster was a contact number for specifics, and Ryan dialed it. After two rings, a soft feminine voice said, "Sheriff's Office, Aspen County. How can I direct your call?"

Ryan turned his head and cleared his throat. "Excuse me, sorry about that. I need to get some more information on a man who is wanted out of your jurisdiction, a man by the name of Adam Holton. This posting I have was released on September 23rd."

"One moment, please."

Ryan could hear the receptionist talking to someone else in the background, although he couldn't make out what they were saying. Then the voice became clearer, as she had apparently removed the obstruction from the mouthpiece. It was a male voice saying, "Joe will be back in a few minutes. He's over at Gert's again. Tell whoever it is, he will call them."

She was back. "Can I get a name and phone number where you can be reached? Sheriff Adcock will be back shortly and he will call you then."

"Sure. Tell him to call Deputy Ryan Markinson at this number, in Missoula, Montana. Do you have it there on your caller I.D?"

"Yes," she answered.

"Thanks. I'll be waiting for his call."

Ryan was alone in the office; the only other people on duty were tied up at a convenience store robbery. He went through some more mail, although his heart wasn't in it. It was Friday, and he had promised his son they could go to an indoor rodeo tonight, so something better start happening soon.

He drummed his fingers on the desktop, as if that would speed things up. Right now the only thing on his desktop was that 'wanted' poster. He took his forefinger and tried to get the rest of the creases out of it. Maybe he could run it through the printer and get a better copy. He was just walking away from his desk when the call came through, and he lunged back, dropping the receiver on the floor.

"Markinson," he almost shouted, and then correcting himself, said, "Sheriff's office, Deputy Markinson."

"Damn, man. Slow down, you almost broke my eardrum. This is Sheriff Joe Adcock from Aspen County out here in Minnesota. You called for me?"

"Yes, and I'm sorry about dropping the phone. It was on the edge of my desk, and when I went to grab it, well, it just slipped out of my hand."

There was a chuckle on the other end of the line. "What is it I can help you with, Deputy?"

"Well, we received this 'wanted' poster sent out by your office and I think we might have a lead on this guy."

"What guy would that be, my friend? We send out a few 'wanted' posters."

"The name is Adam Holton."

It was quiet for a moment, and then Sheriff Joe said softly, "You know where he is?"

"Yes, I believe we do," Ryan replied. "What exactly did he do, and how dangerous is he?"

"Well, it's a long story, Deputy, but this man took the law into his own hands after justice had failed him, and dispatched a little justice of his own, right here on the Aspen County Courthouse steps. In short, he blew the man's head off. Weren't any of us too sad to see it happen, but the law is the law, and you just can't do that."

"What did the man he killed, do to him?" Ryan asked.

"He was a sexual predator who raped, mutilated and killed Adam's fiancé."

"Had he been convicted?" Ryan asked.

"Well, yes and no," Sheriff Joe drawled on. "The man was guilty as hell and we had evidence that proved it. But he was smart enough to get himself a shyster lawyer from Minneapolis who got the evidence suppressed, and the jury let him go."

Ryan let out a low whistle. "Been there and seen that, Sheriff."

"Listen," Sheriff Joe came back. " If he is the right man, use a little common sense. I don't think he would hurt a flea, but damn it you never can be too careful. If he is the man, see if he will wave extradition and I'll send someone out to bring him back. Unless you want us to come and make the pinch."

"No, that won't be necessary," Ryan, said.

"When are you going to do it?"

"Well, I don't think he's going anywhere, and I do want to talk to the lady he is working for one more time, but I would say tomorrow."

"It's your call, Deputy. Have a good weekend."

"Thanks, Sheriff, you too." He hung up the phone and stared at it for a few minutes. Something wanted him to take care of business and get it over with, but if he hurried, he had just enough time to get his son to the rodeo. There were other deputies that could make the arrest, but it would be good for his image right now, if he did it himself.

He would talk to Linda in the morning. Then again, maybe it wasn't Adam Holton. Maybe it was nothing.

When he got back to the ranch from the hospital, Adam started supper for the men. He was getting to be quite a cook. Linda had given him some hints on what to make and how to make it. Tonight they were going to have spaghetti, so he prepared the sauce and put it on to simmer. Then he thought he would see what he could do about getting Blaze's body out of the barn. He had told Ramon that he would take care of it.

There was not a lot of frost in the ground, so Adam dug a hole with a bobcat, and then dragged the dead horse out to it. He wrapped him in a horse blanket and threw in some of his tacking that had been made just for him.

Adam stood over the shallow grave, and looked at Blaze one last time, before he back-filled the hole. He had only known this horse just that one night, but it was a special night, and he had been a special horse.

Linda called shortly after Adam got back into the house. She wanted a couple of other things from the house, although it looked like she might get out on Sunday morning. The things she wanted were her mail and a ledger book she kept in the top drawer of her desk. "I might as well get caught up on my book work," she told him. The doctor was amazed at how well she had recuperated, and she wanted out as soon as possible, herself.

"I'll be there in the morning," Adam said. "Tonight, I need to clean up and take care of my sores. Some of them are getting infected."

"Use my tub, Aaron. You can soak for while, and the water is better there than in the bunkhouse. I've got some good smelling bath salts you can use. Make you popular in the bunk house, tonight."

Adam laughed, but didn't comment. It was good to see her in such good spirits.

"I don't know if Ramon would understand if I start using your things. I just got him talking to me, and if I start doing things like that,

I might be back where I was with him. I told him I would be ready to start working with them again on Monday."

Linda giggled. "Ramon has been with me for a long time, Aaron. I suppose he thinks you're trying to get on my good side. What happened the other night in that storm went way beyond trying to impress me, Aaron."

Like a couple of good friends, they made small talk for a while. Linda wanted to ask about his name, but not over the phone. Maybe she would in the morning.

Supper was quiet like always. Ramon and Adam sat at one end of the table, while the others talked in Spanish and bantered back and forth. They would look at Adam and laugh, but he had no idea what the hell they were saying, and was too proud to ask Ramon to interpret. It was probably better he didn't know.

Ramon told Adam that for now, it would be better if he just stuck close to the ranch, and took care of business. "I have a feed delivery in the morning you can help with, and maybe you can keep a phone with you in case the boss needs anything. She seems to prefer you to the rest of us, anyway." The remark dripped with sarcasm.

Adam, noting the tone of his voice, started to respond to it but thought better of it. "She did say she wanted to talk to you."

"You can tell her everything is fine. We will have most of the cattle ready to ship by the end of next week."

"I took care of the dead horse, today," Adam said changing the subject. Ramon nodded his head but said nothing.

"I need to go into town tomorrow for groceries, is there anything you guys need?"

"Get some things we can take out in the field. The men are tired of sandwiches. Get some soup, stew, or maybe chili. Those kinds of things." Ramon got up and dumped his dishes in the sink and walked out.

Adam finished cleaning the dishes and then thought, "why not?" He went into Linda's bathroom and locked the door. He could always say he was cleaning it, if Ramon came checking.

Her wet clothes from the other night were still lying in a pile next to the tub. Linda's torn blouse was stained heavily with blood, as was the bra. He picked them up and put them in the hamper along with a pair of jeans. Then he ran the tub full of hot soapy water.

The water felt good on his hands, which were in the worst shape. It softened them up and he was able to pick away at some of the loose skin. Adam lay back with his head in the corner of the tub, his hands on his chest, and let them soak. His thoughts went back to that night when he had undressed Linda for the tub. For some reason, the sight of her nearly naked body that night, had stirred no emotions at all, but now he felt himself being aroused by the memory. He had been scared that night that she might die.

Maybe it was different now that he knew she was going to be all right. After all, she was a good-looking woman. Almost as old as his mother, but for some reason that didn't matter either, right now. He was lonely, and needed anyone who would care for him.

Suddenly, memories of Mandy washed over him and gave him a sense of betrayal. It didn't seem right for him to have these feelings. Maybe it was time for him to move on, before he was hurt again. Adam jerked out the plug and turned on the cold water and sat in it until he couldn't stand it any longer.

He cleaned the bathroom, and then, dressed again, headed for the bunkhouse.

Ryan slept in late. They had gone out for pizza after the rodeo and got home way after the boy's bedtime. But it had been Saturday night and it felt good to have fun with his son for a change. He needed to do that more often. He let Dougie ride along with him this morning. He could stay in the hospital day-care for the few minutes he would need with Linda.

The hospital was quiet for a Saturday morning, only a few aides and nurses busy making their rounds.

When he got to Linda's room, she was up, sitting in a chair and looking out the window. He cleared his throat to announce his presence and she turned to look at him.

"Well, what did I do to get a second visit from you? Aren't you sweet!"

"The first time it was to visit, - this time it's business." Ryan smiled, but it was so insincere Linda reacted with a frown.

"Linda, I have reason to believe that the man who works for you, and saved your life, is not who he says he is. His face was on a 'wanted' poster that came through our office." Ryan handed the poster to Linda.

She was shaking her head from side to side slowly, as if to say: no, she could not believe it.

Unlawful flight to avoid prosecution for murder. "Who? Who did he murder?"

"I better keep the details to myself until we determine if this is him or not. I came here to get your opinion. Could this be him, knowing what you know about him?"

"I guess," she stammered. "I don't know." She handed the poster back to him.

"I will be going out to your ranch this afternoon to question him. I just wanted you to know that."

She turned to look out the window again, saying nothing.

"Look, Linda. I know what this man did for you and how you must feel about him, but the law is the law, and I have to act on this." Ryan was standing about two feet behind her, holding his hat in front of him. Sometimes this job sucked, and this was one of those times. "I better go," he said quietly. "I'm sorry." With that, he turned and walked out.

Maybe it was fate that had made Adam go shopping first for groceries, otherwise their paths might have crossed. He had the mail, ledger books, and some clothes she asked him to bring and took the elevator up to her room on the third floor.

The door was open, and she was sitting on the end of the bed staring at him, when he walked in. "Hello, Adam," she said.

At first it didn't register with him what she had called him. "I brought you the stuff you asked for." Then, the look on her face and the tears in her eyes told him something was wrong, and it hit him.

Adam didn't sit, but stood looking down at her.

"How did you know?" he asked.

"Adam, why didn't you tell me? How long were you going to live this charade?"

"You never would have understood," he said, so softly that Linda could barely hear him. "I don't want to cause trouble for you, so maybe it would be best if I just walk out of here right now and don't look back."

She was crying softly, but looking up at him, she said, "Adam tell me why you did this. You don't seem like a murderer."

"I'm not. Well, - maybe in the eyes of the law, but he deserved to die for taking the most precious thing that I had. That same law that is after me couldn't punish him, but now it wants to punish me. Somebody had to do it, - and that was me. Mandy was the most precious thing in my life." He sat down in the chair, after pulling it up to the bed, so he was facing her. "I woke in the morning thinking of her, and I went to sleep thinking of her. I didn't deserve her, but by God she loved me, and I loved her so much." Adam was trying his best not to break down, but his voice cracked and his hands were shaking. "She was a beautiful person, Linda, inside and out, until this hunk of shit, worthless human being, came along and abducted her. He raped her and then he killed her, and then he stuffed her lifeless body into a culvert filled with sewage. He said he did it. But the cops screwed up, and his lawyer took advantage of it, and got him off. I killed him Linda, not just for what he did to Mandy, but so he couldn't do it again. I'm sorry, I better go," he said, his voice cracking.

Linda got off her bed and walked over and closed the door. She came back and wrapped her arms around him, but Adam's arms stayed at his side.

"Adam, they're coming to the ranch today to arrest you. Do not go back there. I'm not sure when they are coming, but they said today.

Please don't run away. Let me help you. Leave the car here in the hospital parking lot. Take a cab to mile marker 47, west of town. There's a road there that goes up to the High Plateau. The machine shed up there has a wood stove for warmth, and there are some blankets in the trunk of the car."

"What then?" Adam asked. "What do I eat or drink? What about my belongings in the bunk house?"

"Adam." She tipped his chin down so he was looking into her eyes. You have to trust me. Right now I don't have all of the answers, but I get out of here in the morning, and I'll find someplace safe for you. Adam, I need to help you. Please trust me." Linda wiped her eyes. "Now you better get going before they come back here. Here, take this." She reached into her purse on the end of the bed and gave him a handful of bills.

He looked at them and stuffed them in his shirt pocket. "Use the phone here, to call a cab, and take my cell phone with you."

Outside in the parking lot, he shielded his eyes from the bright sun. The road passing the hospital was a busy freeway, and cars and trucks were zipping by. It would be so easy just to hitch a ride and be gone. It made more sense than this. But something about Linda would not let him do that. He had to trust her.

CHAPTER TEN

It was two thirty before Ryan could get everything together. There would be four of them, and another car would stay at the end of the driveway in case Adam tried to leave. There would be no shotguns or rifles. Ryan felt this was unnecessary.

The ranch was a big place and he could be anywhere, but Linda had said he was doing the cooking while he healed up from his frostbite. They would start with the house.

Ryan walked up to the house and rang the bell, while one of the other men watched the backside of the house. There was no answer, and there were no lights on. He tried the door but it was locked, so they forced the simple lock with a pocketknife, and entered. The house was quiet, only the rhythmical ticking of a grandfather clock in the hall broke the silence. Ryan had everybody else stay outside, while he took a quick look around. He walked into the office with its big picture window that looked out over the front yard. There was a man walking across the yard toward the house, but it wasn't Adam.

Making a hasty exit out the back, instead of the way he had come in, Ryan gathered all of the men and went around the house to meet the man coming across the yard.

"Sir, can I ask you to come over here?" Ramon stuck his hands in his jacket pockets, while he approached him.

"What's the problem, Officer?" Ramon had a quizzical look on his face.

"Sir, if you would take your hands out of your pockets, please. Thank you," Ryan said. "Who are you, and do you work here?"

"I am Ramon Garcia and I work here. I am the supervisor."

Ryan asked Ramon for his ID and looked the card over.

"We're looking for Adam Holton, or, you probably know him as Aaron Holton. Is he around?" Ryan stepped back and was standing about three feet from Ramon, with his hands on his hips.

"He went to town this morning to get groceries and I don't think he is back yet. Why, what did he do?"

"We aren't sure," Ryan said, "but we want to talk with him. Did he have a car or truck of some kind?"

"He took the boss's car. White caddy with the steer horns on the hood. Garage is open and the car ain't here." Ramon had turned his head for a quick look at the garage.

"Tell you what, my friend, we're going to leave a couple of officers here for when he comes back. I want you to stay with them in the house."

"Fine with me," Ramon said, and the three of them went inside.

Ryan and Bob Kulich, a new deputy, got in the squad and headed for town. "Keep your eyes pealed for that car, Bob. We need to make another trip to the hospital."

Linda was walking the hallway in her robe, and trying to think. She wanted to help him even if it meant breaking some laws. He was no killer, and had only done what a lot of people wished they had guts enough to do.

The doctor had been in and said she could leave first thing in the morning. She could see the Caddy in the lot, from the window in the hallway. She could leave right now, but it wouldn't look right.

Linda walked slowly back to her room and sat on the end of the bed. There were a couple of cards from well-wishers still lying on her table, and she ripped them open. The first one was from a neighbor she hadn't heard from in a while. She was a union official with the Cattlemen's Association and the card said, "By a vote of 32 to 19, we wish you a speedy recovery!" Linda laughed out loud.

The second card was from her mother. She recognized the address in Coeur d'Alene, Idaho. There was a letter with the card.

Her mother had been left very wealthy, and lived there alone since Linda's father died ten years ago. She had been very active in the Coeur d'Alene community, and had donated a lot of money to schools and colleges. Education had been her life's work, and she had been a teacher for most of her life. But a year ago, she received the bad news that she had Lou Gehrig's disease. Amyotrophic Lateral Sclerosis, an always fatal, debilitating, neurological disease that slowly lets you waste away. It starts with some minor muscular weakness and that was what had happened to Anna. She stood holding a cup of coffee one day, when she watched it slip through her fingers and crash to the floor.

Since that time, her legs had grown weaker and weaker every day, and from the sound of her letter, she was going to be in a wheelchair soon.

Linda's hands shook as she read the letter.

Dear Linny,

I was so sorry to hear about your accident. The staff at the hospital called me and filled me in. I hope you are healing fine. I never thought there was any way for you to ever get hurt, as you were always the strong one of my two daughters. I know that a 'get-well-card' and letter are supposed to cheer you up, but I'm afraid this letter probably won't.

Things here haven't been good. I no longer can walk without assistance, and my breathing is also getting more labored. The doctor says it will not be

long before I will need a live-in companion if I am going to stay in my own
house, and that is my wish. I do not want to go to a nursing home.

I wish there was some way for you to get someone else to run the ranch
for a while, so you could come and stay with me, but that might just be
asking too much. Your sister has similar problems getting away, although I
don't think I would be comfortable with her here, anyway. The neighbor girl
next door, who is about twenty-one, just finished nursing college, helps me
in the morning and at night, but she can't stay with me all of the time.

Well, enough about me. I hope and pray we will find solutions to both
of our problems.

Hugs and kisses, Mom

A nurse came in and gave her a pill and she laid down. She was
tired and confused. Outside the window, the last rays of the setting sun
peaked over the tops of the cloudbank that was forming in the west.
More snow, no doubt.

She had barely closed her eyes, when it hit her like a ton of bricks!
Adam! Adam could take care of her. He had said he was a physical
therapist and that's what Mom needs. He needs a place to hide, and
the best thing was that Linda would know where he was! She would
call him right away.

She slid over to the other edge of the bed and grabbed the house
phone. But after dialing the first six digits of her cell phone, she stopped.
It could be traced, couldn't it? It went through a switchboard. She had
to be careful.

She just had to hope that he trusted her, and went where she said to
go. Tomorrow she would call him from home when she got there.

Ryan put the pedal to the metal and they sped back to town. Between
the ranch and Missoula, there was no sign of the white Cadillac. He
needed to get the plate number and call out for the highway patrol to
watch for it. He needed to talk to Linda once more, first.

They shot off the freeway on the exit to the hospital. Bob had his
fingers etched to the dash as he prayed for a safe landing. The tires

squealed and nearly lost their grip with the pavement as Ryan yanked the wheel to the left and they careened into the hospital parking lot, to the wide-eyed amazement of several spectators. The car was still rocking when Ryan jumped out, yelling at Bob to stay put.

But Bob wasn't listening. Instead he was pointing at the white Cadillac parked one row over. "Is that our baby?" he asked.

Both deputies walked around the car looking in the windows before they realized it wasn't locked. There were groceries in the back seat and the keys were under the front mat. Ryan took them and opened the trunk, but there wasn't anything unusual in there.

"I'm going in to talk to her. There's a chance he's still in there, so call another car over here for backup."

He didn't wait for the elevator, running up the stairs and down the hall. A nurse behind a desk shouted, "Walk, and be quiet, please!" but then, seeing the uniform, said, "Oh my."

When Ryan burst into Linda's room she was in the bathroom. The door was closed and the light was spilling out from under the door. He stopped to catch his breath and his thoughts, then walked calmly to the chair beside her bed, and sat down. Crossing his legs, he balanced his hat on top of his knee.

Linda was in her pajamas when she came out of the bathroom, and was looking toward the window, so she didn't noticed Ryan until she turned and was beside her bed.

"Where is he, Linda, and why did you tip him off?"

She calmly turned the covers back and got into the bed. Then, turning to Ryan she said, "I don't know where he is, and I don't know what you're talking about."

Ryan's mouth was open but nothing was coming out. It was obvious she was lying, but what did he expect her to do. Maybe she was right by lying, and maybe he didn't belong here, bothering her. He looked at her as he stood up, and right then and there, they both understood all too well what was happening.

Ryan put his hat back on, walked over to the window and stood with his back to her. "I could probably get into a lot of trouble, if certain people knew that I talked with you about him. You understand what I am saying, Linda."

"Yes, but don't worry. I heard nothing."

He didn't answer her, but turned and walked out the door.

Coming out the door of the hospital, he saw a tow truck hooking on to the front of the Cadillac, while Bob stood by watching. The truck engine was roaring loudly, struggling to lift the heavy car.

"Drop the car!" Ryan yelled at the driver. "There's been a mistake."

"But! What the hell?" Bob was exasperated.

"Like I said Bob, there's been a mistake. Now let it go." Ryan sat down in the squad, and motioned with his forefinger for Bob to join him.

He called the other deputies back to the office, and thanked them for their help.

"We're not sure right now what we're going to do with this man, so if any of you do see him, let me know. But for time being, the heat is off."

Cheryl, who had not gone out to the ranch, but knew what was going on, was sitting on a stool in the corner staring at him as he spoke. Something did not pass the smell test, as far as she was concerned, but she would take the issue up with him later.

Linda was sitting up in bed hugging her knees to her chest. *There were so many questions and so few answers right now.* She needed to think this one through.

She hoped that Adam had gone up to the machinery shed on the plateau as she suggested, but she doubted right now that that had happened.

Tomorrow when she got home she would call up there. If her phone was still working, and Adam had it on, maybe - just maybe, she had a plan. But she was going to have to work fast, because he was not going to be able to stay in that place for long.

Her chest was feeling good and it only hurt when she coughed. It had taken a little while to get used to the cast on her arm, but she had adapted.

Linda was a fighter, and a survivor. Maybe that is why she was still here today, that, along with the unselfish heroic act that Adam had done, to drag her from the jaws of death.

At first she felt that her feelings for him were indebtedness for what he had done for her. But now, sitting on this bed, she understood all too well that these feelings went deeper than that. And, right or wrong, crazy or sane, she wanted Adam in her life.

She dabbed at her eyes with the balled up Kleenex in her right hand before she realized she was crying. She had no idea why she was crying but she was, and she slipped down into the bed and pulled the covers over her head before anybody came in and saw her.

The cabbie left him off at the mile marker with a puzzled look on his face. He was in the middle of nowhere on a busy freeway. It was a fifteen-mile ride for the driver just to find a turn-around so he could go back.

Adam looked to the west for the road, but all he saw was forest. He walked slowly to the top of the next hill carrying his blanket roll and the bag of groceries he had taken. About a quarter mile ahead were both the bridge and the off-ramp.

The wind felt like hot water on his sore face, and he pulled his collar up and pulled down his hat for protection.

He had no idea how far up the road he would have to walk before he got there. *Maybe he was nuts to involve her anymore than he had already. What was he going to do, live up here like a hibernating animal? Sooner or later someone would see them. That was a given.*

It was starting to snow but the skies didn't look that ominous, just a few flurries fluttering down on the breezes coming off the mountainside.

There were two houses on the road on the right hand side. The first one appeared to be some kind of summer cabin and was uninhabited right now. A log was pulled across the driveway.

The second house was still under construction, and logs and lumber littered the yard, but there was no sign of anybody around.

Good, he thought. I don't need any nosy neighbors wondering what I'm doing or who I am.

The road was steep as it made its way up the side of the mountain, and Adam's breath was coming hard, walking into the wind with his arms full.

He had traveled about three or four miles when the terrain leveled off, and as he came over a rise he could make out the vast meadow below, that was the great plateau. The bulk of the mountain rose behind it, gray and forbidding, nothing but rock and snow.

The building was on the far end, and he could just make it out in the falling twilight. If he stepped it up, he would be there before dark.

It was a long way up here, when you came this way. No wonder Dan had made a shorter road.

He thought he heard something behind him, and turned quickly to look, but he was alone, about as alone as he could get. Maybe it was the mountain talking to him.

When he finally got to the building, it was dark. The door was unlocked, and there were no lights to turn on. In fact, the only electricity came from a generator, but Adam had no idea where it had been put. He needed to find the office, make a fire, and settle down with some food, and his thoughts. If there was a chance he would stay here, there would be time to find the generator later. Adam felt his way through the building, from piece of machinery to piece of machinery, in the dark. At last, in the glow of his cigarette lighter, he made out the tiny room built into the far end of the building and headed for the door. Had he walked around the building, he would have seen the outside door that led to this room. There was dry wood inside, and a gas lantern hung over a small table. Adam had both a fire and a light going in a few minutes. In the flickering light of the lantern he could make out the cot in the corner, and the walls full of bins of parts for the machinery. There was a workbench of sorts, full of tools, cans of oil, tubes of grease, and worn out parts and belts. There was also an enamel coffee pot. Not that he had any coffee but he could cook in it, and he did have a can of stew.

He sat on the cot and ate his stew out of the bottom of the coffee pot. He cleaned the gravy out of the bottom with a slice of bread and stuffed it into his mouth. Then, opening a bottle of milk, he washed it all down and lay back on the cot.

It had warmed up considerably since he arrived in his small hangout. There was a window in the exterior door, but it was too dark to see anything, as cloud cover had slid down from the mountain and blanketed everything. That was all right, he didn't want to see anything.

Adam's mind was working in too many directions at once and he tried to sort out his thoughts as he lay there, curled in a fetal position, staring at the hot coals through the partially open door of the stove.

If he didn't hear from Linda by noon tomorrow, he was going to leave. He didn't know where yet, but he was just going to leave. That thought, and thoughts of Mandy, were his last conscious reasoning before sleep came.

On Sunday morning, Linda was up and dressed before it was light out. The doctor had said he would be there early to check her out and he was true to his word.

He, and a nurse carrying an armful of charts entered the room together. Linda was standing at the window and she turned and smiled.

"Graduation day, my dear," said the doctor, as he sat on the end of the bed, motioning for her to come over with a curved forefinger.

"Unbutton, and let me see your chest." He pushed and prodded as he examined her, while she stood in front of him. She had only a small bandage covering what had been the wound from the lever that had penetrated her chest.

"I have two prescriptions for you to take and you can get them filled right here at the hospital, if you like. I want to see you in my office in one week to take that cast off you arm and put on something more comfortable, but otherwise I'm very happy with your recovery. Do you have any concerns?"

"No, I feel fine. I just want to say, 'thank you,' again for everything."

"My pleasure," he said, standing and shaking her hand.

As fast as they had come, they were gone.

Linda didn't wait for the 'goodbye committee'. She packed her bag and left, taking the elevator down to the ground floor. She stopped at 'Admitting' to check out, and get her prescriptions filled.

By 9:00 a.m. she was pulling out of the parking lot and into traffic. Linda drove west on the freeway, passing the exit to the frontage road that would take her to the ranch. She had an errand to run before she went home.

She had thought for a long time last night, and she was sure she had a plan that might just work, if only two people agreed with her, her mother, and Adam. She wasn't going to risk calling him from her house phone and having the record on her cell phone. She was headed to the High Plateau. Ramon had called her last night and inquired about Adam, but she told him she had no idea where he might be.

"He came and dropped the car off yesterday," she said, "and then told me he was going to take a cab home. I wondered why he couldn't just pick me up in the morning, but he didn't say. Either way, I'll be home by noon, so let's you and I meet in the afternoon."

"I think your hombre is in trouble of some kind," Ramon answered. "I never felt right about him from the start."

"See you tomorrow," Linda answered, ignoring his remark.

Off to the left, she could make out the buildings and her house, as she passed by high up on the freeway. This wouldn't take long, and then she would be home.

Most of the snow from the big storm last week was gone, except where it had drifted up, or been piled up, by the snowplows. She let the traffic pass her and then took the exit ramp heading up to the plateau.

The snow last night had erased all tracks Adam might have left walking up here, and she could only pray that he would be where she had told him to go, - and that she didn't get stuck.

At the end of the road she turned in toward the field, but had to park, as the road was covered with too much snow. There was smoke coming from the chimney on the machine shed, and Linda smiled at the sight of it.

Adam heard the car door slam, even though she had parked a quarter of a mile away. But then, it was that quiet up here on the mountain, and you could hear everything. He walked out the door and peeked around the corner of the building.

It was Linda, and she was half running and holding her chest.

Arriving out of breath, she turned the corner to go around the building and Adam swept her up into his arms. He didn't know why. He just wanted to. The sight of her coming across the field had tempered his despair, but beyond that, he was feeling like the only other person in this world who cared anything about him, had just shown up.

Adam held her so tight her chest hurt, but it didn't matter. She wanted him to hold her, and the tighter the better. She had waited all night for this.

At last their heads pulled back from each other, and he stared at her for a second, then touched his fingers to her cheek, as if feeling whether she was real or not. She kissed him softly on the lips and then said, "Let's go inside."

Linda was pacing back and forth talking, while Adam sat on the table and listened. "Adam, you would be good for her and it is a good place to live. I don't know how long she has left, but I promised her I would take care of her, or find someone who would care for her. It's so very important to her to live in her own home for whatever time she has left."

"There is a young woman next door who's been going to college to be a nurse, and would take care of all her personal needs. She has been helping her now, but she can't do it full time. I don't know how often I can get up there myself, but I promise you, it will be as often as possible. Please, give it a try Adam." She was pleading and her faced looked pained.

He walked over and held her hands in his, facing her. "Then what, Linda? Then what comes next, after she is gone? Where will this all end?"

She touched her finger to his lips. "It will all work out. Trust me, Adam."

He was looking for any answer to his problem, and she seemed to be giving him something.

"Ok," he said, his lips muffled in her hair, as she hugged him again. "Ok. Let's give it a try."

CHAPTER ELEVEN

Before she left him, Linda explained that she would leave his backpack and a bus ticket, tomorrow morning. It would be awhile before they dared see each other again. She wanted to smooth things over at the ranch and let things settle down. Right now, as much as she didn't want to leave, she had to, and Adam watched her walk away across the field. She turned once more when she was several hundred feet away and waved. He waved back, and felt bad that he hadn't walked with her, but she insisted he stay put. Someone could be watching.

Adam could still smell her hair. He could still feel the softness of her lips on his. Even though the kiss had been brief, it had not been without some emotion, and that was starting to confuse him. Linda was all he had going for him right now. He was also concerned that their friendship might be headed somewhere he didn't want it to go. Adam stood in the doorway and watched the taillights disappear around the bend in the road. Even though she was gone, for the first time in a long time, he didn't feel alone. Looking up at the mountains, he saw wispy, feathery clouds hiding the summit, and the granite looked colder and more forbidding than he last remembered it. What was in store for him in Coeur-d'Alene, on the other side?

Linda's mother was skeptical at first, but then she was only getting part of the story.

"Adam has a lot of experience working with handicapped people, Mother. It's what he did before he came out west."

"Why did he come out west, Linda?"

She stammered for a moment, and then said, "A failed relationship, Mother." She had to be careful what she said. Adam would be sure to have an explanation of his own if her mother questioned him, and there would be no time for them to co-ordinate their stories.

"I seem to be in a position where I have less and less to say about my destiny. For that reason, Linda, I'll trust your judgment. Send him out, but I am still aware that there are people out there who might take advantage of me."

"I won't let that happen, Mother." She pumped her clenched fist into the air and mouthed: "Yes!"

She met with Ramon in the afternoon and asked him to bring her Adam's personal stuff from the bunkhouse.

"I think I'll give them to the sheriff," she lied.

Ramon just shrugged his shoulders and smiled. He was glad Adam was gone.

The cattle had been sorted and made ready for market. The ranch was ready for the upcoming winter. Ramon had done a good job.

"I need to go to town for more supplies, Ramon, so I'll be gone for a few hours. We're going to have a special supper tonight to celebrate my being home."

"Need me to come along?" Ramon asked.

"No. Outside of this cast on my arm, I seem to be healed up pretty good." Ramon left to go outside, and she had to sit down for a few minutes. Her side was giving her a fair amount of pain. Maybe when she got back, she would take a hot bath and soak some of her soreness away.

Adam heard the tires on the gravel and ran to look out of the door. The white Caddy was just coming to a stop at the same spot where she parked yesterday. Linda stepped out of the car with a paper bag and an envelope.

She had picked up some sandwiches and a bus ticket to Coeur-d'Alene, Idaho. She had also made arrangements for the bus driver to pick Adam up on the bridge, past mile marker 47, on I-90.

He stayed in the shadow of the building as she walked across the field to him. His last Marlboro was in his mouth, the end glowing red, as he took the last drag and flicked it on the ground in a shower of sparks, then ground it out with his boot heel.

She had changed clothes, and wore a brown buckskin jacket with strips of leather fringe that hung down off the sleeves. She had put her hair in a ponytail, tied with a white ribbon that matched her white jeans.

Linda stopped and offered him the bag before he could say anything. "I bought you some sandwiches, and there's a can of soda in there too. I really didn't know what you like, so, I hope that this will------"

His eyes were locked on hers. She held the bag out in front of her, nervously. She wanted him to hold her, but she wanted him to make the move. She knew how she felt about him, but it had to be both ways, to be right.

Adam took the bag and dropped it behind him on the ground, reaching for her hands at the same time. He pulled her to him to hug her, but she turned her face toward his, and their lips met, softly and briefly, more like a brother would hold his sister. His hands were rubbing her back and shoulders. *Strong hands and tender arms,* She thought. He had aroused feelings and emotions in her that she hadn't felt in a long time, but she didn't think he knew that. Suddenly he stopped and released her, wiping his hands on the sides of his pants, as if he had done something wrong.

"I'm so sorry, I just got carried away. I'm just so grateful for what you're doing for me." He was blushing. *What in the hell am I doing?* he thought to himself. He felt he had let his emotions become misguided.

"Adam. You saved my life, and have made me a happy woman. I want you in my life, Adam, more than anything right now. Let's go inside."

They sat at the table and ate corned beef sandwiches, and shared the can of Coke, while Linda told him of her plans.

"My mother is expecting you, and I told her you are a physical therapist and she was thrilled about that. I'm going to come out there for Thanksgiving, which will be in less than two weeks. At that time, I hope to have some other good news for you, but I have to talk to some people first, and I don't want to let the cat out of the bag so I won't say anymore about that, for now."

He looked at her inquisitively, but before he could speak she placed her forefinger across his lips, silencing him.

She gave him the envelope that she brought. "This is your bus ticket to Coeur-d'Alene. They will pick you up on the bridge tomorrow morning around eight, so watch for the bus. There's some cash in there too, to tide you over until I see you again. I will try to call when I can, but you understand the situation, so I have to be careful. Your pack, with your belongings is in the trunk, and I'll leave it where the car is now parked. It was too heavy for me to carry and you need to stay in here until dark."

Adam remained silent through all of this, but taking her hands once more, he said, "Why would you do this for me, Linda? Why would you risk all that you have, to help me, a fugitive?"

She stood, and biting her lip, said, "Adam, you saved my life, and also because I, … I care for you, and I want you safe." Her eyes were brimming with tears. The table was between them, but reaching across, she grasped the sides of his head and pulling him forward she kissed him gently. "I have something else for you," she said, reaching into her coat pocket.

He smiled as he saw the two packs of Marlboro cigarettes she held in her hand.

The election was over, and Ryan won in a close race. Tony Winters had called Ryan late last night and conceded defeat. Ryan thanked him for that and for being such a good candidate, running a clean campaign. He told Tony that anytime he needed an attorney, Tony would be his attorney-of-choice. They made it a point to have lunch in a couple of days.

As for Adam, and where he was, had been put on the back burner. Not entirely forgotten, but close.

Cheryl had mixed feelings about Ryan being sheriff. She had worked with him for nearly ten years, but now she would be working for him, and she hoped that it wouldn't change him. They had many good times together, and even dated just last week. Was that all going to change?

They had a supper date on Saturday night and Cheryl was going to ask Ryan straight out if it wasn't time for them to take their relationship to the next level. She was tired of being *buddies*. She wasn't getting any younger, and although there were things to think about, such as their children, she was sure they could work it out. Today she had taken the day off to put her thoughts in order.

Joe would be in charge until the first of the year, but he was leaving for Arizona on New Year's Day, and he told Ryan he wanted him to take over as soon as possible.

Linda sat at her desk looking out over the vast front yard, her head in her hands, thinking. This ranch had been her life, but ever since Dan died it just wasn't fun anymore. Ramon was a good foreman, hand picked by Dan, but Linda just didn't trust him to run the operation the way she would like it done, and the responsibility she didn't want, was all hers.

Since Dan's funeral, her outlook on the ranch had changed. One moment she had been in partnership with a man she loved with all of her heart. They had worked side-by-side sharing so many successes and failures, and then he was taken from her and it became just a monotonous job for survival, with so many worries and uncertainties.

Linda picked up the picture of her and Dan from the desk, and slowly ran her fingertips over his face, as if she could still feel him there. How many times had she sat and looked at this picture, sometimes ending up in tears? But lately, he seemed to be more of a distant memory. Those same feelings were harder and harder to bring up in her mind. Could it be because someone else was taking up that space in her heart? She blinked and looked at the picture again. For a second, she had pictured Adam in that frame. Linda laid the picture face down on the desk, and picked up the phone. She needed to talk with Tony Winters. He had helped her through some legal messes before, and maybe, - just maybe, he could help her now.

Adam was afraid he would oversleep so he kept waking up all hours of the night to look at his watch. It would take about an hour to walk out to the highway, and Linda said the bus was due around 8 a.m. It was now five a.m. His ticket was in his shirt pocket and he had emptied out his pack, looking for clean underwear.

He dumped it all out on the table, and in the glow of the gas lantern he inventoried his meager belongings. There were his clothes, his letters and pictures, - the gun was not in there. Either Linda had taken it, or the renegades he worked with, had. The clothes were all folded and smelled clean like they had been freshly laundered. He held a tee shirt to his nose and inhaled. It smelled like Linda's house. It was a comforting odor, but again he wondered about the gun. As he picked up his papers to put them back into the pack, wrapped up in the bundle, but right on top, was a new envelope he hadn't seen before. It was a small blue envelope, sealed with a tiny red heart sticker on the back. It was addressed: Adam, from Linda.

His hands were trembling as he tore open the flap and pulled out the letter. Folded inside the letter was a picture of Linda, sitting on the front steps of the house. She was wearing the same buckskin jacket and white jeans she had been wearing the night before when she came to see him. The print was a Polaroid and was simply signed, *Love, Linda*. She must have taken it before she came out last night.

Adam stared at the print for a long time and then slowly opened the letter. It was one page and hand written.

Dearest Adam,

I hope that you find this before you get to my mother's, but there are some things I must tell you because I fear you might be confused. Adam, we haven't known each other for very long, but we've shared an experience that I can never forget. Without your heroic efforts I wouldn't be here today. For that, I am eternally grateful. But you know all of that, and that's not why I am writing to you.

While you are on your way to Coeur d'Alene, I am contacting an attorney to see what can be done to get you free of the charges against you. You cannot spend the rest of your life running from this, and I'm certain that there are things that can be done. Your location at my mother's will be kept a closely guarded secret, and you must trust that what I am doing is right.

I need you in my life, Adam, and not as a hired hand on the ranch. I need you because I want to be with you and care for you, and let you care for me. Right now, I envy my mother having you there with her.

I'll see you at Thanksgiving, and I hope to have more information for you then.

Love, Linda

He read the letter again and then put it into his pack with everything else. He had given some thought to not getting off the bus in Coeur d'Alene, and to keep on going to the west coast, but now he realized she was fighting for his existence. He would be running from the only person he knew, that cared what happened to him.

She had said last night, "Adam, I love you."

Well, Linda, he murmured, *I think I love you too, but I'm not sure if it's the same way.*

Adam made it to I-90 a little after seven. He sat on a hill next to the bridge where he could see a long way down the winding highway, watching for the bus. It was cold and he pulled his collar up, and tried to protect his still-sore face and ears.

A state trooper drove by, and Adam tried to duck behind some cover, and hoped he hadn't been seen. The trooper was talking on the radio and paid little attention to him, even though he had seen him. A lot of people walked along the highway. Adam realized his evasive actions were more suspicious than simply being there, and decided to squash his fears and look normal. He pulled his pack to the edge of the road and sat on it.

Not long after he sat down, a man in a blue pickup stopped and asked him if he was looking for a ride.

"Thanks," Adam said, "but I'm waiting for someone."

The man gave him a cheerful smile, waved and drove off, his old truck belching smoke, one loose fender shuddering from the vibrating engine.

He could see a long way down the interstate, and caught the sun reflecting off the roof of the shiny bus, long before it reached him. Adam stood and held his hand up to get the bus driver's attention. He heard him decelerate, pulling around him off on the shoulder, with a hissing of air brakes. The diesel exhaust pipe was blowing dust and smoke in his face as he walked by.

The entrance door swung open and he stepped onto the first step, holding his ticket out in front of him. It was warm in the bus and it felt good after two days and nights without much heat.

"Good morning, Cowboy," the portly bus driver chuckled. "Let's see what you got," he said, grabbing the ticket from Adam. He pulled his cheaters out of his shirt pocket and then, after scanning the ticket, tore the stub off, handing it back to him, and motioned to the seats behind him. "Have a seat, my friend, if you can find an empty one." He laughed at his remark because there were only three other people on the bus.

CHAPTER TWELVE

Tony Winters reclined back in his desk chair as Linda Pendleton talked, his hands clasped over his slight paunch of a stomach. He was dressed in a three-piece, gray flannel suit with a black string bow tie over a stark white shirt. His feet, though out of sight, were in his favorite boots: a pair of six hundred dollar cowboy boots with two-inch heels.

His disappointment at losing the election had passed and now it was back to taking care of his law practice. Hell, he never thought he could win anyway, but he just wanted to keep Ryan Markinson honest. Yes sir, he was an honest lawyer and proud of it, and just to show there were no hard feelings either way, Ryan was sitting there right in front of his desk next to Linda. Tony had asked that he be there, and Linda hadn't objected.

Linda finished talking and was looking toward Ryan to see if he had anything to add to what she had said, but he just sat holding his hat in his lap with a sheepish grin, almost a sick grin, on his face.

"Well, let me get this straight," Tony, said. "You hired this drifter to work on your ranch and he turned out to be a murderer, and now you want me to represent him, because you feel he got the shaft from the law."

Ryan shifted nervously in his chair, as Tony's gaze shifted to him.

"And you, Sheriff, after talking with the powers-that-be, back in Minnesota where the accused is from, would also like to see what can be done for him. I find this a hard one to believe. I've been accused of ignoring a person's guilt because I was representing him in a court of law, but you're the first sheriff I've run into who seems to be in a similar circumstance."

Ryan cleared his throat, and crossed and uncrossed his legs, before speaking. "Look, Tony. I'm not advocating we help this man get off. Like Linda, here,"- he paused and cleared his throat again, -"ah, Mrs. Pendleton here, - I want to see that he gets a fair trial. Nobody's talking about getting him 'off' from anything."

Tony got out of his chair, and was rummaging in a drawer in a credenza behind his desk, his back to both Ryan and Linda, who were sitting quietly waiting. Finally, he came back with a yellow legal pad and sat back down again, his pen poised over the paper. He had made a big number one on the pad and underlined it. " Let's get some information here before we talk about doing anything. Where is this man?"

Ryan shrugged his shoulders and looked at Linda, saying nothing.

"Well damn it, people, we can't do squat without the person, can we?"

Linda was twisting her handkerchief in a knot. "Look, Tony - I may know where he is and I just may know how to get hold of him. But I want a plan of some kind here, before I say anything more about that."

"Sheriff? You're willing to pass over this part of aiding and abetting, for the time being?"

Ryan was on the spot. He nodded his head, yes, slowly, and then defensively said, "Damn it, Tony, stick to the point for a moment! I'll decide when laws are being broken, not you!"

Tony looked up at him, somewhat startled by the outburst. He had touched a sore spot and it was time to move on "Who's the sheriff in Minnesota and how do I get in touch with him?"

"I'll send you over all of the information," Ryan replied. He was uncomfortable with this whole conversation. Ryan stood and put his hat back on. "Look, Tony. For obvious reasons I am not going to get that involved in this. Linda came to me with good intentions of getting this man to turn himself in. But at the same time, she wants him to get the best shot he can get to beat this rap, and I don't have a problem with that. Either way the case gets cleared up. I think he was somewhat justified in doing what he did, but the law won't see it that way, unless you or some other attorney can plead his case and convince a judge somewhere to see the injustice that's been done here. You'll have to excuse me, I have to go now." Ryan turned and walked out, closing the door behind him. It was so quiet in the room; the only sound was the ticking of the clock on the wall and the soft whoosh of an overhead ceiling fan.

Tony spoke first. "Linda, I'll look into this and get back to you. I guess I need to get more information and talk to some more people here before I say anything else. Let's get together on Friday," he said, paging through his desk calendar. "How about 10 a.m.?"

"Sounds good to me," Linda said.

She drove home, her head spinning with thoughts. As much as she wanted to help Adam, she was going to have to be careful here. She had to live and do business here in Missoula, and although she was well liked, Adam was a stranger. But then her thoughts went to their embrace in the machinery shed last night, and the feelings she had experienced. There were deeper reasons here than Adam's freedom, and she was slowly realizing that.

He sat way in the back of the bus, next to the last seat. It was not that far to where he was going, and Adam settled in watching the scenery through the tinted glass. From Missoula to Coeur d'Alene was only a couple of hundred miles, but it was all mountains, as both cities were in the Rockies. It was not the high mountain passes of the central

Rockies, but still, the freeway twisted and turned its way through the passes as it headed west. For a man from Minnesota who had never been in the mountains, it was an eye opening experience.

The bus left him off in Coeur d'Alene twenty miles south of Anna's house, but Linda had given him directions on how to get there. He stood at the cabstand outside the bus depot and waited for a cab to show up. It made Adam nervous each time someone looked at him, but such was the life of a fugitive. He would feel better when he got back out of the public eye.

The battered red and white cab pulled up, and the Muslim cab driver jumped out and opened the door for him before he could even get off the bench. "Where too, Mun?" he asked, with a heavy Middle Eastern accent.

Adam just handed him the directions, pointing at the address, but saying nothing.

"Hokey dokey," the man said. "Hop youself in."

Adam tossed his bag across the back seat, and sat down. The driver threw the cab in gear and they were off with a slight screech of tires. The man was very short and his head barely stuck up above the steering wheel. The radio was tuned to some talk radio show and he seemed to be quite interested in the conversation, turning the volume up a little more. Good, Adam thought. *He didn't want to talk with him anyway.*

Coeur d'Alene was a beautiful mountain community and the road they were traveling seemed to be going up into a mountain canyon around a huge blue-water lake. It had snowed last night, and the roads were wet and slushy, so the rear end of the cab fishtailed from time to time as the driver maneuvered on the curvy road. The windshield wipers were scraping on a dry windshield, - the driver engrossed in what was being said on the radio in some foreign language. At last, with a jerk, and the screech from worn out brakes, he stopped in front of a large white house that sat just across the road from the huge lake. The house seemed to be falling into disrepair, but it was obvious that at one time it had been a stately home in a well- to- do neighborhood.

"Here you be, Mun," the driver said, turning around and smiling with a mouthful of yellow and black teeth. "Sixteen dollar, Mun."

Adam gave him a twenty, muttering, "Keep the change," and grabbing his bag stepped out onto the street. Just then, the sun came out from behind some clouds making him squint as he looked up the hill towards the old house.

The cab took off, and a shower of slush from the rear tires sprayed Adam's feet with a wet mess, and he stamped them in disgust.

He walked slowly up the walk. Up to this point he had no reservations about coming here, but right now the thought of turning and walking away was very tempting, but then what?

He stood on the porch nervously, and for a minute before he rang the bell, looked behind him at the lake across the road. The houses on both sides were some distance away, separated by the vast yard, now filled with mulched over flower gardens, statues of animals, and bird baths. In back, but close to the house, he could see a huge garage with at least four stalls, with what looked like living quarters above it. The driveway came in from an alley.

Turning around, he could see a glow through the lace curtains from a lamp in the house, and the outline of a person in a wheelchair who seemed to be reading. As he walked over to the doorbell, the person looked up as if alerted, closing the book in her lap.

The bell rang once, a rasping noise not at all like a doorbell should sound, and it was almost startling. The wheelchair moved behind the curtain and a frail voice said, "Come in, the door is unlocked," The voice came over an intercom and through a small speaker next to the door.

The door stuck a little, but with a slight nudge of Adam's shoulder it opened, and he was standing in a small entry that looked into a large living room, cluttered with piles and piles of boxes and books. He was also face to face with Anna Banotchik, Linda's mother.

The day had been a whirlwind of activity for Linda. First, she met with Ramon and laid out the work schedule for the next two weeks. They would have to let two men go, because the winter season was the slow time, but there were still calves that were vulnerable to winter's harshness to be taken care of, and feeding was a daily chore because the snow cover made it hard for the cattle to graze.

She had written to her mother this morning, and hoped that the letter would arrive about the same time as Adam. There were still meals to be cooked and a business to run, although things had slowed down considerably. Tony Winters had called and left a message reminding her about Friday's meeting. Linda made a note to call him in the morning, before she left.

She was still hampered by her sore ribs and the brace on her arm, which she had taken off while she soaked in the bathtub. The faucet on the other end of the tub was running slowly, keeping the water hot, and she could hear the steady gurgling of the excess water running into overflow drain. She had lit a candle and it flickered in the corner by her feet. The tub was warm and soothing, and she allowed her tired mind to wander. Pushing her worries to the back of her mind, and Adam to the front. Linda wished she had been conscious the night that Adam had undressed her and laid her in this tub. How had he felt when he did that? Had he felt desire for her? She had conveniently forgotten that she was dying and badly hurt that night, and he was hurt too.

She fantasized that he was sitting on the edge of the tub right now, looking down at her with those dark eyes slowly searching her body, but always coming back full circle to meet her eyes. A few of his fingers were dangling in the water making slow swirling motions above her stomach. His mouth was partly open and she saw the tip of his tongue slowly moisten his lips. He wanted to reach in and kiss her in a different way than he had, she could just sense it.

Linda looked down at her body she visualized through her half closed eyes, what he would be looking at if he were here now. Her dark nipples were just above the water, more erect than they had been in a long time, even though she was very warm. They glistened wet in the flickering light from the candle that seemed to burn with a new intensity. A few lingering soap bubbles hid them momentarily, and then dissolved. Her breasts longed for his touch, as if they too, wanted to see him, and be seen. Why not, he had already seen them, hadn't he?

Linda knew she shouldn't allow this fantasy to go on. My God, she was behaving like a lovesick teenager, but she just didn't care anymore. It had been so long since a man had desired her. Way too long. She did love him, she was sure of that, and she wanted him here with her right now. She needed him physically as well as emotionally. Her hand, with her sponge in it, was washing slowly in a place that needed no more washing. Linda's eyes were now closed, and her face was flushed, her breath racing, and then the telephone ringing brought her out of her trance.

She sat up and reached over the edge of the tub, picking up the phone. It was her mother. Linda hugged her knees to her chest, suddenly cold and aware of her nakedness. She pulled part of the shower curtain around her.

"Linda, I hope I haven't caught you at a bad time."

"No, no Mother, I was just washing up and getting ready for bed." *Playing with myself in the bathtub,* came to mind, and brought a slight smile to her lip.

"Well, I just wanted you to know, that the young man you sent out here arrived this morning. He seems to be nice and he's going to stay in the old servant's apartment above the garage. He wanted a day to get settled, and then he promised me that we would sit down tomorrow and work out a program to keep me active."

"I think you will like him, Mother," she replied. She was standing in the tub now reaching for a towel, and embarrassed that her mother had caught her at such a time. "He did some great things for me while he was here at the ranch, but we just didn't have a lot for him to do, with winter coming," she lied. "I wish I could be there with you, Mom, but hopefully this will help you until I can make arrangements to get there and spend some time with you."

"I just thought it was strange that he travels so light. Why, he only had a backpack that I saw. Don't you think that was strange?"

"He has a lot of things here, Mother, and I'll be sending them out after he gets settled." *It was just one little lie on top of another,* she thought.

"We'll have a good old fashioned Thanksgiving, Mom."

"That's nice," her mother replied.

Fortunately, her mother was tired, and Alice had come to put her to bed, so they said goodbye.

She lay in bed hugging her pillow for a long time, before her mind would settle down and let sleep come. All of her thoughts were about Adam. Did he feel the same way about her? That question plagued her mind, and she had to find out the answer.

Tony Winters met Linda at the Perkins restaurant in Missoula for breakfast, and to talk about the information he had gotten from the sheriff in Minnesota. They sat in a green, tufted, leather booth next to a large window, facing each other across the table. After finishing her meal, Linda looked outside, dabbing her mouth with her napkin, deep in thought. Huge snowflakes the size of cornflakes seemed to be covering everything out there for good.

A young waitress stopped just long enough to take their dirty dishes and refill their coffee cups. "Can I get you anything else?" she asked. They both shook their heads saying *no* at the same time.

"Just think, in another few weeks the Christmas season will be upon us," Linda said, as she watched the snow coming down.

Tony looked up from the notes he had been shuffling through and said, "Christmas must be hard for you since Dan passed away."

"At first it was, but time has a way of healing those things. This year will be better I'm sure."

"Spending Christmas here?" Tony asked.

"No, I think this year I'll be going to Coeur d'Alene to be with my mom," she said, and then wished she hadn't.

If Tony had heard her he didn't seem to be particularly interested, taking a big gulp of coffee while engrossed in a note he had written.

Looking up, he said, "You know, Linda, I, - for the life of me, don't have any idea why you want to get involved in this, but if you must, this is what I've found out. The man who killed this young man's fiancé was a third degree sexual predator, who should never have been let out of prison. When he was arrested for the crime, he confessed to what he had done. There were things in his confession that only the killer would have known, so it pretty well proves he was guilty although he never was tried in a court of law."

Tony stopped talking long enough to take another swig of coffee. Linda, who was listening intently, showed no emotion outside of some wrinkles in her brow at the moment, her chin in her hand, looking straight at Tony.

"The sheriff admits that they never should have listened to this guy without warning him about his rights, but that happens a lot in this type of situation. Nevertheless, he got himself a good lawyer who jumped on that fact, and then he was released."

"Why would a lawyer do that, Tony? Why would they want a man like that back out in society, no matter what had happened?" Linda looked angry as she questioned him.

The sudden outburst caught Tony off guard, and not wanting to get into a discussion on legal ethics, he just shrugged his shoulders.

"Back to the discussion on Adam," he continued. "In order for me to help this young man, I need to talk to him."

"Right now, I don't think that's possible," Linda replied curtly, and somewhat upset over Tony's use of the word young.

"Look. Linda. Let's be sensible. If this man doesn't want to be seen, there is nothing I can do for him. At some point he is going to have to turn himself in to the authorities, and go to court. That's the way the system works."

Linda had a hooded sweater on, and she was playing with the drawstrings around her neck, while she stared at Tony.

"If I talk him into coming back and turning himself in, and I'm not saying I can, where would he be tried, and would you represent him?"

Tony looked at her for a moment before answering. "Minnesota, and maybe," he replied. "I'm very busy right now."

Linda reached into her purse and brought out her checkbook. "What do I owe you for a retainer?" she asked.

Tony laid his hands on top of hers and squeezed them gently. "We'll work it out."

CHAPTER THIRTEEN

It took Adam a while to get the heat on, and clean up his newly obtained living quarters, but Anna had insisted he do that first, and leave her alone for the day. The place had not been used in a long time. Over fifteen years, according to Anna. The furniture was covered with dust and spider webs, and there were boxes of stuff everywhere: mostly books, papers and boxes of knick-knacks. He took all of the bedding and towels over to the house and washed them, finding the laundry in the basement, on his own. He thought he would stop and talk with Anna while things were washing and drying, but she was asleep in her chair, so he left.

By evening it had taken on a bit of a homey touch. The air was heavy with the smell of cleaning products that he borrowed from the laundry. Adam sat on the edge of the bed and looked at Linda's picture in the glow from a small bedside lamp. He could still smell her hair and feel her softness, and he wished she were coming sooner. Not being able to talk to her like he had, was a bitter pill to swallow, but maybe she would call sometime when he was in the house.

In the morning he would need to go to a lumber company for

supplies, because he needed to buy some spindles and rails to make some kind of apparatus for Anna to walk alongside of, daily. She needed to stay active. He was also hoping she had a car he could use, but he would find out in the morning.

At this stage of the game, all he could do for Anna was try to keep her going as long as she was able. For a daily schedule, Adam thought he would come in the morning, after Alice had Anna up and dressed, and leave in the evening when she had her dressed for bed.

He hadn't met Alice, the girl who was taking care of Anna yet, but thought he would go back over tonight to talk with her, and see about a bite to eat.

Anna was watching television when he came into the living room. She had grown very thin, but her dark blue eyes still glistened as if nothing was wrong. "You need to find us some food, Adam," she said. "Usually I ate when Alice came at night, but I told her, you and I would take care of meals now."

Becoming the cook had not been talked about, but Adam smiled and said. "What do you want, and where do I find it?"

"Let's go in the kitchen and look," she smiled, spinning her wheel chair around.

They had pancakes and breakfast sausage swimming in maple syrup. It had been Adam's specialty back at the ranch when he was cooking. Anna loved it.

Anna was sitting next to Adam with a dishtowel in her hands, while he stood in front of the sink. He would wash a dish and then put it on the towel in her lap and she would dry it, slowly and painstakingly, running her towel-covered hands over it. She couldn't hand it to him, but Adam would take it and place it back in the cupboard, replacing it with a wet dish. She had very little strength left in her hands and arms, and maybe what he had planned for tomorrow would be too little, too late.

The back door gave a slight shudder and then opened, as Alice Kennedy stepped into the kitchen, followed by a blast of cold air, before she could shut the door. She had been told this morning that Adam would be here, but it still caught her off guard, and for a second she stood by the door staring at him, speechless. She wore blue jeans, a light blue winter coat and a dark blue stocking cap that she was pulling off as she looked at Adam. Her cheeks were rosy from being out in the cold, and they were nearly a perfect match for her long red hair that spilled down her back, flowing out of the stocking cap she was now stuffing into her pocket.

Adam broke the awkward silence by stepping around the table and extending his hand, saying, "You must be Alice." She was short and had to look up at Adam.

"Yes, yes I am," she said, and took his hand limply. "You must be Adam. Anna told me you would be coming. I understand you're a physical therapist."

"Amongst other things," Adam smiled. *Like a fugitive,* he thought.

They both looked down and realizing they were still clasping hands, let go of each other. Adam stuffed his hands in his back pockets while Alice turned her attention to Anna, who had been sitting silently, some silverware still in her lap.

"We better get you ready for bed," Alice said, pushing her wheelchair out of the kitchen and into the bathroom, closing the door behind them.

When they came back out, Anna's hair had been braided and hung down her back, and she was wearing a long, yellow flannel nightgown. Alice wheeled her into the bedroom, which was equipped with a hospital bed, and parked the chair alongside of it. Adam followed, not sure what was expected of him, but wanting to be close by to help if he could.

"We tried to find a way that Anna could be alone, and still get a hold of someone if she has to," Alice said. So we came up with these cell phones. There, on the nightstand, were two cell phones sitting in a charger. "At night I've been taking one of them with me, so she could call me if she needed to get up. It's yours now." She handed him one of the phones. Alice had gone around behind the wheelchair and helped Anna stand. "Would you help her into the bed?" she asked.

Adam reached down and picked her up, and laid her in the open bed. Anna smiled, but said nothing. He had handled her like a child.

Alice covered Anna, and then kissed her goodnight. "See you tomorrow," she said.

"Good night, Anna," Adam said, and he and Alice went back to the kitchen.

"I better get going," Alice said. "I still have some schoolwork. I used to stay and do it here at the table until she fell asleep, but you're here now."

"What are you studying?" Adam asked, not wanting her to go yet, but at a loss for what to talk about.

"Nursing," replied Alice, stuffing her hair back in her stocking cap and zipping her coat.

"I took a few nursing courses," Adam replied.

"Well, if I get stumped, maybe you can help me," she laughed. "See you tomorrow."

For a few minutes after she left, Adam stood in the empty kitchen. He drained the sink and wiped it out and then dousing the lights, walked through the rest of the house, shutting off lights. He passed Anna's open door and in the faint light of a night-light above her bed, he could see she was sleeping. He let himself out the back door, lighting a cigarette on his way to the garage. The night was clear and cold and he shivered in his shirtsleeves. He looked across the yard to Alice's house. At least, that is where he thought she had gone. Her tracks in the fresh snow went that way. The house was dark except for a light on upstairs in the front that spilled out onto a porch. She had seemed nice, a no-nonsense form of nice, and very businesslike. But after all, he was an employee right now, and so was she. Right?

Linda and Ramon were going over a schedule that she had made up for the next month. Things had slowed down a lot, and winter was traditionally the time of the year when they made repairs that had been put off. The list this year was longer than years before, and Linda knew they would never be able to afford it all, so they had to pick and choose.

"We're going to have to hold down purchasing a good deal of material, and try to do what we can with what we have," she said. "I also need you to take a man with you and work on equipment up on the high plateau. A lot of that stuff got put away last fall without much maintenance. I need to go to town tomorrow, so make me a list of the things you need up there, and I'll pick it up for you."

Okay was all Ramon said. He slid his chair away from her desk and walked to the door, but before he opened it, he turned with his hand on the knob. "Have you heard anymore about the search for Aaron?" he asked.

"Who?" The name, Aaron, had confused her for a second. "Oh, him. No, I haven't, but maybe I'll stop and see the sheriff tomorrow and see what they've found out. Although that seems to be a chapter we should close, doesn't it?"

Ramon smiled, his white teeth showing proudly. He said nothing, but opened the door and went outside. She sure could get defensive, whenever Aaron's name was brought up, he thought.

Linda watched Ramon disappear around the corner of the house. Why was he worried about Adam? Adam. The mention of his name brought a whole flood of feelings, and she had to sit down for a minute. Next week was Thanksgiving, and she would see him then. Could she talk him into cooperating with her and her lawyer? Or would such talk scare him away for good. She had to be careful here that she didn't get too involved, in case things went bad. But on the other hand, what she wouldn't give to bring him back here to run this ranch. Not to sleep in that bunkhouse out back, but to sleep in this house with her.

She thought about what had happened the other night in the tub and there had to be a reason why she had acted like that. There had to be a reason for the feelings she hadn't felt, since before Dan died. It had to be more than sex.

She looked at herself in the mirror by the door. *I'm still a good looking woman and have a lot to offer him*, she thought. *If only he was willing to overlook a few things, they could be so good together.*

By Monday of Thanksgiving week, Adam was starting to feel more at home around Anna. It felt good to be back doing what he did for a living, before this all started. The big difference was, he used to take care of many patients each day, and now he had only Anna.

Along with her therapy, Adam made an attempt to make life more normal for Anna. Alice, because of her lack of time, had been forced to take a lot of shortcuts. The easy way to do it was good for Alice, but not always good for Anna. Adam had Alice remove the catheter and bag she had taught Anna to use. He could take her to the bathroom and set her on the stool. Anna could handle the rest. He made a tray that he clamped on her wheelchair to hold her food. It had a strap to keep her hand in place and she could now feed herself. It was more like shoveling it in, but she took pride in the fact that no one was spoon-feeding her. That day would come soon enough.

Adam took Anna downtown, where she bought some new clothes and took her to have her eyes checked for stronger glasses. He made a dental appointment for her for two weeks after Thanksgiving to repair a chipped tooth, and last week, they had just gone out for a drive in the hills. Adam spent a good part of one day getting her old Lincoln town car running. It had sat in the garage for over a year without running, but with a fresh battery charge and some fresh gas, it ran great.

Alice was taking longer with Anna in the mornings now, fixing her hair, and adding a touch of perfume and make-up, so she would look good and feel better about herself when they went out. She seemed to not be in such a hurry as she was the first few days after Adam arrived. She stayed later at night too, and she and Adam talked about school, and what else they could do for Anna. They also seemed to be genuinely interested in making this job as easy as they could, for Anna, and for each other.

On Wednesday the day before Thanksgiving, Adam braved going out alone once more. It made him very nervous to be out in public. It was almost like everybody who even casually glanced at him, had the potential to recognize him. From what, he didn't know. Adam had no idea whether his description and picture had been splashed around heavily or not. Surely there were a lot of fugitives out there they were looking for: people who were cold-blooded murderers or kidnappers, and not someone who had just evened the score. The thought of evening the score brought anger back. How could you call it 'even,'- when all that that animal gave up, was his worthless life, while Mandy gave up so much goodness? She had so much beauty and grace. He slammed his hand down on the dash of the Lincoln to clear his mind, wiping his eyes with the back of his hand. He just couldn't forget her, no matter how hard he tried.

The book was in the medical section of the library. He had borrowed Anna's library card. Amyotrophic Lateral Sclerosis, Lou Gehrig's disease. He had worked with patients who were suffering with it back in Minnesota at the clinic, but still didn't know much about it. All he knew was it was terminal, and some patients lived longer than others. Could his therapy help Anna live longer? He needed to find out.

Adam found two books, on the disease, and checked them out. On the way home, he picked up groceries and cigarettes, and the fixings he hoped would suffice for a small Thanksgiving dinner. Alice would be there and so would Linda. She had called Anna and told her she would be there by early morning. He also filled the Lincoln with gas.

The roads were crowded with holiday shoppers as he made his way back to Anna's. This was so much better than the ranch, but he knew, in the back of his mind, that it could change abruptly. Maybe Linda would have some good news. He still didn't know what she was doing for him, but from what he gathered from talking to her, she might be trying some legal strings, if that was possible.

Linda left for Idaho about four in the morning. She had told Ramon that she wouldn't be there for Thanksgiving, but arranged for a cafe in town to bring dinner out for the crew. There were only five of them now. She also told Ramon where she was going, and not to look for her back, until Sunday. She had talked to Tony the day before, and he told her bluntly that there was nothing more he could do for her, or Adam. Adam had to turn himself in to Ryan, and be extradited back to Minnesota to face trial. Then he could help him. It was what Linda had expected she would hear, but dreaded hearing just the same.

Adam had been dealt one dirty hand by the law already. Was he ready to believe it would be different this time? She bit her lip and shook her head slowly, as the white Caddy headed west through the mountain passes in the early morning darkness.

There was another problem. Anna had called her just a day ago for no other reason than to tell Linda how much Adam was helping her, and how much she thought of him.

"Oh what tangled webs we weave." Linda's Shakespeare was shaky at best, but it described how she felt right now.

It was eight a.m. when she pulled up to her mother's house. The sight of the house always brought a flood of memories of her childhood and her family. There had been so many good times, but as always, time had stripped them of all the good ingredients, and now she was left with the spoils: a sick mother, a dead father, and a sister who had divorced herself from it all. She had to be honest; it would be the easiest thing to do.

This was her first trip back since last Thanksgiving when her mother was well. *But let's be really honest,* she thought, *Adam wasn't here before either, and that has a lot to do with why I'm here now.*

She had done her best to look young again. Yesterday she had her hair cut short, and dyed a little darker. She was wearing black slacks that fit her trim form just right, and a white blouse with an extra button undone on the bodice. She had taken the brace off her arm and wrapped it with an elastic bandage under the blouse sleeve. She would just be careful.

Adam was upstairs changing bedding on Linda's bed in her old room. It was his first trip up there and Anna had told him specifically which room to go to. There were three other doors off the hall and they were all locked.

Linda's room looked like the day she had left it in the early eighties. Her class annual was still lying on the bedside table along with a picture of her with some boy. Was it Dan? She had been a beautiful young lady with long flowing hair and a radiant smile. In the picture she was dressed in a red sweater and a very short black skirt. He had his hand on her shoulder and for some reason it seemed posed. *What the hell, all pictures are posed, aren't they?*

He slid open a dresser drawer, and found it full of old clothes that smelled of mothballs. *Time to quit snooping,* he thought. Adam finished with the bed and was dusting the room, when he heard the door open downstairs, and Linda's voice calling out, "Hello, anybody home?"

She walked through to the kitchen where her mother was sitting with a book on her lap, a shaft of sunlight coming in the window.

"Hi, Mom," she said.

"Linda," Anna replied softly. "You startled me." The paperback book fell from her lap to the floor.

Linda reached down, picked up the book, then leaned over and kissed her mother on the forehead. She pulled a chair up so they were facing at each other, and then pushing Anna's hair away from her face, said, "I miss you so much, Mom, and I feel so bad that I can't be with you more. Especially now."

Anna smiled, and speaking so softly that Linda could hardly hear her, said, "I was so worried about you and your accident. Adam told me you were badly hurt, but you made a great recovery."

"Speaking of Adam," Linda said... but before Anna could answer, someone behind Linda cleared his throat, and she turned to face him.

He was standing there with a smile that could pass for a smirk on his face. His hands reached for hers. She pulled him to her and they exchanged hugs and a brief kiss. Then, as if she was uncomfortable with the affection in front of her mother, Linda held him back at arm's length and said, "I smell something cooking. It must be my Thanksgiving dinner."

CHAPTER FOURTEEN

Alice came over a few minutes later, and while Adam finished with his cooking, she and Linda reminisced. Alice had always lived next door to Linda's parents, but she was just a small child when Linda left home.

Over the years, however, when Linda and Dan had visited, she had watched Alice blossom into the young lady she was now, and had talked with her on many occasions. They always exchanged Christmas cards, and Alice and her parents had stopped at the ranch once, on a trip out East. Alice's parents still both worked, her mother as a cook at a school, and her father as a police officer in Coeur d'Alene. He was looking to retire soon.

Alice was an only child, and although she still lived at home, and got along well with her parents, they had little in common. They did very little together, and she seldom talked about them, or to them.

Adam normally saw Alice in her street clothes, or a nurse's white outfit that she had to wear to school. But today she had on a long, black velvet skirt and a red blouse with a black vest. A silver brooch in the shape of a large "A" was pinned to her vest, and she wore a silver chain with a small cross around her neck. In her hair was a red bow with a little silver arrow through it. She looked very festive, *and* Adam had noticed.

From that chilly reception Alice had given him on the day when he first arrived, there had developed a much warmer friendship. Adam noticed that also, and he was glad, because the feeling was becoming mutual.

The dinner was not elaborate, but nice. Instead of turkey, Adam had cooked a goose and made some wild rice dressing, per Anna's instructions. He had an apple pie that he warmed in the oven, served with cinnamon ice cream on the side, and whipped cream on top.

After dessert, they sat in the living room and had coffee. Alice sat close to Anna and helped her with hers, until it became obvious that Anna was tiring and it was time for a nap. Then Adam took her into the bedroom and laid her on the bed. As he removed Anna's shoes, he could not help but think that Linda had not spent much time with her mom, instead, talking with him and Alice. He knew that Alice would be leaving shortly, and maybe if he left for a while, and they were left alone, it would give them some quality time with each other.

"I guess I'll be leaving for a while," he said to Linda. "Leave you women to your gossip. Give you someone to talk about."

They both laughed at his remark, as he stepped out the back door and lit a cigarette. He felt like a square peg in a round hole right now. That, and he was tired. What would his first Thanksgiving have been like with Mandy? The thoughts of her were incessant. They just kept coming. He drew down deep on the cigarette and blew the smoke out the side of his mouth. Then, Adam snapped the butt, with his forefinger and thumb against the side of the house, in anger. It fell apart in a shower of sparks, as he headed for the stairs alongside the garage.

He was lying so he could see through the window, and his view included the back door of the house. It was not long before Alice emerged, stopping on the top step to look up at the window he was looking out of. It was dark in the room and she could not see him, but Adam wished she had. He also wished she had stopped by to talk, like she had yesterday. They seemed to have a lot in common.

He dozed off, and when he woke it was with a sense that he was not alone. Linda was sitting in a recliner across the room. She had taken off her coat and shoes and was sitting with her feet tucked under her, smiling at him. "Hi, sleepyhead," she said coyly. "Mother is still napping, so thought I would come and talk with you for a while, if that's ok? Your door was unlocked, so I just made myself to home. I used to come up here when I was a little girl and play house. That is, before my mother got a maid and a nanny for me. Not two people. They were one and the same."

Adam was still laying propped up on one elbow wondering what she was talking about. He rubbed his eyes and said, "Huh? I'm sorry, I guess I dozed off." He swung his legs to the side of the bed and taking an ashtray off the nightstand, lit a cigarette and inhaled deeply, holding the ashtray in one hand and the cigarette in the other. Linda stood up, crossed the room and sat on the edge of the bed next to him. "Do you have an extra one of those?" she asked,

"I didn't know you smoked. I've never seen you smoke before."

"I guess I'm just a sociable smoker. I brought treats." She walked over and opened the back door to the outside and brought in a paper bag with a twelve pack of beer that she set on the nightstand.

"It is Thanksgiving. What would Thanksgiving be without a little beer, huh?" She twisted off the caps on two of them and handed one to Adam.

Linda explained what Tony had told her, about Adam having to turn himself in, to clear things up. How there was a defense for what he had done, and if it was handled right, he might get off with a hand slap, or possibly just a very light sentence. "I didn't come here tonight to ask you to do that. I just wanted you to know about it and to think about it."

Adam didn't comment. He just sat looking at her out of the top of his eyes, while his head was still slightly bowed.

Linda also told him how much it meant to her to have him here; with her mother "Mother has called me and talked about you. It's not just the medical help and advice that is so good for her, Adam. It's your friendship that seems to be impressing her the most."

Adam had not said much. He just sat there in deep thought. "I guess you can't have it both ways," he said. "You're confusing me. I genuinely enjoy the chance to help your mother, even though I know it's only temporary. But to throw myself on the mercy of a legal system that has failed me once already, - well, I don't know if I'm ready for that, Linda." He leaned back on the bed, his feet still on the floor, staring at the ceiling. Linda laid down alongside of him, but on her side, propped up on her good arm. With her other hand, she reached over and turned his face toward her. She bent over and kissed him tenderly.

"Let's forget it all for the time being, and just enjoy each other," she whispered.

The statement caught Adam off guard, and before he could react to it, she bent and kissed him again. This time her lips lingered for a few moments. Her mouth was slightly open, and more eager. She was now partially on top of him and Adam could feel her breasts against his chest. His hands went to her back, and he could feel tenseness there, ebbing out like tiny electrical impulses from her body to his.

Now Linda was kissing his forehead, while her hands explored his hair. Adam opened his eyes and discovered that the only place he could look was down the front of her blouse. Her breasts, crushed against his chest, seemed to be bursting out of the lacy bra that restrained them. For an instant he stopped questioning what was happening, and became caught up in the moment. His hands were on the small of her back and wanting to slide down. Her body seemed to be urging him to do so. His body was responding, without his mind's permission. In fact, his body was out front, and the gap was widening. Then a memory of those same breasts he was looking at right now reminded him of another time, a time when they hadn't seemed sexy at all, but part of a badly injured body. He had not wanted her in this way then, and a minute ago, he wasn't sure that he wanted her that way now. But it had been so long, and she was so beautiful and willing right now, and resistance, what there had been of it, was already galloping off ahead of him.

Linda's fingers were now opening the buttons of his shirt, and then going from his shirt to hers, in a hurry-up effort to undress them both. His hands had found their way to her bottom, and she pulled one leg up, suggesting something else. Like a puppy, showing its belly in friendly surrender, she was welcoming the way. She reached in back with one hand to release the clasp on her bra, and her breasts loomed even larger in his face. Just the very ends, were hidden in lace, and fighting to get out of their restraint.

Adam was boarding a runaway train he was not entirely sure he wanted to be on. He knew by the reaction he was getting from his body, that the train was about to leave the station. He was not in love with her the way she was with him, but he was a man with blood, that right now was gushing through his veins, carrying the testosterone his glands were dumping in copious amounts. It was impossible to ignore.

Her kisses were warm and inviting, and her tongue had found its way to the end of his. Her mouth was sweet and tasted of peppermint. Everything about her was so sensuous. Her good hand was fumbling with his belt, but she was lying on top of her arm, and him, leaving little room to maneuver. Slowly Linda raised herself with her other arm, just enough to work her fingers around the buckle, and he felt it release. Her breath was coming in gasps and her mind was racing ahead of her fumbling attempts to undress him, when the arm snapped, and Linda screamed.

They both realized what had happened, as Linda rolled over onto her back, her face grimacing in pain, holding her broken limb with her other hand.

Adam jumped up and stood beside the bed, his shirt hanging open. "Oh my God! I am so sorry. I forgot all about your arm, Linda." He unwrapped the bandage she had put on when she took the brace off. Running to the refrigerator, holding his pants shut with one hand, he found some ice in his tiny freezer. He filled a towel and wrapped it around her arm.

"We need to get you to a hospital. I'll go get the car out, and you get your, - uh, blouse, and... here, let me fix your clothing."

She sat up while he clasped her bra. She was sobbing now, her shoulders pulsing up and down, her head hanging. Adam came back to the front and tipped her head back to button the top of her blouse. She wasn't sobbing! She was laughing hysterically!

He fell to his knees in front of her, next to the bed, not sure what was happening, and then buried his head in her lap, laughing with her.

It was two a.m. before they got back from the hospital. Linda's arm was in a new plaster cast she that could not remove. Adam walked her to the top of the stairs and kissed her forehead. "Once again, I am so sorry," he said.

Linda smiled, and kissed him lightly on the mouth. "You should be. Breaking a lady's arm in the throes of passion," she said playfully.

"Do you need any help?" Adam asked, as he switched on the bedside lamp.

Linda laughed. "No, you had your chance. Leave."

Linda left on Sunday afternoon, after dinner. As much as she wanted to stay, she had a ranch to run. Her attempt to seduce Adam had left her confused and frustrated. There had been a time in her life when a bat of her eye, and the flick of her tongue, would have brought a man to her loins with all of the desire of a Brahma bull. Dan and she had made love insatiably when they first met. What had happened the other night, that made Adam play more "defense" than "offense?"

At first, she wanted to believe that he did want her, and that he was just shy. But the longer she thought about that, the more she realized it wasn't true. He didn't want her. Not in that way, at any rate. But she was not through with him yet. She had told him she would be back for Christmas

The day after she returned, she met with Tony once more and told him that Adam was not ready to turn himself in yet. "Maybe after he thinks about it," she said.

Tony only shrugged his shoulder, and said, "Whenever he's ready. I'm not looking for work at this point." Then, stopping Linda before she could leave his office, and with his hand on her shoulder, Tony said seriously: "Linda, you know that you could be in a world of hurt, if you are harboring a criminal. I hope that wherever he is, you're not involved."

Linda could only smile, and nod her head that she understood.

The next month was bad for Anna, and her health went downhill rapidly. Adam and Alice worked her limbs and muscles, but no amount of massaging and therapy seemed to help her. Her breathing also suffered and Adam had oxygen brought in for her at night. Her appetite was almost non-existent and both Adam and Alice would spend hours trying to get her to eat something. It had to be ground and blended, to almost the consistency of baby food, for her to swallow it. Alice would read to her every night before she went to sleep. Her body was dying, but her mind was still sharp, and still craved to know what was going on.

Whenever there was time from Anna's needs, Adam and Alice would sit at the kitchen table and do her schoolwork together. His knowledge was a big help to her, but something else was happening, and it wasn't unbeknownst to either of them. They could feel it. They were becoming more and more infatuated with each other. At first it had been the playful pushing and shoving, almost like kids with their puppy love. But then it had led to handholding while they talked. Then a quick, goodbye kiss at the door one night, followed by a more prolonged kiss the next night. Tonight it had led to a make-out session on the couch that may have culminated in something even more sensuous, had not Anna had a choking session, and they both ran to help her. Alice was almost relieved it had happened, because she was fast becoming powerless to keep from doing what she so desperately wanted, and knew was going to happen, eventually.

It would be Christmas in just a few days, and Adam had braved the crowd's downtown, and bought Alice a beautiful white cashmere sweater and a tiny gold locket. In the locket, he put a picture of himself, taken in a machine at the mall.

The thoughts of Mandy were starting to fade from his mind, but they were not completely gone yet. Alice was starting to take her place, despite the resistance. Mandy had been, to his mind, almost perfect. But Alice was bringing to him comparisons that showed faults in Mandy that Adam hadn't thought existed, and was left with a puzzled feeling

They bought a Christmas tree and decorated it while Anna sat in her wheel chair and smiled, as they cloaked it in all of the old bulbs and decorations she had accumulated over the years. Each one of them told a story from years gone by, and the twinkling lights reflected in the wet pools of Anna's eyes as she took her trip back on memory lane. She cried, because she couldn't help it, and she cried because she realized that this would be her last Christmas. But they were also tears of happiness, for the two young lovers sharing their love for each other, with her. She loved them both for what they were doing to make her life as comfortable as they could.

CHAPTER FIFTEEN

Linda arrived at her mothers on Christmas Eve day. Anna was now on oxygen a good share of the time. Adam, although he was trying, was at a loss to explain Anna's rapid decline, but her doctor said it was not unusual for the disease to progress in a hurry, once it reached a certain point.

"I wish there was more I could do to help her," Adam said. Linda and Adam were seated at the kitchen table with cups of hot chocolate, while Anna napped in her bed.

Linda did not answer at first, taking small sips of her drink and looking at him with raised eyes. She knew something was bothering him. "You can't take it personally," she said. She had strong suspicions that something was blooming between Adam and Alice, from their actions, and although she was powerless to stop it, she had come prepared to throw a wrench in the gears if she had to. She was a woman used to getting her own way, and not used to sharing.

"I talked to Tony the other day," Linda said, shifting uneasily in her chair. "He says the longer we put this thing off, the harder it will be to resolve. With Mother going downhill the way she is, it might be better if we put her in a home. There is also the chance that they will find you Adam, and if that happens, versus turning yourself in, we lose any negotiating we might be able to do."

She had taken his hand in hers, across the table, and was holding it loosely while her other hand rubbed the top of it. "I want you to come run the ranch Adam. It's more than I can handle, and Ramon is giving me more and more problems everyday."

Adam had been quiet until now. But slowly he took his hand back from Linda, and rubbed it through his thick, curly hair. For a moment it was quiet, and the soft ticking of the clock on the wall was the only sound in the room. He was still being quiet, but seemed uneasy now, and confused. Like he wanted to say something, but just didn't know how to say it. "Maybe you're right," he finally said. "Let's get through these next few days and celebrate Christmas for Anna. Then I'll make a decision."

Just then, the back door opened, and Alice came in, stomping her feet to get rid of the snow from her boots. "It's so cold out there you would swear your lungs would freeze.... Linda! You're here! What a nice surprise."

Alice had a shopping bag with some gifts in it, and she went over and placed them under the tree before saying anything else. Then she walked over and hugged Adam from behind, her arms clasped over his chest. Her cheeks were rosy from the cold, and she was rubbing his chest to warm her hands. "You're so nice and warm." She bent over and whispered in his ear. Still hugging Adam, she asked Linda, "How long can you stay?"

This show of emotion between Alice and Adam had Linda off balance for a second, and she said, "Just a couple of days. Why do you ask?"

Alice sensed some hostility in her voice, and for a moment she was uncomfortable, but as she started to release Adam and back off, he reached up and put his hands over hers, holding her there.

It was Adam who answered, in an effort to change the subject.

"I think you gals should get supper ready while I go get some wine. I was going to do that this afternoon, but I forgot." After he said it, he had misgivings about what he had done. Not for Linda's sake, but for Alice's.

Adam had no way of knowing what was discussed while he was gone, but when he returned, Alice was getting Anna up and into her chair, and Linda was putting supper on the table. She had put a cassette in the kitchen radio, and Christmas Carols were playing softly. Tony Bennett was singing, "I'll Be Home For Christmas," and Linda was humming along with him.

After supper, Alice helped Linda clean up and then the two of them put Anna down for the night. Alice hooked up all of the breathing tubes and the catheter while Linda watched with a very concerned look on her face. It was almost like it was too distasteful to watch what was being done to her own mother.

The gift exchanging would be done the next morning on Christmas Day. All three of them sat for a while with glasses of wine, and watched the bubble lights on the tree, as they went through their never-ending percolation. Soon they were all yawning. It had been a long day for Linda, with the drive over, and Alice didn't seem to show any sign of going home. She sat next to Adam on the couch with her feet curled under her, and her hand on his leg. Alice smiled, and looked overly interested at every comment Adam made.

Linda took it all in, while becoming more and more irritated with her. She wanted to be alone with Adam. She had fantasized about it on the trip here, and it had been on her mind constantly since Thanksgiving, when she had experienced her aborted seduction attempt. If only she had accomplished that, she might have a better idea where she stood with him right now.

Linda had stood nude in front of the mirror this morning, when she arose to leave from the ranch. She posed sideways, looking at herself. *I think I still look good,* she thought. *My breasts are still firm and so is my butt. My stomach is flat.* She had spent some extra time in the shower trimming and shaving away the wild hairs that seemed to come with age. *What man in his right mind would not be interested in this?* Just thinking about being with Adam, had stirred that anxious longing in her loins.

"If you guys will excuse me, it's been a long day and I think I'll go to bed." Linda walked into the kitchen, put her glass on the table, and coming back through the room, headed upstairs. Both Adam and Alice said softly, "Goodnight."

Linda sat on the edge of the bed and quickly undressed, pulling a tee shirt over her head for a nightshirt. *There was only one thing she could do to break them up and that was to put her mother in a home and get him back on the ranch. It was time anyway. Anna's quality of life was fast eroding away. But first, she had to get him free of his charges.* Linda walked to the window and looked out on the front yard. All of the garden statues her mother had loved so much now stood in snow part way up their girth. The full moon made it so bright she could make out the details in the sculptures from way up here. A small rabbit hopped from garden to garden, looking for spoils from summer to eat. Linda's mind went back to another day, and she could visualize her mother in her baggy clothes and her wide brimmed hat going from flower garden to flower garden cutting and pruning. Always finishing up with a fresh bouquet for the kitchen table.

The back door closed downstairs. *Alice must have left. Adam might still be here. Maybe she needed a glass of water or, - what other reason could she come up with to go down there?* Linda pulled a robe on and walked to the top of the stairs, but all she could hear was the hissing of the air from her mother's breathing apparatus and the ticking of the clock. She walked down the stairs part way and stopped. It appeared to be dark downstairs, except for a night light in her mother's room. Walking the rest of the way down, she walked slowly through the large room. She needed no lights; the moonlight coming in the large windows lit the room so well it was almost like an eerie daytime. Making her way to the back of the house, she looked out toward the garage. There was a light on upstairs. Was he alone?

Linda slipped on her boots and coat by the back door and stepped outside, clutching the front of her coat to her body, even though it was buttoned. It was cold in the clear night air, and ever since her ordeal in the blizzard she didn't tolerate cold very well.

She walked to the bottom of the steps and looked toward Alice's house, but it was dark. *She must be asleep,* she thought. Looking back at the garage, she wondered what she would say to Adam. *"Hey, I'm here to screw your brains out."* She would pretend to be upset about her mother, and in need of comforting, not able to sleep and looking for a soft shoulder to lean on.

It was only a short walk to the stairs but she could feel the cold rising up inside her short coat on her bare legs. She was only wearing a tee shirt, panties and a short robe under the jacket, and there was not much warmth in them. *But there would be warmth inside. Yeah, there would be lots of warmth, and as for her lack of clothing, well… it was all the less to take off.*

Linda walked up the steps in her soft boots making very little sound. Should she knock? Maybe the door would be locked and she would have to knock. There was a small landing on the top and she made out a bucket sitting by the door. Otherwise the landing was empty. There was no storm door, and the apartment door had a window in it. Inside, curtains hung on both sides of the window, but they had been tied back with ribbons. Linda rested for moment, as she was breathing hard. It was more from the growing anticipation of seeing him, than the climb up the stairs. Even though the moon was full and bright, she was in the shade here and it was dark. Suddenly, out of the corner of her eye, she was aware of a rapid shadowy movement inside, and she leaned closer and looked through the small window. The light she had seen from outside was in the kitchen, over the sink on the side of the room, but it did spill over into this area, a little. Enough so that she could make out Adam *and* Alice.

They were on the couch straight across from the window. Alice's naked back was to Linda, as she peered through the window. She was leaning toward Adam, her naked thigh thrown across his lap. He had his fingers threading through her long red hair, and as Linda watched, was trailing his lips from hers down to the tender spot on her throat and then back to her lips again. Linda could hear their gasps of passion, and knew where this was heading. She jerked her head back away from the window, and quietly backed away from the door. For a moment she thought she would fall backwards down the stairs. Her hand gripped the railing in a death grip and her body started to tremble, half from the cold, and half from the rage within. Finally, she backed down the stairs one step at a time. When she came to the bottom, she ran to the house and inside the back door. Linda slammed the door shut in the process and collapsed on the kitchen floor, slumped there on the rug beside the door. She was biting her lips to keep from crying out, and rubbing her eyes to destroy the image she had just seen. Suddenly realizing she would wake her mother if she wasn't careful, she rose to her knees. Gone was the initial shock, but not the anger. But now, the anger was being controlled and channeled away from the reaction she had had, to strike out. It was being channeled to the part of her that said, "I will get even."

Adam was exhausted and spent. Alice's head was nestled under his chin and she leaned in to plant tiny kisses on his chest and neck. Her arms were around him, and her small hard breasts were pressed into his side. She hadn't been a virgin, but she'd never experienced anything like this before. He had brought out all the fireworks, all of the shooting stars, and an electrifying release that had come in waves. This was making love, not just having sex, - and the fact that she loved this man so much, made it even more beautiful. She didn't want to move and separate their bodies. This is where they belonged... together.

Adam could feel the warmth of her small supple body pressed against him, in a perfect fit. He could feel her heart beating through her breasts, as if they were telegraphing a coded message to him. Her sweet breath was on his neck, mingling with the scent of their lovemaking, drifting up between their bodies. Alice's hand was gently rubbing his chest, trying to calm them both down. Then he heard the door slam on the house. Adam picked Alice up as if she was a child, setting her on the couch and covering her with a blanket, then went to the door. Looking out the window in the moonlight he could see nothing wrong.

"What is it?" Alice asked.

"I heard a door slam. I better check it out." He found his jeans in back of the couch, where he had thrown them. Grabbing his coat off the hook by the door and slipping on his boots, he was zipping up his coat and pants as he went out the door. He had been sweating, and the cold dry air made him grimace and shiver as he went down the steps. It was probably nothing. Maybe Linda had looked out to check the temperature. Adam reached for the knob on the door and turned it. It was locked, and he had purposely left it open. Linda must have locked it. Maybe she felt safer that way. Adam shrugged his shoulders and went back upstairs to Alice.

Meanwhile Alice left the couch and snuggled into his bed. She turned on the bedside lamp and it set off a sparkle from the ring she was admiring on her left hand. It was the nicest Christmas present she had ever received. She held the bed covers to her chest with one hand and held the other hand with the ring under the lamp to admire the sparkle again. It was not a fancy ring, but it was a big, thoughtful gesture on Adam's part. They never really talked about an engagement, and this was the first step, but their whole relationship had been a whirlwind romance. From those awkward days when they had first met, had come a realization that they desperately needed each other. They came close to making love several times, but always, Adam would stop them. It was like he was waiting for the perfect moment.

"I guess it was nothing," Adam said, as he slid into the bed beside Alice. "Linda's been acting kind of funny, don't you think?"

"Not as friendly, that's for sure. But you seem to be friendlier than I've seen you in a while."

Adam laughed and grabbed Alice's hands that were reaching for his manhood. She relented and snuggled against his chest. Adam held her close, stroking her hair, but saying nothing. This girl was becoming very important to him and that felt good. But he had a past to face up to, before he could get on with his life. How was he going to handle this?

Linda was too upset to sleep. She had found a bottle of Johnny Walker Red in the liquor cabinet before she came upstairs, and right now she was sitting in a chair, tipped back with her feet propped on the windowsill. Her legs were slightly spread holding the bottle of scotch between them, one hand cupped over the top of the bottle. She was staring out over the front yard, sipping right from the bottle, and brooding. Like the moonlight that was coming in that garage window, reflecting off Alice's ring, that same moonlight was coming in her bedroom window, casting back an image of her legs and snow-white lace panties. The ones she had chosen just for this ruined occasion. She had made the decision: her mother was going to go into a nursing home. Alice was fired! No longer needed! She could take her little, happy, twirling bottom and go back where she had come from. Linda drank again as she tried to get that image out of her mind, wiping her mouth with the back of her hand, and shoving the bottle back between her cooling thighs. As for Adam, he would have a job yet, but only back on the ranch, and then only after he got his name cleared. He was going to turn himself in or she was going to turn him in. His choice. Linda took another pull on the bottle, and then opening the window to the cold winter air, hurled it out, where it broke against a stone lamb that was in the center of the flowerbed. She turned and crawled into bed.

It was evident from the start on Christmas morning that things were unsettled, to say the least. Alice had come over early with Adam, and the two of them had Anna up and dressed when Linda came down from upstairs. Anna was sitting by the tree smiling, one of her favorite shawls wrapped around her shoulders. From the kitchen came the aroma of bacon cooking, along with the sounds of giggling, and horseplay.

Enjoy yourselves while you can, Linda thought. She cleared her throat to announce her presence as she walked into the room. Linda had put on blue jeans and a white sweatshirt and looked more like she was getting ready to clean the barn, than celebrate Christmas.

"Linda, look!" Alice was holding her left hand out in front of her, as if she wanted Linda to kiss the ring. Adam turned at the sink with a smile on his face to watch her reaction.

For Linda, it was like a dagger in the chest and she quickly sat down before she fell down. Her face was frozen with a look somewhere between astonishment and terror. She had planned to wait till just before she left for home to announce her plans for her mother and Adam, but right now, she wanted to just lash out and freeze this celebration in its tracks. She had come here to have a happy reunion with the man she wanted to take home as her Prince Charming. He would have made her young again. They would have been so good, so happy together. He had saved her life, and now she wanted to change the course of his life, and make him successful. Make him hers.

Linda, in a moment that would have qualified her for an Oscar, looked up and smiled. "It's beautiful. Congratulations. You'll have to excuse me, I left my watch upstairs." She swept out of the room and up the stairs, and fell face down on the un-made bed, burying her face in a pillow. Tears were coming in torrents, and a huge sob that had been stuck in her throat erupted, and she stifled it in the pillow. The toughness she had shown was collapsing, and she didn't know how to get it back. She sat on the bed, still holding the pillow to her chest, rocking back and forth. But then she stopped, holding all of her emotions in check. Had she wanted too much? Had she misinterpreted Adam's friendliness for love? Was he using her? So many questions to answer.

Linda fixed her face with fresh makeup and went back downstairs. She sat down on the couch across from her mother, and took the older woman's limp hand in hers. "Mom," she said calmly, "I need to talk to you about something."

CHAPTER SIXTEEN

Adam knew something was up, but he never expected it to be what Linda was saying right now. "It's time to put my mother in a home where she can get the care she needs." They were both sitting at the kitchen table. Alice had gone home to spend the day with her parents. They opened their gifts early this morning, but instead of a happy occasion, it had been overshadowed by Anna's health, and Linda's coldness. Christmas seemed like something she just wanted to get out of the way.

Alice and Adam went together, and purchased a painting of a ranch in the 1800's done by a famous artist, for Linda. It had been very expensive for them, and she acted less than appreciative when she opened it.

Alice received her gifts from Adam the night before, along with the ring, and Adam had received his gift from Alice, - in winning her. For the moment last night they had seemed inseparable, sitting together and holding hands.

Anna interrupted it all with breathing difficulties, so they had to rush her back to bed, and the oxygen equipment.

Now Linda sat across from Adam at the table, her legs crossed and her arms folded over her chest. "You knew when you came here that this was just something temporary, Adam. I too, thought that it would be longer than this, and mother's health going downhill so fast, was unexpected, but the fact remains that it is done and over. I've come to grips with it, and we need to move on."

Adam took another sip of his coffee and looking up at her, said nothing.

"I can no longer take responsibility for your safe keeping from the law, Adam. You need to make a decision, and you need to make it now, to go back and turn yourself in. Tony stands ready to be your counsel, and I stand by my offer to pay for his services, but only if you come back to the ranch with me."

Adam cleared his throat, and then said. "Linda, why are you so interested in helping me? Sure, I helped you out, and we're both grateful things turned out for the best, but you've more than repaid me with money and friendship. I agree that I need to go back to Minnesota and straighten things out, and I *have* spent a lot of time thinking about that. Something else has happened in my life right now, that has changed everything. I have you to thank for that, too. Alice has given me a new look at life. She means a lot to me, and I need to make some decisions to clear things up, without hurting her." Adam stood and walked over to the kitchen window, with his back to Linda. "Linda, Alice doesn't know about my past, and I intend to tell her tonight. I've been invited over to meet her parents this evening for supper. I'll talk to her before that happens."

Adam turned slowly to face Linda. Her face was frozen, her demeanor, stoic. She uncrossed her legs, but did not get up. Pointing her right forefinger at Adam, she almost spit the words out: "If you think, for one minute, that I am going to finance your defense so you can come back here to live with *her*, you're very wrong." Her lips were trembling and it was obvious she had reached her breaking point, and had nowhere to go. Her eyes were filling with tears, and she wiped them with the back of her hand.

"Adam, I love you! And I've told you that. I don't love you like an Aunt Martha kind of love, Adam. I love you like a woman loves a man and I want you to come back with me and live with me. I know I am forty some years old, and you're in your twenties." The tears were running down her cheeks now. "I came over to tell you this last night, but you were busy, being sexually assaulted by her. No. I 'm sorry I said that. You and Alice were busy," she said sarcastically.

Adam remembered the noise of a door slamming last night, and now he knew what that was all about. He walked over to the back door, and was standing with his hand on the knob. "Linda, I'm sorry for the confused feelings. I'm sorry if you've been hurt. It would be the last thing I wanted to have happen to you. But it would never work out, not the way you want it to. I don't love you in that way. There may have been things I said, and did, that made you think otherwise. I've been on an emotional roller coaster for way too long. It's time to stop that ride." Adam opened the door, but before he went out, he said, "Thank you for everything. I'll pack my stuff and be gone by the end of the day." He closed the door silently behind him.

Alice was surprised when she answered the door, and Adam was standing there. She had just left him a few hours ago, with a supper invitation, and hadn't expected to see him until then. "Adam, is anything wrong?"

"I need to talk with you," he said. "Something has changed."

"Mom and Dad would like to meet you."

"Why don't you grab your coat and I'll come in when we get back. I need to clear this up first." Adam was clearly nervous and upset.

It was a nice warm winter day, so they decided to walk to a park a few blocks away. They locked arms and walked slowly, Alice listening with a look of concern, while Adam told her about Linda's plans to put Anna in a nursing home.

"I guess we all knew that was coming," she said. "You could get lots of jobs Adam, with your skills. Maybe it is time to move on."

He was at a loss as how to explain the rest. They kept moving, without speaking for a few more minutes and started down a walking path into a park. Being Christmas day, the park was empty, except for a few youngsters gliding down a hill on their new snowboards. The black and white landscape was spotted with their colorful snowsuits, and their shrill voices echoed everywhere. Adam thought how nice it would be, to be that age again, with no worries.

A small pond in the center of the park was open in the middle, and some geese were noisily chasing each other around in the water. They walked over to a small shelter building, and Adam swept the snow off a bench so they could sit down. "Alice, I love you, and for that reason I need to talk about something right now. But before I do that, I need you to hear a little bit of my past.

He was quiet for a second. He really didn't know how he was going to explain or how to begin. Adam ran his hand through his wavy hair and looked down at Alice, who was giving him her undivided attention. She looked so cute, with her auburn hair spilling out of her white stocking cap. Her dark brown eyes were wide with concern. What could be so important, to drag her way out here, on Christmas day?

"Alice," he began, stopping to take her hands in his, "less than a year ago I was engaged to another woman. A woman named Mandy. She was my life then, Alice, as you have become now. We were so happy together, and everything had been planned for our marriage."

Alice was getting nervous. *Was he getting cold feet and going back to another woman? She knew last night was too good to be true. He had tricked her.* She tried to take her hands from his, but Adam held tight.

"No. No, Alice, hear me out."

She relaxed, but now her concern was giving way to tears.

"Don't cry, sweetheart," Adam said. "Listen to me please. A few days before we were supposed to get married, Mandy was murdered."

Alice was shocked, and she gave a soft little cry, but Adam went on.

"It's a long story, but the man who did it was let loose because of a technicality in the law. This psychopath was freed, to prey on women again. The law was more interested in this killer's rights, than they were in Mandy's rights, or in justice." Adam stopped to wipe his eyes. It hurt to even talk about it. "I did something that was not me, Alice. I took the law into my own hands and killed that man. I was out of my mind with grief, sweetheart."

"They didn't arrest you?"

"I ran. I fled the state and I've been on the run ever since. I know now that I need to go back and clear this up. But now you've come into my life. I don't want you to get caught up with my baggage, and that's why we're here right now. I'm so sorry for letting this happen. But you, and your love...and my love for you... just snuck up on me. A couple of months ago I realized for the first time that Mandy was gone, and that I had to let go of her, and let go of all the hate that I was harboring. But I was confused, and didn't know how to deal with it."

"How did you get involved with Linda?"

"Well, while I was on the run, I ended up on her ranch looking for a job, and she hired me."

"Does she know about your past?"

"She does now, and that's another problem. She wants me to go back and turn myself in, and I am ok with that. But she wants to pay for an attorney to represent me, and in exchange, she wants me to come and live with her, and I won't do that. I owe her a lot, but that would be a huge mistake."

Alice was overwhelmed with everything Adam told her, but remained calm. She stood, and turning to face him with a look of sadness, asked, "Do you want your ring back, Adam?"

"No! Please, no. I just want you to know what you're getting into."

"Let's walk," she said. They walked down along the footpath that went around the pond. Alice put her hands in her pockets and seemed deep in thought. Adam sensed she had a decision to make, so he too was quiet.

They were almost to the exit of the park when she stopped and faced him. "Adam, you do love me? I'm not just somebody you caught on the rebound? Please be honest with me."

"Alice, I love you with all of my heart. I know we haven't known each other very long yet, but I do know this is real. And all the time in the world isn't going to change my feelings for you. I just don't want to lose you, but I have to tell it like it is, and let you make your own decision."

They started walking again, but this time she took his hand in hers.

Alice stopped again, next to a huge oak tree and stood with her back to the tree, on top of a clump of snow, that made them both about the same height. "Adam, let's both go back and fight this thing together. But my rules would be the same as Linda's. I want to marry you when this is all over."

He reached for her, and wrapping his arms around her twirled around in circles until they both fell into a large snow bank. They sat on the snow, kissing and hugging, while all of the kids on the slope stopped sliding and whooped and hollered. Adam, laughing, gave the kids a thumbs-up, and then pulled Alice to her feet and started brushing her off.

"Keep your hands off my butt, buddy," she said, laughing.

When he got back to the house, he kissed Alice on the nose. "I better get my stuff out of her garage and then I'll be over. I also need to say goodbye to Anna."

Adam didn't know how Linda had reacted to his departure. Had she called the police? Her car was still parked out front. At first he thought about walking up to the house and trying to explain, but then he thought maybe he should pack up first. He didn't have that much stuff and it wouldn't take long. He did accumulate a few things in the weeks he had been there, but it still all fit in the backpack that he came with. He stood by the back door, taking one more look around, the door slightly open, when he heard a car in the driveway below, and turned to look out the window. It was an ambulance. There were two men inside, dressed in white, with matching brown coats, and they went to the back door and knocked.

"We are here for the transfer to Golden Gates," one of the men said. Linda was standing far enough back in the kitchen that Adam could not see her. He only heard her say, "Thanks for coming so quickly."

He wanted to run down and hug Anna one last time, but the thought of confronting Linda again, held him back. He looked across the room once more, and then saw the boots at the foot of the bed. Adam walked over and picked them up, sitting on the end of the bed briefly. These were the boots Linda had bought him when he first came to the ranch. He turned them over in his hands, and then set them back down. He wouldn't need them where he was going. He heard a car door slam and an engine start. Going back to the door and looking out, he saw Linda pulling away from the house; the big white Cadillac sending out a steam of white exhaust. He could see her head through the back window, as she pulled away. She didn't look back.

CHAPTER SEVENTEEN

Alice's parents, Clayton and Eva Kennedy, greeted Adam with warmth and friendliness. They had long ago trusted their daughter to make good decisions and they were not going to question her choice now.

She spent the afternoon explaining what had happened to Adam back in Minnesota, and how she, for one, wanted to do all she could to see that he was exonerated of all the charges filed against him.

Alice's father, who had been a police officer all of his life, had long been an advocate for tougher penalties for sex offenders. He made a note to call the sheriff in Minnesota and throw his support behind Adam as soon as he turned himself in. That is, after he checked out Adam's story. For now, he believed Alice's story, but he was still a cop, and needed proof before he would make his final decision.

That evening Alice's mother made a feast fit for a king, and they ate their fill of ham, scalloped potatoes, and homemade dinner rolls, followed by mincemeat pie, hot out of the oven. The two men retired to the living room while Alice helped her mother with cleaning up.

"I know it must be hard for you to talk about this," Clayton said, "but what if you don't get set free and have to go to prison? What would Alice do then?"

"I think that decision has to be made by her, sir, and I promise you I will do nothing to influence it. I don't deserve to have her, and I realize that. But if things do work out, I will reward her for what she has done for me by being the best husband a woman could ever have."

"How soon are you going back to turn yourself in?" he asked.

"We want to leave tonight. This seems funny to say to you, sir, you being an officer of the law, but Mrs. Pendleton seems to have an axe to grind with me. I think she may turn me in, if she hasn't already." Adam went on to explain everything that had transpired between him and Linda. Clayton Kennedy could only shake his head and smile after hearing the whole story.

"It seems, that if you didn't have bad luck, you wouldn't have any luck, son."

"Well, not true," Adam said. "I did meet your daughter."

Clayton made a phone call to police headquarters, and as discreetly as he could, found that there were no bulletins out yet for the arrest of Adam. Alice and Adam packed her car with clothing and food, and shortly after eight that night they drove away, heading toward the midwest.

Alice would arrange for a leave of absence from school. She had her degree but was taking some advanced classes that she could continue once they were back in Minnesota. They had the name of an attorney in Minneapolis who had agreed to meet with them at the Public Defender's Office when they arrived. This man was a friend of Alice's father, and was a well-known public defender in the Twin Cities. He could not be Adam's attorney, but he would see that he was taken care of. It was about all anybody could do for Adam right now.

It was dark when they drove by the ranch on the freeway, but Adam could make out lights from the house. *Was she looking out the window?* The thought went through his mind, along with a lot of other memories from the ranch. Adam felt sorry for Linda. She had done a lot for him and right now, turning himself in, was something her motivation had brought about, and got the ball rolling. When this was all over, he would try to make amends if he could.

They didn't stop in the city of Missoula, but kept heading east. Adam was sleeping while Alice was driving. When he woke up they were half way across Montana.

They switched places, and Adam drove while Alice slept during the day. She had reclined the seat, wrapped herself in a blanket, and curled up on the seat, facing him. Adam reached over and with his fingertips, gently touched her sleeping face. She smiled in her sleep. Something still wanted him to just turn the car around, and head south. There was so much uncertainty ahead, and he had so much to lose if things went wrong. But he could no longer live with being a fugitive either, and he felt if he could just get someone to listen to him, he might have a chance.

They made stops for gasoline and snacks, but otherwise kept driving until they reached the North Dakota-Montana border. This would be their one stop.

They found a small motel behind a truck stop, in the middle of nowhere, and decided to stop here for the night. The motel was a collection of quaint cabins, set into a hillside, in an area where the Badlands began. There was a sign advertising the Badlands and another sign that said, "Welcome to North Dakota." On the right, and off in the distance, stood a lonely, rusty oil well pump, slowly dipping itself into the ground to extract the precious crude. A few other wells were scattered around, but none of them appeared to be pumping at the time.

They drove past a little flower garden frozen in time, next to the driveway, as they turned in. There was very little snow around, unlike parts of Montana that they had driven through. The landscape in front of the motel was pretty much like the surrounding countryside, patches of sagebrush and prairie grass. A sign in the middle of the flower garden flashed, VACANCY, and advertised 'clean cabins with hot water.' There were no other cars parked outside any of the cabins. An old pickup was parked by a building with a sign indicating that it was the office. The driver's door of the truck had the words 'Elmer's Cabin's' painted on it, but it was hard to read, because the door had a huge dent in it. An old yellow Lab with more gray than yellow on his face, thumped his tail on the board steps in front of the office door, but didn't get up, preferring to stay curled up in the cold. The storm door slammed behind Adam as he sauntered up to the desk, where an old white haired man, with over-sized dentures, stood up and folded his hands on the counter top. He wore a patched denim shirt and a pair of green cords, held up with yellow suspenders that mimicked tape measures. A pocket protector in his shirt pocket was filled to overflowing with pens and pencils. "You look tired, Son," was all the old man said.

"I am, and so is my wife," Adam said, as he watched the old man's eyes checking his fingers for rings, but maybe it was just his imagination. Everything and everybody seemed suspicious to him.

"I can put you in Cabin Three," the old man said, looking at the full keyboard behind him, while pushing a form in front of Adam to fill out, along with a pen with a plastic fork taped to it.

Adam resisted the urge to say, "Shit, we had our hopes set on getting cabin five." It did bring a small smile to his face.

Adam filled in the information, but before he was done, the door slammed again and Alice appeared alongside him. She took his arm and clung to it, but said nothing. Adam pushed the form back to the man, along with a fifty-dollar bill from his pocket. The old man reached behind him and took a key down from the board that held them. They all had their own number painted over their respected hook, but each one came with a different key chain decoration. He also fished a twenty-dollar bill out of his worn billfold, overflowing with papers, and gave it to Adam.

"Check-out time is noon," the old man said. He pushed his dentures forward with his tongue and then clicking them back in place, said, "Have a good night."

"Thanks," was the only comment Adam made.

Alice took the key and walked right over to the cabin, which was situated about fifty feet from the office, while Adam moved the car so it would be parked in front of it. By the time he had parked, and grabbed a suitcase from the back seat, she was inside.

It took a moment for his eyes to adjust to the near darkness as he stepped into the room, throwing the suitcase on the bed. A toilet flushed, and Alice came out of the bathroom taking off her blouse. "I need a shower so bad," she said. "First things, first." In her bra and panties she went back into the bathroom, but closed the door only part way. Adam sat on the bed pulling off his shoes. It was warm in the cabin when they came in, a small gas space heater on the wall next to the door whirled noisily, and the heat felt good. They had some sandwiches they could eat, and several cans of pop, and Adam set them on a small nightstand, next to the bed. That stand, the bed, and one chair, was the extent of the furniture. There was no television, and no dresser. A picture on the wall over the bed, showed a large peacock with his tail flared, standing in a patch of green grass. The picture had a three-corner tear in one corner that must have been the aftermath of something being thrown at it. An attempt had been made to tape it, but the tape hadn't held, and was now sticking out in several directions.

From his perch on the bed, and through the half closed door, Adam could see into the mirror over the bathroom sink. Right now, the mirror was reflecting back a steamy image of the tub with a partially drawn shower curtain. He could see Alice's backside as she faced the shower spigot, the water running from her head down her back. Her smooth back shone in the fluorescent light with the wetness from the water, and soap foam was running down her back and legs. Then she slowly turned and he was looking at her front. They had been naked before in front of each other, but this was the most sensuous he had ever seen her. Maybe it was so sexy because she was washing, and he was being a voyeur. She looked so innocent, he was almost embarrassed he was watching her, but then she looked up, smiled seductively, and waved at him in the mirror. Then he realized what was happening.

At first, he let her wash him, while he explored her body with his hands, his tongue and his eyes. She was becoming aroused, Adam could tell by the flush on her face and on her fair skinned chest, but her symptoms were no match for his, and it embarrassed him that his excitement had to be so obvious. She laughed and tucked it between her thighs, which only made matters worse. Their mouths slid together in the spray of warm water. Her breasts were firm and slippery and they pressed against his chest, his kisses led down her chin and then to the curve of her neck and were lowering to her breast when she cradled his chin with one hand, to stop his descent, while she shut off the water with the other. Alice pulled his head back up until their mouths met once more, and she said only one word: "Bed."

Adam was sitting on the car hood in the cold, his coat collar pulled up around his neck. It was so much colder here in North Dakota, than Idaho, but he needed to smoke and to think, outside, away from Alice, who was still sleeping when he slipped out of bed. Brilliant slivers of sunlight were emerging cautiously over the eastern horizon, absorbing the last vestiges of night's darkness. They seemed in no hurry to bring the new day.

He had thought about Linda last night, as he lay exhausted in the dark, and knew that he should try to write her and explain things better, if he could. Maybe he would write today while Alice drove.

They made love last night several times. They both sensed the separation that would be forthcoming, although they hadn't talked about it yet. At first they had been insatiable, behaving like there would be no tomorrow. But then as fatigue set slowly upon them, they tempered their wildness with tenderness, and then blissfully exhausted, they slept in each other's arms.

For Adam, his night of frolicking with Alice had only made things worse for him and played games with his mind. He thought about Mandy again. Mandy had set the bar so high. So damned high.

He flicked his cigarette butt onto the frozen gravel and shook out another from the pack in his pocket, his shallow breath escaping in small white vapor clouds, into the cold morning air. He leaned back on the car hood once more, his head on the windshield, and stared at the skies overhead. Tiny, cumulous clouds were now popping over the darkened western horizon, as if they'd been puffed from an armada of magic canons filled with cotton, sitting just behind those low hills. The clouds drifted rapidly east, and for each one that made the journey and disappeared, two more took its place. They seemed to be getting larger, and the blue patches of sky were slowly being filled. Was it the beginning of a storm?

Was it fair to Alice? His love for Mandy had bordered on an obsession. No, not bordered, he was obsessed with her. Could he ever love like that again? Alice was leaving her family, her schooling, and her friends, to follow him ... a murderer wanted by the law, back to Minnesota to an uncertain future. There was something wrong with that, and he needed to think this out. Enough people had been hurt already, and for a second, he thought of Linda again. He had to write that letter before they got to their destination. It would be so easy right now to leave Alice the rest of their money, and drive away from here. She could take a bus back to Idaho, and he could go to Canada. Hell, the border was only two hundred miles away. She would be hurt, yes, but she would get over it. But would he? He did love her, the more he thought about it, but it was so different from his love for Mandy. Then, we are all different, and so is every day and every place. We sort through life's experiences as we go along, and we keep what is good, and discard what we don't like, and maybe what we keep will be someone else's discard, maybe he was Mandy's discard. There was good in everything, - if that was what you needed, and wanted. He was so confused. Just so damned confused. He looked back at the cabin's lone window and saw the curtains part. She was watching him, wrapped in a blanket clutched to her chest. She pointed her forefinger at him, and then, curling it back, motioned for him to come back inside.

Linda's anger had subsided a little, and that, plus the business of running the ranch again, kept her mellower than she had been when she arrived home. The cattle had all been brought down to the lower range where they could be fed during the winter, and all of those due to be shipped, had been trucked away. Ramon had gone home to Mexico for a few weeks, and although there was plenty of help on hand, without his direction they pretty much did nothing. So it was up to her to fill the spot of foreman. At the present time, she was riding her four-wheeler around the fenced in property, making sure everything was all right with the cattle and the fence. There was a lot of grazing grass still exposed, so the cattle seemed to be doing fine without too much supplemental feed. She drove between the snowdrifts, trying to choose a safe path as she went. Normally she wouldn't have ridden alone, but Ramon was the only one she was really comfortable riding with, and he was still in Mexico. Adam would have been so good at this. She shook her head to clear the thought, just as she topped a small rise, and the snow collapsed under her machine. She rode onto some hard pack that she had taken as ground, with a slight snow cover. Actually, it was snow about six feet deep. The machine slid down into the snow under it, pinning her leg under the machine. The engine killed. Linda tried to lift the machine, which was too heavy, but by scraping away the snow under her leg, she was able to free herself, and crawl out of the hole. One look told her she was not going to get that machine free without some help.

Linda was mad. She should have taken a horse. Dan would have always used a horse in situations like this. But damn it, Dan was dead, and she was five miles from home, and cold. She kicked at the snowdrift in frustration, and then started walking back the way she had come. She was dressed warmly, but still the cold winter air burned at her cheeks and lips. Ever since the accident she could not tolerate the cold on her skin. Linda tried to walk backwards to keep the wind out of her face, but then she couldn't see where she was going and fell down several times, the last time cracking her elbow on the frozen ground. She sat on the ground holding her stinging elbow, her eyes welling with tears. This was a tough way for a woman to live. How was she going to continue to do this when she got a little older? Adam would have been the real answer, but now that was a dead issue, wasn't it? Or was it? Maybe there was a way to get Adam back here yet, if she played her cards right. He was stuck on Alice right now, and there was no changing that. But first he had a murder rap to beat, and if she could help him with that, the way she had intended to in the first place, well, who knows what could happen. She wasn't going to burn her bridges with Adam.

Linda wiped her tears and nose on the back of her mitten as she started walking once more, toward home. She felt a little better now. Even the wind didn't feel so cold.

Alice drove, while Adam wrote, holding a small suitcase on his lap to write on.

"Writing your memoirs?" she asked.

"No. I'm writing to Linda. I'm not comfortable with the way we left things in Idaho. She tried to help me a lot, Alice, and I'll always be grateful for that. She wanted more from me than I could give. Especially after you came into the picture." Adam reached over and squeezed her arm.

"This is just a *thank you* letter, and a *I love Alice letter*. I think she knows that, but I want to make sure."

Alice took her eyes off the road for a moment. "I think you still have the hots for the old gal," she said, and then she broke out laughing.

Adam winked at her and then laughed with her.

When he first started writing the letter, it was hard for him to say what he meant, but the more he thought about it, the more the words flowed. When he finished, he laid his head back against the headrest, to think if there was anything he had forgotten.

The car thumped across the frozen expansion strips in the freeway and he could feel each one coming through the headrest into the back of his head. He scanned the skies for the inclement weather he thought was coming, but it seemed to have blown south. Adam closed his eyes to ponder some more. The rhythm of the bumps, and the night of lovemaking, had left him so worn-out he soon fell asleep. His hands were resting on the letter.

"Adam, do you think we should stop for gas, pretty soon?"

There was no answer from Adam, just a soft snore.

Alice reached over and pulled the letter from under his hands. She tried to look at the letter as she drove, and read it at the same time.

Dear Linda,

I wanted to write you because I felt bad about the way we left each other back in Idaho. I am writing this as we travel back to Minnesota, expecting to turn myself in and put an end to this mess, one way or another. This is scary for me, yet at the same time there is a great sense of relief, because I'm tired of running. I will always be indebted to you, Linda, for taking me in and providing me with work, food, and shelter, also for being my friend and my confidante. More than that, however, is the bond that will always exist between us that was forged on the mountainside, on that cold miserable night. We both bear the scars from that, physically and emotionally.

Alice looked up from the letter, first at the road and then over at Adam. He had turned away from her a bit, and was now sleeping with his head facing the passenger window. What had happened on that mountainside? Adam had never talked about it with her. He had talked about being caught in a blizzard when she asked about his frostbite scars, but he never mentioned Linda being with him. Her eyes went back to the letter.

I now need to try and salvage what is left of my life. There was a time when I didn't care if I lived or died after Mandy was killed, but time has helped heal that, and of course, meeting Alice has also helped in that process. I firmly believed once that no one could take Mandy's place in my life, but now I know that isn't true. I do feel bad about Alice having to change her life around to help me get through this, and I still wonder if she knows what she is getting into. I wonder if I know what she is getting into, or what I am getting myself into, for that matter. I question if I'm doing the right thing, bringing this much conflict into her life.

Once again she looked over at Adam. She was getting emotional, and a tear ran down her cheek and hit the bottom of the letter as she clutched it to her bosom. Why would he doubt her resolve about what they were doing? Didn't he know? Hadn't she explained well enough about how she felt? She wanted to wake him up right this minute, shake the letter in his face, and yell: "Explain what you mean by this, Adam!" She bit her lip to keep from crying out loud, but a small sob escaped her throat, surprising her. There was more of the letter, but she was not sure she wanted to read it, so she drove on, just staring at the road ahead, and thinking. Then at last she brought the letter back up and read on.

I sometimes question what kind of a man I am, for doing what I did that day back in Minnesota, but there is a point in a man's life when you can't play 'Life's Game' anymore by the rules. The rules that were made to bring justice to situations like this have been exploited and misrepresented by lawyers and judges. We all have a breaking point and - right or wrong – I had reached mine. I will never regret what I did… only the consequences. I hope, Linda that someday our paths will cross again under better circumstances. I pray that what I am doing is the right thing, for both Alice and me.

Your friend, Adam

Alice wiped away her tears and suddenly realized the car was barely moving. It was a good thing they weren't being followed by a Highway Patrolman. They would have thought she was drunk. She brought the speed back up to sixty-five, and then noticed the gas gauge was almost empty. Good thing Jamestown was just ahead. It was a good time to stop; she needed to use the bathroom.

CHAPTER EIGHTEEN

Adam woke up, somewhat surprised that they were stopped, until he saw the gas pumps and the station beyond. Alice was nowhere in sight but the nozzle was running in the side of the car. Right beside them was an old pickup truck, with a small calf tied in the back, also refueling. A young man with his coat collar pulled up was stamping his feet to keep warm as he watched the pump. A black, Collie type dog watched him through the back window, with a look of concern on his face. They were in a good-sized town, judging by the buildings, and Adam guessed it must be Jamestown. He had looked at the map before they left this morning, and judging from the time, this must be it. There weren't a lot of towns out here in the North Dakota prairie. His letter was laying on the dash of the car, the defrosters blowing it up and down slightly. Funny, he didn't remember putting it there, but then he fell asleep and maybe Alice did. He picked it up and folded it in three folds. Maybe they would have an envelope and a stamp he could buy, inside. His fingers felt something damp and he noticed the paper had a wet spot on it. Condensation from the windshield, he reasoned.

Alice was at the back of the store waiting for the microwave to heat a couple of breakfast sandwiches. He walked up and pinched her behind and she jumped, but smiled when she saw it was him.

"Get us some coffee, you pervert," she said with a grin.

He paid for the food and gas, and then asked the young man behind the till if he could buy an envelope and a stamp.

"Sure thing, mister. In fact we can sell you an envelope with a stamp and you can mail it right here. We're also the local post office." He smiled, put on a post office uniform hat, and posed again.

Adam took the wheel and they got back on the freeway headed east again. Alice seemed quiet and subdued, and after eating her sandwich curled up to nap, with her head leaning toward the door, not next to Adam.

At first he chalked it up to the stress they were both under on this trip. There were so many unknowns. He could be in jail for the rest of his life, or he could be set free. What were the charges going to be against him, for fleeing this crime, or for the crime itself? He had not thought about that before. His best chance for a defense had probably been with the help of Linda's lawyer, but that had too many strings attached. Most likely his punishment was going to be somewhere between two extremes: life in prison, or getting off, - but there was just no way of knowing. He just wanted it over. Adam shook a cigarette from a fresh pack, lit it, and blew the smoke over his head away from Alice. Reaching back, he massaged his neck. His muscles ached from the tension, and it was giving him a headache.

The hilly, grazing land and beef cattle herds of western North Dakota had given way to the plains and grain farms of the center of the state. Snow was more abundant here and the ditches and gullies had drifted over. The wind had blown it away from the hilltops, but snow had collected in the frozen furrows of plowed fields. He remembered little about coming through here when he was fleeing the police.

The storm that had been chasing them all day was catching up to them, and the sky was now an ominous gray. Almost as soon as Adam noticed the darkening skies, they responded by opening up, and big white wet flakes started to splatter the windshield. The wipers pushed them to the side where they collected into rivulets of frozen slush, cutting down his field of vision. The roadway was becoming covered except for the wheel ruts from the traffic, and the left lane was becoming treacherous to use. Eighteen wheel trucks carrying their heavy loads roared by in the left lane, threatening to blow them off the road under an avalanche of wet slush.

Adam reached across the seat, taking hold of Alice's shoulder, and pulled her upright, over and against him. She laid her head on his shoulder and he softly kissed the top of it. His lips lingered there, inhaling the freshness of her shampoo. She looked up at him and smiled a weak smile. "I do love you, sweetheart," Adam said. "I want you to always know that, no matter what happens to us."

Alice didn't answer him, but she snuggled closer under his arm and smiled.

Lyle Jackson had been an attorney for over forty years and was now in the twilight of his career. He was once part of the prestigious law firm of "Cain and Williamson," but now he just worked for the public defender's office in Minneapolis. His long time friend, Clayton Kennedy, had called him about helping a friend of his daughter's, a couple of days ago, and he promised to do what he could.

Lyle and Clay had been buddies in Viet Nam. They had shared the same foxhole the night their platoon was almost annihilated. Clay once carried Lyle to safety on his back when Lyle could walk no farther because of his wounds. When the war ended, they went their separate ways, but they kept in touch, vacationing together in Las Vegas, and a cruise to Hawaii. Alice had been a bubbly young teenager the last time they had gone, and Lyle and his wife were like an aunt and uncle to her. He smiled as he thought about her. "I'm going to lunch," he said to his secretary, "but if you get a call from a woman named Alice, have her call me on my cell."

He had no idea when they would be here in Minneapolis, but he wanted to be available when they did arrive.

The sign said, "Welcome to Minnesota." Adam looked at his watch. It was a little after noon. He figured they had about four hours of driving ahead of them, and they would be there. It was time to stop for gas and lunch.

Alice sat up and looked around somewhat perplexed. She had been sleeping hard. "Where are we?" she asked.

"We just crossed the border. I thought we would stop for lunch and a bathroom break. When do you want to call that attorney? We'll probably make Minneapolis about five."

"I'll call, while you do your chores," she said. "I'm not hungry and I don't *have* to go potty, thank you." She was still sitting under his arm, so she slid over and reaching to the back seat, got her phone out of her bag.

Linda had no idea where Adam was right now. She knew he was going to turn himself in, but she had never heard where that would be, and the state of Minnesota was a big state. She didn't know when that would be, either. If she was going to help him, she was going to need some help herself.

The snowstorm that had passed through yesterday was tapering off, and the boys were outside right now plowing the yard. She wanted to help them, but the long walk home yesterday in the cold had taken it's toll on her, and today she had her face covered with Vaseline, where the cold wind had burned her skin. Linda had been exhausted by the time she made it home, but the ordeal only served to strengthen her resolve to find, and help Adam. She needed a man in her life, and she wanted this one. She was digging through her desk now, looking for the Kennedys' phone number. Alice had given it to her when she hired her to be her mother's nurse. Maybe they knew where Adam and Alice were going, but then again maybe they wouldn't share that with her. She was going to have to be convincing when she talked to them... if she talked to them. *That number has to be around here someplace. Aha!* She exclaimed

162

as she held up the piece of paper with Clayton Kennedy's phone number on it. *Now what to say?* She had better think awhile about this.

"Miss Kennedy, yes," The soft voice replied. "Mr. Jackson is out at a late lunch, but he did tell me to give you his cell number and that you should call him there right away, as he's expecting your call. Do you have something to write with?"

"Uh, just a moment." Alice dumped her bag partially out on the seat between her legs while Adam watched her, somewhat perplexed. Grabbing a pen, she said, "Go ahead please." She scribbled the number down on a scrap of paper. "Thank you, I'll call him there."

Alice smiled at Adam, her look giving off just a hint of frustration, but she started punching in the number she had written down.

Adam was thinking not about how many miles they had to go, but how many hours of freedom he might have left. Every police car and highway patrol car they passed, sent him into a near state of panic, as he assumed they were all sitting with his picture taped to the dash of their cruisers, while they looked for him. He reached in the back seat and grabbed an old cap and put it on, and Alice looked at him out of the corner of her eye, making a quizzical face but saying nothing. The phone was ringing.

"Hello, this is Lyle Jackson."

She identified herself, and before she could say anything else, he started talking.

"Alice! How are you, sweetheart?" His voice was so loud and crisp, that Adam could hear him three feet away.

"I'm fine, Mr. Jackson." There was a slight pause because she didn't know what to say next, even though she had rehearsed it just a few minutes ago. Finally, just as Lyle Jackson started to break the silence, she blurted out. "We're about three hours away from Minneapolis and need directions to where we can meet you." She felt stupid. She could have talked a little more about her folks, or anything, before saying that. But done was done, and she waited a second while he was talking to someone else. Just saying goodbye to someone.

"Alice, yes, I'm sorry. I had to say something to a friend for a moment, but I did hear you. Look, why don't you two come to my home when you get into Minneapolis? I live close to downtown in the Kenwood area. Can you write this down?"

"Yes, I've got a pen right here."

"Okay, the address is 420 Wilson Terrace. It's a brownstone house on the corner with a wrought-iron fence around the yard. Just come into the cities on Interstate 94. Are you on 94 now?"

Adam nodded his head yes when she looked over at him, even before she could ask him. He could actually hear every word they were saying, as Alice had the volume on the phone turned up.

"Well, stay right on 94 all the way to downtown, and then get off on exit 54-B and take the first right. I am looking forward to seeing you both, Alice."

"We're looking forward to seeing you too, Mr. Jackson."

"Lyle, Alice. Just call me Lyle, please. Don't stop to eat, I'll have supper ready for you."

Lyle Jackson was the "Ironsides" of Twin Cities lawyers. Had he been confined to a wheelchair he would have fit the part to a T, but he wasn't. Tall and broad, he was as big in stature as he was in the legal system. He was a feared competitor who always gave his best in every case. The only problem now was, he was bound by contract to the public defender's office in Minneapolis, and was not allowed to take on any outside cases. He knew this when Alice's father called him, but still, he had a plan for Adam, and until he could put that plan in place, he would help him all he could. He walked out of the downtown restaurant and hailed a cab for home. He had some phone calls to make, but he could do them from there.

The sparsely populated prairie land of North Dakota disappeared as if a curtain had been dropped behind them, and the fertile earth of the Red River Valley, now frozen in winter's grip, panned by their windows as they continued eastward toward Minneapolis. Farms dotted the landscape; smoke curling from the chimneys of white clapboard homes that were surrounded by red barns and outbuildings. Their doors were all closed against winter's wrath, protecting people, animals and machinery as they waited for spring. The snow that had been falling was diminishing, but was still coming. They were just traveling faster than the storm. The Weather Service reported that eight inches had already fallen in Jamestown.

For Adam, it was a relief to be back in Minnesota. If he was going to be arrested before he could surrender, this is where he wanted it to be.

Alice moved back to the middle of the seat and was sitting as close to him as was safe. She had a pen and was doodling on the back of a paper bag to pass the time. They both seemed to be talked out, and the mood was subdued, because of the uncertainty that lay ahead, more than anything else. Adam looked down at the instrument panel. They would have to stop for gasoline one more time and that would have to be soon. They had less than a quarter of a tank.

Adam was thinking about the home he had left just a few months ago. It would be nice to see his family again. *They did allow that in prison, didn't they?* His parents were deceased, but he had a brother, two sisters, and friends he longed to see. Then there were Mandy's parents. He had been close with them; right up until the day he had pulled the trigger from that rooftop sniper post. He could still see Mark Stevenson's head exploding as he stood next to his lawyer. He had never heard the shot, zoned out the way he was. It was not the way he would have wanted to do it, given his choice. He would have preferred torturing and killing him slowly; the same way that monster had killed Mandy. But you take what you can get. Adam remembered standing, to watch the body slither down the steps, and then seeing the deputies outside of the courthouse pointing at him as they drew their guns and rushed across the street. Stevenson's lawyer was screaming, while kneeling over his dead client, until a stream of vomit came out of his throat and quieted him.

From there, things happened in so much of a hurry that they all blurred together, until he walked onto the ranch in Montana. His thoughts went back to Mandy's parents, and to Alice, and how awkward was that going to be.

Linda waited until almost nine p.m. to call Clayton Kennedy. She wanted to make sure he was home, if possible. She had spent the afternoon thinking about what she was going to say, and the best approach still seemed to be in telling the truth. She wanted to help Adam, and Tony Winters was the best lawyer money could buy. She didn't have a lot of money, but she was willing to use what she had to achieve the right results.

He had fallen asleep in his chair and phone rang three times before a sleepy male voice said, "Hel-," then Clayton cleared his throat and said, "Excuse me, hello?"

"Mr. Kennedy?"

"Yes, speaking." *Who the hell could be calling this time of the night*

"This is Linda Pendleton. Is this a bad time?"

"No, no, - what can I do for you?"

"Well, after Adam and Alice left the other day, I remembered that I still owed Alice some money and I need to get it to her. In fact I owe them both money, and I was wondering if you could get me an address so I could send it to them?"

She had caved. *What had happened to the truth, and where did this cock and bull story come from? Well, she was committed now.*

"Right now I don't have an address for them, Mrs. Pendleton, but I am expecting a call from them, so I guess I could relay your message and see where they want it sent."

She was silent for a moment. *This was just great. They were going to know something was up if he talked to them. They knew she owed them nothing more.*

"If you would, that would be great. Can I call you back tomorrow?" *What a mess she had made of this. Maybe it was better to just shut up right now, and re-group. After all, this guy was a cop and he would naturally be suspicious.*

"Thank you, Mr. Kennedy."

"Clayton," he countered. "Good night, Mrs. Pendleton."

Clayton Kennedy sat in his recliner nursing the last of his brandy, and thinking. Her story was a front for something else, he was sure of that. He had no intentions of letting her know where Alice was, but Adam? If Adam turned himself in, that would be no secret. Adam had said she was after him. She didn't know when to quit, did she?

Linda hung up the phone. She sat on the edge of the bed, thinking for a moment, and then the old temper came back. Linda picked the phone up and slammed it down on the nightstand. Then, just as quickly as she had lost her composure, she gained it back. Acting coy-like, she played with a strand of her hair and lay back on the pillows, smiling. What the hell was she getting all worked up about? Tony Winters would know where Adam was. He had access to the law, and Adam would have to contact the law if he was going to square things up.

When Lyle got home, his wife was still out, so he talked with Gloria, the cook and housekeeper, to let her know they would have guests for dinner. She was also told to prepare the guest room for overnight visitors. The radio had mentioned snow tonight that could be significant, so the trip to northern Minnesota to meet the authorities would have to wait until morning. He looked out the window at the street in front of his house. Christmas lights still twinkled on the lawn of his neighbor's mansion and the large circular drive was filled with cars. *Must be having a party, he thought.*

Alice and Adam had traversed through the farmland of central Minnesota and were now approaching the metropolitan area. The lights of the city could be seen ahead of them and the vast stretches of empty lands and fields were broken up with suburban homes and strip malls. Where there had been exits off the freeway every several miles, there now seemed to be one, right after another.

It had been a quiet afternoon, with both of them alone with their thoughts. Adam, from time to time, gave her a slight hug to let her know he was still close to her. Just preoccupied. The weather seemed to be catching up with them, as the sporadic snow flurries that had fallen all day now turned into a moderate snowfall. Already a few sanding and salting trucks could be seen driving the freeway, their blue strobe lights announcing that they were there.

It was the evening rush hour, but lucky for them, the traffic flow was going the other way. The images and lights of the tall buildings of downtown became clearer and clearer as they skirted the outside of the loop, until Alice said, "There's the exit."

Adam had been somewhat mesmerized by the lights and came out of his little trance long enough to say, "Thanks, I almost missed it."

They stood on the sidewalk in front of the big brownstone, looking up at it and holding hands. There was not a lot of front yard, so the house sat close to the street. Just a small circular driveway accented the portals in front of the house. The house was lit up in every room on the ground floor.

Large, white snowflakes stuck to Alice's long eyelashes and she brushed the back of her hand across, to clear them. It was Adam who spoke first. "Well, we better go in. Alice, no matter what happens from here on in, I want you to know, that without you, I would still be running back there in Idaho, somewhere. You have given me hope, sweetheart, and courage to face whatever comes." Adam reached down and kissed her nose. He ran his hand through her hair and looked deep into her tearing eyes. "I love you, Alice."

At first she did not answer him, but just bit her lip, and tears ran down her cheeks, mixing with the wetness from the snow. The red and yellow Christmas lights from across the street reflected off her wet cheeks.

"It will be worth it, Adam. It'll all be worth it. I'll wait for you, forever."

He didn't answer her, as they turned and walked up the steps and rang the doorbell.

It was Gloria who answered the door, but Lyle was right behind her, and before she could say anything, his big booming voice said, "Come in, come in." He hugged Alice and then held her at arm's length. "Let me look at you! My God, you're a beautiful young lady, but then you were a pretty girl before, so why wouldn't you be?" He grabbed Adam's hand and shook it vigorously. "Welcome to my home, Adam."

Gloria stood back while they exchanged greetings, and suddenly Lyle realized her uncomfortable position.

"Adam, Alice... this is our friend and trusted employee, Gloria." She smiled and said, hi, then left the room.

Lyle's wife Ellie came home a few minutes after Adam and Alice arrived. She seemed to be cordial but quiet, and said little as they ate supper and discussed tomorrow. She was a large, matronly looking lady with lots of blond hair and an overly made up complexion. She seemed preoccupied with her charity work, and talked about it to Lyle, who smiled and pretended he was interested.

The plan tomorrow was for Adam to turn himself in to the authorities in Aspen County, in the morning. Lyle had made all of the arrangements and they would have to get an early start. The weather might necessitate an even earlier start, as outside the snow was piling up. It was unusually warm right now, but the television warned that cold weather and wind was right on the heels of the storm

Lyle would represent Adam until he could find the right man to defend him. But by law, he could not be his attorney during the trial. He was bound to a contract where he now worked, that prohibited it. But it didn't stop him from helping Adam find the best help possible, and lay out the strategy for a defense.

Adam picked at his roast beef, and tore his dinner roll into little pieces, putting them into his mouth one by one and chewing slowly. He had to force himself to eat. From time to time, he would look across the table at Lyle, but said very little, just nodding his head in agreement most of the time as Lyle explained what would be happening. Alice sat beside him, her plate almost clean, except for some crumbs from a croissant she had eaten. She too, wasn't hungry. Gloria hovered over the group, ready to run and get whatever they needed, and Mrs. Jackson went on talking, mostly about herself. It was as if she didn't know Adam and Alice were even there.

They retired to the living room after eating, for coffee and more planning for the next day. Lyle sat with a yellow legal pad on his lap, in a Queen Anne chair next to an oversized Tiffany lamp that glittered like a pile of precious stones. Adam and Alice sat on an overly ornate couch and held hands as they seemed to be glued to his every word. This was going to be serious business, and the more they listened to Lyle, the more they realized what they were getting into. At last, Lyle seemed to be finished with his questions and planning. "I know you two must be tired after your trip, and I know you'd probably like some time to yourselves. Gloria has prepared a room for you upstairs, so if you like, I'll show you the way."

"That's really nice of you," Adam said.

Alice smiled, but didn't answer. She was gripping Adam's arm so tightly, she was nearly cutting off the circulation.

"Someone will get you up in the morning," Lyle gestured to the inside of the bedroom. "I hope this is okay with both of you."

The room was huge, and an oversized four-poster bed occupied center stage. There was an assortment of chairs and bureaus around the edges. A large window, flanked by white satin draperies and sheer curtains, looked out over a snow-coated street below. The suitcase they had brought in, and left by the back door, was now sitting on a bench at the foot of the bed.

"This is wonderful, Lyle." They were the first words Alice had spoken in a while. "Thank you. And thank you, for everything that you're doing for us."

Adam just nodded his head in agreement, but remained silent.

Lyle smiled and said, "Good night." He turned and disappeared down the stairs.

Adam stood by the window for a while watching the snowflakes fall. He was thinking about the day that had started all of this, months ago. His thoughts went back to waking up that fateful morning and walking downstairs in the little townhouse that he and Mandy had picked out to start their life together. It was to have been their honeymoon cabin, a stepping-stone to that quiet house somewhere in the country that they would have filled with babies and love. Now it sat cold and lonely, and led to nowhere.

*Adam was standing in front of the gun cabinet he had made in high school woodworking class, looking through the glass doors. The side of the case had routings of wild animals carved in the wood and a shiny lacquered finish that accented the yellow knotty pine wood. It had been designed with slots for four rifles, but his Browning deer rifle was the only one inside, sitting snugly on the green velvet cloth that lined the case. Someday he had hoped to fill it with a fine assortment of rifles and shotguns. He had bought the rifle when he was sixteen, with money he made on his uncle's farm baling hay one summer. For a second, he thought of the day he had walked out of Chalmers Hardware with it in his hands, and how proud he had been. He opened the door and took the weapon out, his hands sliding down the smooth stock. He remembered picking up the clip with its four rounds in it, and snapping it in place sliding it into the leather case that was folded in a drawer underneath the gun rack, and walking out the front door of the townhouse into the bright summer sunshine. It was a half-mile to the courthouse down a busy street, but this was hunting country, and hunting season, and a rifle in a case was not out of place. The walk was just a blur in his mind until he got to the Federal Building. Then he walked up the stairs to the third floor, past the office where he worked, to a door that was marked, **No Admittance,** but was never locked. He met no one in the building and had no idea what he would have told him or her, if he had been challenged. The stairs went straight to the roof and he remembered walking across the tar roof that was getting sticky from the radiating sun. His shoes were making little sucking sounds as he walked to the front of the building and looked down on the courthouse steps, across the street. It was less than a hundred yards. An easy shot for him. He knelt behind the parapet wall to stay out of sight and unwrapped the rifle. Peering through the scope at the back of the building he zeroed in on something about the same distance away as the courthouse steps and made a small adjustment to the scope. Adam was calm as he waited. He had a job to do, and do it he would, as soon as the son of a bitch showed his face.*

171

"Adam." His name being called startled him, and he whirled around quickly, and just as fast realized where he was.

Alice had undressed, except for her panties and bra, and was sitting on the end of the bed. "Come and hold me," she said.

He stood beside the bed for a moment, taking his clothes off slowly, and then they slid under the heavy covers and into each other's arms. They clung to each other and cried together. There was no love making, just an intimate, tender embrace that lasted all night long.

CHAPTER NINETEEN

It was still somewhat dark outside when Adam awoke. The room too was dark except for the filtered light coming through the window from the rising sun, peeking over the eastern horizon, signifying that day was breaking. Adam stared at the ceiling for a moment to get his bearings. His left arm had no feeling in it, from Alice lying on it all night long. He turned and looked down at her and she opened her eyes, almost as if on cue.

Outside, the sound of a steel blade on a snowplow scraping down the street, reminded Adam of yesterday's storm. He wrapped himself in the sheet and walked to the window. Today the sky was clear and the smoke from several neighborhood chimneys drifted lazily away.

A slight tapping on the door interrupted his thoughts, and Gloria's voice announced it was time to get up.

"Be down in a few minutes," Adam said.

They showered and dressed in silence, the tension of the events yet to come that day was too much to mask with anything but reality.

Gloria was placing a platter of French toast and sausages on the table as they came in, followed by Lyle, who seemed to be the only one in an optimistic mood. "Well, the snow was not as bad as we thought it might be," he mused, taking a sip of coffee. Then, sensing the tension, Lyle reached over and touched Alice's arm. "It's going to be fine," he said. "It's going to be just fine. I've been in this business long enough to know that justice is not always served, but it's usually the ill prepared who fail. We are *not* going to let that happen."

Adam tried to swallow the bite of sausage in his mouth, but he was eating just to be polite. There was no desire for food in his anatomy.

Alice had gone one step farther and took nothing from the platter; just preferring to take small sips of her coffee. She had pulled her hair back into a ponytail, and tied it with a green bow and was wearing a black pants suit with an emerald green blouse that matched. She wore very little makeup, and her eyes showed the effects of a night of troubled sleep. It was hard not to feel that she had made a mistake falling in love with this man, but done was done, and falling out of love, was not an option. She needed to stay strong and support him.

The guilt Adam was feeling for what he was putting Alice through, was worse than the fear and uncertainty of what was going to happen to him. He felt like he had let her down, and her choosing him, was choosing damaged goods. She deserved much better, someone without all of his baggage. He still didn't know if turning himself in was the right move. The system had failed him once already, and his faith in it was at an all-time low. If Alice had not been here, he would have bolted and run. No, scratch that. He would never have come back in the first place.

Lyle's white Lexus had been idling in the driveway and a large frosty patch had appeared under the exhaust pipe. It was toasty warm inside as they entered and settled back on the leather seats. Adam and Alice sat in the back on the left side, as Lyle squeezed his body behind the wheel, adjusted the rear view mirror, and backed out of the driveway. There was no turning back now.

They skirted the edge of downtown and headed north out of the city. From gleaming downtown skyscrapers, the neighborhoods changed to factories and warehouses, and then to the duplexes and old homes of the old city. Before long, they were driving through the suburbs, filled with tract houses and ramblers, broken up by occasional shopping centers and malls. Gradually, they too thinned out and there was more and more undeveloped land, with strip malls out front of new housing developments, and fancy houses of all descriptions and styles. Maybe someday they would live like this, Alice thought, and then choked back a sob that formed, as she thought about the years she might have to wait for him. She looked over at Adam who was sitting with his head back, staring at the headliner in the car almost as if he was hypnotized.

Lyle broke the silence with a question to Adam, about Mandy's parents. "Adam, are her parents still alive? Or the rest of her family? Amanda, I'm talking about."

"Yes. Yes, they are."

"Do you think they would support you?" Lyle was looking in the rearview mirror at Adam as he drove.

Adam cleared his voice before answering. "I'm not, sure. I was on good terms with all of them, but after this happened, and I ran.... well, it's been a long time since I talked with them."

Lyle's cell phone rang and he snatched it off the dash. It was his secretary from work.

The countryside now was woods and fields that looked dazzling in their new coat of white snow. A whitetail deer stood on the side of the road and watched them go by, as Lyle slowed and changed to the left lane to keep his distance from it. Deer were unpredictable, and could bolt in front of a car at the last minute.

About thirty miles south of Duluth, they exited the freeway and headed west toward the Iron Range and Aspen. This was familiar country for Adam, the area where he had grown up and lived for most of his life. Small hamlets that were home to many summer people dotted the many lakes, and soon the towns of Harmon and Kingsley came into view. These were Iron Range towns that once were bustling settlements in their day, but now with the ore depleted, were nothing more than havens for old retired miners and their spouses.

Next would be Jobson and then it was fourteen miles to Aspen.

Aspen was still the biggest city for miles around with about fourteen thousand people. It had suffered with the closing of the mines, but being the county seat and still possessing a thriving paper mill, had changed little over the years.

Lyle had talked on the phone for about forty miles now. He seemed to be a very busy man. Coming into Jobson, Lyle pulled the car over to the side of the road and put it into park. He turned in the seat so he was facing Adam and Alice, and then hesitated for a moment, as if he was thinking about the best way to verbalize what he had to say.

"Before I go any farther, Adam, I need to ask you if there is anything that you want to tell me about this case that you haven't already. We might not get a chance to talk again for a few days. I can't be your lawyer, but I will do my best to find you the best possible counsel that I can. To do that, I need to be able to tell them exactly what we're up against. I'm not going to speculate as to what kind of a defense you could or should use. That will be up to your new attorney."

Adam lowered the window a few inches and lit a cigarette. His hands shook, and his lips seemed to tremble a little. His eyes were watery, but not spilling over. His complexion had turned red. "How much is this going to cost?" he asked. "We don't have a lot of money."

"There isn't any charge for what I'm doing, but you will have to work things out with your new attorney. Most of them will work with you on that." Lyle paused again, and then said, "They're expecting us in a few minutes. The sheriff was the person I was talking to on the phone."

Adam flipped his cigarette butt out the window and put the window back up. "Let's not disappoint them," he said.

The short trip to Aspen was over before he could think much about anything. Alice was weeping quietly but not getting overly emotional. They held hands and kissed from time to time. They had talked late last night, and there was really nothing more to discuss. Alice would go back with Lyle and try to get work right away. There was a lot of call for nurses in the metropolitan area. They would pick up a local paper and see if there was anything closer, but that might not be a possibility. The hospital in Aspen was quite small.

They came into Aspen from the east, which was the part of town Adam had grown up in. The road came up over a hill and just like that, the scenery changed from woods to town. He could make out the upper half of his parent's old house from the elevated roadway. Smoke was drifting from the chimney, and he wondered who lived there now. There was St. Ann's Church where he had been confirmed, and Leman Brothers Auto Dealership. He once worked part time there, washing cars after school. He looked in the direction of Jimmy's Pizzeria, where all the kids used to shoot pool and hang out, and then high on a hill, the cemetery where his folks and Mandy were buried. His eyes locked on the stones and monuments as they passed, until the corner of a building blocked his view. His eyes scanned the streets as if he was looking for someone he would know, but the streets seemed to be almost deserted today. Dirty snow banks lined the curbs and were piled up around the metal streetlights with their white round globes.

Lyle stopped for a red light, and then almost as an afterthought, flipped his left turn signal on and turned on Hazel Street. The courthouse was in the center of the block six blocks away. The sheriff's office and the jail were behind it.

Adam lowered his head. He didn't want to see any more, and most of all he didn't want to be recognized. Alice was gripping his hand so tight she was almost shutting off the circulation.

Several Aspen County patrol cars were sitting at the curb in front of the courthouse, and two deputies were looking over a map on the hood of one of the cars. Their breath was making little clouds of steam in the winter air, and one of them looked up as they passed and smiled, giving a mock salute.

Lyle drove around to the right, past the steps where Adam had taken care of Stevenson with 180 grains of lead through his head, but Adam didn't look up. His head was still lowered.

The sign said, 'Parking for County Business Only.' Lyle pulled up to it and shut off the engine. Alice gave a small whimper, as she pulled Adam to her and kissed him tenderly. He put his arms around her and held her tight. She sobbed into his chest and he stroked her hair. Lyle sat patiently until they released each other, and then getting out, stood on the sidewalk waiting for them.

Adam had expected to be horse-collared, shackled and handcuffed at the city limits, but it was strangely quiet. Another deputy walked beside them on the sidewalk and said cheerily, "How's it going?"

Lyle answered, "fine," and they started up the walk to the building. He held the door as they stepped inside, and walked up to a counter where a young lady with a pleasant smile asked if she could help them. "Were here to see Sheriff Martin," Lyle said. He handed her a business card.

She looked at the card, and then smiling, said, "Take a seat and I'll go see where he is." She pointed to a row of chairs behind them.

Percy Martin struck a magnificent pose when he walked into a room in his white uniform shirt, and brown pants with a gold stripe down the leg. On his chest above the left shirt pocket was a gold badge that read, **Sheriff of Aspen County**. His collar sported a row of gold stars that signified he was the commander, and on his pocket flap was a simple gold bar that read, Sheriff Percy Martin. It was a job he had looked forward to for many years, having been groomed by Joe Adcock, the former sheriff, to take over the job. He still called Joe a lot, and as a matter of fact had just talked to the former sheriff last night, about Adam coming in.

He was a big man, more than six feet in height, with broad shoulders and black curly hair complimented by an dark complexion and green eyes. Today he stood in front of Adam, and extended his hand. "Adam, you remember me, don't you? We've wanted this to happen for a long time. I'm glad you came in this way." Another deputy, who was equally as large in stature as Percy, came in and stood off to the side smiling, while Lyle introduced himself and Alice, to the sheriff. Percy turned and nodded toward the deputy and said, "Adam, this is Blaine Stewart. He will take you into custody. Let's all go into my office."

Once in the office, Alice and Lyle stood to one side, while Blaine said to Adam, "Adam Holton, you are under arrest for unlawful flight to avoid prosecution for murder. I must warn you now, here and in front of your attorney, that from here on, anything you say can be used against you in a court of law. Do you understand this?"

Adam nodded his head, and then said, "Yes."

"I must also tell you that you have the right to an attorney, and one will be appointed for you, if you cannot afford one. Do you understand that?"

Again, Adam said yes.

"Please put your hands on the desk in front of you and lean forward."

Adam stepped back a foot or so, and did what he had been asked. Blaine patted him down and then reaching into his utility belt, brought out a pair of handcuffs and gently cuffed Adam's hands behind him. "Do you want to say goodbye to your friend?"

Adam turned to Alice, and she put her hand to his cheek. Tears were running down her face.

"It's going to be fine," Lyle said, putting his big arm around her shoulder and leading her out of the office.

Alice walked back one last time and kissed him softly, then she and Lyle turned and left. Blaine pointed to a second door that was in the office and said, "Through there, Adam."

Linda read the letter for the third time. She had been confused after talking to Alice's father and didn't know what to do, or if there was anything she really could do. But right here, and right now, she had made up her mind and time was wasting - she had to get to town. *No, I better call Tony first and make sure he's there.* She grabbed the phone off her desk and dialed. It rang several times before Beatrice, his secretary, answered.

"Bea, this is Linda Pendleton and I need to see Tony as soon as possible." Linda's words were jumbled and hurried and Beatrice was under the impression that something was terribly wrong.

"Well, he's right here, Linda, hang on and I'll get him." She held the receiver to her chest to muffle the earpiece. "Tony, its Linda Pendleton and she sounds upset."

He walked into his office, and closing the door behind him, sat down behind his huge oak desk, and put his feet up on one corner, then picked up the phone.

"Linda, what's the problem, sweetheart?" They had never been sweethearts, but they were more than just friends, and Tony had a genuine interest in her.

"Tony, I need a big favor and I know you're busy, but this can't wait. Can I come talk to you?"

"Well, yes. You know that. When do you want to come in?" He sat up in his chair and was paging through his calendar.

"I'll be there in fifteen minutes."

"Uh, wow. Okay, fifteen minutes it is." He closed the book as the phone cut off. Tony pushed the intercom button to his secretary. "Bea, call Mr. Callahan and cancel my 11 a.m." He listened for a second: "I know, I know. Tell him something. I don't care what you tell him. Just cancel it!"

Linda pushed the old Cadillac as fast as she dared drive on the slippery roads heading for downtown Missoula. Tony Winters was the "best in the west" when it came to criminal law. He was also an old family friend in more ways than one. When Dan was alive, they had been hunting buddies, and their families socialized a lot. Then a couple of years after Dan's death, Tony's wife also had left the picture; not dying, she just headed East with another man, and never came back. For a while they lost touch with each other, but then a while back, Tony called Linda and asked if she would like to go out. At first she resisted, but steadily he persisted, and she did go out with him, and they had fun. But Tony had one thing in mind, and it had to do with getting into Linda's bed. Not that she was against that entirely, but she just wasn't ready for that then. She was well aware that she might have to give in now, to get what she wanted this time, but if that was what it took, so be it.

Alice finally calmed down, sitting in the passenger seat, as they drove back to Minneapolis. She was tired from all of the turmoil her mind had gone through in the last few days. "I was expecting more of a reception than that," she said to Lyle.

Neither Alice nor Adam had noticed the plain brown Chevy sedan that fell in behind them about thirty miles outside of Aspen when they were coming in, but Lyle had. He also saw the squads on the side streets in the town itself, and the two officers, looking at the map on the hood of their cruiser, getting into the car as they turned the corner. There had been no reason to mention it at the time and he wasn't going to now.

"I was surprised too," he said. "Are you hungry?"

Adam walked down the narrow hallway to a room marked 'Booking' on the frosted glass door. Blaine walked directly behind him, his right hand lightly on Adam's right shoulder, and his left hand lightly gripping the cuffs. "In here, buddy," he said.

The room was stark white with a sterile look, and had no furniture except a wooden bench that was bolted to the wall. Another deputy sat on the bench, seemingly relaxed. He didn't get up or acknowledge them in any way, but continued reading a magazine.

"Adam, I want you to stand here for a second while I take your cuffs off. Then you need to go into that bathroom over there and remove all of your clothing. There is a live camera, no film, that will be watching you, and there's an intercom in the room. Tell me when you're unclothed and I will come in. I am sorry for this embarrassment but it's our procedure." Blaine took the cuffs off one wrist only.

Adam walked into the bathroom and stood in front of the stool. Feeling the need, he relieved himself. Then, after flushing and putting the lid down, he sat and started undressing. He knew what was coming next and the body search didn't bother him, or being examined. What bothered him the most was putting on the prison clothes they would give him, and being seen like that. He was not a criminal. He was just a man who did what he felt he had to do, to keep that psychopath out of circulation. Something the law couldn't do.

As soon as he was nude, he stood and told Blaine, "I'm ready," hoping someone heard him.

The body search was rude and disgusting, but Blaine did his best to help him keep some self-esteem. When he was finished, he threw the rubber glove in the wastebasket, almost as disgusted as Adam was. He hated doing that. "Here's your new clothes," he said.

He was handed a pair of white boxers, an orange jumpsuit, with **Aspen County,** stenciled across the back, and white work socks. He could keep his shoes.

"As soon as you're dressed we have a couple of other things to do, and then I'll let you get settled in."

"Okay," was all Adam said.

The other things consisted of getting a 'mug shot' taken, finger printing, and signing a receipt for his possessions. He was allowed to keep his smokes, but he would only be allowed to smoke with supervision. A light would be provided for his cigarette at these times. They took the elevator to the fourth floor, and Blaine and Adam walked down a narrow concrete floor hallway. Once again, Adam was cuffed until they got to the room: a solid steel door with a small window opening, a stainless toilet and sink, and a single bed with some sheets and blankets folded on the end.

Blaine took the cuffs off. "This is home for a while, buddy," he said. " The County Attorney will be up to see you soon. You don't have to talk to him unless you want to." Blaine paused to let that statement sink in. "Visiting hours are 7:00 p.m. to 8:00 p.m. each evening, and you are allowed one phone call a day, during that time only. We'll bring your meals. There is a switch that turns a light on above the door here. If you need anything, turn it on, - but don't abuse it, - and no, you can't have any Hustler magazines, or anything to drink, but water, and that's right there." He pointed at the sink.

Blaine closed the door on Adam and left him standing, looking at the far wall. Adam sensed he was still there, and he turned and looked out the small barred window in the door. Blaine, standing there, smiled and said, "I hope you win, buddy."

"Thanks,"

"Jeez, Linda, is this the same guy you were busting your butt for last fall? I thought that was a dead issue." Tony was sitting behind his desk, leaning back to get the best view of Linda's legs, while Linda did her best to give him enough of a shot up the side of her skirt, to keep his interest, among other parts of his anatomy. She wasn't sure what was going on in his trousers, but she was damn sure what was going on in his head. At the last minute she had deliberately gotten this little denim skirt out of the back of her closet, even though she was a blue jeans gal most of the time.

"Yes, it's the same guy, Tony, and for a while I did have second thoughts about helping him, but now I know it's the right thing to do. He did save my life you know"

"I don't know, Linda. Shit, I'm so busy right now - and where the hell is this guy now, anyway? Last time I talked to you, it was some big-ass secret."

"Minnesota, Tony."

"Whoa. Just a moment. I don't know if I can even work in that state. What the hell is he doing in Minnesota?"

She let her skirt hike up a little farther, and saw Tony's eyes drop to her legs again. "What do you say we go to supper tonight, and talk this whole thing over, Tony?" Linda was being coy with him now. She turned in the chair and caused her skirt to ride a little higher. Tony's face was getting red, and he was having a hard time thinking about what he was going to say.

"Tonight? I can't go tonight. Maybe tomorrow night, I could." He was paging through his appointment book.

Linda had crossed her legs slowly and was now smoothing her skirt down.

"All right, tonight! But I'm not promising you anything, as far as this guy is concerned."

"Pick me up."

"Yeah, yeah, I'll pick you up."

She was laughing out loud as she drove home My God, it had been twenty years since she had done that. *What was it Dan used to call her? A big tease. Yeah, that was it, - she was a real tease.*

She laughed again, then flipped her skirt up, and laughed some more. Damn, she still had it. Men were so easy to manipulate, especially if you knew how to use what nature provided. Her right hand was in a ball in her lap, pressing against her crotch. This whole scene was getting more than just Tony excited.

Adam was brought down to make his evening phone call. He had five minutes, and had been told that his call might be monitored. He called Lyle, but there was no one at home, and the call went to his answering machine. He stood up and gave the deputy a look of hopelessness, and the deputy said he was sorry. He took Adam back to his cell.

It was so different from what he imagined it would be. He was accused of murder, and Adam had expected to be treated like a murder suspect, but everybody was so nice, and this place was like a hotel in some respects.

Adam leaned back on his bed looking at the steel door and tried to imagine the people who had been in this room before him. What kinds of deviants had used this room? Did they treat everybody this nice? There was a knock on the door and he looked up. He saw a face he recognized, but from where? From Stevenson's trial, that's where. This was the County Attorney who had botched the case.

"Adam. Francis Heitla, County Attorney. Can I talk with you?"

When Adam stood to go to the window, he noticed the deputy standing by the side of the door, trying to be inconspicuous.

"About what?"

"Your case," said Francis, "and how we would like to proceed. You don't have to talk to me if you don't want to. I am not going to ask you anything about the case."

"Okay," said Adam

"Okay what?" asked Francis.

"Okay, come in, or whatever you want to do."

He heard some keys in the door, and the deputy opened it and let Francis in. He left it open and stood on the far side of the hall where he could observe, but not be a part of the conversation. Francis stood, while Adam sat on the bed looking up at him.

"Adam, the arraignment will be tomorrow." Do you remember me? I remember seeing you at the trial for---"

"Stevenson?" Adam asked. "The one you let get away?"

Francis was taken aback by this, but didn't take the bait. He was not here to get into any discussion about the Stevenson trial, and he knew now he should never have brought the subject up. He cleared his throat, and looked through his papers. "Do you have an attorney? I have the name of Lyle Jackson from Minneapolis. Is he your attorney? -- No, he can't be."

"Just for now," said Adam.

"Well, tomorrow at the arraignment you will be charged with unlawful flight. That is a felony and will allow us to keep you here until we work out the other charges with your attorney, when, and if, you get one. Bail may be set tomorrow. I don't know for sure, and it's basically up to the judge if he is going to allow that. He may wait until all the charges are filed. Mr. Jackson has been notified about the arraignment, so I would expect he will be here tomorrow, and maybe he and I can meet to go over the other charges. Do you have any questions, Adam?"

"No. Not right now."

Well look, Adam," Heitla looked tired. "I want this to be as painless as we can make it under the circumstances. There's a part of me that understands why this happened, but there is also a part of me that has a job to do, and right now that's all I am trying to do. My job."

Adam did not answer him, but his attitude had softened from where it had been a few minutes ago. He just nodded his head, slowly. Heitla extended his hand and Adam took it, but he didn't shake it. He just held it a second, and dropped it. The old attorney touched Adam's shoulder and said, "Good luck my friend."

Alice spent the day job hunting and had several prospects lined up. Tonight she was going to the library to work on her resume. Lyle told her about the arraignment, but he suggested she not attend. Tonight she was going to call Adam, and she was excited about talking to him and telling him all about her job leads. It had taken her some time to find out the procedure for talking to him, but she finally figured it out.

Lyle and Alice had talked a lot on the ride back from Aspen. Not just about Adam, but about Alice's folks and old times. He also talked about his relationship with his wife, or a lack of one. As so often happens with professional people, they seem to go their own way, and he and Ellie had been no exception. So, for now, Lyle buried himself in his work, and Ellie lived in her own little world, a world, which for the most part, did not include Lyle. Alice only half listened to this part of the conversation; she didn't feel comfortable discussing his personal life.

Not far from Minneapolis, they stopped in a small town for dinner at a quaint cafe that advertised, 'Real Home Cooking.' It was there, that Lyle told Alice he was having trouble finding an attorney to take the case, but she shouldn't get alarmed. There were a lot of people he hadn't spoken with yet. The restaurant's advertising lived up to its slogan, and the food was great.

CHAPTER TWENTY

Adam lay on his cot, staring at the light coming in the small glassless opening in the door. It was only 9:30, but the jail seemed to have quieted down for the night. About ten minutes ago, a deputy had stopped by his door and wished him a good night.

Adam hesitated in answering back, but then said, "thank you." It was all he could think of to say. He listened as the man's footsteps went down the cement hallway and faded away, leaving him alone with his thoughts. Something sure seemed to be strange, and not at all like he had thought it was going to be. His treatment by the guards and deputies was almost cordial. It was as if he was a guest, not a prisoner. Another thing that seemed strange was the lack of other prisoners, at least on this floor. There didn't seem to be any, and on his trip down to the phone this evening, the other cells were all dark.

He folded his pillow over and shoving it into the small of his back, sat leaning against the wall. *What was Alice doing tonight?* He missed her so much already. *The arraignment tomorrow, what would that be like? Did his brother and sisters know he was here? Was it in the papers?* He wanted a smoke so bad, but he was going to have to wait until morning.

Tony went to pick Linda up at seven in his Lincoln Town Car that was loaded with amenities and ultra soft leather. He popped a disk of the Carpenters into the CD player just before he shut the engine off and walked up to the door. She was a big fan of Karen Carpenter, he remembered.

The ranch was quiet tonight, with a single light on in the bunkhouse, but nothing much else showing any kind of activity. His cowboy boots clopped across the wood porch as he reached the door and raised the big brass knocker. A Christmas wreath still hung crookedly beside the door and Tony straightened it. He pulled his collar up a little as he waited. The night sky was clear as a bell and there was a bite in the air. Somewhere, a dog was barking. He could hear somebody coming, and when she opened the door, his hormones did a little back flip. This country bumpkin looked every bit the part of an elegant lady tonight. She had on a black sheath with a thin silver belt that tied and hung down one side, like a slender glittering sash. The dress had a deep V and she wore a necklace, with a small circle of flashing diamonds that rested between and drew awareness to her cleavage. It was getting the attention she planned,

"Damn!" was all Tony could say. "Damn and double damn, Linda! You make a man just sit up and take notice. You are a treat for sore eyeballs. You are one beautiful woman, you know that?"

Linda smiled. For now, she hoped that his eyeballs weren't the only balls that were taking notice. It had been awhile since a man had noticed her, that she knew about anyway.

"Let me grab my coat and we can get going, Tony. You look nice, yourself."

The car was warm and comfortable. Tony drove slowly, savoring the ride, and the fragrance of her Estee Lauder perfume, that seemed to drift from Linda to his nose. Linda smiled when she heard Karen Carpenter singing, "It's Only Just Begun." *He was trying hard, wasn't he?*

The restaurant was five star and very upscale, located in the magnificent Hilton Hotel. Tony handed the valet his keys, and then took Linda's hand, and they walked inside to total elegance. Their table was waiting, along with a bottle of Dom Perignon in a bucket of ice. The wine had been bottled before either of them were born. Their waiter took their coats with a promise to be right back to pour their wine. A string orchestra played melodiously from an inconspicuous spot in the club. A soft mixture of The Blue Danube and some other rendition, that seemed to be a little out of place in a cow town, but smacked of a long lost culture they both enjoyed putting on for the evening.

Their glasses poured, and their orders taken, Tony broke the quiet mood first. He knew the subject was going to be discussed, and he wanted to get it out of the way. "I looked back in my files and found what information I did have on your friend. Adam Holton, I believe the name was."

"Yes," Linda said. "He worked for me for a couple of months but, more importantly, he saved my life at a great risk to his own. I owe him a big favor, Tony. But more than that is the fact that what he did back there in Minnesota was justifiable and he does not deserve to be punished anymore than he already has been."

"He blew a man's brains out," said Tony.

"Correction, he blew a madman's brains out, before the madman could kill and rape again. The law failed him, Tony, in the way it fails a lot of victims, and it failed his dead fiancé and, and, ---" Linda was at a loss for words to finish her sentence.

Tony saw seriousness in her eyes he hadn't seen before. Eyes that were getting moist, and sparkled like the jewelry she wore. He reached over and touched her arm. "Tell me all about him."

Alice lay in the big four-poster bed that she and Adam had shared the night before, staring at a white luminous crucifix on the wall across the darkened room. She had been raised in a religious home, but like many young people and their busy lives, had drifted away from it. But now, the sight of the cross and the feeling of despair in her heart, reminded her that there was a greater power that was there to help.

She found a simple prayer forming on her lips. *Please, God, help us. Help Adam to cope, and help me to support him in this difficult time.* She pulled the covers up to her chin. Without Adam's arms to comfort her, they were all she had. The pillow was damp from her tears, and she grabbed it and turned it over. She had to do a better job of facing her problems. This crying and feeling sorry for herself was not going to solve anything.

Tomorrow, the plan was for her and Lyle to leave for Aspen first thing in the morning. Lyle told her about the arraignment and how the formal charges would be read against Adam, and that he would have to enter a plea. A trial date would be set if he pleaded "not guilty." Maybe not right away, but soon. That was their plan for now. When a new lawyer took over, it would be up to him and Adam if he wanted to continue with that strategy.

The night had been filled with a little bit of everything when it came to emotions. It had been settled. Tony would take the case. Linda's arguments had won him over, even easier than she had hoped. Tony would only take the case pro bono. It had been a long time since he had done something to make him feel good about himself, and his ability as a defense attorney. This was going to be his chance. They had finished most of their rare wine, and ate their meal as they talked over the details.

Tony ordered a buttery lobster, surrounded by a row of specially prepared scallops, and Linda, true to her rancher roots, ordered a small steak that had been sautéed in a special garlic sauce, with a vegetable medley that was to die for. They deferred dessert for a while, and he led her to a small dance floor. Tony was in good shape and she could feel the hardness of his body, as one of her hands found his shoulder, the other resting in the middle of his back. Then, her head soon found his shoulder, and the music found them both. They were a little clumsy at first, but they both knew how to dance, and after a small period of adjustment, they began to move together as one, with the music. They were the only couple on the floor. Her hair smelled so fresh and felt so soft, and the delicate aroma of her perfume that he first noticed in the car, now drifted back on a soft cloud of Linda's other subtle scents. Like Linda, it had been a long time for Tony too, and he had forgotten how good it felt like to hold someone like her. His wife had ignored him for years, before she ran off with…whoever that wonderful guy was. God, he hoped they were both miserable. They danced until the orchestra took a break, then returned to their table for a raspberry torte dessert, hot chocolate coffee, and after dinner drinks, topped off with a few more drinks from the bar.

It become obvious that Tony was in no shape to drive, so he called a cab and arranged for his car to be put in the ramp for the night. He thought about a room at the hotel, but he wanted Linda to make the move if one was going to be made. They rode out to the ranch snuggled in each other's arms, and the cabbie had to almost shout to wake them up when they got there. "Come in, and I'll take you to town in the morning," Linda whispered. There was seduction in that voice if he wasn't mistaken.

It had been so long for both of them that, they were like a couple of sex-starved teenagers tearing at each other's clothes in the back of a car, until they both lay naked, their clothes strewn around the room. All inhibitions for Linda, if there had been any, had disappeared back there on the dance floor, and that was two hours ago.

Tony's hands were gentle as they caressed the soft skin of this woman that he'd daydreamed about for so long. All the fantasies he'd had were all coming true. Linda was a very passionate woman and it had been a long time for both of them since they'd enjoyed sexual fulfillment. The need to feel loved and cherished that Linda had longed for, - for so long, - had been satisfied. As she lay there in the dark after their lovemaking, she could only think: *Maybe Tony was a better fit than Adam.*

It was a little before nine when Blaine came to get Adam to take him to the courthouse. "You need to wear these, Adam," he said. "I'm sorry." He leaned over and clamped leg irons on him.

"Not your fault," said Adam

He had to walk with short steps, and with his hands cuffed behind him. It just seemed hard to get coordinated, but it wasn't far and soon they were there. When they got inside the cuffs were switched from behind his back to the front.

Adam sat at a small table facing the judge. There was an empty chair beside him, but not for long. He felt Lyle's hand on his shoulder as he sat down. "How they treating you, sport?" Lyle had a grin on his face.

"Good. Almost too good, Lyle."

Lyle made a note to ask him what he meant by that, but right now the bailiff was asking everyone to stand. "The Honorable Oscar Persons is presiding, and this Court is in session."

Adam stood to witness the judge's entrance, but then as he sat back down, he looked behind him and Alice smiled and waved. He couldn't wave back, but he smiled and nodded. She looked scared, and a little out of place.

Lyle asked for permission to approach the bench, and he had a few words with the judge then sat back down. "Just had to clear up a couple of things before he begins," he smiled.

The prosecuting attorney had not yet arrived, so they just sat for a moment looking at each other. Adam used the time to turn and smile once more at Alice.

Francis Heitla finally came down the aisle, and before sitting, apologized to everyone for being late.

Lyle Jackson smiled and shrugged, and the judge said nothing.

"Mr. Heitla, the counsel for the defense has asked for a couple of days postponement of these proceedings, to allow for the defendant's new attorney to get into town. Would you have any objection to that?"

"None at all, Your Honor."

"Then I am asking that these proceedings be postponed until January 6, which is next Monday. Will that work for you, Counselor?" He looked at Lyle with his question.

"Yes, Your Honor, that will be fine, but it will not be me."

"Court is then adjourned for today." Judge Person rose and left the courtroom.

"That's it?" asked Adam.

"For now, yes. Look, Adam, I received a phone call this morning from Tony Winters of Missoula, Montana. He is asking to represent you in this case, and will be flying in tomorrow to talk with you."

Adam was confused. "Who? Why?"

"I told you I couldn't do it, but if I were you I would talk with this man, Adam. He's the best of the best. If anybody can help you, it would be him. I have never met him, but I've heard a lot about him."

"Let's go back, Adam." It was Blaine standing there waiting.

"I'll come see you in about an hour," Lyle said. "I have a few calls to make."

"Can I say "hi" to her?" Adam asked Blaine, - nodding at Alice, who was now standing in the aisle, waiting for him to leave.

"Sure, buddy. Take a few minutes. I'll wait right over there."

When Tony woke up, the clock was blinking 6:22. His head was pounding and he was sure someone, or something, had crapped in his mouth. But then, he remembered last night. He lay still for a second, recollecting his thoughts. Linda's side of the bed was empty, and he could smell coffee brewing somewhere. He had had a few one-night stands in his time, but last night was different. This time, there was some chemistry to go with it. Linda had been a willing partner, not just a performer trying to please him, He had always thought a lot of her, and never realized how lonely she really was. It was all too obvious last night. They would have to work on this relationship a little, and see what might happen. He padded out to the kitchen on his bare feet, but Linda, standing at the stove, stopped him in the doorway before the boys in the lunchroom spotted him. She pushed him back into the hall with a whispered *shush* - and a giggle. "Don't let them see you, Tony," she laughed. "They'll tell the whole town. They should be done in a few minutes and then I'll come and get you."

He watched her walk away. Damn, she did look good in those jeans didn't she? Just then the phone rang and Linda came into the office, where he was waiting, to answer it.

"Yes, yes I'll tell him, and have him call you right back, as soon as I can get a hold of him, that is," she added, realizing she had almost given away her secret. She hung up the phone, and then turning to Tony, said, "Lyle Jackson, the man who has been handling the case for Adam, wants you to call him right away."

"Why didn't you just let me talk to him while you had him on the-----oh." Tony laughed. "I'll call him as soon as I get to the office."

It was all set. Tony would be there for the arraignment, and Lyle was off the hook. Adam was still confused about the whole thing, and he had a lot of questions for Tony when he met him. Why, and who is paying the bill were just two of them? Til then, he would keep his mouth shut. He had a lot of time to think right now, and that was bad in some respects. The one question he could not give up on: was he doing the right thing to Alice? He had such a long-time relationship with Mandy, and then she was gone, and almost *too soon*, he was with Alice. It just didn't feel right. Not his feelings for Alice, but the suddenness of it all.

His sister, Noreen, and his brother, Jason, had been there last night to visit. He felt embarrassed to be seen in jail clothing, but it was nice to see them. Noreen cried a lot and showed him pictures of her new baby. Jason just seemed mad about what "they" had done, to make Adam mete out justice on his own. They both promised to visit when they could, and Adam asked Noreen to tell the rest of the family. On Sunday night, Alice came by herself. There was a piece of Plexiglas between the partitions they sat at, with holes in it, and Alice put her fingers through the holes, so Adam could feel them and kiss them. She cried some, but seemed more composed about the situation then she had been before. Alice told Adam she would not be able to attend the arraignment, because she was starting the first day at her new job at University Hospital. She also had a lead on an apartment, close enough so she could walk to work.

When Adam came into the courtroom on Monday morning, Tony was sitting at the lawyer's table, tapping the eraser of a pencil on the wooden top. Adam walked straight to the table, choosing not to make eye contact with anyone else in the courtroom when a muffled cry caught his attention. When he turned to look, it was Linda. She was holding a handkerchief to her mouth and her eyes were brimming with tears. The pieces of the puzzle were coming together.

Before Adam could sit all the way down, and ask the questions he wanted answered, Tony started talking. He had his hands on Adam's shoulders and was holding him in a position where eye contact could not be averted. "Look, Adam. I apologize for not getting here earlier and meeting with you, but things happened so fast, I did the best I could. This thing this morning is just a formality, and then we'll have time to talk."

Before Adam could do much more than nod his head, yes, the bailiff came in and announced that court was in session, and for all to stand.

Judge Persons looked ornery today, and pointing his finger, asked Tony Winters to explain who he was.

"I am the new counsel for the defense, Your Honor. I am taking the place of Lyle Jackson." Tony smiled, as he stood straight as a ramrod addressing the judge.

"You need to present your credentials to the court, Mr. Winters. I have no information on you."

"Yes, Your Honor. I apologize for not doing that before now, but this all came up very fast."

"Counsel for the prosecution, do you have any objections?"

Francis Heitla shuffled some papers, and then stood. "No, Your Honor, I don't at this time."

"Well, let's get on with it then, shall we?" The judge was on a fast track today. "Adam Holton, you have been charged with one count of fleeing to avoid prosecution, and one count of murder, in the first degree. How do you plead to these charges?"

Adam, standing along with Tony, looked at Tony for help. Tony whispered in his ear and Adam said,

"Not guilty, Your Honor."

"To both charges?"

"Yes, Your Honor, to both charges."

"That being your plea then, you shall be held over for trial and shall be judged by a jury of your peers. The trial date shall be set within two weeks. Are there any objections from the prosecution or the defense?" Francis Heitla said, "no," loud and clear, and the old judge's eyes went to Tony.

"No objections about that, Your Honor, but we are asking for bail to be set."

The old judge looked at Tony, and said, "Your client has already run from the law, Counsel, and because of that, bail will not be issued or discussed. This Court is adjourned." He banged his wooden gavel on the block that sat right in the middle of his desk, with a resounding swing.

Adam was led out a side door, so he did not pass by Linda. Tony had arranged for a meeting with Adam this afternoon.

CHAPTER TWENTY-ONE

Alice loved her new job, and tomorrow she was moving into a new apartment. She had been grateful to Lyle and his wife for the board and room, but it was time to leave, before she wore out her welcome. Lyle hadn't really talked to her in two days, and seemed to have washed his hands of Adam and his problems.

The new apartment was small. Just an efficiency apartment, but it had all of the comforts of home. There was a small kitchen to cook in, a nice cozy bathroom, and a comfortable living room with a small balcony that overlooked a city lake. The apartments were offered furnished or unfurnished, and her plan was to slowly replace their furniture with some new, as soon as she started earning money. The hospital was within walking distance and that helped a lot because she didn't want to drive in the big city any more than she had to.

There was one drive she did have to make, and that was the hundred mile trip to Aspen, to see Adam. Wednesday nights, and the weekend, was her schedule. At first they sat on opposite sides of a partition touching fingertips through the holes, until Adam asked for the privilege of at least sitting at a table together. The first time he asked, it had been denied, but he tried again, and this time it was granted.

The sight of Linda in the courtroom the day of the arraignment had unnerved Adam, but in their meeting, when he asked about it, Tony explained about how much she wanted to help Adam. Tony also explained that he was taking the case for free, because Linda was a very good friend of his. Right now, she preferred to stay in the background, but when the time was right she wanted to talk to Adam.

For now, Tony would be leaving, but he had hired a private attorney from the Twin Cites by the name of Able Brandon to do some research for him and from those results, they would build their case. "I think your defense should be that you were driven to do what you did. We need to put the blame for this whole thing where it belongs, on the courts of this county." Tony paused, to let Adam think about what he had just said.

"I was driven to do what I did," said Adam. "That is the God-awful truth."

"I know," said Tony. "But now we need to make it a good enough reason that a jury is going to buy into it. I've asked for a speedy trial, so this thing doesn't get tried in the papers. I don't think this county's docket is too backed up with cases, so I think we will get that."

"What's a 'speedy' trial?" Adam asked. "I mean, what kind of time frame are you talking about?"

"I hope by summer," Tony said.

"That's speedy?"

"It is for the legal system, and especially in this type of case. But we *will* need some cooperation from the judge and the prosecuting attorney. Right now, they seem to be very accommodating."

Back in his private plane heading for Montana, Tony smiled, and reaching over put his arm around Linda. "I have a good feeling about this case, sweetheart, and I have a good feeling about us too."

Linda looked up from the window she had been peering out of.

"Let's hope so, Tony. Let's hope so. Is that Bismarck, North Dakota down there?"

"You betcha, honey, and you know what? I know a steak house down there that has the best ribs you ever ate. Shall we give them a try? Getting too late to fly, anyway."

Linda giggled, and with her best southern accent, said. "Why Tony Winters! I do think you are trying to seduce me... *again*."

Tony dipped the right wing sharply as he turned in the direction of the lights of the Bismarck, North Dakota airport.

In early March, Judge Persons set a trial date of April twentieth. Jury selection would start in the middle of March and the trial would be held in Aspen County. Tony Winters had expected the prosecution to ask for a change of venue, but none had been forthcoming. He flew back to see Adam twice, but most of their planning had taken place over the phone, or by mail.

The publicity in the papers had been minimal. For one thing, the sheriff's office released little or no information. They acknowledged that they had Adam in custody, and the trial date, but both attorneys refused to discuss the case with the media.

Tony, who always looked forward to a good fight, was perplexed by the lack of enthusiasm the prosecution was having for the case. It was almost as if they were going through the motions but their hearts weren't in it. Were they going to try to pull a fast one? It made him suspicious that they were going to spring something on him at the last second, because good lawyers just didn't normally act like this. At least, he had never experienced it.

Francis Heitla and Tony had exchanged information several times, and even met once, at Tony's request. And the outcome just left Tony shaking his head.

For Alice, life had been as good as it could be under the circumstances. Her job was a much better one than she'd had in Idaho, or ever dreamed about, and she loved the people she worked with, and the work itself.

On one of her visits to Adam she had said, "Adam, you don't know how much I miss not being with you, but things have gone so well for me at work and home. That's helped me so much. I feel bad talking to you like this, knowing you're locked up here, but I don't want you to worry about me."

Adam smiled, and reaching across the table, took her hands. "It does make me happy to know you're doing well. Things in here aren't that bad. The food is good, and they treat me like a guest. The only thing I worry about is, if I get some prison time it might not be so nice, and I do miss my freedom. I guess that was something I always took for granted."

Alice gave him a weak smile, as if he had ruined the atmosphere. "Let's not worry about that right now." But in her heart, she was worried. Worried that, as fast as they had fallen in love, they might fall out of it.

Life for Adam at the jail settled into a routine. A routine he would just as soon break. The thought of being incarcerated for a long stretch of time scared him; he refused to deal with it. Whenever those thoughts surfaced, he pushed them aside and picked up one of the books Alice had brought him, and started to read.

Blaine would stop by when he was on jail duty, and they would talk for hours about life in general, and what had happened to both of them since they'd left high school. Even though he was just two grades behind him Adam didn't remember Blaine from school, He had gone into the service for a couple of years, and when he got out, went to college, getting his degree in criminal justice. Working in Aspen didn't give him much satisfaction, but some day, when he had more experience he planned to move on to a larger city. They tired of talking through the little window, and after dark when the traffic around the jail slowed down, Blaine would come into the cell and the two of them would sit on Adam's cot and talk. Blaine seemed to be oblivious to the fact that Adam had been charged with murder. Well, actually the County Attorney had settled for second-degree manslaughter. But it still carried a sentence of five to eight years. He could get ten years for the illegal flight.

Adam missed Alice so much, and their meetings did little to curb his feelings of despair and loneliness. They parted, both crying, several times. Adam would go back to his cell and daydream about the day this would all be over, and they could melt into each other's arms again.

Alice had her work and her new friends to keep her busy and ease the loneliness somewhat, but there were many long drives back when she drove with one hand, and wiped away her tears with the other.

On March twentieth, jury selection began. Tony flew in the day before and had a long meeting with Adam. Tony seemed confident and in charge, almost as if this was no big deal. Maybe he knew something Adam didn't.

The jury pool had about fifty people in it, which was not a lot but they had been pre-screened so there wasn't much to disqualify them. Adam sat quietly, as one after another, they came forward to be interviewed and questioned by the two attorneys. Judge Persons seemed to be bored with the proceedings and spent most of his time doodling on a piece of paper. The courtroom was closed to all spectators and reporters. The first four people were accepted without question: three women, and an elderly man who appeared to be very religious. The fifth candidate, however, seemed to be having some trouble convincing Tony that she held no opinions about the case. Tony's detective work had turned up evidence to the contrary. She worked in a "greasy spoon" restaurant on the edge of town and had been overheard talking about the case. Tony wasn't sure which way she was leaning, but decided to pass on her.

"Your Honor, we object to this candidate being on the jury. It is our opinion that she has some pre-conceived opinions that would keep her from being fair and impartial."

"Do you have any objections to us excusing this candidate?" the judge asked Francis Heitla.

"No, Your Honor," he said. He had a pile of papers in front of him, and looked like he was busy doing his taxes or something, instead of paying attention to the proceedings.

"You are excused," the judge told the woman. "Thank you for coming in and good luck to you."

The lady looked at him with a blank stare, and then got up and walked out, as if she could not believe she hadn't been selected.

Tony chuckled and whispered to Adam. "Can you believe that she's irritated? Most people will go to any lengths to get out of jury duty."

"Next," said Judge Persons. "Raise your right hand and do you solemnly swear-------."

Linda couldn't go to Minnesota with Tony this trip. She and Ramon had a huge falling-out, and Ramon quit, so she had her hands full with things at the ranch. It was a good thing it was winter and the work was minimal or she would have been frantic. "I do want to be there for the trial though, Tony, or at least part of it," she said.

"That would be nice for both of us," Tony answered, smiling that big smile with all of those white teeth. He reached out and took her in his arms. "The last couple of weeks have been wonderful for me. Every hour we've spent together has been pure pleasure," he said. "You make me look forward to each day."

Linda stretched up on her tiptoes and kissed him tenderly. "You lawyers know all of the right things to say, don't you? It has been very nice, Tony, and I enjoy being with you too. But being a lawyer, you understand about suspicions and how they work. Although most of mine have melted away, there remains just a tiny bit I need to work on." She touched the tip of his nose with her finger. "I'll keep trying, if you do."

At last, the final juror had been selected. He was one of only three men on the jury: a retired Duluth police officer, who had moved to the area to live by a small lake outside of town. The former officer was questioned about his feelings on the subject of people who broke the law. He answered truthfully: "I was hired to catch the criminals, not judge them."

One other man on the jury was a former farmer, who now ran a business in town, and just coincidentally, had three daughters. The rest of the jury was a motley group of women, including one who would not look up from her knitting to answer questions, and a sarcastic woman in her seventies, who shouted every answer, while playing with her hearing aid. There were two alternates selected: one man, and one woman.

Tony Winters was ecstatic about the jury, believing they exceeded his expectations for a panel that would be sympathetic to Adam.

Judge Parsons was instructing the now seated jury: "Ladies and gentleman, you have been selected to serve as a jury of peers, to judge the guilt or innocence of the defendant in this upcoming trial. I am instructing you right now not to discuss this with anyone. Not even your own family. I will not be sequestering you for the time being, and I will release you today to go back to your homes, until the onset of the trial, You must remain impartial about anything you read or hear. I expect it to be a couple of weeks before the trial starts. You will be notified by registered mail. I also expect that the trial itself will last about two weeks. Do any of you have any questions?"

The nine women and three men, plus the alternates, all looked at each other, but none of them said anything, except one sarcastic old woman named Bernice, who said, "Yeah, I have a question. Where's the bathroom?"

The bailiff, laughing, pointed to a sign with the word **restrooms,** on the west wall of the room.

"You are all excused," the judge said. "Would the two attorneys remain? Deputy, please take the prisoner back to his cell."

"I'll see you in a few minutes," Tony said, as Adam was led away.

Judge Persons came down from the bench and approached the two attorneys. "I must warn both of you that you may not approach the jurors in any form or fashion until this trial is concluded. If you do, I will declare a mistrial and we will start over with new attorneys. I would like this trial to move right along, so have your witnesses and material ready. Be prepared: just like a good boy scout. Now if you will accompany me to my chambers, I will go over some dates with you, and maybe I can rustle us up a beer or a cup of coffee."

Tony and Adam sat side by side in his cell. Adam smoked incessantly, taking deep drags off his cigarette, as if he didn't want to waste any of it. Alice brought him a carton once a week, and the staff here had given him permission to smoke in his cell. Tony talked about the dates for the trial and how he wanted him to act and dress, while waving his hand in front of him to disperse the cloud of smoke. "I might get you set free, but your going to kill yourself with those heaters, my friend." Tony smiled while he said it.

"The day I walk out of here, or out of prison, will be the day I quit." Adam threw the butt in the toilet and put the package away.

"Trial will start the twenty fifth," Tony said. "I'll be back the day before, and we'll go over some things. We did some in depth research on Mark Stevenson. By 'we,' I mean Able Brandon. He's the attorney that I hired to do a little detective work for me. Did you meet him?"

"Who do you mean, Able Brandon? Name seems familiar."

Just the mention of Stevenson's name made Adam cringe.

"Seems this Stevenson guy had been after girls for a long time. One of the names that came up might be somebody you know. Ruth Ann Holton."

Adam's head jerked up, and his eyes were intense. "My sister? That bastard touched my sister? No! How can that be? I would have known that!"

Ruth Ann was Adam's younger sister, and she had been the pride of the family. She was married now and lived out east in Cleveland. Come to think of it, she *had* started acting strangely about two years before Stevenson had stalked and killed Mandy. She and Adam were never real close, but why the secret?

"She didn't report him until *after* you killed him," Tony said. "But it might work to our advantage, if the judge will allow it."

Adam was pacing the cell now, like a caged animal. He took the package back out and lit another cigarette, flipping the match into the toilet. "Tony, I need to talk to her."

"I hoped you would say that. We need her for a witness. Let me know if you need my help."

After Tony left, Adam lay on his cot with his head at the foot end of the bed. There was an elongated window close to the ceiling that let some light into the room. It was about three feet long and about eight inches high. Constructed, so light could come in, but nobody could get out.

All he could really see lying at this angle were the tips of some tall white pines that stood close behind the building, and the evening sky beyond. It was a very dark sky right now, intermittently illuminated by a yellow half moon that slid from behind the jagged clouds from time to time.

That's the way life felt to Adam right now. He spent so much time in the dark but every so often the light would break through and give him short glimpses of the world around him: The real world.

CHAPTER TWENTY-TWO

"**R**uth Ann, I need to talk about this. I know I haven't been much of a brother, but I need your help. I need you, sis." Then Adam proceeded to tell her about turning himself in. She already knew about the shooting and his escape out west.

The line was quiet. She had been surprised to hear from him, and at first she had been all bubbly and cordial, but when Mark Stevenson's name had come up, she clammed up.

"Please, Ruth Ann, I have only five minutes to talk to you and then they'll cut me off. That man was an animal, Ruth, and someone had to stop him. Your story would go a long way to help me convince a jury that what I did was right."

"If you were right, why did you run?" Ruth Ann's voice was clear and concise.

"I was scared, Ruth. I was scared that they wouldn't understand why I did what I did. After I turned myself in, I found out that they did understand. They treat me like a hero around here, at least, as much as they can without getting into trouble. But the law is the law, and right or wrong, I did take a man's life, Ruth, and although there are ways around most laws, I need all of the ammunition I can get. I know that's a poor choice of words at a time like this, but you know what I mean."

"Adam, I wish I could help, but you have to understand. Billy, my husband, knows nothing about what happened to me. I'm not sure how he would react. Maybe he would see me as damaged goods, and I've kept this secret from him for so long, that he might even see me as dishonest. I never should have called the sheriff and told him about this, but it happened before I married Billy. It was old news, because it had happened two years before. The sheriff just filed a report because there was nothing else he could do, with Stevenson dead. I thought it would help you, Adam, but it didn't turn out that way."

"The only way you can help me, Ruth, is to come and testify. If you would have turned Mark Stevenson in, when he did this to you, Mandy might be alive today."

It was a harsh thing to say, but it was true, and Ruth broke into tears when she heard it. She had been living with that guilt for a long time.

Blaine had his hand on Adam's shoulder. His time was up.

"I'm sorry, Adam. I am so sorry." Ruth, sobbing, hung up the phone.

Adam sat and looked at the receiver. A dial tone sounded and he hung it up.

"Trouble?" asked Blaine.

Adam just nodded his head, and then stood up to be escorted back to his cell.

Alice stepped off the plane in Cleveland with a map of the city, and an address. Blaine ran Ruth's phone number through a cross directory, that gave them William Cross's address.

Alice visited the day after Adam talked to Ruth, and he told her everything. She bit her lip and grimaced when she heard it. Then she asked Adam for Ruth's address.

"I can't ask you to do that," Adam said. "Let's tell Tony and maybe he could send somebody to talk to her."

"If she isn't going to do it for you, she isn't going to do it for Tony either. But maybe- just maybe- I could get through to her. Stevenson took away a woman that you loved, Adam, and now the law is threatening to take you away from me. Let me try to reason with her." She booked a flight the next day. Adam got the information down to her and she took a sick day from work.

According to the map, it was about five miles from the airport to Ruth Ann's house. At first Alice thought about calling her and asking to meet with her, but then she had second thoughts: that might just make her bar the door. *No, she needed to surprise her, but even that had some risks. She might not be home, or her husband might be there. If anyone was going to have to explain this incident to him, it had to be Ruth Ann. It couldn't just come out in a discussion in their foyer.*

A blue and white cab was approaching and she raised her hand and whistled like a New York doorman.

"Where to, Mum?"

"4405 Euclid."

He flipped the meter on, and they lurched into traffic. There was a throaty roar from under the cab indicating that the exhaust system was not in the best shape. The windshield was cracked on the right hand side, and a piece of chrome was whipping in the wind from the side of the front fender. The license fastened to the headliner in front said that Bareek Baruke was her host for the trip.

Alice was extremely nervous. She was in a strange city, about to confront someone she had never met before. It didn't get much worse than this.

Bareek weaved in and out of traffic, the toothpick in his mouth changing sides every time he changed lanes. Outside of the initial conversation for an address, he had said nothing, but his eyes in the rear view mirror kept glancing at Alice in the back seat. Whenever their gaze met, he would smile a large toothy smile, but still remained quiet They skirted the downtown area and headed south to Cleveland's east side. The weather was much warmer than Minneapolis, and there were no snow banks left. The trees were already leafed out, and lilacs, crocuses, and irises were blooming in yards along the way.

"You visiting Mum?" They were the first words Alice had heard from the driver since they had left the airport, and his heavy accent was noticeable.

"I… I'm here to see my husband's sister." She kept her hand hidden in her jacket pocket so he wouldn't notice the missing rings. *It just sounded better than saying boyfriend or fiancé.*

Bareek crossed three lanes of traffic amid horns blaring, and shot down an exit ramp. "Sorry, Mum. Came up kinda quick."

They were now on a frontage road, and about three blocks down, they turned on Euclid. The street was narrow with cars parked on both sides, and in some places that left only a single lane to squeeze through. Judging by all of the kids in the street, and the run down condition of the houses, it seemed a poorer section of the city. There was a tangle of bikes and plastic three wheelers in the yards spilling onto the street. *There was a place like this in every big city, wasn't there?*

Bareek pulled the Crown-Vic over to the curb and said, "Here you goes Mum."

"Can you wait a minute?" Alice asked.

"She flew to Cleveland to talk her into it? Why didn't you say something! I was working on getting a subpoena, and then she would *have* to testify. We have to work together here, son." Tony was sitting across from Adam at a table in an interrogation room.

"No, -- no, I don't want that. I want her to come under her own free will. Not be dragged in here with threats." Adam had a look of disapproval on his face.

"Did you talk with her?"

"Yes," Adam said. "But I didn't have any luck with that part of it. She has her reasons for not testifying. I just needed to hear her side of the story."

"What makes you think Alice can convince her to come?"

"I didn't think that, Tony. Alice did."

Tony was silent for a second as if he was forming his thoughts to whatever he was going to say next. "Well, you keep me posted, will you Adam? Ruth Ann's testimony could prove critical to your case. Now lets take a moment to talk about *your* testimony." Tony reached across the table and covered Adam's hands with his. An elaborate ring on his left hand sparkled in the light from the overhead florescent. They both looked at each other, and their eyes made firm contact. Both men appeared to be extremely serious. "Adam, there are only three ways I know of that we can go about establishing a defense for you. The first is insanity, or some form of momentary insanity. The second is self defense, and the third, is what is known as justifiable homicide." Tony relaxed for a moment, releasing Adam's hands, and sat back in his chair, nervously fingering a fountain pen. Adam remained as he had been, with his forearms learning on the tabletop and his head slightly bent, staring at Tony out of the tops of his eyes. "Insanity," said Tony, "is hard to prove in this state. It's a defense that is rarely used. In your case, most people would say you had to be insane, even temporarily insane, to do what you did, but the problem would be proving it. The entire case would hang on the testimony of a bunch of shrinks and experts who would examine you, and cross-examine you for weeks. It would, for all practical purposes, take the case out of our hands. Self-defense is self explanatory, and there is no way the jury is going to believe that you were threatened from this man. Not when you blew his brains out from across the street with a high powered rifle." Adam now sat back in his chair, still staring at Tony with a look of dead seriousness.

"But justifiable homicide, might just fill the bill." Tony was standing now, with his hands gripping the edge of the table. His knuckles were turning white from the pressure of his weight. "There have been numerous cases where women have been battered and beaten by a man, and then they just snapped. They have taken all they can take. They have reached the end of their rope and feel they have no other options. Some of them have stuck a knife in the abusers back as he slept, and still got off. I'm speaking metaphorically of course, when I apply this to your case, but with the right twist, it might just work."

A deputy came to the door, and opening it, said, "Ten minutes, Counselor."

"Gotcha," said Tony, and waved him away. The deputy left without closing the door and Tony walked over and pulled it shut. "We need to make this jury believe that you killed Stevenson before he could kill any more women; That, Adam, is why your sister's testimony is so important to this case. We need a pattern established. You didn't know about your sister's assault at the time you killed Stevenson, but they don't know that. Now we can't lie and say you did, but if we're careful, we can make them think you did. Stevenson killed Amanda. He had admitted it, right? His confession was thrown out on a technicality, not because it wasn't true. But the sad fact remains that we are not going to be able to use that in this trial. I will try to use it, and maybe plant a small seed in the jury's mind. Let's see what happens."

Through all of this, Adam had remained quiet, but now he spoke quietly. "Tony, I killed Stevenson for lots of reasons, but most of all I killed him because he took something very precious from me and had no remorse about it. One of those reasons included the failure of the law to put him away, but there are other reasons. I am not sorry I did it. Even knowing what might happen I would probably do it again."

Tony held up his hand, to stop Adam right there. "Adam, as much as what you're saying is the God awful truth, we cannot use that to defend you. You have to believe in me, son, and follow my lead!" He was nearly shouting the last sentence at him. Tony looked at his watch and then the clock on the wall. "We'll continue this conversation later. My time is up for now, but you think about what I've told you, and get the right mindset, or you *are* going to jail. I guarantee it."

Alice was standing on the front steps ringing the doorbell. No one came to the door, but she could hear somebody moving around inside. She peeked through the window, but the lace curtains that covered the glass gave her a distorted view of what was going on inside. This time she knocked, and a chair scraped on the floor, and somebody was coming.

A television was going in the background but the sound was so low she could barely hear it.

Ruth Ann opened the door just a few inches and looked out as if she was irritated for being interrupted. She was strikingly pretty, but with no make up on, and her hair hanging loose to her shoulders, there was an air of plainness to her delicate features. She had on an old flannel shirt with a red and black square print, and blue jeans. "Can I help you?" she asked.

All of the words Alice had rehearsed, and was going to say, suddenly vanished, and her mind was a blank.

"Are you Ruth Ann?" she asked.

Ruth did not answer, but indicated that she was.

"I want to, ---that is, if you don't mind, --- I'm Alice," she finally said, and put her hand out. Ruth Ann did not grasp her hand, but continued gripping the edge of the door. "I'm your brother Adam's friend."

Ruth Ann still did not say anything.

"Please, can I come in for just a minute?" There was a desperate look on Alice's face and Ruth sensed something was wrong. She stepped out onto the porch, quietly closing the door behind her. Her arms were crossed across her chest. A button was missing on her shirt, and on her collarbone a black bruise was visible against her pale skin, but Alice tried not to notice too obviously.

"Ruth Ann. Your brother desperately needs you! Without your help, he could go to prison for a long time!" Alice blurted out.

Ruth turned to look behind her through the window. "Let's go somewhere else," she said.

"I have a cab out front." Alice turned to make sure the cab was still there.

"Let me grab my purse, and my daughter," Ruth said.

Linda had gotten the news this morning that her mother had passed away in her sleep the night before. Although she had expected it, she still felt sad, and had taken a walk to think, and cry a little. Something was happening with her and Tony that felt comfortable, and for the first time in a long while she felt that there was somebody else in her life to share her grief and aspirations. Tony was coming out later today for a while, and she needed to talk about some things. Not just her mother's passing, but the trial, and their future... if there was going to be one.

The cab driver was still waiting patiently for Alice, and seemed a little surprised when three of them came back.

"We're just going to have you take us to a coffee shop and then you can go," Alice said, as she got into the cab. "You name the place," she said to Ruth Ann.

"Mama Casimos?" Ruth Ann said, almost making it sound as if she was asking a question.

"Mama Casimos it is, Mum," Bareek said.

"This is my daughter Chelsea," Ruth Ann said as she sat the little girl on the seat between them. The toddler looked unhappy about being wakened from her nap.

Alice took the child's little hands in hers. "Chelsea, you are adorable," she said.

"Her father works nights, so I didn't want to disturb him," Ruth Ann explained.

"Not a problem," said Alice.

The neighborhood turned from white clapboard houses to more of a commercial landscape and Bareek pulled into a small strip mall where, next to a pizza place, was Mama Casimos. The neon sign above the door flashed from "coffee," to "espresso" to "cappuccino." White curtains were strung midway across the windows so you could see only the tops of people's heads through the glass. Alice paid Bareek and gave him a five-dollar tip for waiting.

"Thank you, Mum," he said, and gave her a big toothy grin.

"Thank you, Bareek, and have a good day." She reached in the window and touched his shoulder with her fingertips.

It was warm in the coffee shop and the rich aroma of brewing coffee and chocolate smelled delicious. They slipped into a booth, and Ruth Ann asked for a high chair for the little girl.

They ordered cinnamon rolls, coffee, and some juice for Chelsea. Ruth Ann tore off some of her roll and put it on Chelsea's tray.

Neither of the two small women was tall enough to see over the curtains, and Ruth Ann seemed to relax a little here, shut off from the eyes of the world.

"You said Adam could go to prison for a long time?" Ruth Ann asked.

"I understand you talked with him," said Alice

"Yes I did. Look, Adam and I haven't seen each other for a long time, not since he left home, anyway, which was right after our mother died. I was very surprised to hear from him the other day. I knew what had happened from the newspapers, but I didn't know that he turned himself in."

"A lot has happened since the shooting," said Alice. "He wants to make amends, and get on with his life, - our lives - if he can."

Ruth Ann gave Chelsea a sip of juice. "Alice, my husband might do some awful things if he knew what happened to me. He's not a patient man, and my not telling him about this a long time ago would only add fuel to the fire. Chelsea was born before we were ever married, and in some ways, I need him and so does she." She reached over and touched the toddler's face, wiping her mouth.

"What if he doesn't have to find out?" Alice countered. "What if you just happened to take a little trip home to see your family about the same time as they would need you to testify? How long has it been since you've seen your family?"

Ruth understood what she had been asked, but did not answer the question. "Do you love Adam? Are you engaged?" She was changing the subject.

"I love him and would marry him tomorrow, if he was a free man. And yes, we are engaged." It was quiet for a few minutes. They both sipped their coffee and looked at each other. Alice could see more bruises on Ruth Ann's neck and arms, but left the subject alone, for now. *What was it like to live with someone who treated you like that, just to have a home?* "I'm not sure he loves me as much as he loved Mandy. I say that because he has never gotten over her, but I see that as a quality in Adam, not a hindrance to our relationship. I haven't known him very long. If he goes to prison for an extended length of time, Ruth Ann, then he might lose me, too. I do love him a lot, but I could never wait for him for years and years, and I know he wouldn't expect me to do that. I might think I could, - I might say I would, - but the logical side of me says, it wouldn't happen."

Ruth Ann was nervously balling up her napkin, and then smoothing it back out. Her gaze seemed to flick from the tabletop, to Chelsea, to Alice. She seemed on the verge of tears but was tying hard to remain calm.

Alice reached across the table and gently held Ruth Ann's hands. "Please, Ruth, I'm begging you."

"I have no money. How am I supposed to pay for this trip?"

"I'll send you tickets and money. Please!" Alice was the one with tears streaming down her cheeks.

Ruth Ann took a deep breath, and held her head higher than she had all day. "All right. I'm going to do it," she said, loud and clear. They hugged over the tabletop, and Chelsea clapped her little hands and smiled, then they both looked at her and laughed.

"She is so beautiful," Alice said. "Maybe, some day." she murmured.

They decided to walk back home. It was a great spring day with the warm sunshine melting away the last of winter's dirty snow piles. You could hear the gurgles as the water from the melting snow found its way down the gutters to the storm sewers below. Bright green leaves adorned the trees, and sap was running down their trunks. The chirping of birds was everywhere, and a few squirrels dashed across the street between the cars in their daring little games. A few early lilacs had already burst into flowers, and they stopped to admire a tulip garden that had just bloomed. A block from the house, Alice found a cabstand. "I better wait here," she said.

"During the week, Billy sleeps during the day and I pick up the mail, so send the tickets to arrive during the week, please! I don't want him to see them."

"I will," Alice said, "and I'll call you with the dates, as soon as I know more. When is a good time to call?"

"Mornings," Ruth Ann said. "Not on the weekends."

Alice once again held Adam's sister's hands. "Ruth, don't let him abuse you." She had wanted to leave the subject alone, but could no longer keep quiet.

Ruth nodded her head to acknowledge she understood, but didn't reply, and Alice didn't pursue it. She kissed Alice on the cheek and said, "Thank you for coming."

"No, thank *you*, from Adam and me. It takes courage to do what you are doing." Alice held up her hand as a cab pulled up, splashing water, and they both jumped back. She got in and waved once more to both of them, and then they melted away into traffic.

CHAPTER TWENTY-THREE

It was the trial of the decade for Aspen County. The local media didn't go overboard on it, but the papers in St. Paul and Minneapolis gave it front-page coverage. On KLOX in Duluth, a liberal talk show host did a weeklong series on sexual predators, and how the state had done so poorly at keeping track of them.

As for the two attorneys, they had no comment when they had been approached for their spin of the upcoming trial.

Tony seemed to be primed and confident when he arrived in Aspen on the Friday before. He rented a whole suite of rooms in the local Holiday Inn, as he brought along three members of his staff, and Linda.

Francis Heitla was still keeping a low profile. He had the list of witnesses that Tony planned on calling to the stand, and a couple of them puzzled him. One, in particular, was Linda Pendleton, who seemed to be a friend of Tony's, who was coming from Montana to be a witness for the defense. He could only guess what that was all about. Apparently, Adam's sister was also testifying, and he expected some other character witnesses to show up and plug for Adam's reputation.

Tony was back in Adam's cell and they were sitting on the edge of his bunk the night before the trial. "Are you nervous?" he asked Adam.

"I am, but only because there is so much uncertainty for me. Before this happened, Tony, I had never been in any courtroom anywhere, so I'm very naive as to how this whole thing works."

Tony laughed that big, boisterous laugh that was his trademark, that, and those six hundred dollar cowboy boots he always wore. "Look, little buddy, I have never been more confident about a case. Linda told me about the night of the blizzard, and the part you had in saving her life Adam. I'll be bringing that up in the trial and I just wanted you to be aware of that."

"What does that have to do with this?" Adam asked.

"Very little," Tony replied, "but it has a lot to do with you, and the type of person you, are and you are the one on trial here. We're not fighting to change the law here. We're fighting the way the law was mis-used, to make you do what you did. The very laws that were in place to protect us all, failed you Adam, and that was wrong."

Changing the mood and the subject, Tony said, "I brought you a new suit and shirt. You need to look your best." Tony handed him the garment bag that he had hung on a pipe when he came in. "There will be times when you will want to stand up and yell, "That's not right!" - or a lot of other things, but you must stay calm and not speak unless you are asked to testify. I'm not sure if we are going to put you on the stand or not. We'll see how the trial goes and how the jury is reacting. Cross-examination by the prosecution can be brutal. I'll coach you when we get to that, if we do."

'Is Linda here?' Adam asked.

"She is, Adam. By the way, her mother, whom you and Alice took such good care of, passed away last week. We flew back for the funeral and had a nice talk with Alice's parents. You've got a lot of fans buddy. Look, Alice is going to be here in a few minutes to see you, so I'm going to leave. We'll have a chance in the morning to talk before the trial, so write down any questions you have. Get a good night's sleep, and we will see you tomorrow." Adam stood and hugged Tony. It didn't feel awkward at all.

Alice was not allowed in the cell, like Tony was. They had to go to the visiting center, but they were given a small room to talk in. It was a room with a large one-way window and no way to know if they were being watched or not, not that it mattered, They both understood the seriousness of tomorrow's trial and they were both visibly concerned about it. She was already in the room when Adam came in, and she hurried over to embrace him. She smelled so fresh and clean. Adam buried his head in her soft hair and stroked her back. They were both near tears. Alice spoke first: "Tony seems optimistic, Adam, and I'm so impressed by him."

They sat down facing each other. "I have a lot of confidence in him. It's the courts I don't trust. What did Ruth Ann have to say when you called on her?"

"She said she would be here, Adam. I sent her the tickets and two hundred dollars last week. Are you aware of the abuse she is getting, living with this Billy guy?"

"I wasn't, but my other sister told me about it. I hope she knows what she's doing."

Alice leaned across the table, kissed him, and brushed the hair out of his eyes. "They have the cutest baby, Adam."

Adam smiled and asked. "Where are you staying?"

"Tony got rooms for both Ruth Ann and me at the Holiday Inn."

Ruth Ann sat at the small kitchen table and wrote the note. She was not sure how he was going to react, but she would be long-gone before he got up. Suddenly the bedroom door opened, and she quickly pushed the note under the tablecloth as Billy came out, squinting in the sunlit room. He was wearing an old pair of boxer shorts, and scratched himself with his right hand, while he opened the refrigerator with his left, to take out the milk. He drank right out of the carton, and when he finished it, he threw the empty carton on the floor next to the waste container. Then, turning around, he stared at Ruth Ann as if he had something to say to her, but only belched, and went back into the bedroom, slamming the door behind him. She retrieved the paper and resumed writing.

Billy,

I thought I cared for you at one time, but now I know that was just a lie I made myself believe.

I'm going back to Minnesota to help my brother out at his trial and then I am staying there. I never told you what the man that Adam killed did to me before we were married, because I knew you would never understand and would probably whip me for it anyhow. Now it's time for the truth to be told.

I'm tired of living like this, Billy, and Chelsea is not going to grow up seeing you beat me anymore, because we are both leaving you. If you follow me I will do to you what Adam did to the last man who abused me. Maybe it runs in the family, Billy. I realize now that you are not much better than the man that Adam killed.

Ruth Ann

She was crying as she folded the letter and wrote "Billy" on it, and then left it on the tabletop. She was not crying for the loss of her marriage, she was crying for regaining the dignity that she lost a long time ago. She sat for a moment and gazed at the gingham curtains she had sewn. Billy called them prissy, and tore them down every time he got upset. The broken plasterboard by the door was where he had rammed her head into the wall, then ripped her clothes off, and had his way with her, while Chelsea cried in her high chair. She tried to make the marriage work, but the more she thought about it, the more she knew that could never happen. Billy was an animal and she knew she couldn't live like this anymore.

Ruth Ann went to the back porch and got the suitcase that she packed the night before when Billy was at work, and set it by the front door. She checked her coat pockets for the tickets and money. Chelsea was sleeping on the couch and she picked her up and whispered to her to calm her fussing. She opened the door and, cradling Chelsea in her right arm, grabbed the suitcase with her other hand and started down the sidewalk. The tears had stopped, and her head was high. She was convinced that she was doing the right thing. When she got to the corner, she turned right, and walked down one more block to the cabstand and sat down and waited. She watched back down the sidewalk, still scared that he might have woke up and followed her, but just some little kids riding their big wheels was all she could see. It seemed longer, but it was only a few minutes before a cab pulled up, and Ruth Ann, with her sleepy child, slid into the back seat while the young black driver put her suitcase in the trunk. "Cleveland Municipal Airport," she said.

"Yes, Ma'am," he said. "Taking a little vacation, are you?"

"Yes we are. We're taking a little vacation, aren't we Chelsea? A vacation from hell."

The cab driver did not answer, but studied her in the rearview mirror. Maybe he had said the wrong thing. He turned the music up a little on the radio.

The big day was here. Was it the day of atonement, or the day of conviction? Time would tell. At nine-fifteen, Adam was escorted over to the courthouse from the jail. He and Tony were given a few minutes to talk, and then they both entered the courtroom through a side door with their escort. Adam did have leg irons on, which forced him to walk in little shuffling steps, but his arms were free and he looked good in his new Brooks Brothers suit that Tony brought. The suit was dark blue, with a faint pin stripe, and the light blue shirt was a perfect match. His tie was dark blue, with touches of light blue and red. They went straight to their table and sat down.

It was very bright in the courthouse. The huge windows set up high in the walls, let the sunlight stream into the big room, which was painted a stark white. White ceiling fans turned lazily in the air making small whispering sounds. The fans were set in the midst of round globe light fixtures that hung on slender rods about every ten feet. Back of the judge's bench was a painting of "Washington Crossing The Delaware," that fateful night. To the left of the painting, hung a replica of the "Declaration of Independence," and on the right, a copy of "The Preamble To The Constitution."

Adam turned and looked behind him into the gallery. He could see his older sister and her husband. To their right sat Linda and Alice and, yes, Ruth Ann! Ruthy gave him a small wave and a smile. Adam smiled back and mouthed, "Thank you." It had been so long since he had seen her. She looked so small and delicate. He scanned the rest of the crowd, and then the judge walked in and the bailiff asked all to rise.

"District Court 371 - in and for the County of Aspen, is in session," the bailiff announced.

Everybody was still standing when the nine women and three men were led to the jury box. Judge Persons then asked that the jury be seated and the rest of the courtroom followed suit. Adam didn't recognize any of them, except for Ida Pribbinow. She had been a teacher at the high school in Aspen. Not his teacher, but if you went to school there, you would have known her. She always had a stern, austere look about her.

"Here is a list of things I will not tolerate in this courtroom. I am telling you right up front so there will be no confusion." The judge looked down his nose through his reading glasses, from his high perch, while he read from a laminated sheet of paper he held in his right hand. "First of all, to the spectators and interested parties in the audience, let me just say: keep quiet. That means what I just said, and I will not elaborate." He went on to address both attorneys and the jury. Ida Pribbinow was the only one taking notes, and she was writing furiously.

"Now lets get right into this. This trial is to determine the presumed innocence or guilt of one Adam Holton. He must be seen as innocent of the crimes he is accused of, in this courtroom, until such time as he is proven guilty beyond the shadow of a doubt. The crimes I am referring to are the killing of one Mark Stevenson, on October seventh of last year, and the defendant's subsequent flight to avoid prosecution.

Would the tall lady from the jury in the red dress, who is taking notes so intently, please look up here?" Ida stopped writing and looked up at the judge.

"Madam, we do have a court transcriber. That would be this young lady sitting right below me, pecking away on that machine. I am afraid you are going to miss something if you do not pay attention up here." He pointed to himself. "You can take notes, but you don't have to write down every word that is spoken. That's what she is here for." He pointed down to the young woman, who was visibly embarrassed. "That being said, lets get on with it."

Ida, looking ruffled, closed her notebook but still held the pencil in her hand, poised for writing.

"We will ask the prosecuting attorney to make his opening statement to the jury at this time." The judge then blew his nose, before turning off his microphone. The courtroom reacted with giggles and he rapped his gavel once. "I apologize," the old judge said.

Francis Heitla walked quietly over to address the jury. The only notes he had were written on index cards he palmed in his hand. He appeared meek and diminutive, but his voice had an air of authority in it. He now transformed from his passive look to a more "in charge" look.

"Ladies and gentleman of the jury. In the next few days I will attempt to explain to all of you, why this man," he stopped to point at Adam, "is guilty of murder in the second degree, and the other charges against him. We will show and prove to you that he premeditated the killing of Mark Stevenson last October, and then fled. Never mind his reasons for doing what he did, that will come out in this trial. He broke the law, and that is all there is to it. He has admitted to that. His vigilante behavior took the life of a man the courts had already acquitted. In fact he was acquitted in this very courtroom, and was standing on the steps outside, when Adam Holton gunned him down. I ask that you keep in mind that the law is the law, and no one is above it. He has pleaded not guilty to this crime. The only way that can be true is if he didn't do it." Francis looked at his index cards and shuffled through them, but then, as if thinking better of it, he put them in his jacket pocket. "Thank you," he said, seeming to revert to his meek posture, and walked back to his chair.

Tony waited until the judge indicated that is was his turn, then rose and walked to the jury. In contrast to Heitla in his crumpled gray suit, Tony seemed dominating and regal. He wore a navy blue corduroy blazer with gold buttons, and leather patches over the elbows, gray slacks and a western shirt, with a black string bow tie, that Bat Masterson must have put in style. His cowboy boots echoed across the courtroom, off the hard wood floors, as he approached the jury box looking bigger than he already was. The jurors, who had treated Heitla with some indifference, seemed to be locked onto him.

"My fellow citizens of the jury," Tony said. "As the prosecuting attorney brought up, Adam Holton is accused of killing Mark Stevenson. We do not need to spend much time proving that in this courtroom, do we? He has admitted to it. He is a self-professed killer. But that is not the whole truth. And the truth is what we are after. The truth is what has to come out here, or there will be no justice for anyone. Murder is condoned in some instances in our society. When it happens, it usually is not called murder. Webster calls it a lot of things: Homicide, annihilation, slaying, putting an end to, - but it is all murder. Counsel says that Adam broke the law and that is all there is to it. If he killed someone, he was wrong, end of story. Well, people, I am here to tell you, it's not that simple." Tony stood in front of the railing that separated the jury from the rest of the courtroom. He leaned over, putting his big hands flat on the rail and made eye contact with each of them, as he talked.

"Every day in this country, many people are murdered, and the reasons for doing so most of the time are not in accordance with the law. But there are exceptions, my friends, and I intend to show them to you. I ask that you have an open mind and follow this trial closely."

Ida Pribbinow had been listening so intently she seemed to be hypnotized. One of the three men on the jury, the youngest of them, sat with his finger pursing his lips, deep in thought, slowly moving his head up and down in agreement.

Tony had been watching the Judge out of the corner of his eye and saw him pick up his gavel. He knew that he was about three words short of getting a lecture. The Judge would tell him, *Just make an opening statement, counsel. Do not try the case right here and right now.* But that was what made him a good attorney. He knew how to push the jury's buttons, and he also knew when not to push the judge's.

"I want to thank you all before this trial ever starts, for serving on this jury; For taking time out of your busy lives to help us find the truth. In the end, I know we will." Tony glanced at the Judge again and saw him roll his eyes, as if to say: *Why don't you just lean over and kiss them?*

Judge Persons sounded his gavel and looked at his watch. "I am going to call a recess for lunch. Let's all be back here at one thirty."

Adam stood to be escorted back to the jail for lunch. He had sat passively through the morning procedures, stealing glances from time to time at Linda, Alice, and Ruth Ann. He was still not sure what part Ruth Ann was going to play, but Tony was adamant that it was necessary for her to testify. Tony's confidence bolstered Adam's, and right now he was feeling good about things, but he knew they had a long way to go.

CHAPTER TWENTY-FOUR

Linda and Alice both listened as Tony talked across the supper table at the Mine Shaft, one of the few nice restaurants available to them in Aspen. They were not talking about the case, because Tony forbade them, but instead had been talking about Linda's ranch, and Tony was trying to encourage her to sell it. Linda listened to him but didn't really agree, and Alice had been lost in the conversation for the last few minutes.

"You know land prices in that part of Missoula have never been higher and, ---just a moment," he said as he dug in his pocket for his cell phone. "Tony Winters here." Tony's face showed a look of concern at first, but now it was breaking out in a subtle smile as he listened to the caller. "You sure about this? Well, I'll be damned. I knew we were only scratching the surface. Look, get me her name and number. Leave it on my voice mail at the hotel, but don't mention in your message what it's about, - and great work, Brandon." Tony slapped the table with his big palm, almost spilling their water glasses. "Remember that half-lawyer, half private-dick, I told you I hired?" Alice and Linda both said that they did. "He's the one who found out about Ruth Ann. Well, he's been doing some questioning around town about Mark Stevenson for me. Long story short, he found another victim."

Her name was Laura Erickson, and she worked in housekeeping at the Holiday Inn in Aspen, the same hotel where Tony and his party were staying. She was also a good friend of Francis Heitla's wife, Amy. Amy had been Laura's tutor in school, and their friendship continued until the Stevenson trial, when Francis lost the case, and Stevenson went free, Laura had been very disappointed and stopped seeing Amy. She had never understood the connection.

Laura was a short, slightly pudgy young woman of about thirty, who had been diagnosed with a learning disorder when she was twelve. Through special tutoring from Amy, she had made a lot of progress, and after graduating from high school she got this job at the hotel. She had worked here now for over twelve years and she loved her work, and they loved her. But it almost came to a halt a little over a year ago.

Mark Stevenson had stayed at the hotel for a few days, and one day, under the pretense of needing more towels, he lured Laura into his room. Once in the room, he made advances towards her, and when she refused, Mark became violent. He had raped her repeatedly and then held a knife to her throat saying: "If you tell anyone about this, I will kill you."

When Stevenson was indicted a few months later for killing Mandy, she had planned to break her silence and tell her story, but before she could get her act together, the case had been thrown out of court, and he was free again. Laura remembered his threat, and clammed up. After Adam killed Stevenson, she thought it was time to get on with her life and forget about the whole thing. He was dead and no threat to anyone, anymore.

The next morning before the trial started, she repeated her whole story to Tony at the hotel. She saw Francis Heitla as defending Stevenson, not prosecuting Adam. The truth about this man had to be told, even if it came from someone as simple as Laura, and even it came in someone else's trial.

For Tony, it was a day of mixed emotions. He had the witness that could push the verdict over the edge, but how could he use her? There was no way he could put this fragile woman on the stand. He took the risk of destroying her emotionally. Just her talking to Tony this morning had been gut wrenching to listen to, and the courtroom would be a whole different scene. One other question nagged at Tony, and that was how close Francis Heitla was to this whole thing. After all, it was his wife who had been this girl's mentor. He had to think about this and there wasn't a lot of time. The prosecution was only calling a few witnesses.

Day two of the trial was a cold, blustery northern Minnesota day, and the spectators in court were all dressed in last winter's jackets. It had rained during the night, but as daylight came over the small rural community, the sun poked over the eastern horizon with its usual promise of warmth. But instead, the day became windy and colder. From time to time the rain would change to snow pellets, a mixture between snow and sleet.

Adam had spent a restless night. Watching Tony work yesterday had bolstered his confidence. But when Francis Heitla's said the words; *He took a man's life, and no matter the reason, it was against the law,* still rang in his ears.

The prosecution would go first, so after all of the daily formalities with the judge and the jury was completed, Francis Heitla called his first witness to the stand.

"Your Honor, the prosecution calls Attorney Jerome Klein to the stand." Jerry Klein was all of eighty and maybe closer to ninety years old. He had practiced law in the Aspen area all of his life, and at one time had been known as a reliable defense attorney. The only thing he was known for now was falling asleep in court.

The bailiff presented the Bible to him. "Do you swear to tell the truth, the whole truth, and nothing but the truth?"

"Huh?" muttered Kline. "Oh that, yes... yes I will. Where do you want me, Judge?"

"In the witness chair, please." Judge Persons gave him a disgusted look. *"Sixty years in a courtroom and he still hasn't a clue,"* he mumbled under his breath.

Francis Heitla approached the witness, and clearing his throat said, "Mr. Kline would you tell this court who you are, and what your occupation is?"

"I am an attorney at law, and have been for longer then most of you can remember."

"Yes, Mr. Kline. Would you state your name, please?"

"Jerry Kline and that's with a J, dear." He leaned over and smiled at the young woman who was transcribing.

"Mr. Kline, were you hired to represent Mark Stevenson at a hearing on October fifth, nineteen ninety nine in this court room?"

"Yes... yes, I was."

"What was that hearing about?"

"I believe he had been accused of income tax invasion." Kline wiped his face with a red bandana he had taken out of his jacket pocket. He had a habit of drooling.

"Was he released?"

"Yes."

"You and Mr. Stevenson then walked out of the courtroom together, is that correct?"

"Something like that."

"Would you tell this court what happened next?"

"Well, some damn fool shot him in the head and damn near shot me too. Scared the shit out of me." Judge Persons shook his head slowly to show his disapproval, but said nothing.

"Mr. Kline, did you see the man who did that?" Francis figured he better keep it rolling.

"Bet your ass, I did."

"Mr. Kline," Judge Persons interjected. "You, of all people have been in courtrooms enough to know that you can't use language like that. Now clean it up, or shut it up. Strike that last comment," he said to the transcriber.

She looked at the judge, confused.

"Not what I said! What he said."

Kline meanwhile, looked at the Judge with an angry, confused look but did not comment.

"Francis took over again, before he did say something else that would get him thrown out of court. "Mr. Kline, do you see the person who shot Mark Stevenson here today?"

Kline stared at Adam for a moment. "Sure I do," he said. "Sitting right there!" and he pointed at Adam, his hand shaking from the results of Parkinson's, or anger, Francis wasn't sure.

"Mr. Kline..." Francis wanted to ask him something else, but at the last minute, changed his mind. "No more questions, Your Honor."

"Would the defense like to cross examine the witness?" the judge asked Tony.

"No, Your Honor. In light of the fact that my client has admitted to killing Mark Stevenson, I find it not very relevant."

"Suit yourself, Counselor. Can't say I disagree. Witness is excused."

Kline either did not hear or was not paying attention, so he remained sitting, smiling at Ida Pribbinow in the jury box.

"Mr. Kline, you are excused!" the exasperated judge almost shouted.

Kline got up and shuffled down the aisle and out the door.

The next witness was Todd Belling, a deputy who had been standing on the steps when the fatal shot was fired. Todd took his testimony very seriously and had the demeanor of a Nazi Storm Trooper.

"I was standing on the front steps when the shot was fired, and looking up at the roof of the Federated Building, I saw the defendant still standing there holding a smoking rifle. Another deputy was standing there talking to me." Then, as if qualifying his statement, he said: "The other deputy hadn't seen where the shot had come from. I yelled to the other deputy to follow me and we rushed to the building, but by the time we found our way to the roof, he was gone." Todd, sitting rigid in the witness chair, waited for the next question.

Ida Pribbinow used the moment of quiet to sneeze, and the jurist next to her said, "God bless you." Ida reached over and patted the woman's sleeve and smiled. Judge Persons shook his head, as if to say, *what next* and ran his fingers through his thin gray hair.

"Your Honor," Francis said, "The prosecution would like to enter into evidence this rifle which was found on the roof of the Federated Building by Deputy Belling and his partner. This is the rifle you found, is it not, Deputy?"

Belling made a point to get up and walk over to the table and pick up the rifle and examine it. "Yes sir, I would say this sure looks like the one we found. Got that nick in the stock that I noticed. Same scope on it, damn fine rifle it is."

"Thank you, Deputy. Do you see the man who was on that roof, holding this rifle, here in this courtroom?"

"Yes I do." He pointed at Adam.

"No more questions, Your Honor." Francis walked back, and sitting down, went back to his notes.

"Any cross examination from the defense?"

"No, Your Honor," said Tony.

"I don't think we have time for any more witnesses this morning, so I am gong to ask for a recess for lunch. Court will resume at one-thirty, sharp." Persons rapped his gavel once, and left in a flurry of black robe.

Tony washed down his club sandwich with a glass of milk, while Alice and Linda had tuna salad. Most of the lunch talk was about the prosecution's witnesses, and what a waste of time it had been, but he did understand that his perception of the trial, and the jury's take on it, were two different things. Waste of time or not, you had to go through the paces. He glanced at his watch, and then told Alice he would call her as soon as the case went to the jury. She had to leave tonight because she simply could not get any more time off work.

"I have to have a conference with the judge and Heitla today," Tony said. There is no way I can put Laura on the stand, and I'm hoping they will allow a video- taped interview, with both attorneys present."

Linda asked, "What about Ruth Ann?"

"Nope, she definitely needs to take the stand. The big difference here is, she is his sister. We need to use that to our advantage, but it will have to be done carefully." Tony waved his hand for the check and then gave the waitress his credit card. When she returned with his receipt he handed her a five-dollar tip. He checked his watch again and said. "We better hurry back."

Court was back in session just like the judge had promised, at one-thirty. The prosecution called its third witness, a man from the State Bureau of Criminal Apprehension.

John Plummer had been an agent for the B.C.A. for over thirty years. He was a tall, handsome man who looked a lot like Cary Grant to those who remembered Cary Grant. He was dressed in a gray pinstriped suit and a white shirt. He entered wearing a dark gray trench coat, which he shed before he took the stand, taking the time to drape it carefully over his chair. Then he approached the witness stand and was sworn in.

"Please tell the Court your name and occupation," Heitla said.

"My name is John J. Plummer and I am a Special Agent for the Bureau of Criminal Apprehension for the State of Minnesota. I work in the Ballistics Lab."

"Agent Plummer, you were the one who did the tests on the rifle that was used to commit this crime, is that correct?"

"I did the testing of that rifle. That is correct." He pointed to the rifle on the table.

Judge Persons raised his eyebrows at his carefully worded answer. He hated these so-called experts, with there hoity-toity ways.

Heitla was back. "What were your conclusions?"

"The bullet that killed Mark Stevenson, although badly damaged, was fired from that rifle. It was a one hundred and eighty grain

Remington rifle slug. The marks on the slug matched the marks on the casing that was still in the rifle. There were still three bullets in the clip of the same brand and size, and there was half a box of the same kind in the defendant's home."

"I have no other questions, Your Honor." Plummer looked as if he had been cheated out of his performance by having such a short time in the witness chair.

"The witness may step down if there is no cross-examination. Is there, Counsel?" He looked at Tony.

Tony just shook his head and chuckled. "No further questions from me, Your Honor."

"Are there any other witnesses or evidence to be admitted by the prosecution?" asked the judge.

"No, Your Honor," said Heitla. "The prosecution rests."

"Your Honor, I ask for permission to approach the bench," Tony said.

"Permission granted, Counselor, and Mr. Heitla please come up, also."

"Your Honor I have a witness that we would like to have testify, but she has a mental condition that would make this very hard on her. So hard, that I am reluctant to use her if she has to testify in this court. Her testimony is very relevant to our case and very important to this case, I might add. I am asking permission to video-tape it for the jury."

Adam was sitting forward in his chair, trying to hear what was being said. Tony had coached him about Laura, and told Adam what he was going to try and do.

Judge Persons asked Francis Heitla, "Do you object to this form of testimony, Counselor?"

"Not as long as I can be there when she is interviewed."

"Agreed, Mr. Winter?"

"Agreed," said Tony.

"When do you intend to do this, Mr. Winter?" asked Heitla.

"How about this evening at this location?"

Francis said that it was okay with him.

Tony returned to his table and motioned to Brandon, who was sitting behind him, to lean forward. "Set it up with Laura for this evening," was all he said. He turned and squeezed Adam's shoulder and smiled.

Judge Persons shuffled some papers; his reading glasses perched on the end of his nose. "Because it is late, we will not get into the defense portion of this trial today. We will resume tomorrow morning at ten a.m. Once again, I caution the jury to not discuss this case with anyone. Not even your families. Ida, you hear that?"

Ida looked up from digging in her bag, and smiled. She drew her finger across her lips in a symbol of silence.

Judge Persons leaned over the bench and said to the court reporter, "She said she wouldn't say anything. Put that down."

"Court is recessed!" the bailiff hollered.

They had an early supper, and then Tony returned to the hotel to get ready for tonight's interview with Laura. Brandon called and said it was all set. Laura and her parents, who insisted on being with her, would be there at seven.

Tony said goodbye to Alice, and urged her not to worry about things. Like the shadows of night, things are always darkest just before the new day comes. He asked Linda to call Ruth Ann, and have her stay with her tonight in place of Alice. Linda was a little surprised by this, because she didn't know Ruth Ann, and because she had wanted to reward Tony for all of his hard work tonight, but right now that was the last thing on Tony's mind. He had to stay focused.

Adam sat in his cell and pondered all that had happened so far. It all seemed so insignificant to him when he thought about the prosecution's case, but in a sense he was also disappointed. He had expected Tony to blow the prosecution's case out of the water, not ignore it. A copy of today's paper was on the foot of his bed, and it seemed slanted toward the prosecution in their coverage. He opened a new pack of smokes, and lit a new one off the butt of the one he had just finished. He was tired, but sleep wouldn't come easily tonight. He thought of Alice and her concerned look in the courtroom today. He thought of Ruth Ann going on the stand tomorrow, and he thought of Mandy, buried up on the hill, at the other end of town.

They all met in the courtroom, and then Judge Persons told them they would be going over to the jail for the testimony. They had all of the necessary video and audio equipment over there.

Laura was dressed in a red dress with a flowery blouse. She held her mother's hand almost all of the time and said little, except to smile and say "hi." Her dad gripped his hat and only murmured, "glad to meet you," when he was introduced to Tony and the judge. They were a quiet family.

Francis was late, and burst into the room at the last minute, apologizing for his tardiness. He saw Tony and the judge when he rushed in, but then turning, saw Laura and her family. He seemed confused. Turning to Tony, he asked, "Is this your witness... this...Laura?" His face was ashen. He fumbled for words.

Laura seemed unmoved and unconcerned, by his startled reaction.

"Judge, can Mr. Winters and I talk for a moment, before we start?" Francis seemed annoyed.

"Certainly," said Judge Persons. Turning to Laura and her parents he said, "Mr. and Mrs. Erickson, Laura, we're going to do this over at the sheriff's office at the end of this hall. They have the equipment we'll need. If you want to start over there, we'll be right with you. They're expecting you. Now, what is it, Francis?"

Turning to Tony, Heitla seemed to stand a little taller. "This young woman is testifying for the defense? About what?"

"You seem to be upset," said Tony.

"Never mind me. How is Laura Erickson involved in this case?" Francis was getting more worked up by the moment, talking louder and waving his hands.

"She was raped by Mark Stevenson. Do you know her?" Tony said it very softly, but the words hit Francis like a ton of bricks.

He sat down on one of the benches. Regaining his composure, and ignoring Tony's question, he became defensive. "You do know Mark Stevenson is not on trial here? Adam Holton is."

"I assure you, this girl's testimony is relevant."

Judge Persons had remained neutral up to this point. "Let's take her statement, and if it's not proper I can rule on that before we let the jury see it."

Heitla shook his head, no, slowly, but he didn't mean, "no." He didn't know what he meant right now. He was thoroughly confused. The three men walked over to the sheriff's office.

CHAPTER TWENTY-FIVE

The technician from the sheriff's office had all the equipment set up for them. She was a female officer, no older than thirty, and that helped to ease Laura's fears. She joked with her, and told her how pretty she looked in her new dress. Laura giggled and said, "thank you." It was obvious to the others in the room, including the camera operator, that Laura was handicapped.

From the time Tony had talked to Laura yesterday, until now, he worried about how he could interview Laura and get her to open up. He knew he was opening up something else. Some deep emotional wounds, and he had to be careful.

If Laura was aware of Francis Heitla being in the room, she didn't show it. It was as if she even forgot who he was. Tony had worried about that, so he tried to keep her focused on him. Judge Persons, along with Laura's father, stayed in the background being as inconspicuous as possible. Her mother sat next to her, but off camera.

Tony pulled a chair up, so he was facing Laura, trying hard to smile through his concerns.

"You will need to move back, Counselor," the deputy behind the camera said. "I have the back of your head in the picture."

Tony slid his chair straight back a couple of feet and slumped a little, saying, "How's this?"

"That's fine, but you're still blocking the shot and Laura isn't very tall, Maybe if we found her a higher chair. I would like the picture to come almost straight on." She left the room and returned with a stool. Finally, with everybody in place, they were ready to start the testimony. "Camera is on," she said.

"Let's swear her in," the judge said, and came forward with a Bible and handed it to Laura's mother. "Laura, would you put your hand on the Bible your mother is holding, and repeat after me. I will tell the truth tonight about everything I say, so help me God."

"I will tell the truth tonight," she said. "I always tell the truth." She looked at her mother, who nodded, yes.

There was a knock at the door, and a striking older woman in a gray business suit, stood there. The judge went to meet her and announced to the others that this was Patricia Sanderson, a Clinical Psychiatrist for Aspen County. She was there only to observe the questioning. She smiled, and waving her hand, said, "hi."

Tony looked from her, to Laura. He was ready to start.

"Laura, I would like to ask you a couple of questions about yourself before we get started. First, I will say for the camera: that I am Tony Winters, the defense attorney, and I represent Adam Holton in this trial, and that I have talked with you on one other occasion, Laura. Do you remember that?"

Laura nodded her head.

"You will have to say yes, or no, Laura."

"Yes."

"Will you tell us your name and where you work?"

"My name is Laura and I work at the Holiday Inn."

"Your full name, Laura?"

She seemed confused for a moment and looked at her mother who whispered "Erickson," loud enough so they all heard it.

"Erickson. Laura Erickson," she repeated.

"What is it you do at the Holiday Inn?" Tony asked.

"I wash bedding and towels and sometimes they let me help make up beds, and put the towels in the bathrooms.... soap too, sometimes." She seemed nervous, but was smiling, and clasped her hands together and pushed her dress down between her thighs with her hands, while holding her legs tightly together.

"Laura, I want you to think about a time...no, just forget what I said for a moment." Tony paused to think, and then came back with a different question. "If I said the name Mark Stevenson to you, do you know who I am talking about?"

Her smile disappeared. "He's bad," she said, looking down at her lap. Then brightening up a bit, she said, "Mom says he's dead, and.... and that I don't have to worry about him anymore." She straightened her dress and put her hands back up on the table.

"Did he hurt you, Laura?"

"Yes!" She said very emphatically.

"Where were you when he hurt you, Laura?"

She was on the verge of tears.

"Have a drink of your water," her mother suggested.

Laura sipped from the glass of water and then she smoothed out her dress again.

"I was at work."

"Did you go to a room where he was staying?" She nodded her head, looking at her feet.

'Look up here, Laura," Tony said, holding his hand to his face. "Yes, or no, - you went to his room?"

"Yes. To bring him towels."

It was hot in the room, and Tony stopped to wipe his brow. Francis Heitla had taken off his jacket, and sat down in the corner of the room behind Tony, and next to the judge. He seemed deeply disturbed by the questioning, refusing to make eye contact with Laura.

"When you went to the room, did you knock?"

"Yes. I knocked and said, "Housekeeping." That's what Brianna told me to do."

"Brianna is your boss?"

"Yes," she answered.

"Did he come to the door, or where was he in the room when you got there?"

Laura seemed to be thinking very hard. Those terrible memories that she tried to forget, and now they wanted her to talk about them. It was so hard. So hard to do.

Tony turned to look at those behind him. Laura's father was biting his lip; the judge seemed stoic and unmoved. Francis was sitting with his head in his hands, listening, but not watching. Patricia remained standing, her arms crossed over her chest, her coat and bag hanging from one arm. She, like the judge, seemed impassive for now.

"He was in the bed."

"Then what did he do?"

"He held up some money, and said, here's a tip for being so nice and bringing me the towels."

There were tears in her eyes now, but Tony knew he had to continue, or he might lose her.

"Did you go to get the money?"

"Yes. Brianna said it was all right to take tips."

"Did he give you the money?"

"No! He grabbed me and pulled me into the bed!"

"Did he have clothes on?"

Laura was staring straight ahead, and the tears were running down her cheeks. Her mother reached across and gently wiped her face and kissed her cheek.

"He didn't have any clothes on. And told me to take mine off! I didn't want to, but he ripped my dress, and I didn't want to have my clothes ripped, so I took it off. I only have two white dresses."

"Did you take off everything you were wearing?" Tony asked.

"He took off my underpants," she said, "and my brassiere. He tore that too, and it hurt me."

Francis Heitla shook his head in his hands and moaned. The judge asked him if there was a problem, but he didn't answer.

"After he took off your underclothes, did he touch you anywhere?" Tony asked.

Laura started crying again, and once again her folded hands went between her thighs, and her legs were clenched tightly together.

"He put his fingers inside of me, and told me how pretty I was. Then he got up on his knees, and put a pillow over my head so I couldn't see! I could hardly breathe! He put something inside of me that hurt very bad." She was sobbing now, and Tony told the Tech to shut off the camera for a moment.

"I think we have the idea, Counselor, why don't we quit?" Heitla looked at Tony with an almost pleading look.

"Just a couple more questions," Tony said. "Patricia?" he asked, looking for her support. She just pursed her lips and shrugged her shoulders.

"Laura?" Tony said. Her mother had seemed to quiet her down. Mrs. Erickson moved her chair closer to Laura and had her arm around her daughters shoulder talking quietly to her. Laura's mother was almost in tears herself, her eyes were also pleading with Tony, but she said nothing.

"Laura, we are almost done, honey. Can you sit back in front of the table for just a few minutes?"

Laura sat up straight on the stool, snuffling.

"Turn the camera back on," said the judge.

Tony gave her a few more seconds, and then continued.

"Laura, after he hurt you, did he talk to you?"

"Yes."

"What did he say to you?"

"He told me if I ever told anyone what he had done, he would kill me."

"Did you ever see him again?"

"No. He's dead, and I am glad he is dead! He is dead, - right, Mom?"

"Yes, Laura," she said.

"No further questions," Tony said.

"Would you like to ask anything, Counselor?" The judge was talking to Francis.

"No. My God, no!" he said.

"Please shut off the camera," said the judge. The tech running the camera had also been crying, and she wiped her face on her sleeve as she reached up and shut it off.

Tony was kneeling in front of Laura, who had moved to a chair closer to her mother. "You were so brave," he said, his eyes threatening tears. "You are right, sweetheart, the man who hurt you is dead, and now, we need to keep the man who stopped him from hurting anybody else, out of prison. You have helped him so much. I am so proud of you." Tony hugged her, biting his lips to hold back the tears. There were things about this job that disgusted him, - and this was one of them.

Francis lived in a large white duplex high up on, what the people of Aspen called, Snob Hill. He and his wife Amy had lived there in a secluded way for over thirty years. They often sat on the porch in the summer; in a big white porch swing that hung right by the front door, and watched the traffic go by. In the winter you could always see Francis at night sitting in his chair by the window, reading his paper, and Amy across the room doing needlepoint or knitting. Before being elected to the County Attorney's Office, Francis had had a practice downtown, with a partner.

Amy, on the other hand, busied herself with her teaching career. She had wanted children of her own so much, but it wasn't possible because Francis had been left sterile from childhood mumps. She tutored Laura privately for many years, and after Laura graduated from school, they remained friends, until Mark Stevenson's trial. Laura had kept her secret for over two years, but promised herself, if Mark Stevenson went to jail for killing Mandy, she would tell on him, and the first person she would tell would be Amy Heitla.

As soon as Stevenson beat the rap, Laura would no longer talk to

Amy. She saw the failure of the justice system as Francis Heitla's failure, and Amy was an extension of him. At first Amy didn't understand and was hurt, but gradually she thought maybe Laura was just striking out on her own, and she was happy for her.

Francis dropped his briefcase on the floor by the door and threw his coat over a chair. Amy could tell he was troubled, but she wasn't alarmed. He was moody from time to time, but he always got over it.

"Long day, dear?" she asked, looking up from her needlepoint. "There's some veal in the oven for you, if you're hungry."

Francis didn't know where to start. He sat down in his chair and stared at Amy for a long time. Long enough to make her nervous.

"Franny, what's bothering you?"

"How long has it been since you saw Laura Erickson?" He looked irritated.

"I don't know," she said. "Is there a problem?"

"There was a problem. I'm not sure there is one now."

Now Amy was getting confused, and even more nervous. "You're scaring me, Franny. Come out and say what you have to say, and quit playing games."

Francis told her the whole story, everything that had come out in the deposition tonight.

Amy was shocked, but now it made sense why Laura had quit coming to see her. "We failed her, Franny. You failed to convict Mark Stevenson and she never understood why."

"How would that affect her relationship with you, Amy? I lost the case, not you."

"Francis, you would have to know Laura, like I knew her. She would never figure that out. She saw us both as one, sweetheart. Yes, come to think of it, it was about that time that she quit calling. Oh! I feel so bad now."

Amy was sitting curled in the corner of a love seat, and Francis went over and sat down beside her, but not before he poured about two inches of scotch into a glass from a crystal decanter sitting on the bar across the room. "Why did I ever run for this horseshit job, Amy? Why did

I ever leave that office on Barton Street, and Harry, the best partner you could have? I had it made. I wish I could have given you a child, darling." He tipped his glass back and drank about half of it. Then he loosened his tie. Setting the glass down on the end table, he put his arm around her. He took her glasses off and set them in her lap with her needlepoint. She transferred all of it to the end table. Francis loved this kind, gentle woman totally, and he had been rude to her. Not directly, but still rude. He kissed her lightly. Her lips were soft and moist. Then he unpinned the mother of pearl broach she wore on her high collared blouse, and opened the garment a couple of buttons.

"Why Franny, are you looking for something?" she asked, smiling coyly.

He lay down and curled up with his head in her lap, while she unfastened the rest of her blouse and unhooked her bra in the front. Her tiny breasts stood out as perky as they had twenty-some years ago, when he had first laid eyes on them. Her nipples were the same pink hue they had been way back then. Those breasts had never nursed a baby, but should have. She would have been a terrific mother. He closed his eyes and she deftly cradled his head in her arms. Francis drew his legs up and was soon fast asleep. She stroked his hair and sang softly to him. *"Lullaby and good night Oh my darling sleep tight. God is with you through the night. ----"*

CHAPTER TWENTY-SIX

Tony awoke refreshed. Yesterday had been brutal, but today he would get his turn to show his stuff, and so far this trial had gone better than he expected it would. He stayed away from Linda last night on purpose; he had to stay focused even though the prosecution seemed to be out of it.

Ruth Ann and Linda spent the evening in the hotel's pub having a couple of get-acquainted drinks. Ruth Ann's sister was taking care of Chelsea.

Adam experienced a good night too. He had a surprise visitor last night after visiting hours were over. He was reading in his cell when he heard footsteps coming down the hallway. Two pair. Then, there was Blaine's familiar face at the door's window asking if he was asleep. Some nights Blaine stopped to visit, so Adam said, "No, come on in."

"Well, I can't stay, but I brought you a visitor." Then, as quickly as they arrived, the two men stepped inside the cell. It was dark, and the visitor was in the shadows, but suddenly Adam's pulse quickened as he recognized the man. It was Joe Adcock. Sheriff Joe. Blaine turned on the light and left. Adam was speechless, but Joe quickly broke the ice.

"How are you, son? I heard about you turning yourself in a few days ago, so I called Percy and he said, Yup! He's right here, right now. I kind of got out of touch living down there in Arizona. You know, I'm retired now. Adam, I am going to cut right to the chase here. I came back to help you, son."

"Help me, how? The last time I remember you, you were chasing me across the countryside."

Joe smiled. There were still two dimples in that old weather-beaten face "Got a cigarette? Let's talk about it." Adam fished out a couple of beat up Marlboros from his shirt pocket, and they shared the lighter Joe had in his pants pocket. Joe took a deep drag and then said, "Let's sit down. This might take a while." The two men sat side by side on the cot, flicking their ashes into the toilet stool.

Smiling slightly at Adam, Joe said, "You know, you scalawag, when you killed Mark Stevenson you did what almost every man in my department wanted to do for a long time, but couldn't. In law enforcement, we called it poetic justice. But it isn't always poetic because those same laws that protect the innocent, sometimes help the wrong people, and that's what happened to you."

"I had a twin brother, Adam, and we both were good football players. But in our senior year, my brother Lonnie went to a different high school in Duluth where we grew up. He had made up his mind to become a priest. When football season came along, my dad was so damn frustrated because we both played on the same nights, in different towns. That is, until the last game of the season, Central against Cathedral, both undefeated. Dad was in his glory that night. Both teams played hard, and it was still nothing to nothing with a minute left in the game, when Central kicked a field goal for three points. I was playing linebacker, and Lonnie was a fullback. Got any more smokes?" he asked. "I left mine in the car."

Adam reached under the bed and pulled out a carton and flipped Joe a pack. "None for me, thanks," he said.

Joe was quiet while he patiently unwrapped the pack of cigarettes, shook one out, and lit it, blowing a smoke ring that drifted over his head.

"There was very little time left when we kicked off to them, and they got the ball on about their own forty. They were out of 'time outs' and had maybe a couple of plays left. We figured they would pass, but Lonnie got the ball, and broke around the right end, at the same time that our safety, and outside linebacker, blitzed, and over-ran the play. It was Lonnie and I, heading for their goal line, diagonally across the field."

Joe leaned back against the wall. "You know, Adam, on my worst day I could catch Lonnie in a foot race, but we rambled for those forty yards. I dove for him at the ten-yard line, but came down hard and dislocated my shoulder and broke my collarbone. I heard it snap, as Lonnie went over the goal line. The next thing I could remember was lying on that ten-yard line in my brother's arms, while he cried and told me how sorry he was. Hell, the stadium didn't have a dry eye in it. My dad came out on the field crying too, and hugged us both. He was so damn proud of both of us." Joe stopped to reflect and scratched his head. "What's this got to do with Adam Holton, you say? I was the only one who chased you across the county that day, Adam. You had a ninety-mile an hour, at best, beat up Chevy pickup that was smoking so damn bad I could hardly see the road behind you. I had a new Ford Crown Vic, with a police package that would do one hundred and forty. I had a radio that could have called help from everywhere, but I shut it off. I didn't catch you, son, because I didn't want to. Just like I didn't want to catch Lonnie on that ten-yard line that night."

It was quiet for a moment. "I came back to make it right, Adam. I'd like to talk to your attorney before tomorrow."

"Sheriff, I..."

Joe held his hand up. "Joe. Not sheriff anymore."

"Tony Winters is his name. He's staying at the Holiday Inn."

Joe got up and stuck out his hand. "I'll let myself out, Adam, and I'll tell Blaine to come back and lock the door. See you in court."

Francis was adjusting his bow tie in the vanity mirror while Amy put on her make-up. "I'm so glad that you're coming with me today, dear," he said.

"Why is that, Franny?" she replied, plucking an eyebrow in the mirror in front of him.

He came around behind her and held her close to him. Both of them were now looking in the mirror, him over her shoulder. "You saw me lose a trial I wanted to win so badly, a couple of years back. It really wasn't my fault that we lost that trial, but I always got the blame for it." Turning her around to face him, he said, "Now you get to see me lose a trial I want to lose. This is much easier, sweetheart." He kissed her on the cheek. "I wrote a letter this morning to the County Board and I'm resigning after this trial. I hope Harry will take me back, but if not, we can always go somewhere else. I could use a fresh start."

"That would be nice, Franny."

"We better get going. Yesterday, I was late."

Tony and Linda were just sitting down to breakfast, when the tall old man in the western shirt approached their table, and introduced himself. "Hi, I'm Joe Adcock. I was the Sheriff of Aspen County when Adam Holton allegedly killed Mark Stevenson. I'd like to talk to you for a minute, if I could, or is this a bad time?"

"No...no, it's fine. Sit down." Tony pulled out a chair for him.

The waitress came over, and Joe ordered coffee. "Not much of a breakfast person," he said.

"How did you know about me?" Tony asked.

"From Adam. I went to see him last night."

The waitress showed up with their food, and Joe's coffee, and everybody was quiet until she left.

"Tony, I'm here to help Adam. It's that simple. I told him why last night, and he agreed the best thing I could do was to see you."

Both Tony and Linda were now giving this tall stranger their undivided attention. Joe looked nervously at Linda, and then, Tony realizing he had not introduced her, apologized. "I'm sorry, Joe-- this is my friend, Linda Pendleton. She too, is a friend of Adam's."

Joe told Tony and Linda basically what he had told Adam the night before. While he talked, they both ate, listening intently.

"Sheriff, could I put you on the stand?"

"Just Joe, now, not sheriff, but yes I would like that."

"Where can I reach you?" Tony asked, wiping his mouth with his napkin as he pointed at his watch, with a worried look at Linda.

"I'm ready, when you are," she said.

"I'll be at my brothers place," Joe said. "I wrote his phone number on the back of the card."

It was one of his old business cards that said, Joe Adcock, Sheriff of Aspen County, with a gold badge on one side of it. The numbers on the front had been crossed out.

"Thank you," said Tony. "Thank you so much. I will be in touch; right now we need to rush to get to court on time." The two men stood and shook hands. Joe tipped his hat to Linda.

Running to the car, they settled inside, and headed for the courthouse. "This could be a big break if the judge will allow it," he said to Linda. "Last minute witnesses can be a problem if the prosecution wants to make a fuss about it. I just might talk to Francis beforehand. I wish I knew what that guy was thinking, anyway. In all my years of trying cases, I have never seen a prosecutor so laid back. It's spooky. They have a phrase up here called, 'Minnesota Nice,' but this is ridiculous."

Linda, who hadn't said a word since they left the restaurant, just smiled and shrugged her shoulders.

They ran up the long flight of steps to the courtroom, passing under the words inlaid over the huge oak doors: 'Justice And Liberty For All.' Had the words been reversed for a reason? How many people had come here looking for justice and were turned away? How many guilty people had been set free because of high-quality lawyers and legal maneuvering? Tony knew of one case, that was for sure.

It was dark and drizzly outside, but it was bright in the courthouse, and both of them stopped for a moment to let their eyes adjust. Linda spotted Ruth Ann, and walking down the center aisle slid in beside her and took her hands in hers. She was first up on the stand this morning and she was very nervous. She had borrowed a black business suit from her sister, and she looked very professional.

"Wow, look at you," Linda said. "Those men on the jury are going to love you."

"One of them is old enough to be my daddy," Ruth Ann giggled.

"Sugar Daddy," Linda replied, and they both laughed.

There was just enough time before the proceedings started, for Adam and Tony to talk about Joe. "I hope this guy is for real and I hope we can use him," Tony said. He went on to explain how witnesses that come forward at the last minute are not usually allowed to testify. He had two choices: ask the court for a recess and add him to the list, and then give the prosecution time to weigh his impact on the case, or get Francis to just waive him through right up front. "For some reason, the judge just doesn't seem to give a shit what we do, as long as we both agree," he told Adam.

For today they were not going to worry about it, as Ruth Ann and Linda would both be testifying.

The door banged open and the bailiff called everyone to stand and come to order. Tony took the opportunity to glance behind, into the gallery. There was a good crowd today with a few more still coming in. Tony nodded, *good morning*, to Francis, who seemed to be especially chipper this morning. He was leaning over the rail talking to a slender, matronly looking lady in the front row who seemed to look very prim and proper. For some reason, Francis reminded him of Mr. Whipple, the toilet paper man. Suddenly Amy pointed up front, and Francis made a hasty retreat to his chair, both of them laughing. Judge Persons didn't seem to notice, or care.

Ruth Ann was looking very fragile as she took the stand. Not just in appearance, but in the tone of her voice. For Tony, this was going to be a challenge. He wanted the jury to believe that her rape had just been the start of Adam's wrath. His questions could not be misleading, but he wanted her testimony to be. He just had to hope Francis didn't ruin it all in his cross-examination.

"State your name, please, and where you are from," Tony said.

"My name is Ruth Ann Cross and I live in Cleveland, Ohio." *Not anymore, she thought,* knowing she could not say that.

"Ruth Ann, I want you to tell this jury what your maiden name was."

" Holton," she said very softly.

"You need to speak up," the judge interrupted. "The jury is way over there, darling and some of them don't hear so well."

"Holton," she repeated loud and clear.

Ida Pribbinow smiled at her and mouthed, 'Thank you.'

"Ruth, you are the defendant's sister, is that correct?" Tony looked around first to make sure there were no other interruptions.

Adam was sitting back in his chair, watching his little sister, and wishing he didn't have to put her through all of this.

"Yes, I am three years younger than Adam."

" Do you love your brother, Ruth Ann.?"

"Very much," she replied, blotting a tear from her eye.

"But that's not the only reason you are here today, is it? You have another story to tell that has never been told, a story that might have contributed to Adam's state of mind when he killed Mark Stevenson. Ruth, I want to take you back to May of 1997, two years before Mark Stevenson was killed; to a day that you decided to walk over to your sister's house, just before dusk. Do you know what I am talking about here?"

"Yes."

"Tell this jury what happened to you on that day, Ruth Ann."

"Mark Stevenson chased me down, beat me and raped me. Then, he took me to his house and raped me again and again. He finally let me go the next morning, but he told me if I ever told anyone, he would kill my family and me. I firmly believe he meant it." Ruth seemed to sit a little taller in the chair right now, as if she had found some backbone she didn't know she had.

"You didn't go to the police?"

"No, I was afraid."

"After Mark Stevenson was killed, did you then go to the police?"

"Yes."

"What did they tell you?"

"They told me they would make a record of it, but with him dead, there was little they could do beyond that. They said if I wanted to sue his estate in civil court that it would be there for evidence. The sheriff said if I wanted, he would dig the guy up and hit him in the head with the shovel."

Judge Persons hid his laugh in his handkerchief, pretending to blow his nose. Both Tony and Francis smiled at the comment. Several jurors also laughed, and the judge rapped for order.

Tony became serious again. "Ruth, how did Adam find out about this?"

"I don't know," she said, "but he did. He called me and told me he knew."

For Tony, this was a gamble. If Francis asked Ruth Ann when Adam called her, and asked her about it, it would not be good. He had been watching Francis closely throughout Ruth Ann's testimony, and he had taken no notes. Francis seemed to be paying more attention to the woman in the front row than the trial.

"I have no other questions for this witness, Your Honor."

Judge Persons looked at Heitla. "Cross examination, Counselor?"

Francis walked slowly and methodically up to Ruth Ann's chair.

"You live in Cleveland?" he asked.

"Yes."

"Married? Children?"

"Yes, we have a little girl, Chelsea."

Francis took a deep breath as if he was contemplating asking something else but then turned to the judge and said, "No further questions."

Tony was confused. Heitla's questions seemed meaningless. As if he had asked them, just to ask something... because it was expected of him.

"Witness is excused," said the judge. "Next witness."

Tony stood and faced the bench. "Your Honor, at this moment I would like to approach the bench along with the prosecutor, if you don't mind."

The judge motioned them forward with his index finger.

Your Honor, I would like, at this time, to submit the taped testimony from yesterday, which you are aware of, to the jury. I ask, for reasons to protect the witness's identity, that only the jury be allowed to see it."

"Any objections?" he asked Francis.

"No, Your Honor. I was there yesterday. I don't want to see it again."

"You don't want to see it, or you don't want anyone to see it?"

"I have no problem with the jury seeing it."

The judge stood. "Ladies and gentleman, Court will be in recess for awhile, so the jury can see some taped testimony in another room that has been set up for that purpose. Unless people on the jury care to share what they see when this trial is concluded, this testimony will remain undisclosed." He turned and marched out, followed by the jury.

Tony went right over to Francis. "Another witness has come forward for the defense, and I know that it's not legal or ethical for me to call him without your permission. I guess I am asking for your permission, if the judge allows it."

"Who is it?" Francis asked, all of the time holding Amy's hand over the rail. By the way Counselor, have you met my wife Amy?"

"No I haven't," Tony replied. "It's a pleasure." He nodded at Amy.

"Mine too," she said with a shy smile.

"Man's name is Joe Adcock," said Tony

"Sheriff Joe. Why I'll be damned! No. No problem with him taking the stand as far as I am concerned. Where did you find him?"

"I didn't," Tony replied, "he found me." Tony thanked Francis and went and sat down next to Adam. Tony didn't want to see Laura's testimony again either. He didn't want to see the tape, but he told Adam all about it.

CHAPTER TWENTY-SEVEN

There was not a dry eye among the jurors when they came back in. It was nearly time to break for lunch, so Tony felt now would be the time to talk to the judge about Joe. "Permission to approach the bench, Your Honor."

Judge Persons wrinkled his brow in a sign of irritation "I was going to call for the lunch break, Counselor. Can it wait until after that?"

"Ah…it may just affect that, Your Honor."

Exasperated, he waved his hand at Tony. "Come on up. You too, Francis and let's make this quick. I'm damn hungry."

Tony stood as close to the judge as he could, so the gallery couldn't hear. "I would like to call a witness who is not on your list, Your Honor. I have spoken to the prosecutor here, and he's not against it."

"What has that got to do with me calling a lunch recess? This better be damn good, Counselor."

"I would like you to recess until tomorrow, so I can notify the man I would like to have testify that he can give evidence. He is not in the courtroom today, but he can be tomorrow."

"Who is this? Do I know him?" The judge was now standing, holding his gavel like a weapon out in front of him.

Before Tony could answer, Francis did. "Joe Adcock."

Judge Persons had a look of disbelief on his face. He sat back down, staring at Tony.

"Court is recessed until tomorrow morning at ten a.m." said the judge.

Tony got in touch with Joe Adcock minutes after he left the courtroom. It seemed as if Joe was just waiting for his call. "Joe, can I meet you tonight in town? I'd like to buy you dinner. We need to talk before you take the stand tomorrow. That is what you want to do, right?"

"Do you think I would have traveled sixteen hundred miles if I didn't want to? Sure Tony, name the time and the place."

"Let's do this Joe. Come to the hotel, and we can meet in my suite. I'll have supper sent in, that way we'll be assured of privacy. Let's say about six."

Tony was waiting on the courthouse steps, and now, just for a minute, he sat down to collect his thoughts. Everybody else but Linda had gone home. She went to get the car and was now parked at the curb waiting for him, and examining her fingernail polish. She thought she would be on the stand today and was anxious to hear why the change in plans. She had spent a lot of time preparing for today.

It was a warm, humid spring day, the bright blue sky broken up with some of those puffy cumulous clouds floating slowly overhead, the kind that herald the coming of summer. A couple of kids, who either skipped school or were out early, were skateboarding up and down the sidewalk. Like a new calf that gets out of the barn for the first time in the spring, they were just happy to be outside enjoying themselves. They both waved at Tony and he smiled and waved back. Slowly he raised himself to his feet and started down the steps to the car. Just then a sheriff's car pulled in behind Linda, and lowering the passenger window, the man behind the wheel motioned Tony over to his car. Leaning across the seat he shoved his hand out the window and motioned again for Tony to get in.

"Percy Martin," said the sheriff. "Need to talk to you for just a minute."

Tony grabbed the extended hand and shook it vigorously. "Tony Winters. Glad to meet you, Sheriff. I hope we haven't done anything wrong?"

"No, not at all. I wanted to give you some information that I just found out about this morning that might help you. Tony, we've had two other women call in to my office and say they were victims of Mark Stevenson. They were both willing to file a report and we're in the middle of that right now. Once they do, then that information is available to you."

"Thank you so much," Tony said, shaking Percy's hand again.

"I know that Joe came back to set things right, Tony, and I hope he does. I was also part of that problem and I feel terrible about it too. But I need my job. I have a family to provide for, so I need to be careful. I've stayed away from the trial...and Adam, on purpose. But no one wants to see that man found guilty. He's a hero, not a criminal."

"I guess I don't know what to say except, thank you, again." Tony said.

Percy answered with a short salute, and the clicking of the door lock next to Tony. "Got to go," he said.

Tony walked slowly to the car and Linda slid over to the passenger's side. He sat down in the car and looked at her with a grin on his face.

"What?" she said. "You look like the cat that swallowed the bird or something like that."

"I love you," he said, "and when this is all over, I want you to marry me."

"Wow," Linda exclaimed, "You need to talk to the cops more often."

Adam was in a state of confusion. As much as he too, believed that things were going his way, nobody was talking to him about what was actually happening and it was frustrating him. He sat on the edge of his bed and picked up a magazine that Alice had brought him, then, aggravated, threw it back down. He was just too keyed up to read and somebody was coming to pick up his dinner tray. He hoped it was Blaine.

It wasn't Blaine; it was someone he had never seen before. The new deputy unlocked the door and asked Adam if he was finished. He had hardly touched his meal.

With the tray in one hand he turned to face Adam. "Keep your chin up, buddy, you have a lot of people pulling for you. I knew Mandy from school."

Adam's head jerked up. "You did?"

The deputy looked out the door to make sure they were alone. "Yes I did, and she was one of the nicest girls I ever met. I don't want to make you sad talking about her. I just wanted you to know what you did was so defensible. The whole town feels that way."

Adam stood and took the deputy's free hand in his. "Thank you. Thank you for saying that."

With his boyish face masking a small grin, he shook Adam's hand. "I'm not just saying it, it's true. Let's hope it's a slam dunk for you, buddy." With that he left.

Adam sat back down on the edge of his bed. He had been skeptical when Tony did not want him to testify. He wanted to tell his story so bad. He wanted to clear the air once and for all. Now though, he was starting to understand why Tony did not want to take that risk. This town knew his story, and they were not going to let him down. He could just feel it. He was starting to cry, but not tears of sadness. They were tears of overwhelming gratitude for the decent people of this community who believed in him, and believed in justice. When he first wanted to come back here he felt it was a mistake that the laws would not allow him to be acquitted. These were the same laws that had set Stevenson free, why should he trust them? It seemed now though, that if they could be manipulated to protect scum like Stevenson, they could also be manipulated to protect decent people. He'd just never felt it would happen to him, and true, it hadn't happened yet. But he felt more optimistic tonight than he had been in a long time.

When Joe finished telling how he felt about Adam, and how he knew he had let the whole community down with the way the Stevenson case was handled, there was absolutely no doubt in Tony's mind that this could break the case wide open. All Tony needed to do was to convince the judge and prosecutor that all of this was relevant to Adam's situation. After all, this case was about what Adam had done, not what Stevenson had done. But he had strayed into this forbidden territory already and found little opposition. It was going to be a word game, and he was good at them. Tony had come back here to defend Adam, but so far he had done a first-rate job of trying Mark Stevenson all over again, and that was what he intended to do, if they would let him. The two men sat at a table in Tony's suite. Their empty, greasy platters with the remnants of a prime rib supper sat in front of them. Tony reached into his pocket for a couple of cigars and saw Joe's eyes light up. "Cubans," Tony said. Joe bit the end off his and then looked at it like it was going to be a sin to smoke it. He put half of it in his mouth and tasted the sweet tobacco. Then pulled it out for Tony's waiting match.

"When this trial is over and Adam is set free, there will be plenty more of them where these came from," he said.

Joe smiled and inhaled deeply.

Today was as beautiful as yesterday. Song birds seemed to be everywhere in the trees, singing about it, and a big fat robin leaned back with all of it's might and pulled a night crawler from the green lawn in front of the courthouse, then fluttered away with the long worm dangling between it's feet.

Tony and Linda walked to the top of the steps and turned to survey the scene before them. If all went well, today would be the end of his witnesses. He didn't expect much rebuttal, but that was up to Francis. The jury might even get the case today. Before they went through the doors, Linda squeezed his hand. Tony had told her they best not have any public displays of affection.

The courtroom was packed. Adam had not been brought in yet, and Francis was once again leaning over the rail talking with the woman he had introduced as his wife. The jury was seated, all of them with looks of dead seriousness on their faces. All except Ida Pribbinow, who seemed perplexed by the whole thing, and was working on a piece of cross-stitch.

Linda was seated once again, next to Ruth Ann and Adam's older sister Noreen.

"All rise. District Court 371, in and for the County of Aspen, is in session."

Judge Persons came in with flowing robes. He slapped the gavel once and said, "Be seated," then leaned backwards into his chair. "More witnesses for the defense?" he asked.

"Yes, Your Honor, the defense calls Joe Adcock." Tony was dressed in a gray three-piece pin strip suit today, more reminiscent of a Washington lawyer than himself, but elegant just the same.

A slow murmur went through the courtroom as Joe rose and made his way to the stand. To most of the people in Aspen, this man had been their Wyatt Earp. He had kept them from harm for more years than they could remember. Francis smiled at him and Joe smiled back, as he passed. There had been so many trials, when they had always been on the same side of the room. They had spent long nights going over evidence and planning strategy to keep the criminals of this county behind bars, where they belonged. All except Mark Stevenson.

"Raise your right hand please. Do you swear to tell the truth, the whole truth and nothing but the truth, so help you God?" The bailiff was smiling broadly as he spoke. Joe was a friend of his, and it was so good to see him.

"I do," Joe retorted and sat down in the witness chair. Joe was dressed in khaki slacks and a white shirt with collar straps. All that separated him from the sheriff's uniform he had worn for so many years were some pins, patches, and that big gold badge. His brown boots were the same as always.

If he was nervous, he didn't show it. He looked like a man with a mission, but then he had always looked like that. He thought of all of the times he had sat in this very chair; hundreds of times, but seldom for the defense. His job back then had been to bring criminals to justice, not help them go free. That is, until Mark Stevenson's trial.

Tony usually stood in front of the witness, but today he stood to one side so the spectators and jury would have the clearest possible view of Joe. Tony's voice was the only sound in the room as he spoke. "Will you tell this court who you are, where you live, and what you do, please?" Tony was wasting no time, lumping three questions into one.

Joe pulled himself higher in the old oak chair. He spoke loud and clear. "My name is Joe Adcock, I live in Sedona, Arizona, and I am the recently retired Sheriff of Aspen County."

Judge Persons seemed to be in his usual thoughtful pose, leaning back in his chair with his left hand massaging his chin, and his right hand holding his ever-present gavel, poised relaxingly in mid air. He and Joe went back a long, long way. They had drank together and fished together, sometimes doing both. Many a hand of five-card stud had been played shoulder to shoulder in the smoky back room of Simon's bar, with some of their old crony friends over the years. Then the Stevenson trial had brought it all to a crashing halt. Joe had left after that a broken man, but their hands had been tied on that day.

Tony ran his hand through his hair while he spoke to Joe. "Joe, you were kind of a surprise witness, both for me and the prosecution, I might add." He glanced over to Francis, who showed no emotion, but was taking notes on a yellow legal pad.

"Maybe it would benefit this court and the jury, for you to tell us why you felt compelled to come back here and testify in this case. You were not subpoenaed by anyone, were you?"

"I came back to do what I could do, to make things right. I kind of thought it was my last chance to undo a great wrong. I fought for justice all of my life. Maybe this is my last hurrah."

"Joe, in your years as the sheriff, how many times did you run across

Mark Stevenson? I am only talking about legal matters, or when he was afoul of the law."

"Wow!" Joe shook his head as if he didn't know exactly what to say.

"More than a dozen?" Tony asked.

"I would say many times more than a dozen, and a lot more than a dozen different offenses."

Ruth Ann emitted an audible sigh, and Linda put her arm around her.

A dull buzz of murmurs had come over the courtroom and Judge Persons rapped his gavel once, lightly. He settled back in his chair again keeping the gavel poised, as if to say: *Don't make me use this again.*

Tony briefly checked his notes. "Joe, I want you to tell this courtroom what happened to this town the day Mark Stevenson was released for 'allegedly' killing Mandy Severson.

Francis slid his chair back nosily, and stood up. His hands were shaking and there was a sense of agitation in his voice. He could only let this go on so long, even if the judge didn't care. "Your Honor. This trial is, and has been, more about Mark Stevenson's acquittal, than the charges here before us against Adam Holton. Let's get back on track here." His words seemed to be somewhat hollow, almost as if he was a bad actor and Tony sensed this. In a way he felt sorry for the role Francis was being forced to play, but Tony had pushed too far, and Francis had made his point loud and clear.

"I apologize, Your Honor. Where I was going with this is relevant to my client's troubles here, and his shooting of Mark Stevenson, I assure you, but I will re-word things."

"Then get there," the judge said. "Counsel for the prosecution, do you have anything you want stricken from the record?"

Francis was quiet for a second, deep in thought. "No, I just want to have a level playing field here." Francis sat back down. He felt compelled to, at the very least, make it look like he wasn't rolling over and playing dead. He needed to leave here with some of his reputation intact. He looked back at Amy sitting in her usual chair in the front row. She was smiling broadly, her dimples showing, and fanning herself with a magazine. It wasn't at all hot in the courtroom, but she did look a little flushed.

Tony, who had walked back to his table to check on something in his papers, now came back and faced Joe again. "Joe, what was the mood that you and your deputies were in, when you had to pursue Adam Holton for killing Stevenson?"

Joe did not hesitate. "We had a job to do and we tried to do it to the best of our abilities. Most of us were glad he had killed Stevenson. I'm not going to lie. Cops are human too, you know."

"Did you do all you could do to apprehend him?"

"I think so. Some people might not agree. But yes, we issued the same bulletins we always did, and sent out the same fliers we always did, around the country."

"Keeping in mind, Joe, about this being Adam's trial, tell me what you think happened here to make him take the law into his own hands."

"We all have a point we reach when we no longer care what the rules are. Especially when they are being used to foster more evil. That's how Adam felt, I'm sure." Joe looked at Adam while he talked, but Adam's head was bowed.

"As police officers, deputies, and troopers go about their jobs each and every day, they constantly see the same people committing most of the crime. With the right lawyers and intricate laws full of loopholes, there's not much you can't get away with anymore. For us, it's kind of a 'catch and release' program. It has ruined countless good law officers. It demoralizes them, and gives them a feeling of helplessness. Some go on. Some quit, thinking: anything is better than this. Adam did what every man with an ounce of caring and responsibility would have done. This worthless man had taken Adam's life away from him. Not his physical life, but his spiritual life, because you see, he worshiped Mandy, and now here was Stevenson smirking and flaunting his ill-found freedom. He would have raped and killed again. That's a fact you can take to the bank." Joe slammed his fist down on his chair arm, to emphasize his point.

"I don't know what else to say, except, Adam I'm so sorry for putting you in this situation." The two of them were now looking straight at each other.

"That is a good man," he said, and turned to face the jury, his finger shaking, as he pointed toward Adam. We need to do what is right here and skip the technical bull crap." His voice was shaky. "This is Aspen, not New York. Everything that happens here happens for a reason; some good, some bad. Adam had a good reason."

The jury was moved, and Tony could sense it. Time to stop right there before something was said to ruin it.

"No further questions, Your Honor."

"Counsel for the prosecution, do you care to cross-examine the witness?"

Francis stood, leaning on the table, trying to formulate an answer as best he could. His lips were pursed, his brow furrowed with wrinkles. He too, had been moved by Joe's testimony. " No further questions from me, Your Honor." Then, in a moment of lightness that caught even Tony off guard, Francis said, "Good to see you, Joe."

Joe walked back and took a seat in the audience, shaking several hands on the way. He looked embarrassed about the attention, but relieved he had said what he did.

That left only Linda, and Tony approached the Judge.

"Your Honor, the last witness we would like to call, is Mrs. Linda Pendleton."

Linda walked to the stand and quietly sat down. She was nervous and it showed, winding and unwinding her scarf around her fingers.

The bailiff, who was daydreaming, had forgotten to swear her in and suddenly realized it. After a stern look from the judge, he ran and retrieved his Bible and completed the task.

Tony walked slowly up to Linda. He realized that his mind was not where it needed to be right now, while looking at her, and he stopped for a moment to compose himself.

"Mrs. Pendleton, how did you first get to know Adam Holton?"

"He wandered on to my ranch looking for work."

Tony had told her last night not to elaborate too much, keep her answers short and simple. The more you say, the more the other side has to work with.

"Was that unusual?"

"No, lots of people drift in looking for work."

"You had a job for him?"

"We're always short of help."

"Check his references?"

"No. Most of the people we hire are just laborers, so that's not too important in this kind of business. I did ask him about his background and he told me he was raised around cattle and horses."

"You had no idea he was a fugitive from the law?"

"No."

"Mrs. Pendleton,"-- Linda smiled, it sounded funny for him to address her that way, -- "I've brought you before this court to tell the jury what this man did for you, so you could attest to his character. I think you have an interesting story to tell that will show us what Adam Holton is really made of. Let's go back to a stormy, snowy night in November, a night when Adam and several other men were working high on a mountain plateau. Tell us what happened that night."

"I had brought supper up to the men and on the way back down this steep one-lane road, my pickup got into some ruts and I was pulled over the side. I fell about thirty feet down, and if my truck hadn't got hung up on a tree, I would have fallen to the bottom of an abyss."

"Were you hurt?"

"Yes, badly. I had several broken bones and a punctured lung. I was trapped in the wreckage and no one knew where I was. The men passed by me sometime during the evening on their way down, but the wind and snow had erased all my tracks." She paused to drink from her water glass, wiping her hands on her skirt, wet from the sweating glass. She was dressed in a gray suit with a white frilly blouse, the black silk string tie keeping a little bit of the West, in her looks.

"How did this involve Adam?" She had stopped, and Tony needed to get her started again.

"Well, when the men got back, apparently Adam noticed my truck was missing. The other men were asleep by this time, except for one, who would not help him when Adam wanted to go back out looking for me. The storm was so bad at this time you couldn't have gone back out on any kind of motorized vehicle."

"Then what happened?" Tony gently prodded her.

"Adam saddled a horse and went looking for me. He found me about an hour later, and by this time I was nearly dead from hypothermia and my injuries. He was suffering greatly too, from exposure, but he managed, with great effort on his part and the horse's, to get me home and call for help."

"How much longer do you think you would have lasted out there that night?"

"Minutes. I had given up. I owe him my life and--- and---" Linda broke down at this point.

Tony wanted to go to her and hold her and comfort her, but that was not a side he dared show. The court reporter, who was sitting right there, gave Linda a Kleenex, and she composed herself.

"Your Honor, I am not going to question this witness any further. I think we all get the picture here." He had wanted to tell them about Adam's injuries and the subsequent death of the horse, but right now it didn't seem that necessary.

"Any further witnesses, Counselor?"

"No, the defense rests, Your Honor."

"I will, at this time, ask the prosecution for their redirect."

Francis was sitting with his arms folded, seemingly relaxed, chewing gum. "I have no questions of the witness, Your Honor."

"Mrs. Pendleton, you may step down." Linda walked back to her seat, touching Adam's shoulder as she passed him. Ruth Ann waited for her with open arms, and they comforted each other.

"We will recess until tomorrow morning, at which time we will have your final statements to the jury, gentlemen. I realize it is early yet, but I want to give you both time to work on your summations. Court is adjourned." The gavel fell. Judge Persons made an exit as hasty as his entrance had been.

Tony sat talking to Adam. "Tomorrow will be it, son. It will be Friday and the jury will have the case. I feel very good about the way this trial has gone, but juries always worry me. They can be unpredictable, sometimes. Let's keep the faith though." He patted Adam on the back as the deputy came to take him back to his cell.

CHAPTER TWENTY-EIGHT

It was a quiet evening for Tony and Linda. His summation had long been written, and it was time to relax. They walked the streets of Aspen like a couple of tourists, looking inquisitively in the little shops and stores. They still were careful not to look too chummy, that would come later. Linda went into a souvenir shop and bought a small lamp that had a northern Minnesota scene on it. It was a small waterfall that seemed to flow into a pond when the light was turned on. They stopped and ate a greasy hamburger at a restaurant where only a few locals were sitting and drinking coffee. They sat in a back booth trying to be inconspicuous. If it were not for the trial, this would have been a beautiful part of the world to visit. Linda's feelings for Adam had tempered. Her new found love for Tony was pushing away all of those foolish thoughts that she'd had for too long.

Adam ate supper in his cell again that night. He was waiting for Alice to come, and was in no mood to talk with anyone else. She had called and left a message that she had three days off and would be there sometime Thursday night. He sat and chained smoked while he waited, and a thousand thoughts seemed to race through his mind. He had always been a little pessimistic, but the suspense of the trial had left him depressed, wishing for the best, and pondering the worst. His thoughts went back to Linda. He had felt so sorry for her today when she broke down on the stand. It was a side of her he had never seen. She had always been so stoic in front of him, and it had a big impact on him. That night in the storm would always be there, but Adam had never thought that he had done anything that most men wouldn't have done under the circumstances. Maybe he was wrong about that. There were many times he wished he had never involved Linda in his life, because of all the trouble he seemed to bring, but, had he not been there that night of the storm, she would not be alive today.

He heard the door open at the end of the hall, with a rattle of keys, and then he heard Alice talking to the deputy as they came down the hall and stopped in front of his door. Adam stood as she came in and they both held each other for a moment, saying nothing. She smelled so good. She felt so soft. Things just seemed more bearable when she was around. The deputy told them that he would be back in one half hour and closed the door. Adam never heard him lock it.

"It's nearly over, honey, and Tony says things have gone real well, but we still need to pray and hope for the best. The jury could still change their minds." He brushed the hair from the side of her face and tucked it behind her ear as he talked.

They sat down on the edge of the bed, fully aware that they were free to do whatever they wanted to do, but right now nothing was on their minds except talking, and holding each other.

"I brought you something," Alice said. She fished in her pocket for an envelope and brought out a check for ten thousand dollars, made out to both of them. "It's from Anna's estate, Adam. We were in her will!"

For the first time all day, Adam smiled. "A house, Alice?"

She shrugged her shoulders and smiled. "One thing at a time, Adam. Let's take one thing at a time."

For the rest of their allotted time they talked quietly about what might be ahead for them. Alice's job was turning into such a good job, and she loved the people she worked for, and with. She gave him the carton of cigarettes she had brought, and a new Outdoor Life magazine. "Were they out of 'Playboy?' he joked. They even shared a few laughs, and then the deputy was back, and it was time.

I'll be here tomorrow, Adam, so let's hope it brings you luck and that soon we walk away from this together. She kissed him and held his face between her hands, and kissed him again. "I love you. Goodnight, Adam."

Ruth Ann lay in bed looking out the bedroom window at her sister's house. Chelsea was sleeping beside her and she could hear her soft breathing. She had prayed tonight for Adam's release, and her release from the bonds she had been in. She believed that God would find a way to help them both. The moonlight was shining bright over the farmyard and she could make out things as small as bicycles and toys left lying in the yard. A cat was creeping stealthily alongside a granary pursuing some small rodent. This was all she wanted, a place of her own. A place to start over and get things right this time. She wanted a home for her and Chelsea, with their own sneaky cat, and Chelsea's own toys.

Linda stayed the night with Tony but they had not made love. They even stayed in separate beds. She wanted Tony to be on top of his game in the morning, and nothing was going to distract him, if she could help it.

They were early for court, so Tony sat at the table and practiced his speech, while Linda sat behind him reading the local paper. There was not much there about the trial, except to say that by the end of the day it could be in the jury's hands. There had been little in the Twin Cities' papers since Adam turned himself in. Small town news in Aspen rarely got out, because most people up here had the theory that, what happened in Aspen, stayed in Aspen.

Slowly the courtroom began to fill with people, one by one, and couple by couple. It was basically the same people that had been there all week. Adam was brought in, looking more cheerful than he had in a long time. Tony wrapped his arm around him and said, "Let's get this over with and get you out of here, son."

Adam laughed, and said, "I hope so, Tony. I really hope so."

With his usual flurry, the judge came in with all of the usual formalities, and it was time for the rubber to meet the road. Judge Persons cleared his throat and wiped his face with his handkerchief. "The counsel for the prosecution will address the jury with his summation, and then the counsel for the defense will have his turn. The prosecution can then readdress if he wishes. Do you both understand, gentleman?"

Both lawyers stated that they did.

"Then let's go!" the judge nearly shouted.

Francis walked tentatively to the jury box and faced them. He had no notes or papers. He seemed upbeat and confident, but before he said anything he looked at Amy in the front row and gave her a knowing smile. She responded with a thumbs-up gesture.

Tony watched the whole thing and whispered in Adam's ear. "That's one strange couple."

"Ladies and gentlemen of the jury. The county of Aspen elected to bring Adam Holton in front of his peers, to explain his actions, and initiated this trial. The actions I speak about are the assassination of Mark Stevenson on the steps of this very building. These proceedings were a hard thing for a lot of us. As you have heard and seen from the testimony in this trial, there are not many people around who cared about what happened to Stevenson. In fact, they rejoice in it. The prosecution did not bring forth many witnesses, because it was hard to find anyone who believed that what Adam did was wrong." Francis stopped for a moment to glance at the paper in his hand. "But I have been charged with prosecuting this man." He pointed at Adam.

"My summation will be short and to the point. We have laws in this land that were passed by our leaders to hopefully make this a better place to live. Vigilantes are not legal, or welcome, and if we want it that way then we need to go back to our legislators and get the laws changed. As the County Attorney for Aspen, it fell into my hands to prove to you that Adam should be held accountable for his deeds. I am here to tell you today that murder is murder, and the character of the person being murdered is not sufficient reason to allow it. The defense has given the reason for Adam's actions: that his grief, and his feeling of hopelessness forced him into it. That may well be, but it isn't the way the law sees it. I have never told a jury that they should do anything but the right thing, and I am not going to start now." With that, Francis smiled, said, thank you, and returned to his seat. It was as quiet in the courtroom as a Sunday afternoon in the town library. No one moved or talked. It seemed to the jury as if they had just sat down, and Francis was done already. Even Judge Persons had a look of bewilderment on his face. They had not expected this. They had not expected Francis to say, "do the right thing, vote your consciences and make the right decision." They had expected him to say: "The law is the law, and don't you forget it." This was Aspen, not Minneapolis. People up here stood up for what was right. The law didn't always apply to everything. At least it didn't in their minds, and in their town.

Judge Persons said nothing, but gave one rap with his gavel signifying the end of the prosecution's speech. "Counsel for the defense, you may proceed."

It was Tony's turn, and he well realized that this was where many cases are won or lost. Right here, in the summation. He was ready, primed, and pumped. He slid his chair back slowly and stood up, an aura of self-confidence on his face. Reaching down, he squeezed Adam's shoulder and walked to the front of the jury box. The sound of his heavy boots echoed in the big room. Perry Mason, in all his glory had never looked this confident. He approached the jury box with a few note cards in his hand, but as he reached for the rail, he slipped them into his coat pocket.

Tony looked back at the audience and his eyes found Linda, Ruth Ann, and Alice. They lingered there for a second and then he turned to face the twelve people before him.

Linda, biting her lower lip, had never seen Tony work before, and she was awe-struck. They had been friends forever, and now they were lovers. Now, in this moment, this defining moment, she had a tremendous amount faith in him, and the love she felt for him had grown beyond belief.

Francis sat back in his chair to watch Tony work, gently stroking his chin, and looking more relaxed than he should have. He said what he was forced to say to the jury. But secretly, he hoped Tony would shred his summation. At this point he had no plans to object to anything reasonable.

Tony walked from one end of the jury box to the other, his hand lightly running the length of the wood railing, his eyes never leaving the jury. One by one he stared at them, as if to say: *you listen to me now*. He remained silent, but he was intimidating, to say the least.

Ida Pribbinow smoothed out her skirt and adjusted the bun of gray hair on the back of her head. Her pencil and paper were ready in her lap. Zip Collins, the youngest of the three men on the jury, sat with his arms crossed, looking irritated and defiant. He wanted this damn trial over, so he could go back to his business in town. Each day was costing him money. Who was this big shot in front of them right now, trying to get under his skin?

Adam sat with hands folded on the table in front of him, his eyes never leaving Tony. His heart was racing and he could feel it beating in his temples.

Judge Persons was reclining in his usual pose, his gavel in his right hand, his left hand holding his robe against his chest. He admired Tony, but felt that the man was a tad arrogant

Tony ceased moving and let go of the rail. He took one step back and stood tall. With one hand in his trouser pocket, and the other hand held out in front of him to direct his oration, he was ready.

The court reporter hovered over her keys, and examined her fingernail polish as she waited for Tony to begin. This was just a job to her, and she refused to get emotionally involved in any trial.

Tony's voice was soft when he first started talking, so low that the judge was on the verge of asking him to speak up, when suddenly his tempo increased. Like Mancini directing an orchestra, he wanted them to relax before the main movement began. "Ladies and gentleman of the jury. Before I begin, I want to tell you a little bit about my firm and myself. We are not a big firm by Washington or New York standards, but we are well respected in the state of Montana and the surrounding territory. We are also a very busy firm, and we are not actively looking for more business. When Adam's case came across my desk, I was too busy to even consider taking part in it." Tony switched hands in his pockets, and coughed softly into his left hand. "There was something inside of me that made me take a second look at this case, so I dug around for the facts. I was appalled at what I saw. And, busy or not, I made a decision to do whatever I could do, to get justice for Adam."

"Sexual predators are all over this nation, in one degree or another. Some of them are voyeurs who never go beyond their peeking and looking. Some of them are 'dirty old men' looking for that last thrill, but even they never cross the line between legal, and moral, in the eyes of the law. But all of them have one thing in common. They prey on women, in one way or another. Then, once in a while, a Mark Stevenson comes along; a man not content to look and fantasize, but a man who is a cold blooded, scheming, deliberate killer with no conscience whatsoever." This moved some of the women on the jury visibly, and Tony was watching all of their faces, carefully. He needed all twelve people on his side. He still had much to say. "I am not going to show you pictures of what Mandy Severson looked like when she was found by Adam, with her panties stuffed in her mouth and her hands lashed behind her back. This trial is not about that." Tony looked at the judge to see if he had crossed any lines, but the judge just nodded to proceed.

"What I am going to show you today is why Adam Holton did what he did, and that is what this trial is all about. It's not about *if* Adam killed Stevenson, - we all know the answer to that. Each of us has a point where we can no longer tolerate what is happening to us. But the majority of us will walk away from whatever it is that bothers us, to escape it. Maybe it is a marriage with an abusive spouse." Alice reached over and took Ruth Ann's and held it tight. "It might be a bully who likes to beat up on you, or a neighbor nobody can tolerate. There are lots of 'for instances' out there." Tony was talking softer again. "The common sense that we are born with, tells us how to behave and react in these times. But there is no chapter in the Book of Common Sense that tells you how to react when you find the love of your life has been raped, tortured, and stuffed into a mud-filled culvert to rot with the trash and garbage that collects there." He was talking louder than ever. "But still, Adam rose above all of that, and let the law handle things and take its course. We know what happened. The law failed him. Failed all of you, and it failed Mark Stevenson's next victim. Oh yes! There would be more. You can bank on that. There is no therapy for these people to make them stop. They can't quit cold turkey, either." Tony was angry and his face showed it. He turned and looked at Adam, who was wiping his face on his sleeve, a face that was covered with a grimace of sadness. His hands were shaking. He was visibly upset.

Turning back to face the jury… a jury that seemed spellbound and hanging onto his every word, he began talking again. "We all heard Sheriff Joe's testimony yesterday." He gestured at the empty witness chair behind him "This was a man you all trusted to protect you, for thirty years. An icon in Aspen, you might say. You also heard Joe's frustrations with the law. I don't think I need to repeat any of his testimony for you. Sheriff Joe was trying to do the right thing here, and undo a great injustice. He's retired now, and not bound by the same oaths and codes of behavior that bound him when he was your sheriff. That's somewhat unique, but it does make for a truthful trial. Not everything gets said that should be said in most trials." Tony took another step back and surveyed the spectators in the courtroom.

"Adam Holton did not kill for revenge. He killed to stop the raping and killing. You heard other witnesses describe what had happened to them at the hands of this man. Adam's own sister was raped, and threatened with death, if she told anyone. Left to live with her shame and fear, a fate almost as bad as death. You heard the taped testimony of a handicapped woman, with the intelligence of a twelve year old, left the same way. Mark Stevenson had no favorites, and he had no master plan. If a girl had a vagina, - she was fair prey for him!" Tony stepped forward and pounded on the rail for emphasis and Ida Pribbinow jumped, sat up straighter, and crossed her legs, holding her pad of paper to her bosom. Tony reached over, touched her arm and smiled.

Then he came back at them softer, and gentler. "Yesterday, I learned of two other women who have called in since this trial started. The sheriff is in the process of taking statements from them now. I hope if there are others, and I know in my mind there are, they too, will come forward. Mark Stevenson is no threat to anyone now, thanks to Adam Holton. It won't help Adam, but it will help the victims get some closure. Sheriff Martin stands ready to take your statements."

He changed direction for a second and told them of a case in Michigan, where a jury found a woman innocent in the killing of her husband. "She didn't kill him in a fair fight," said Tony. "She stabbed him in the back while he slept, with a knife from her kitchen. Lawson verses Collier, nineteen seventy-three. She proved that it was the only way she could stop him from killing her. He had told her he was going to do it the next day. Once again, that is what Adam did. Mark Stevenson did not name his next victim, but there would have been one. It might have been one of you, or one of your loved ones, maybe a daughter." At this he looked at the man in the jury who had three daughters, then continued on, or a sister, a niece or a best friend." Tony's hand swept the jury for emphasis. "You heard another witness describe to you how Adam nearly died in a raging blizzard to save her from certain death. Does that sound to you like a man who takes life lightly?"

The court reporter stopped to look at the back of Tony's head, her hand hovering over the keys of her machine. *This guy sure knew how to talk.*

Tony had the jury mesmerized. He had them right where he wanted them. He was playing them like a fine Stradivarius, and he knew it. This was his forte. When it came to addressing juries, he was the best. The jury in Aspen that day was getting a course in Summation 101.

He paused for a few seconds to let things sink in. Linda was so proud, so impressed, and win or lose, she knew now she deeply loved this man. *This was no fling. This was the real thing.* She smiled at her little poem.

Adam had never been in a courtroom before this trial. He had avoided Stevenson's trial because the sight of the man drove him mad. But he knew right now, that if he had a chance, this was the man who could pull it off.

Even the old Judge, who had presided over countless trials, was getting a new lesson from the Book of Litigation.

"Let's just imagine for a moment that there was some redeeming social quality in Mark Stevenson's life, shall we?" Tony had toned things down again. He held up a copy of a rap sheet that he had gone to his table to retrieve. "I don't know what it would be though, because it's not in here. This list of offenses goes back to his eighteenth birthday." The sheet was two feet long. "Sheriff Joe told me his juvenile file was at least this long, but we aren't allowed see that. His parents still live in this area, and deserve some respect, but their absence at this trial tells me they gave up on him a long time ago. All Adam wanted was for the law to lock Stevenson up and keep him there. There is no death penalty in this state. Adam Holton had no record before this situation came up. But this very court could not lock this man up." He held the rap sheet at head-height. "Instead, they want to lock Adam up." Tony hung his head, and shook it from side to side, as if he was bewildered. "I am a lawyer, and proud of it. I despise the attorney who wanted this man freed."

The whole courtroom was deathly quiet. People were even suppressing their coughing, so as not to interrupt this drama. All you could hear was the whirling of the ceiling fans, and the traffic outside.

"Adam Holton deserves to live as a free man, just as you are all free of Mark Stevenson. He will not be able to do that, my friends, if he is found guilty of anything more than bad judgment, which he admits to. He will, in his lifetime, leave a positive mark on this society or any society he chooses to live in. You mark my words." He was on a roll, but there is a time to stop before you lose your edge. Now he stood there, silent in front of the jury. He had blown Francis out of the water and he knew it. No one on this jury would remember what Francis had said to them. It was time to put it to rest. Then, Tony simply said, thank you, and went back to his chair.

It took a moment for the old Judge to realize Tony was finished, but he suddenly came around and banged his gavel. What for, no one knew. "Would the prosecution care to redirect the jury?"

Francis smiled, and said, "No, Your Honor."

"Then this portion of this trial is concluded. The jury will remain seated while the courtroom is emptied, and you will receive your final instructions before your deliberations. Bailiff, clear the courtroom." Once again, the gavel came down.

CHAPTER TWENTY-NINE

Judge Persons came back after the room had been cleared, and instructed the jury to carefully pay attention to the testimony they had heard in the trial, in order to reach a fair verdict, simple instructions but undisputable. They would deliberate for the rest of today, Friday, - and if they did not reach a verdict they would be housed in the hotel downtown, and resume deliberations on Saturday morning. If they were still undecided, they would resume again on Monday morning. He shed his heavy black robe and was dressed in slacks and a gabardine sweater. With a pair of penny loafers, instead of tennis shoes, he would have looked almost casual. They were to call him at anytime that they had questions… or seemed to be bogged down. Otherwise, Adam's fate was in their hands.

The jury deliberation room was in the back of the courthouse on the second floor above the Judge's chambers. Off to one end were the bathrooms, a small kitchenette with a coffee maker, and some other essentials. Right now, a large box of pastries from Roman's Bakery was on the counter. Fresh coffee had been made, but they were on their own for more. No one else was allowed in the room, and the deputy, parked outside the door, would see to that. Lunch would be delivered today at one, and then they were free to deliberate as late as they liked. Supper would be at the hotel.

Two pitchers of ice water were on the middle of the table, and in front of each of the twelve padded chairs were two pencils, a pad of yellow legal paper, and a napkin. One chair, on the end closest to the door, had a place card that read, **Reserved for the Jury Foreman**. Five chairs were down each side, and one sat opposite the Jury Foreman. They filed in and took their seats. The first order of business would be to elect their leader. They would go around the table and each would state his or her preference for this person. A simple majority would be the winner. Mrs. Diana Klose, who was chosen on the first ballot, just happened to be in the right chair. She had the procedural laminated card in front of her, plus a copy of the witnesses' testimony from the court reporter

The first thing they were going to do was to take a vote and see where they stood. Zip Collins, the youngest of the three men, sat in the chair opposite Klose, staring at her. They had been the only two who had voted for themselves. Elmer Craig also voted for Zip, but none of the women had, and he was irritated about that. As far as Zip was concerned, women belonged at home, canning and raising kids, not taking charge of a jury. Diana sensed his hostility, but was overlooking it for now. If it got to be a problem, she would address it, she had already made up her mind about that. Her first order to her fellow jurists was to grab some coffee and a roll, and then they would talk. Everybody but Zip got up and helped himself or herself. He preferred to pout.

They chatted about things unrelated to the trial while they had their refreshments, and then the Jury Foreman called them to order, except for Elmer, who had been in the bathroom for a long time.

"Would you care to check on Elmer, Zip?" asked Diana.

"Check yourself, you're the boss."

Just as she rose to go over there, Elmer came out smiling, and took his seat.

The first initial vote was ten for acquittal. The two dissenters were Ida and Zip. Ida believed that only the Lord God himself had the right to take a life, and Zip, - well he was just being the opposite of Diana. At least it seemed that way. His "no" vote was so loud, it was almost shouted, and they all stared at him. It was time to deliberate and they did, for the rest of the day. The day ended with only Zip still stubbornly holding out.

The jury had the case, and all Adam could do was hope and pray. He alternated from one to the other, wishing he had paid more attention in Sunday school when he was a kid. He believed in God and Jesus, he just didn't have a lot of experience talking to them. He promised both of them he would be more faithful, and a better Christian if he got out of this mess, then, thinking he sounded too much like somebody making a deal, he recanted, and prayed that he was going to do that even if he wasn't lucky enough to be set free.

It was hot in the cell; Even Alice had said so when she visited in the evening. They were both nervous and on edge, and it was hard for them to find anything to talk about. It was as if the tension had robbed their minds of looking beyond anything but the upcoming verdict. It was here and now, and they had to deal with it.

Adam tossed and turned on his cot after Alice left. Sleep was going to be elusive. His mouth tasted appalling from all the cigarettes he had smoked, and he gave thought to getting up and brushing his teeth, but he couldn't even concentrate enough to do that. Blaine brought him a late snack, and stayed for a while and chatted. He too, had seemed nervous and ran out of words. The snack still sat right where Blaine had left it, on the shelf. Adam just wished he could be as optimistic as they all were.

Around midnight, he finally went over the wall he had built inside him, and sleep did come, but it was a fitful kind of sleep.

He parked the truck at the end of the logging road, and they walked hand in hand down the trail to the pond. Actually, it wasn't really a pond, but a wide spot in the river, and their old swimming hole for as long as he could remember. June was so pretty here in the north woods, and maybe a few mosquitoes would come for their drop of blood, but otherwise it didn't get any better than this.

Mandy carried the blanket from the truck seat, and the lunch she had made this morning was wrapped inside of it. Deer sausage, homemade bread, and some Toll House cookies baked late last night. They walked hand in hand, Adam swinging the six-pack of beer in the other one, and stopping to kiss her every few steps, laughing and giggling. God was truly in his heaven and all was right with everything, - not just the world. Her yellow flip flops slapping the grass, and the swishing of her flowered sun dress, were the only sounds in this sun-bathed paradise, with the exception of the birds, and soft summer breezes. Adam was dressed in cut-off shorts, old worn tennis shoes, and a faded red tee that said, **Moss's Place. Where Beer is King.**

They stopped on a grassy knoll that overlooked the pond below them. They were alone, except for a couple of wood ducks that sensed their presence and slowly paddled to the middle of the pond, and then realizing that was not far enough, took flight downstream and disappeared around a bend. Adam walked to the water's edge, and when he returned, Mandy was lying on her back with one hand shielding her eyes from the sun. Adam stretched out along side of her, facing her. From a foot away he could smell the freshness of her body. She smelled like lilacs and Irish Spring soap. He bent down and buried his face in her hair, looking for that special soft place on the side of her neck, and coved it with soft kisses. It was the path to her delicate willing mouth, and soon, lips found lips. Their hearts started that race. Mandy rolled onto her side facing him, and her hand caressed his face as he continued kissing her. His hand had found her thigh but went no further. They were to be married soon and although it was hard to wait, they wanted their wedding night to be new and special. He would never do anything to destroy the trust she had in him. Her dress had been pushed up and he still had his hand on her thigh. It was as smooth as a newborn's skin. Their kisses became more intense, their hearts were racing as if they had climbed Everest, - almost reached the summit, - and now they were uneasy to go back down, but too afraid to go farther up.

Then suddenly, Mandy broke away and stood up, smiling tenderly at him. It felt colder for some reason, and Adam was confused as to what she was doing. She turned her back toward him, facing the pond. For a second he was content to just watch her, with no desire to follow, but then, trying to rise, he couldn't. His legs wouldn't work. Mandy walked down the hill to the water's edge. There was an aura of fog surrounding her that was growing denser, and within it, was a bright light that created a halo effect around her. The flowers in her sundress had vanished and the dress seemed longer and dazzling white. He had never seen a white, so vivid before. Mandy's feet no longer seemed to be on the ground, as if she was levitating a few feet over the water. He tried to drag himself, but his arms collapsed like rubber. She was a goddess, and so beautiful. "Mandy!" he tried to scream. "Please don't go!" But nothing came out.

The cold, damp feeling was getting worse, and as Mandy drifted away, an ever-thickening fog came off the pond and began to collect around her. It was getting harder to see her, and the light seemed to move with her. She had not looked back, or beckoned in any manner for him to accompany her. Adam tried to call to her, but his voice was non-existent. He was terrified! Nothing seemed to work but his mind. Then another step, and she disappeared into the fog.

Something cold was touching his shoulder when he awoke, startled and trembling. He was sweating profusely, confused and frightened. The light from the hallway spilled through the tiny opening in the door. He was on his knees in the bed, his bare shoulder against the cold concrete wall. Although he was sweating, Adam felt cold and shaky. He lay back down and pulled the blanket around him. He fluffed up his pillow and lit a cigarette, calming down now, becoming more rational. It all made sense when he thought about it. Mandy had come to him one last time, and he now knew it was over; She didn't need him where she had gone, she had left him and this world behind.

Adam lay awake for a while and smoked his cigarette. He thought of Alice. He missed her so much. He had not been fair to her, but the charade was over. It was time to move on, and he would, with Alice if she still wanted him.

On Saturday morning the jury met at nine a.m. to start once more. Zip had called his wife last night because she had left an emergency message. They were in danger of losing the business if he didn't get back, and quick. "Let's go over the testimony again and see if the things that are bothering you can be explained better, Diana said, looking straight at Zip. We would all like to go home today I'm sure, but we must be fair. In fact, maybe we should take another vote right now and see if anybody changed their mind, overnight." Zip was looking at his paper pad in front of him. He had written only one word all day yesterday, and that word was **No!** About two inches high. He hated Diana; he hated this jury and all it represented. He just wanted to get out of here and go home. He had to share a room with Elmer, who was up all night moaning and groaning in the bathroom in the cheap hotel room. Damned if he wanted to do that again.

He didn't answer to Diana's comments, but reached down and tore off the sheet of paper on top and crumbled it up. Then he wrote YES in letters that covered the whole page and held it up so everybody could see it.

"What is that supposed to mean, Zip?" Diana asked.

"What part of 'yes' don't you understand?" was said in a sarcastic sounding voice.

"Is that 'yes' for acquittal, or 'yes' for guilty?" Her brown eyes were staring him down. Zip squirmed in his chair. *No woman had ever intimidated him before, but this one was coming damn close. This bitch must have invented 'the look.'*

"Yes, for acquittal," he said. "On both charges."

"Let's all vote once more," said Diana.

At eleven a.m. Judge Persons got the message. They had a verdict. He got in his car and headed for the courthouse. On the way, he called the court reporter, and Francis, telling them to get over there. His office called Tony for him, and got the news out to the public over the radio. The verdict would be announced at two p.m.

There were some faithful followers who had camped out around the courthouse, and they were now filing back in to get a good seat. Tony and Linda called Ruth Ann and Adam's sister Noreen, and told them the verdict was coming at two. Alice heard from Linda at the same time.

Blaine gave the news to Adam a few seconds ahead of Tony's call. Tony was on his way over to talk with Adam and would stay with him until the time came, in a couple of hours.

At 1:45 p.m. the courtroom was full, but not packed. Adam had been brought over and was now sitting at the table with Tony, wearing the familiar leg irons that would not let him forget that even if he was 'presumed innocent until proven guilty,' he was still being treated as a criminal.

At five minutes to the hour the bailiff came in and called the courtroom to order. They all stood while Judge Persons walked in with a grumpy demeanor, and sat down. He did not stand, but read from a statement he had prepared.

"This trial was put in motion by an indictment against Adam Holton for the killing of Mark Stevenson, - and Adam Holton's flight from prosecution. He has been judged by a jury of his peers who listened to testimony for, and against him. This jury has made their decision and their ruling will be held as the verdict. It is subject to appeal by the County Attorney's office or the defense's legal team if they feel they have been wronged." The judge put the paper down and picked up his gavel.

"Bailiff, will you usher in the jury?"

They, nine women, and three men, walked in, in single file. Zip was the last to appear. They were smiling and looking at the spectators, and at Adam, Tony and Francis. Francis appeared to be relaxed, sitting with his arm thrown over the back of his chair, and his tabletop clean and clear. Amy was in her usual place, but appeared to be biting her fingernails. Adam's older sister decided at the last moment that she didn't want to be there if the news was bad so she was in the hall holding Chelsea.

Judge Persons banged his ever present gavel, and said, "Would the defendant please rise and face the jury?"

Both Adam and Tony stood. Tony's right hand was on Adam's shoulder. Adam was opening and closing his hands in a sign of nervousness, but his face remained calm. Tony seemed composed and confident.

"Has the jury reached a verdict, and was it unanimous?"

"We have, Your Honor, and yes, - it was undisputed." Diana spoke loud and clear.

"It is the wish of this Court that you now read your verdict." The judge leaned forward, and rose to his feet, as Diana held the paper high in her hand. "It is the verdict of this jury, that the defendant, Adam Holton, be found not guilty of both charges against him."

For a few seconds the people all remained silent, but then they rose to their feet in a tremendous ovation. Linda, Alice and Ruth Ann looked like a rugby scrum, holding each other in a small circle while jumping up and down, and screaming. Amy was crying openly, and clapping her hands, hardly what you would expect from the losing side. Francis had not moved one inch, sitting just as he was, but he was smiling.

Lost in the celebration was Adam and his lawyer, who had engaged in a huge embrace. Adam's face was hidden in Tony's shoulder, while Tony smiled and clapped him on the back.

Judge Persons stood smiling, with his gavel poised, and let them celebrate for a few minutes, then the gavel came down for the next to the last time. "Order!" he hollered, and everybody took their seats. "I want to thank the jury for serving so well. I want to thank the alternates and I want to thank both attorneys for their cooperation. I now direct the deputies to unlock the defendant's shackles and release him. You are a free man, Adam Holton, acquitted of all wrongdoing. Go forth and prosper. The jury is dismissed, and this Court stands adjourned. His gavel fell for the last time, and he disappeared from the room, in a flurry of black robes. It was Sunday, and he had a golf date.

Blaine had asked to be with Adam, good or bad, and now he knelt and unlocked the shackles. He rolled them up in his hand and handed them to Adam. "Souvenir," he said. "Congratulations."

Adam smiled and handed them back. "No thanks, but I do want to thank you for all of your support."

Then he turned to embrace a tearful Alice. "I love you so much," he whispered in her ear. "Let's get away from here."

He hugged Linda, and said, "Forever. That's how long I will be indebted to you."

"Maybe it was pay back time," she said, and kissed him on the cheek. "Don't you and Alice forget about us."

"Not a chance," Adam responded, and Alice said, "Thank you so much to both of you." Tony had joined the celebration.

When they walked down the steps into the bright sunlight, the flash of a camera and a few handshakes were waiting. But at the bottom of the steps was Ruth Ann, looking happy, but confused. Where did she and Chelsea go from here? Adam swept her up in his arms, and then holding her at arm's length he said, "I will never forget your bravery and what you did for me. You are my hero until I die. Alice and I talked last night, and we want to do something for you. I want you to know this was decided last night before this verdict was announced."

Alice smiled, and handed Ruth Ann the check for ten thousand dollars that Anna had bequeathed to them. They had both endorsed it. "Let's just say we inherited some money from a dear lady, and we want to share," she said, as she handed Ruth Ann the check.

"I...I don't know what to say," Ruth Ann said, kissing them both. Just then, Adam's older sister came hurrying over, carrying Chelsea, and they all hugged together. The system had worked this time, and there had been justice for Adam.

CHAPTER THIRTY

Tony was driving though the town with Linda at his side. Adam and Alice sat in the back, holding hands, and talking. They had never been happier. They drove down the main street of Aspen, past all of the streets that Adam had walked and played on while growing up in this town. There was a memory in every block. They drove past the motel where Tony and Linda had stayed, and where Laura worked, past the barbershop Adam had gone to for twenty years, and the cafe where he had eaten many greasy hamburgers, and drank gallons of coffee. They even drove past the school where he had spent half of his life.

They had only a single stop to make, and Alice had agreed to accompany him this one time, but it was with reluctance, and it showed. A gentle rain was falling and the wipers were squeaking on the windshield, smearing around the dead bugs that had accumulated. "It's just over the hill, and then take a left," Adam said.

The cemetery sprawled out before them, taking in about an acre of land behind the small white church that sat on the south end. The church might just as well have been in the hills of Vermont, with its tall steeple and large oak front doors. The marquee in front advertised next

Sunday's service, and listed services at eight and eleven. Adam had gone to Sunday school here, and so had Mandy, but he tried not to think about that now. His folks had been married here and were buried in the graveyard just over the hill. He hadn't forgotten where. He made a silent vow that some day he would come back and visit their gravesite, but not today. Today was going to be the end of one chapter of his life and the beginning of another. The Alpha and the Omega.

The driveway that led around the church to the cemetery was just a dirt lane, with grass growing down the center. The car splashed through shallow puddles as it wound its way to the far end, and then Adam said, "Stop here."

Alice looked uncomfortable but she followed him, taking the umbrella that was stashed under the seat. They walked hand in hand, almost to the base of a large oak tree that was just forming buds, and then Adam pointed to the hillside in front of it.

"I'll stay here," she said, walking under the tree's naked canopy. Adam dropped her hand and walked down the hill, stopping in front of a white stone marker about forty feet away. The shoulders of his blue denim shirt were turning dark from the rain, his hair falling in his face. He brushed it back and knelt by the gravestone. **Amanda Severson 1976-1996. Gone but not forgotten**.

Adam moved about two feet from the front of the marker, and taking out his pocket knife, cut a round plug of grass from the ground and set it aside. Alice could see his face and he didn't appear to be grieving, just very serious. With one hand he started to dig in the soft sand until he had made a hole that seemed to be about a foot deep. Then he sat back on the heels of his boots, and taking out his billfold, he took out a photo and a wad of what appeared to be tissue paper. Alice could see him from this distance, but not clearly because of the rain. For just a second Adam held the two rings up, and then placed everything in the hole, filled the sand back in, and set the grass plug back in place. He stood and paused for just a moment, and then walked back up the hill to Alice. "Let's go home, sweetheart," he said, taking her hand in his gritty one. As they walked back to the car they stopped, and Adam kissed her, the soft rainwater mixing with their tears, made their lips slippery and wet. "Thank you for coming with me," he said. He wiped both of their faces with his hankie. "Now, let's go and get on with our lives."

ONE YEAR LATER

Adam paused to go through the mail as he came in the front door. Alice would be home in a couple of hours and it was his job to get supper started. Maybe tonight they would go out some place to eat. They didn't have anything to really celebrate, and that seemed like the only time they did eat out. *Yeah, she'd like that, going out for no reason.*

Alice and Adam worked at the same place, but different hours. They had moved into their house shortly after their wedding last September and were still remodeling. Ruth Ann stayed in Aspen and had a good job in a beauty shop. Chelsea started pre-school this year. For a long time, Ruth Ann worried about Billy coming back into their lives, but then she found out he had assaulted a police officer, and was sentenced to eight years in prison. She filed for divorce.

There had also been a wedding in Missoula, and Adam and Alice had flown out for it. Well actually, Tony's plane came and picked them up. Linda sold the ranch, and moved into Tony's 'Snob Hill Mansion.' She was enjoying every minute of it.

Francis was now doing corporate law, for a new firm in Aspen that sold paper products and building materials. Amy was still teaching and taking care of her much loved little man in the evenings.

Adam heard the garage door go up as Alice drove in. He was sitting on the couch doing his daily crossword puzzle.

Alice came in and sat down beside him. "Twenty three down, is 'grapes,' she said, reaching over and tickling him.

Adam jumped up, picked her up, and ran around the room blowing spit bubbles in her neck and then plopped back down on the couch with her.

"You need to start being nice to me," she said.

"Why for?" Adam asked.

Alice fished in her blouse pocket, and pulled out a small grainy black and white picture. "This, is why for."

"What's this? Something from work that you swiped from the x-ray department?"

"No, it's a sonogram, Adam, and its something from both of us."

The End.

Breinigsville, PA USA
09 September 2009
223775BV00002B/1/P

9 781440 160615